CHILDREN OF THE SUN

JOHN SLADE

CHILDREN OF THE SUN

ISBN 1-893617-04-1

Library of Congress Catalog Number
99-93657

FIRST EDITION

Cover photograph by the author

Other books by John Slade

DANCING WITH SAMUEL
A JOURNEY OUT OF DARKNESS
THE NEW ST. PETERSBURG
HERBERT'S MOUNTAIN
GOOD MORNING, DADDY!
A DREAM SEEDED IN THE EARTH

WOODGATE INTERNATIONAL
P.O. Box 190
Woodgate, New York 13494

315-392-4508

This novel is about war in the twentieth century, at the end of a long millennium of war. May we demand, and build, a better peace.

This novel is about the conflict between black people and white people in America, four centuries after the first Dutch vessel emptied its cargo of African slaves onto a beach in Virginia.

This novel is about four war victims: a midwife who has been emotionally battered, a soldier who has been emotionally bludgeoned, a petrochemical engineer who seeks ways not to exist, and a Polish refugee from Hitler's war whose twig-thin fingers carve voluptuous sculptures in West Indian mahogany.

This novel, like it or not, is about us.

For Carl Thorne-Thomsen

who left Harvard University to become
a Green Beret in Vietnam,
because he felt that "college deferment" unfairly placed
the burden of war on the poor people of America.
He died on that distant battleground,
and never had the chance to bring his courage and wisdom
to the White House.

ACKNOWLEDGEMENTS

The writing of *Children of the Sun* began and ended in Norway, and I would like to express my lifelong gratitude to the generous Norwegian people. A course at the University of Oslo International Summer School during the summer of 1981 provided an excellent introduction to the study of nuclear weapons. During four of the following nine years, Norway provided me with a job and a home, so that I finally had the financial support and adequate time to write this story. In November of 1990, the Bodø Graduate School of Business provided the funding for me to attend an international conference on nuclear weapons in Stockholm; sharing discussions and dinners with high-ranking experts from a dozen countries for a week, I was able to confirm, after eight years of research, that the facts regarding nuclear weapons in this novel are correct, that the chain of events in the plot is entirely possible, and that in general, the story rings true.

Thank you, Norway, *Mange Takk*, for your sailor's eye, which sees beyond your borders. Thank you for your fisherman's heart, which cares for every man on every boat as the storm draws toward them over the darkening sea. And thank you, Norway, for your poet's soul, a soul nurtured on the mountaintop, a soul nurtured by the sea; as you listen, so shall you tell your tale to the world.

My deep gratitude as well to generous friends who read the manuscript:

Socha Svender, my neighbor beside the sea, whose spirit was made of Polish steel;

Patsy Hylton, my sailing companion, and companion of soft tropical evenings, whose heart is as warm as the Caribbean sun;

Carolyn and Jack Peduzzi, who believed in me and in this book, at a time when the book and I together weren't worth a peanut. Their encouragement, despite the storms at sea, remained as steady and dependable as magnetic north;

Marvin Williams, a Crucian scholar who, with one foot in a basketball court on St. Croix, and the other foot in a stateside university library, turned my rendering of Crucian dialect into a readable version of the real thing;

Roseanne Bell, who read this novel with the eyes of a brilliant black woman;

Roger Peterson, a sturdy Marine whose gruff voice cannot hide his golden heart;

Tom Muchmore, who served as editorial midwife to the earliest chapters;

Pat Scott Dowler, an angel who made copies of chapters as they poured out, at a time when ten cents a page would have dug deeply into my grocery money;

Heidi Honegger, who helped to unsnag several knots in the plot;

Ingmari Øiesvold, who read with a poet's insight;

Dick Eiger, whose wisdom, gentleness, and encouragement have been three gold coins in my pocket;

Toni Mendez, who believed in this book, and who did her best to find it a home;

and thank you, deeply, to the strong, generous, determined people of St. Croix, who gave me a job and a home on their island for four years, 1976-1981, and who thus filled my heart with such richness that I was able to write, with a pen dipped in the ink of love, this book.

CONTENTS

PART III

PART IV

This story takes place between
November 1989 and November 1990.

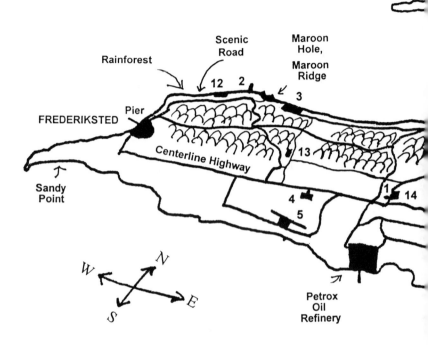

1	Fitzroy's Hot Spot	8	Salt River Bay (Columbus Landing Sit(
2	Lighthouse	9	Witherspoon's home
3	Casa Columbus	10	Seven Hills
4	University of the Virgin Islands	11	Sunny Isle shopping center
5	Alexander Hamilton Airport	12	Twining Vine Restaurant
6	Great Salt Pond	13	Holy Cross Episcopal Church
7	Green Cay	14	Le Reine shopping center

St. Thomas   St. John

CARIBBEAN SEA

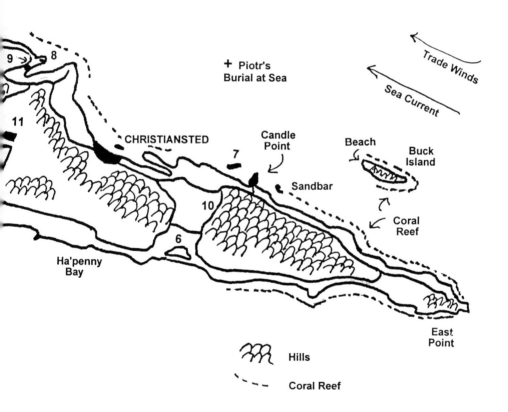

Trade Winds

Sea Current

9 → 8

+ Piotr's
Burial at Sea

11

CHRISTIANSTED

7

Candle
Point

Beach

Buck
Island

Sandbar

10

Coral
Reef

6

Ha'penny
Bay

East
Point

Hills

Coral Reef

ST. CROIX
UNITED STATES VIRGIN ISLANDS
(23 miles long)
Candle Point: Latitude 17° 45', Longitude 64° 40'

When the founding fathers wrote, "We the people," they meant it.

PART ONE

CHAPTER ONE

Three Hats

Driving home from the job that he hated, Karl decided to stop for a barbequed chicken; then when he got to the cottage, he could grab his windsurfer and point it straight out to sea, where the world made sense.

Though he had been on the island only a month, he had eaten at Fitzroy's Hot Spot half a dozen times. He liked the orange-and-white carnival wagon, and the tables beneath a cluster of coconut palms; but he especially liked joining the islanders at their roadside oasis. He nodded to people he recognized and swapped a casual greeting, though he had difficulty understanding their Crucian dialect.

As he parked on the shoulder of the road, he smiled at the seemingly endless dominoes game at one of the tables. An old man was slapping down his dominoes with such flair that every piece seemed to clinch the game with resounding victory. The other players quietly added their pieces, unimpressed, as the game went on.

Karl walked in his green overalls to the window of the wagon. "Hello," he called brightly to the proprietor. "Can't seem to get enough of your chicken."

Fitzroy flashed a smile of recognition. "Ah t'ink yo' ain' never see a chicken till yo' come to Sain' Croy."

"Oh, we've got chickens up north, but we sure don't have that great hot sauce you make. What's your secret, red peppers and dynamite?"

Laughing, Fitzroy passed a paper plate out the window to his son, a shirtless boy with a machete. Karl followed the boy to the side of the wagon, where chickens were jammed neck to tail on pipes over a pit of crackling charcoal. Two girls, wearing maroon-and-white school uniforms and heavy work gloves, stood at opposite ends, cranking handles welded to the pipes. A radio blasted the bouncing beat of reggae. Fitzroy's wife, wielding a paint brush, basted the revolving hens with a thick red sauce. Yelping children darted around the yard in a game of

3

tag. With one chop of his machete, the boy split a chicken's back and dropped the bird onto the paper plate.

"Good work," said Karl with friendly praise.

The boy paid no attention as he shuffled in rubber flip-flops back to the window.

Karl paid for the chicken, an order of fried potatoes, and a glass of Crucian mawbee. The first time he had tried the bitter brown brew, made from local barks and spices, he almost gagged. But each time he stopped at Fitzroy's for dinner, he stalwartly ordered a glass of mawbee as part of his initiation to the West Indies. Now, as he sat at a table in the ragged shadow of a palm, he savored the mysterious drink. Just the ticket, he thought, for washing away a day of oil fumes.

He bit into the hot juicy breast meat. Soon his lips were burning, his throat was on fire, his brow was damp with sweat. He gulped the tannic mawbee, his hand greasy on the glass, and looked forward to that first plunge into the cool, cleansing Caribbean . . . before he launched on a sunset sail far, far out from land.

He noticed a man at the next table staring at him: a strikingly handsome Crucian wearing brown-and-green camouflage fatigues. The man held a rolled newspaper in his hands as he glared at Karl with the eyes of a cobra ready to spit venom. Hoping to avoid a confrontation, Karl nervously continued cleaning his chicken carcass to the bones.

From the corner of his eye, he saw the man had spread the newspaper on a table and was now folding it into a paper hat.

As Karl was finishing a drumstick, the man set the bowl-shaped hat on his curly black hair. Karl heard scattered chuckles at the tables around him. Who is this clown? he wondered, increasingly uncomfortable as the man continued to stare at him.

He chewed the last crispy wing, then walked nonchalantly to the wagon for a handful of napkins and a refill of mawbee. When he returned to his table, the man frowned at him with a silent challenge. Gray at the temples, the Crucian looked to be in his mid-forties, about ten years older than Karl: a middle-aged soldier wearing a child's hat. The man didn't fit together.

As Karl sat down, the Crucian grabbed his hat and set it on Karl's chair just in time for it to be crushed. "Hey!" the man hollered, loudly enough for everyone to hear, "Yo' sat on meh hat!"

Karl jumped up. Masking his irritation, he tossed the flattened paper onto the Crucian's table. "Sorry, pal. Your hat was on my chair."

The soldier held up a pancake of newsprint for everyone to see; he stared at it with mock disbelief, then complained dolefully, "Yo' sat on meh hard hat."

Karl heard scattered laughter. He wondered if he was up against one kook, or a whole gang. "Look, fella, I'm not interested in your little joke. Why don't you mind your business, and I'll tend to mine."

Pointing with his middle finger at Karl's jeep, the man announced, "He got *his* hard hat."

Karl glanced at his green hard hat on the dashboard. "Yeah? So what?"

The soldier leaned toward him and drawled, "Maybe Ah ought to wear one of dem ol' thatch niggah hats, huh?"

Annoyed with the implication that he was a racist, Karl snapped, "Buster, don't pigeonhole me. You got no idea who you're talking to."

The unpredictable man asked in excellent English, "Do I or do I not have the right to place my hat on your chair?"

Wary, for this character was evidently far more clever than he let on, Karl wondered if he shouldn't just get up and leave. But he stood his ground. "No, I do not believe that one person has the right to place his hat on another person's chair. Certainly not without asking for permission."

The man sat back, astonished. "Ah ain' got the right?" he marveled. Glancing around at the crowd focused on him, he protested, "This mahn say Ah ain' got the right to put meh hat on his chair!"

The audience was silent; some of the dark faces were dour, others grinned at the performance. Someone turned down the radio. Cars whizzed past.

The soldier's rage was genuine as he demanded to know, "Then what right do you have to build your oil refinery on our island?"

So that's it, thought Karl. This guy hates Petrox and spotted my green overalls. "Listen, I didn't build that refinery. I just work there."

"During the 1960's, Yankee Doodle destroyed the largest mangrove lagoon on this island," the cobra's eyes burned with fury, "so he could build himself an oil refinery. Boy, do you know what that means: mangrove lagoon?"

Karl played along. "It's a kind of swamp, isn't it?"

The Crucian's fists clenched on his table. "Acres and acres of mangrove lagoon: fish hatchery, lobster hatchery, bird hatchery, the foundation of the fisherman's livelihood on this island. Bulldozed full of dirt, so yo' folks could build yo' oil works cheap."

"Sorry, you got the wrong guy. I just started working there a month ago."

The soldier sucked his teeth with contempt. "Ain' never met a whigger yet who didn't have his excuse."

Whigger? thought Karl. This guy's a real sicko.

He finished his mawbee and began to stand up; the man grabbed his arm with a powerful grip and yanked him back down to the chair. "We ain' done, boy."

Frightened, Karl searched the crowd for a white face; there were none. Even Fitzroy in the window gazed at him sternly. So Karl tried to reason with the bully. "If what you say about the mangrove lagoon is true, then I can see—"

"If?" roared the man, ready to spring from his chair. "*If*?"

"All right all right," said Karl appeasingly, "I didn't mean it that way." Does this nut carry a gun? he wondered.

The Crucian suddenly calmed; he folded his hands on his table and stared deadpan at Karl. "What right . . . what *right* . . . does your Navy have to park its warships at our pier?"

Karl shook his head, again innocent. "I don't know about any Navy ships."

The man mimicked a shrug of helpless ignorance. "Sorry, oh awful sorry, I ain't know nothin' about nothin." Then he pointed a finger of accusation while his voice hammered, "Yo' paid for them ships. Yo' paid taxes for every nuclear missile they got docked at Frederiksted Pier."

"Nuclear?" blinked Karl. "At Frederiksted Pier?" Aw shit. I come a thousand miles south of Miami to get away from Uncle Sam, and end up living with nukes for neighbors. "I haven't been to Frederiksted. The Navy's got a base there?"

"No base. Just a looooong concrete pier, with a ship tied up now and then." Holding up two fingers, the soldier stated for all to hear, "Strategic oil and strategic weapons. What yo' t'ink the Rooskies t'ink about little ol' St. Croix?"

Karl nodded as the picture became clearer. "So that's two hats the Yanks have put on your chair."

Cocking his head back, the Crucian narrowed his eyes. "Without permission."

"Gotcha. Without permission." Karl turned toward the wagon. "Fitzroy, you got a couple of cold beers? This gentleman and I have found a topic we agree on."

But when Fitzroy appeared with two Heinekens and set one on each table, Karl's interrogator seemed not to notice. Instead, he pointed toward the jumble of hills at the northwestern end of the island, tinged maroon by the late afternoon sun. "The mahogany trees in them hills been there since God created the earth. Now yo' folks cuttin' them trees down to build rich man's condos. Tennis courts. Jacoooooozies. Ah hear the bleedin' hearts up north complain about Brazil cuttin' down its rainforest. But Ah sure as hell ain' hear no complaints about buzz saws on St. Croix."

Murmurs of angry agreement surrounded Karl. Hat number three, he thought. "Doesn't this island have any sort of building code? There ought to be an environmental protection plan."

"Yesssssss," hissed the cobra. "The besssssst code money can buy. And money buys any kind of code it wantsssss."

He would have liked to explain that really the two of them, though islander and petroleum engineer, were not so very unlike each other; that most likely if they got to know each other they would find a great deal of common ground, and might even end up proposing a toast of friendship . . . when the soldier with a sweep of his hand sent his beer bottle flying. His lips drawn back from his teeth, the Crucian shouted, "Get off meh island, whigger!"

Leaving his own bottle untouched, Karl stood; he felt his legs shaking. Apparently free to go, he hesitated. He was not going to run with his tail between his legs. Neither was he going to allow this fanatic to include him with the American gang who had arrived uninvited and proceeded to plunder. "Fella, the issue is money, not race. To pick on a guy like me because I'm white is to waste your arguments. You people," he gestured toward the sullen audience, "you people have to organize yourselves into a coalition. Chain yourselves to the trees in your forest. Hire a good lawyer. Take your case to the Supreme Court." He faced the seated soldier; the man's eyes burned with a hatred beyond anything Karl in his life had ever encountered. "By picking on a blue-collar worker like me, you accomplish nothing."

He wove through the tables to the jeep. As he pulled into traffic, he was tempted to toss his hard hat, the helmet that had capped and confined his mind for too many years, right out the window.

Twenty-three miles by six, tapered at its eastern end,
St. Croix points toward the sun rising over the sea.
Some would say it points toward Africa, the Motherland.
Some would even say the island is a part of Africa,
only waiting
to be liberated.

CHAPTER TWO

Sea Devil

The trade winds blow across the Caribbean from the east, and so the sea at the west end of St. Croix is as smooth as a pond. Villagers from Frederiksted often stroll to the end of their pier to watch the sunsets, to catch up on the news, and to savor the tranquil last minutes of the day.

Riding her motor scooter toward the end of the long concrete pier, a Crucian nurse squinted at the orange sun hovering straight ahead of her. She guessed she had half an hour before it set: plenty of time for a swim.

Beneath her shirt and jeans, she wore a bathing suit. When a girl— or really, when a tomboy—her brother had taught her to swim from this pier. Now, as a woman of thirty-two, she still loved to dive from a piling, to frog-kick down through the clear water, and to pat her hands on the sand as she called her bubbling name, "Angelique!" Floating lazily upward, she followed the bubbles as they wobbled toward the surface. She liked to freshen herself with such a swim before she worked the night shift at the island's hospital.

She noticed a dozen people gathered along the end of the pier, shouting with excitement as they pointed down at the water. In the middle of the crowd stood her twelve-year-old nephew, bracing one bare foot on the curb while he tugged against something heavy. She parked her scooter, then hurried to the dock's end and peered over Chester's shoulder to see what he had caught.

The boy gripped the ends of a rumpled red Coke can with fishing line spooled around it. She shuddered when she saw what was at the other end of the line: a stingray flapped its gray wings as it lunged back and forth, ten feet deep. Sea devil! she thought with loathing. The devil heself with a hook in his mouth. And ain' he mad!

The crowd clamored with advice: "Keep that line tight!"

9

"Don' let he get into the pilin's!"

"Oh, ain' it a monster!"

The diamond-shaped fish pulled Chester's arms straight, nearly yanking the boy into the water. Though his eyes widened with fright, he gripped the Coke can firmly and shifted his feet to better brace himself. Puffing his cheeks, he struggled to turn the spool. Finally he tugged the evil creature to the surface, where in a frenzy it slapped the water with its wings. Its stinger, a black stiletto on top of its snakelike tail, thrashed wildly in search of a target. Angelique knew that a touch of that spine would send Chester shrieking in agony to the hospital.

He tried to spool his catch out of the water, but his fingers were too tired to grip the slipping can. Several spectators reached toward him. "Give Ah the can. Ah pull he up, mahn!" With stubborn determination, Chester shook his head; he stared at the sea devil flapping two yards below his bare toes.

Angelique reached over his shoulders and wrapped her hands around the ends of the can, interweaving her finger's with her nephew's. "Ches, don' try to lift him yet. Crouch down while we wind the line as short as we can. Then we lift him up to the pier."

The boy nodded, though he never took his eyes off his deadly foe. As the two turned their hands in tandem, he bent his knees to a crouch. She arched over him; when their fingers nearly touched the curb, she told him, "Now we lift, slow and steady. Don' get scared and jerk the line."

Chester protested, "Ah ain' scared."

Straightening their backs, she and Chester hoisted the heavy ray out of the water. It spun in the air, gray on one side, white on the other, frantically lashing its tail. Her arms trembled with the strain as she raised the spool to the limit of Chester's reach: the ray hung with the bleeding slit of its mouth just above the curb. "Step back," she gasped. The two shuffled backward, dragging the snout and flat body and whipping tail over the curb and onto the pier. As the beast scuffed across the hot pavement, it slapped its wings like a wet cape.

The crowd stretched into a cautious U around the spectacle. "Stand back! He a mean one! Ain' it uuuuugly!"

She let go of the Coke can, then gave Chester's shoulders a proud squeeze. "Good work, Ches."

He looked up at her for the first time and beamed an exultant smile. "Tanks, Aunt Angelique."

"But we ain' done yet," she warned. "We got to cut out that stinger. Ah can borrow yo' knife?"

He set the spool of fishing line on the concrete, then he pulled a knife from a sheath on his belt and offered her its handle. She knelt several feet from the ray's snout—a safe distance from the flailing spine—stretched her arm and pointed the knife at a spot between the eyes. As her brother had taught her years ago, she jabbed the blade into the brain and sprang away, leaving the knife planted in the head.

The stingray's wings arched up and quivered with fierce spasms; its tail whipped berserkly. She grabbed hold of Chester's arm and pulled him further away from the dying demon. The crowd cheered with brutal triumph.

The trembling wings slowly collapsed to the concrete. The tail lay like a dead snake.

She knelt and wiggled the handle: the ray showed no response. She pulled out the knife, walked in a wide half-circle, knelt again and touched the silver blade to the black spine: no reflex. Drawing a red bandana from her pocket, she wrapped a protective wadding around the still-venomous weapon, then lifted the stinger at an angle from the tail. "See how Ah hold it, Ches?"

Watching carefully, he crouched beside her. "Awright."

With a slice of the blade, she cut the stinger free; then she held up the six-inch spine for everyone to see. "That be one less sea devil in these waters."

The crowd whooped, applauded and cheered. "Angelique, yo' a good nurse, but yo' ought to be a surgeon!"

She handed the bundled spine to Chester. "Rinse it well in Clorox before yo' touch it. Then keep it home in a drawer." She added sternly, "Ain' no toy to be passin' round at school."

"Ah know," he replied, his head cocked to show he was old enough to take care of something so dangerous. He placed his prize in a rusty can by the curb, then frowned at several boys watching him. "Ain' no one to mess with that."

Turning to his aunt, he offered, "Half the meat does be yours."

She longed to hug Chester as a proud mother hugs her son. But she would not embarrass him in front of so many people. And of course, he wasn't her son, but Rosemary's. Mindful of her sister's ill-tempered jealousy, she declined his offer. "Ches, Ah ain' hooked that ray. Ah only help yo' the last minute or two. Yo' give half this fine fish to yo'

Grandpa, half to yo' Mama. Yo' show them yo' almost a mahn, able to bring home a feast!"

Grinning, the boy held out his hand: the two shook with an intricate sequence of grips, then both made a fist and they touched knuckles, West Indian style.

Chester slid his foot beneath the stingray and flopped it over. Bits of gravel stuck to the pale belly. He probed with his fingers inside the bleeding mouth, found the hook and worked it loose. Then he reached into a bucket, lifted out a gob of conch guts and fastened the sunbaked, stinking, fly-swarming bait onto his hook. He sat on the curb and unspooled line from his Coke can as the conch guts sank through the crystalline water toward the bottom.

The crowd drifted off, jubilantly informing all latecomers, "Hey, yo' missed the show!"

Wondering if she still had time for a swim, she glanced at the scarlet sun, just touching the horizon. Its reflection stretched toward her across the sea like a river of fire. But now she noticed something strange: silhouetted against the red disk of the sun was a black cross. When her eyes had adjusted to the glare, she recognized the sail and diving planes of a submarine. As the vessel cruised up the fiery river, its black cross grew taller against the sun. She sucked her teeth, then walked to the side of the pier where she knew the American warship would dock.

A white man strolled past her. His blond hair was trimmed to a military brush cut; his nose was coated like a clown's with zinc oxide. She glanced with irritation at the ignorant, arrogant words on his T-shirt,

I SLEPT ON A VIRGIN
(island)

But then she reminded herself not to be so critical. The boyish-faced Yank was no older than her foolish brother had been.

The sailor stood at the end of the pier with his hands on his hips, facing the submarine. Other men, white, black, Oriental and Latin, gathered along the last hundred yards of the pier. On liberty, most of them wore T-shirts, bathing suits and sneakers. Some were suntanned; some were red-eyed. All were clean-cut. They chatted and laughed as they formed a dozen equally-spaced rows perpendicular to the side of the pier, four men to a row.

A burly redhead stared at her—checking her out—then he called, "Say Babe, you better move back. You're standing in the middle of our docking operation." His mirror sunglasses reflected twin blazing suns.

Refusing to retreat, she retorted, "Navy, I learned to swim from this dock. This does be *my* dock."

The Yank grinned with amusement. "Whooeee, ain't she tough!"

His smirking companion warned, "Look out, Frankie. That little kitten'll scratch yer eyes out."

Turning her back to the bully boys, she watched their war machine as it approached her island. Its bow lifted two smooth waves like curls of molten lava. Along the deck stood the crew, evenly spaced from bow to stern; each sailor held a coil of line. Though she had seen many submarines moored at Frederiksted Pier, she was awed each time by their unbelievable size. Nearly three hundred feet long, the steel-plated monster that nosed past her was entirely out of scale to everything else on St. Croix.

Over their blue uniforms, the crew wore orange lifejackets that glowed in the late-afternoon sunlight with a reddish radiance: the sailors looked to her like thermonuclear bees.

The submarine's sail, a square wall twenty feet high, glided to a stop in front of her. The diving plane projected like a canopy over an officer in white. Sweeping his eyes along the pier, he noticed her and called, "Stand back, please."

She folded her arms and stood her ground.

The man scowled, but apparently chose to ignore her. He faced the bow and called, "Prepare to cast lines!" Then he turned to the distant stern and called again, "Prepare to cast lines!"

Each sailor on deck swung a knotted ball at the end of his coiled line: along the submarine's length, a dozen balls whirled in tight circles.

"Cast lines!" ordered the officer. "Cast lines!"

The balls arched over the thirty-foot gap toward the pier, where the first sailor in each row caught them and pulled the lines taut. The ropes were tied to three-inch hawsers coiled along the deck. As the sailors pulled arm over arm with rhythmic precision, the hawsers uncoiled like a dozen pythons that slithered through the air from sub to pier. The sailors grabbed the serpents' heads and necks; the tails remained tightly wrapped around cleats along the submarine's deck.

Now the sailors pulled in a tug-of-war with the broadside ship.

Arching their backs against the sub's great bulk, grunting and puffing, the teams of four moved backward step by laborious step. The stripe of water between sub and pier gradually narrowed, until the hull crushed old truck tires chained to the pilings.

The sailors crisscrossed several of the hawsers: working with practiced precision, they lifted some lines and ducked under others to form a web of triangles. Stepping around her as if she were nothing more than a lamp pole, they secured their spring lines to cleats bolted in the concrete.

Facing the bow, the officer called, "Stations report!"

"Station secured!" answered voice after hearty voice.

He turned toward the stern. "Stations report!"

"Station secured!" rang voices all the way to the tail fin.

The officer blew a three-toned whistle; the crew relaxed. Men on the pier extended an aluminum gangplank from the curb to the deck. Joking sailors ambled aboard.

A hatch opened; a sailor in blue emerged, blinking at the sunshine. He knelt on the deck, reached back down the hole and drew out a plank of wood. Holding it horizontally over his head, he stretched his arms until he fitted its two hooks through rings on the diving plane. She read the varnished nameplate,

SSN 664   SEA DEVIL

She turned and looked across the pier at the dead stingray, its belly speckled with flies. Chester stood with a group of boys who watched the submarine and its crew with fascination. She glanced at the rusty can with the spine in it, then she ran her eyes along the submarine's deck: beneath the sailors' nonchalant feet were hatch covers where the nuclear spines would emerge when they blasted skyward.

Soviet missiles waited in their silos. Waited with fire stolen from the sun. Waited for their journey half-way around the world to a target where, until a few decades ago, islanders had ridden into town on donkeys.

She glared at the officer, busy checking his clipboard while sailors crossing the gangplank called out their names. She fought to calm herself, struggled to control the fury borne of her chronic fear that one day these blithe barbarians would again devastate her family with their unpredictable wars. They had taken her brother; now they threatened her entire island.

Resolved to carry out her solitary protest, she walked to her motor-scooter, reached into its luggage basket and took out a stencil and a can of spray paint. Returning to the spot where she had stood, she unfolded the stencil; kneeling, she laid it on the concrete. Then she shook the aerosol can—the little ball inside clunked noisily—and sprayed an image of a bright orange mushroom cloud, three feet tall. She stenciled the words beneath it,

YOU ARE STANDING AT
GROUND ZERO

"Excuse me, miss," barked the officer, glowering at her. "You are defacing U.S. Naval property."

She lifted and folded the stencil; the gathering crowd of sailors and Crucians could now read her simple message. Then she stood and asked the officer, her voice loud enough for everyone to hear, "What right yo' got to make our island a target?"

He replied with strained politeness, "You are trespassing on U.S. Naval property. I am asking you to please leave the area."

Cupping her hands, she called to the hard-faced sailors on the submarine's bow, "The First World War wasn't supposed to happen, but it did." Facing the stern, she called, "The Second World War wasn't supposed to happen, but it did." Turning to the Crucians gathered behind her, she warned them, "The next war will be the Third World War." To the officer, she shouted defiantly, "And the Third World doesn't want it!"

Two sailors stood beside her, clearly waiting for the order to grab her arms and escort her away. Repressing her urge to spit at them, she picked up her can of paint, then strode through the crowd to her scooter. This evening, she would not swim.

As she rode parallel to the long black egg, the last red limb of the setting sun jiggled in her rearview mirror. Ignoring catcalls from the sailors, she stared ahead at the green hills above Frederiksted. On the highest peak stood the Navy's radar antennas: America's eyes keeping watch over the strategic Caribbean.

Until somebody in this missile-mad world decided to blind them.

CHAPTER THREE

Maroon Ridge

Before she went to work at eleven o'clock, she had a date with a war victim. She had tried with all her love to make him healthy. But he refused to forget, and so she could not purge him of his poison.

She rode along the road north out of Frederiksted. To her right rose grassy hills leading up to the mahogany forest; to her left stretched the pale beach and darkening sea. At the island's northwest corner, she turned east and followed Scenic Road as it snaked up into the hills. Gumbo-limbo and tamarind trees, thibit and mahogany arched overhead, gradually forming a dark leafy tunnel. Land crabs scuttled from the beam of her headlight into the fringe of ferns. She briefly closed her eyes as she rode through a veil of vines draped across the road. She passed no other vehicles, saw the lamp of only one Rastafarian homestead deep in the forest.

She spotted an unmarked turnoff that led north into the tangled gloom, a pair of ruts that few people would have noticed at noon. She turned onto one, and jounced along a serpentine lane, the black trees towering so tall above her that she felt an instinctive fear, of nothing specific, for she had safely passed through this stretch of rainforest a dozen times before; it was a fear that rose from somewhere generations deep, in her soul which was in part her people's soul, of some unknown, unpredictable, otherworldly calamity that must surely be visited upon her people: an unshakable, relentless dread, a certainty of coming horror, a helplessness before the readied weapons of another race of men. She lived daily with a taint of dread, a faint background rumble of approaching thunder; but now, during this passage of three or four minutes through the pungent, night-black forest, dappled by scattered patches of moonlight, dread seeped like black ink into her blood. It was coing; it was coming; what it was she could not say, but when it struck, she would die with a scream rising from her throat.

With a surge of relief, she emerged from the jungle onto the open crest of Maroon Ridge, a long grassy hump of land stretching west along the coastline between the rainforest and the sea. Leaving behind the dank, stagnant air trapped in the trees, she breathed the fresh salty breeze off the sea. Arched across the heavens above her, the stars that she knew so well from nights at the tiller of her sloop now greeted her.

She parked her scooter beside his station wagon, glanced through its window, then looked around at the sweep of moonlit guinea grass and called, "Nicholas?" She expected him to call her name tauntingly from wherever he hid in the waist-deep grass. She took her purse from the scooter's basket, then walked along the ridge toward the lighthouse blinking on its tip. But when she reached the end of the trail, at the edge of a cliff overlooking the sea, there was still no sign of him.

Wind gusted up the wall of rock.

Impatient for the man who made her feel so exquisitely alive with his kisses and caresses, she looked back along the ridge, searching the trail that parted the grass and led to the wall of trees. A round, bone-white moon hovered above the rainforest canopy. She smiled: her lover's magnificent body would tonight be bathed in moonlight.

Resigned to waiting, for Nick had ever been a mysterious friend, she looked in the opposite direction, at the lighthouse perched on the fingertip of Maroon Ridge, fifty yards from where she stood. Its window, open only to the sea, blinked every few seconds like a winking eye.

She gazed down the two-hundred-foot drop to the little bay called Maroon Hole. A ghostly white fringe of foam undulated against the rocky shoreline. The crash and surge of the waves reminded her of the old legend about slaves who jumped to their deaths rather than be taken in chains back to the plantations.

"Hi, Sugah," said a deep voice behind her.

She turned with surprise. "Nick! Ah ain' hear yo' come."

He cocked his head and smiled. "Nobody see Nick, nobody hear Nick, unless he want them to."

Tall and handsome, with beautiful dark skin, sharp eyes, and the touch of gray at his temples that made him so distinguished, he always banished her doubts, at least for a moment, when he smiled at her. He wore his camouflage fatigues with a machete hanging from the belt. In his hands, he carried a blanket and a coconut. He tossed the coconut into the air, so high it disappeared among the stars, though it landed neatly in his hand with a loud PLOCK!

She dropped her purse, gripped his shoulders, squeezed his muscles beneath the rough cloth. He dropped the coconut and blanket, then enveloped her with his strong arms and kissed her. His hands soon moved down her back and wrapped hungrily around her bottom. "Mmmmm," he growled. "Sugahhhhhh."

"Wait." She knew how he would be, wild and determined and impossible to stop once they had their clothes off. "Ah got to put in meh diaphragm."

His face hardened with disapproval. "Trow that damn ting into the sea."

She shook her head, resolute. "No. Ah gon' raise healthy kids, and Ah need a healthy mahn to help me."

He stared out at the sea and brooded in angry silence.

"Nick, Ah thirty-two years old. Ah can't wait forever." She softened her voice, spoke with encouragement. "Will Ah ever hold the hand of Nicholas Cruz, college graduate, teacher, basketball coach, one of the finest men on this island? The good, decent, wonderful Nick Ah *know* yo' got hidden inside yo'. Because it been there before yo' marched off to that damn war."

"College graduate?" He sucked his teeth. "That university be a Oreo factory. Them graduate brown on the outside, but whigger white on the inside."

"Don' use that word!" She almost slapped him, but she knew he was too quick and would grab her arm. Exasperated, she asked, "Why yo' so afraid of that university? Yo' so weak, yo' tink them professors gon' steal yo' soul? Yo' be a Crucian goin' into that classroom, and yo' be a *better* Crucian comin' out."

"Better?" He sneered, "After readin' white mahn's books?"

"Nick, read any books yo' want. Get a degree in black literature, then go into Central High and teach them kids black pride. Not prejudice. Not hate. But some good healthy pride. Which is what yo' ain' got, and what that university could maybe give yo'."

He shook his head stubbornly. "What Ah want bein' a teacher? Ah already got a job."

"Job?" She pointed at his station wagon. "Yo' drive that taxi for one reason: so yo' can blame every white mahn who gets in for keepin' yo' down where yo' can't do better than drive a taxi. Yo' *hate* that job. Ah heard it a t'ousand times. But yo' refuse to give it up. Yo' rather blame and brood and be bitter."

Working his jaw, he stared down at the waves that boomed against the rocks.

"Why yo' refuse to grow up? Yo' a thirty-eight-year-old mahn, Nick." She tugged at the sleeve of his camouflage fatigues. "Not a twenty-year-old soldier still in uniform."

He snapped, "Angelique, yo' say Ah ain' doin' nothin', just drivin' a taxi and cherishin' meh bitterness. But Ah *am* doin' somethin', and doin' it the best Ah can: Ah tryin' with all meh heart not to explode. Ah got so much them Yanks crammed down meh throat, Ah tink Ah doin' real good not to detonate and blow this whole island off the map."

"Nick, Vietnam been eighteen years ago. Leroy be dead and he ain' never comin' back. Ah live with that just as much as yo' do, but Ah re-fuse to spend the rest of meh life feelin' so bitter toward every white mahn Ah meet."

"Ah got so many ghosts." He pleaded, helpless, "How Ah gon' stop them nightmares? Yo' a nurse. Yo' tell me how."

She had tried with every argument and rationale and viewpoint she could think of, and knew she could no more erase his guilt from the war than she could remove shrapnel from his soul.

"And Vietnam," he went on, repeating yet again his litany of com-plaints, "that been only the half of it. What about when Ah come back to St. Croix?" He grimaced, seething with bitterness. "Ain' no parade up King Street. No invitation to speak at Central High. No sir. What Ah *did* find after them long bloody months Ah been gone, was that nothin' had changed on this island. The tourists been still Coppertonin' them-selves on the beach. The refinery pumped its profits to New York. The developers bought more and more land, then sold it to continentals at prices no Crucian could afford. And the best job a soldier could hope to find was drivin' a taxi, chauffeurin' white folks who didn't know Khe San from Kentucky to their seaside hotel." He grit his teeth, then raged, "Angelique, Ah been so angry, so God*damn* angry, Ah had to leave this island before Ah killed some whigger and wasted the rest of meh life in prison."

She cringed at the word 'whigger.'

"And New York?" He frowned with disgust. "Yo' tink Lady Liberty reached down and shook meh hand, said 'Thank You for serving your country' and offered me a job? No, Lady Liberty don' walk the streets of Harlem. She might stumble over the huddled masses, hooked on horse and yearnin' to be free." He stared over the ocean, his gaze reaching north. "Ah lost more buddies to the needle than Ah lost in Nam."

Restless, he began to pace. Though he had all the ridge to walk, a hundred yards between the forest and the lighthouse, he kicked at the grass as he marched back and forth, beating a path no more than ten feet long. She stood out of his way; once he was wound up, there was no stopping him until he wore himself out.

"Fifteen years!" he shouted as if recalling an unjust prison sentence. "Fifteen years drivin' an uptown cab, hopin' Ah could save enough money to buy a piece of meh homeland. Hopin' Denise and Andy might like St. Croix." He stopped pacing and stared at her, his moonlit face filled with anguish. "Hopin' Ah could face yo' parents and not feel so ashamed Ah could die."

That was the part she could never understand. "Nick, yo' know they never blamed yo' that Leroy disappeared. Yo' ain' never had reason to feel ashamed in our household. Yo' spite Mama and Papa when yo'—"

"Sugah, Ah ain' sayin' they blame me. Ah sayin', Ah loved Leroy like meh own brother. And no matter what yo' or anybody say be right or wrong, Ah *feel* Ah could have . . . Ah know Ah could have saved him, if Ah'd stood up to that sargeant." His lips curling back from his teeth, his eyes fiery with hatred, he repeated the line of his everlasting regret, "Ah shoulda shot that whigger through the head."

She grabbed his shoulders and shook him. "Denise said good-bye. And Ah can understand why. She couldn't fight that war any longer, and Ah'm not sure Ah can either."

Stunned, he reminded her, "But yo' love me."

"Nick, Ah want to love a full-grown mahn, a mahn strong enough and brave enough to let go of the past, and to turn around and take hold of the future."

He regarded her with a sudden mix of fright and suspicion. "Yo' gon' leave me?"

"Nick, this be November. Ah ain' want but one ting for Christmas: to know yo' gon' be sittin' at a desk at the University of the Virgin Islands in January." She took a deep breath, hardening herself, then she delivered her ultimatum. "If yo' can't promise me that, Ah gon' say good-bye. No Angelique. No wedding. No family. Yo' on yo' own."

Shocked, he protested, "Ah tryin', Angel. Ah tryin the best Ah can."

She waved her hand, dismissing his excuses. "Ah sorry, Nick, but

Ah done all Ah can to help yo'. There come a time when Ah finally got to look out for mehself."

He was speechless; the soldier could challenge the world, but the vet was desperately afraid of being alone. "All right," he whispered. "Ah gon' sign up for classes."

She studied him closely. Though she remained torn between her love for him, and her lingering distrust of a man so profoundly embittered, she felt a surge of hope. "Nicholas, yo' gon' be one of the *best* teachers this island ever had."

Hesitant, he asked, "And . . . yo' gon' trow away that diaphragm?"

"Not tonight."

His face clouded with disappointment.

She was about to say, On the day yo' graduate. But in four years, she would be thirty-six. She was a nurse and midwife: she knew the risks of childbearing as she approached forty. And besides, his graduation was no guarantee. So she told him, "When yo' can shake the hand of a white mahn—really shake his hand—then," she nodded toward the sea, "Ah gon' trow that little rubber saucer to the waves."

He looked at her as if she were asking the impossible.

She encouraged him, "Ain' yo' the one who used to say, 'Can do'?"

He struggled, but finally nodded with agreement. "Can do." Then he smiled. "Can do, Nicholas Cruz." He held out his hand, ready to shake. "Hello. Meh name be Nicholas Cruz. Ah . . . Ah'm very glad to meet yo'."

She placed her hand in his, and was pleased that he did not shift through the sequence of West Indian grips, but gave her a simple, firm, continental handshake. "Hello, Mr. Cruz. I'm very glad to meet *you*."

Brimming with sudden jubilant joy, he announced, "We got to have a toast." He knelt and hunted in the grass until he found the coconut, silver-green in the moonlight. He drew his machete from its sheath, then with a sharp CHOCK!, he sliced off one end, forming a hole into the hollow center. Standing up, he held the coconut as if it were a holy chalice. "Put yo' hands over mine."

She wrapped her hands over his big beautiful hands, then reached up as he raised the coconut toward the stars. His voice boomed heavenward, "A toast to our children, waitin' to come into this world."

Never had she seen his face so radiant, so full of hope. She too called up, "A toast to our children. May we build a better world for them to come into."

First she, and then he, wrapped their lips around the opening and drank the nectar of their island.

He set the coconut back in the grass. His voice soft with love, he asked, "Shall Ah spread the blanket?"

She almost didn't want to make love. She would rather have waited until that handshake happened for real. But he kissed her cheek with such tenderness, how could she possibly say no? "Ah go get ready."

She found her purse, walked through the grass until she was far enough for privacy, then took out the flat plastic container with her diaphragm in it, and an aerosol can of foam. She held the rubber disk on her palm in the moonlight as she mused with regret—with a stab of loneliness and grief—that it might always be so: Meh shield, protectin' meh precious children by keepin' them unborn.

She undressed, then prepared herself for her lover.

Her clothes wrapped in a bundle, she walked back naked, the grass sweeping pleasantly between her bare legs.

He stood by the blanket, entranced as he gazed at her. She unbuttoned his fatigues. "Angelique," he said, his breath quickening, "meh beautiful, sweet, precious Angelique."

They lay on the blanket deep in the whispering grass, where all the world disappeared except for the glittering myriads of stars, and the sheen of the moon on their dark entwining bodies.

Closing her eyes, she drifted into a fantasy. She imagined herself where Nick would never go, though she had invited him and teased him and even argued with him to come aboard her sloop. But he was terrified of the sea. So she sailed alone, or with one of the nurses from the hospital. And sometimes, though she had recoiled at first from such imaginings, felt them unfair . . . sometimes she let herself dream that the sea was her lover. Wrapped in Nick's embrace, she became her little red sailboat in a building storm, buffeted by the wind of his breath in her ear, tossed by the rhythmic heaving of his body. She loved to be that boat, riding to the crest of his ocean-roving waves, gliding gracefully down into a deep smooth trough, rising up again on the back of a comber to its ragged peak where she shivered and strained . . . then plummeted down into the lovely abyss, only to rise even higher.

As the storm reached its peak, she hugged his powerful back with all her strength. And when his waves broke over her bow, her hull shuddered, heaved and pitched in the wild tempestuous surge.

Then she drifted, swept across smoothing seas by a gentler breeze.

And there upon the infinite billowing pillowing ocean, she was free.

He lifted his head to look at her, his eyes wide with wonder and love. Then he buried his face in her puff of hair and told her, "Angelique, Angelique, Angelique, yo' give me peace."

She squeezed his sweet-smelling body and promised, "Ah love yo', Nick. Yo' meh one and only. Forever."

When she looked up through the ragged black spears of grass at the bright disk of the moon, it was much higher than she expected. She reached into her jeans pocket and looked at her watch. "Got to go, Nick. Meh shift starts in an hour."

"When Ah see yo' again?"

She stood up and quickly dressed. "Me ain' know. Piotr ain' well. Ah t'ink his time comin' soon, and then Ah got to be with Zosia."

He stepped into his fatigues. "Ah phone yo'."

"Fine." She fastened her sandals while he laced up his combat boots.

They stood facing each other. He buried his fingers in her hair. "Ah gon' be a new mahn for yo'." His face was half-lit by the moon, half-dark in the night.

"Let that diploma be yo' peace treaty with the past."

"Yes. Ah promise."

One last kiss, sealing his promise, then she hurried along the ridge toward her scooter. She ached with hope that she could believe him.

CHAPTER FOUR

Casa Columbus

But the ghosts made no promises.

Nick watched her walk away through the grass; heard her kick-start her scooter; watched the red taillight disappear into the forest; listened to the engine disappear into the night. What she tink Ah gon' teach? he wondered. He marveled at her faith in him, her certainty that one day he, failure of failures, might have something to say to a classroom of teenagers. A basketball coach, yes, that he could envisage, that he could truly enjoy. But teacher? What she tink Ah gon' teach?

"Nick."

No, not now. Please, Ah got to tink about meh . . . lectures.

"Nick, when we get home, Ah tink Ah gon' back to school. Gon' be a marine biologist."

No, Leroy, leave me alone. Ah doin' meh best, mahn.

He stared along the path Angelique had taken. Another such path he had known, another Nielsen walking it, into oblivion. Ah could have grabbed Leroy's arm and told him Ah takin' his place, no matter what the sarge say. Ah *could* have just walked up that trail on meh own. Could have been point mahn all the way to Hanoi.

But Pfc. Nicholas Cruz allowed Sergeant William C. Ackerman to overrule him. Nick abided by the rules. And watched Leroy's helmet and backpack and two arms holding a rifle disappear into the sawgrass that swallowed him as a snake swallows a mouse.

Sergeant William C. Ackerman, who made no bones about his hate for niggers. Whose idea of a joke on the most dangerous patrols was to pick a nigger as point man: first on the trail, first to die. Nick could smell the wet sawgrass; he could smell his rain-soaked uniform, the oil on his rifle, his days-old sweat. Felt the muggy heat that turned boots into buckets of water. "Hey, Leroy, m'boy," chuckled Ackerman, "you're number one up the trail tonight." Nick knew the danger. He saw the

24

fear in Leroy's eyes. He argued with Ackerman, "Lemme run point in-stead." But Ackerman *liked* the fear in Leroy's face.

And where be Ackerman now? After twenty years, doin' quite well, no doubt. Maybe he stay on the team and got heself a desk at the Penta-gon. Maybe gone into business, sellin' some hot little item like napalm canisters. Yo' can be sure ol' Attackerman can count bucks as well as bodies. No doubt able to afford a luxury condominium on St. Croix. Why not?

For fifteen years in New York, Nick never gave up his hope that one day the sarge would climb into his Yellow Cab with an abrupt command, 'The Waldorf, and make it snappy.'

Now, each time he met a plane at the St. Croix airport, he scanned the white faces around the luggage belt. One day . . . one dynamite day Whigger Willy would come striding toward the curb with a suitcase and a tennis racket, bellowing, 'Taxi!'

Well, St. Croix ain' got no sawgrass to show the sarge, but the guinea grass does be deep enough. The guinea grass on Maroon Ridge. By the cliff. He'd show Ackerman the view, two hundred feet down.

He stared down the abyss at waves that once washed clean the grave of his ancestors; gazed at the crescent of rocks that formed Ma-roon Hole; watched the restless ribbon of foam, once red with African blood.

With a jolt, he realized there *was* something he could teach. "Leroy," he said aloud, "yo' remember the story yo' grandfather told us? About the Maroons. The history of our people we never learned in school."

He imagined himself at Central High, speaking to his class. He felt that his words filled the souls of a new generation. "From the first days of slavery on our island, the hills in the northwest corner," he would point to a map, "offered freedom to any African who managed to reach their jungle-covered slopes. Freedom to starve, perhaps. Freedom to die of strange diseases. But freedom, nevertheless, from the white mahn's hell." Faces lifted toward him with rapt attention. "And ultimately, when death ended a slave's imprisonment on this savage island, free-dom for his spirit to return to the homeland far across the sea."

He would write on the blackboard, CIMARRON. "The Spaniards called the runaway slaves who lived in the hills, 'cimarron,' which meant wild or savage. Later, the English and the Danes called them 'maroons,' the wild people. No one knew how many there were, livin' up in the rainforest. The Danish planters complained, 'Too many.' They waited for the day when troops would arrive from Copenhagen, a regiment strong enough to march into the forest and round up the planters' lost property." He would scan the back row, where the delinquent boys—himself once—listened to his every word. "The planters needed a full regiment, yo' see, because no white mahn, no matter how many banded together, no matter how well-armed they were, no matter that they took with them dogs as vicious as a pack of wolves . . . no white mahn ever returned from the forest where fierce proud African people hid behind every tree."

He would walk along an aisle among his students. "There been a thriving village in the forest: huts built of bamboo and thatch, gardens growin' yams and cassava. Groves of papaya trees. Herds of goats, flocks of chickens, stolen from the plantations. The men hunted deer. Children filled baskets with crabs. The villagers spoke a dozen different African tongues, worshipped a multitude of gods." He held up one finger: "Some of the people had been born in Africa." Two fingers: "While others had been born on the plantations. Both groups bore scars from the whip." Three fingers: "But a third group, born free in the forest, had never been touched by whip or chains. In one conviction were all these people united: *never* would they allow the white mahn to enslave them. Never would their feet walk the flatlands. Never would they cut sugar cane. Never. And so generations passed inside these sixteen square miles of wilderness, a corner of the island that been truly a part of Africa."

He would stand at the back of the room, sharing his story, his knowledge, his urgent message, with those delinquent boys whom teachers so often ignored. "Slaves down on the plantations listened at night to drums up in the hills that rumbled like distant thunder. Drums that beckoned, drums that promised. The planters too heard those drums, and cursed them, for no matter how carefully they kept watch over their chattel, the next mornin' they might discover that part of their property had disappeared."

The teacher would walk up another aisle to the front of the classroom. "Their letters of complaint posted to Copenhagen finally induced the Danish Crown to send sufficient troops to rectify the situation. Soldiers disembarked from a square-rigger in Christiansted harbor, then marched in splendid blue-and-white uniforms, bayonets flashin', up Kongensgade . . . King Street. The news raced across the island and up into the forest: the army has landed." He would lower his voice to a sinister tone as he repeated, "The army has landed."

"Maroon scouts kept watch in the foothills while the villagers assembled to ponder their options."

He clenched his fists, the rage rising in him until he could have shouted, What options? What options have our people ever had?

But he was teaching. No need to shout. Let the import of this tragedy be conveyed with discipline and dignity.

"Up the eastern slope came the soldiers, up the southern slope, up the western; to the north were the cliffs. Like hands reachin' for a stranglehold, the Danish troops tightened their grip. Readied their muskets. Honed their bayonets.

"A Danish scout reported that he had found the Maroons' village, in ashes. The soldiers followed him through the tangle of bushes and vines, down into a canyon, up onto the crest of a ridge. And yes, there was the site of the village: a clearin' where the earth was still smokin', small fires still burnin'. There was the garden: a dozen crops in neatly planted rows. Bountiful papaya trees. Flocks of chickens, tethered goats, and even a dozen cows. But not a single runaway man, woman or child in sight. The soldiers peered nervously into the branches overhead: nobody was hidin' in the treetops. Warily, they circled the mahogany trunks: nobody hidin' behind them. They poked their bayonets into thickets: nobody there.

"Pressing forward, the Danes stepped out from the forest onto windswept bluffs. They looked down at the rollin' blue sea and wondered what had happened to the savages."

Gazing down now at Maroon Hole, he decided he would bring his students on a field trip to this very spot. So they too could stare down, and imagine.

"A Danish recon patrol scoutin' along the cliff discovered what had happened. Lookin' down at a small bay, they saw bodies smashed on the rocks, bodies tumblin' in the surge, bodies driftin' in the current. The soldiers sent word to their sergeant, who emerged from the forest, strode along the ridge, and stared down with satisfaction at the red foam. He dispatched a courier to Christiansted, informin' the governor that the operation had been a limited success, for though the territory had been cleared of enemy forces, there remained no property other than livestock to return to the planters."

He gazed up the ridge at the black wall of ragged trees that brushed the scattered silver stars.

The classroom vanished; his students were replaced by ghosts more real than any dream of teaching: voices, African voices, clamored in the forest. Grew louder as they emerged from the trees. He heard the cries of frightened children. Heard shouts of defiance hurled back at the Danish invader, and prayers of hope sent up to the sun. The first man leaped: Nick listened to that long empty moment as the Maroon dropped through the air with silent dignity. Heard the screams and wails of those who watched.

Vividly, he envisioned a family gripping hands and plunging together. Saw a boy standing alone, too terrified to move, until he was picked up and kissed and carried by his father into the abyss. Lovers clutched each other and plummeted. Suddenly a woman with a puff of soft hair raced desperately with an infant in her arms back along the ridge toward the forest. She was caught by the village chief and granted immediate peace with a stab of his knife through her heart. The squalling child too was quieted with a plunge of the blade. The warrior carried both of them, limp across his arms, toward the cliff. There he held them, waiting until he stood alone, the last free black man on the island. Then he too leaped, squeezing the woman and child to his chest as he dropped through the rush of wind.

A cry of agony burst from Nick's throat, a long wrenching wail of grief at the annihilation of his people.

Stepping dizzily away from the cliff, for this warrior would not jump, this warrior would gather his forces to fight the invader who— his combat boot bumped the coconut. He stared at the smooth seed in the grass: a helmet, sarge's helmet.

Lemme run point instead.

No way, Cruz. Nielsen's number one boy tonight.

Outranked and overruled, he froze before those blue eyes that gloated with satisfaction, for Ackerman *liked* to see his niggers scared.

Dropping to his knees, Nick drew his machete from its sheath, raised it overhead and slashed the blade down with all his brutal strength, CHOCK! "Whigger!" CHOCK! "Whigger!" CHOCK! The coconut disintegrated into dirty bits of white meat as he bludgeoned Ackerman's skull. "Whigger!"

"Don' use that word!" cried her voice.

Startled, he looked up. But no one was there. The wind off the sea whispered through the grass. Panting for breath, he looked at the

hacked pieces of coconut. He and Angelique had toasted to their children with that coconut. Appalled by what he had done, he slid the
machete back into its sheath, then he tossed the evidence over the cliff.

He decided he would drive home, take a shower and go to bed; he'd
skip the 10:50 flight from Miami. Tomorrow he would visit the University, check out the courses offered in January, maybe take a look
around the bookstore. Then he worried: Might he have already missed
the registration deadline?

Never mind. First ting tomorrow, Ah gon' reserve a desk right up
front.

But as he walked along the ridge toward his taxi, he gazed at the
dark forest beyond it. His boots were drawn toward the one place in all
the world he could call home. His hideaway, his refuge, his realm: his
own piece of Africa.

Slivers of moonlight dappled the mahogany trunks. Treefrogs, his
boyhood pals, peeped as lustily as ever. Overhead, a gust of wind rus-
tled through the canopy. And the air that he loved: he filled his lungs
with deep breaths of the damp, musty, pungent air of his primeval rainforest.

Keenly alert, keeping the moon to his right, he traversed terrain he
knew by heart. To climb and slide and jump with his legs, how good
that felt after sitting long days in the taxi. At a creek where he and
Leroy had often camped, he knelt and cupped his hands in the cool gurgling water for a drink.

The moon rose high into the heavens as he headed east.

Nearing Bodkin Hill, he decided to climb to its peak so he could
look down at the University. He emerged onto a bluff where the trees
had been cleared for cattle pasture. Ever the cautious soldier, he
stopped short of Scenic Road and stood in deep grass, ready to crouch
should the lights of a car approach.

On the opposite side of the road stood a picnic table, popular with
tourists who rented jeeps.

He gazed down at the southern half of his island, a plain speckled
with lights. Along Centerline Highway, diamonds crept in one direction, rubies in the other. The sweeping beacon at the airport blinked . . .
blinked . . . blinked. Near the airport stood a buff-colored building, the
University, its three stories lit by spotlights. He thought with a surge of
pride, That gon' be *my* school. Ah gon' come out of that buildin' as

Mistah Nicholas Cruz, and Ah gon' marry Miss Angelique Nielsen, and
Ah gon' be Papa to enough kids to make a basketball team. Ah gon' be
a dedicated teacher. Might one day be principal of meh own school.
And one day . . . possibly one day, might Ah become governor of the
Virgin Islands. *Then* we gon' see some changes!

As he savored his dream of the future, his eyes were drawn to the
most prominent feature on the plain: the densely packed lights and
cracking towers of the Petrox Oil Refinery. The complex extended for
over a mile along the southern shore, like a Martian City built over the
buried lagoon. Burnoff flames trailed west in the trade winds like tiny
orange flags. Scattered across the Caribbean were the stationary lights
of tankers waiting their turn to dock at the refinery's wharf.

Wonder if Hard Hat be workin' the night shift. Mistah Building
Code. Mistah Environmental Protection Plan. Yes sir, fine for them
who's drawin' their dollar to make a speech about the Supreme Court.

Scanning the refinery as he had a hundred times before, he imagined each tower and storage tank to be a target waiting for the touch of
his magic wand. A one-man night patrol, with a dozen sticks of dynamite and a dozen timers; and then he would be back up Scenic Road,
sitting at that picnic bench, when BOOM! BOOM! BO-BOBOOM!,
fireballs suddenly blossomed into the night over the ruins of Petrox.
Can do, sir! Can do!

But his gloating was brief. For he looked back at the University
and winced; then he turned away from the complicated flatlands and
retreated into the security of the sacred virgin forest.

An owl hooted in the treetops. Looking up, he echoed the call; but
he was rusty, out of practice. As he walked, he thought regretfully,
Tink, if Leroy and Ah had brought our kids with tents and sleepin'
bags. Taught them how to build a campfire, how to steam crabs. We
could have—

Lights winked through the foliage. He was surprised he had come
so far. Crouching, he listened. Above the rasping of locusts, he heard
the pock . . . pock . . . pock of a tennis ball. A faint burst of laughter.

He almost turned around. But he had never visited Casa Columbus
from this direction. Always before, he entered the condominium complex by driving his taxi past the security office, a stone building that
looked like a fortress blockhouse. Then he followed the road to Villa
Pinta, or Villa Niña, or Villa Santa Maria, while he listened to the

happy Yankee chatter in the back seat about all the lovely new bunga-lows springing up.

The forest of his ancestors was deeded property. Zoned for residen-tial development. The chain saws roared, the bulldozers terraced and smoothed, the landscape architects tidied up afterwards with royal poinciana and pruned bougainvillea. A village of another kind was re-placing the ashes and silent drums.

Ol' Nick gon' do a little scoutin'. Gon' recon a hostile village. See what sort of target we got here.

Reaching into a pouch pocket of his camouflage fatigues, he took out a black ski mask and black gloves. He moved along the edge of the forest with the stealth of a panther.

"Love-forty!" cheered a man in white shorts as he pranced on his toes across a spotlighted tennis court. "Ho, I gotcha now!"

The villas were tastefully designed with a Spanish motif: ambulato-ries were capped with archways, facades painted Castillian pink. In front of every hacienda stood an American-colonial lamppost.

A woman practicing her golf swing hit a glow-in-the-dark whiffle ball on a short green arc. Her husband on the balcony of their holiday home hooted advice, "Straighten that left arm! Wiggle that fanny!" He howled with laughter as she swung her ample bottom, then guffawed when she sliced the ghostly ball into a bulldozed hole at the construc-tion site next door. "Ya gotta play it where it lies!"

Across the lawn, a man appeared in pajamas on his balcony; he surveyed his realm while brushing his teeth.

Jovial Joe called from balcony to balcony, "Howdy, neighbor! Where ya from?"

"Down from Cos Cob. Yourself?"

"Put 'er there, pal! Bernice and I hail from Ashtabula. Finally got the air conditioners in today, thank God."

Many of the two-story houses were dark, waiting for the Christmas season, and Easter, the taxi driver's bonanza months. Otherwise, these quarter-million dollar boxes often stood vacant. December was prime time for tinkering with the real estate market. The trick was to pick bungalows far enough from the trees that no fire would spread to the forest. A rainy night, just to be sure.

Scouting further along the periphery, he came upon something odd: a boardwalk leading from a sodded lawn into the jungle. He could smell the freshly sawn planks. The underbrush along both sides had been trimmed. He stepped onto the walkway and followed it for fifty yards until it ended, though he could see something in the brush beyond it. Taking a penlight from his pocket, he shone the beam on two rows of orange flags attached to stakes, outlining the future path. The forest would soon be laced with walkways. Picnic tables. Brass name plates on the gumbo-limbo trees. Even the Cong, he thought with respect for his old enemy, at least walked on the earth.

And she want me to shake hands with the white mahn.

Ah gon' bring meh students here on a field trip. Teach them they got to become lawyers.

Or warriors.

Basketball players. Or guerrillas.

He heard voices: a man and a woman, approaching on the walkway. Unable to resist, he crouched in the ferns. Let the folks know they got neighbors they ain' met yet.

White faces appeared. "Think of it, Vikki, our own little patch of paradise!"

With a fierce ululating howl, Nick sprang onto the boardwalk and flailed his moon-glinting machete over their heads. The woman screamed as if she would turn inside out; she crashed backward into her husband, who gripped her in his arms and pleaded, "Pl-pl-pl-pl-please."

Nick *liked* the fear in their faces.

He stepped off the boardwalk and strode in his combat boots into the forest. As he passed among the giant mahoganies, he remembered an old phrase from Nam, an often-used justification that tonight was filled with sweet irony: We had to destroy the village to save it.

CHAPTER FIVE

Candle Point

Braking her scooter at the crest of a hill, Angelique paused wearily to look down at a pastel turquoise bay, a graceful scallop where the gentle Caribbean nudged her gentle island. In the early morning sunshine, the yellow sail of a windsurfer skimmed across the water like the bright wing of a butterfly.

Flanking the bay at its far end, a rocky peninsula pointed due north like a long black finger. Two centuries ago, slaves from a sugar plantation had built a bonfire every Saturday night on the elevated fingertip. Their Danish master, looking down from his greathouse verandah, (on the hill where Angelique now rested,) had named the peninsula Candle Point. On that fingertip now stood two houses built of stone, their copper roofs tarnished green by the sea. This pair of houses had been constructed over a century ago by a retired sea captain for himself and his West Indian mistress; and though that faithful couple had passed on to another paradise, their two stone houses had successfully weathered a century of hurricanes with no more damage than the loss of an occasional sheet of copper.

Following the last stretch of the road home, she coasted down the grassy hill, then rode along a sandy lane at the upper edge of a broad white beach that cupped the belly of the bay. A parade of pelicans flapped along the shore; though they peered down, none folded its wings to dive.

Now she turned north, due north, for the peninsula pointed north as unfailingly as the needle of a compass, and she rode along a gently rising and dipping concrete lane wide enough for a horse-drawn carriage, or a car. The fresh sea breeze cooled her face, swept the hospital smells from her white uniform. Waves from the bay broke against the jagged black rocks along this first portion of the peninsula; their briny spray misted her face, and brought a smile of peace and gratitude.

33

To her left, westward, in the lee of Candle Point, the water of another bay lay flat as glass, pastel green, and so crystalline that she could see clumps of brain coral.

Halfway to the fingertip, the concrete lane now sloped steeply upward; throttling to full power, she felt she was about to rocket into the blue morning sky.

The ramp carried her up to an oval table of rock; the fingertip had been flattened over a century ago by a crew of Crucian workers with dynamite, pick axes and shovels. Then, with his own hands, the captain had built upon that sea-wrapped promontory the two houses of stone. Hoisting with a ship's pulley grey blocks of granite which he had brought by frigate from the coast of Maine, he laid two parallel rectangular foundations, fifty feet apart on the outermost tip, then he built layer by layer two parallel boxes, their windows open to the Trade Winds. He hewed the roof beams with an axe, and nailed into place shiny copper sheets from a shipbuilding yard in Boston. His home stood on the sunrise bluff, for he was a man up early in the morning, and her home stood on the sunset bluff, for she was a woman who, like certain tropical flowers that open their petals with a burst of perfume in the cool darkness of evening, came to life at night.

The steep concrete lane leveled on the tabletop, then divided into a circular driveway that looped past the two houses. In the center of the circle grew a blaze of pink-orange bougainvillea bushes, where the bonfires of slaves had once leaped and flickered toward the stars.

Angelique's home, on the sunrise side, stood two stories tall: upstairs were the gabled windows of the residence, downstairs were the weathered stable doors of the carriage house.

Honeggers' home, on the sunset side, had only one story, though its peaked roof provided, at its northern end, room for Zosia's loft, overlooking the sea.

The southern peak, facing the island, framed a round stained glass window, its colors dull from the driveway. But when viewed from Honegger's bedroom, the round window high on the bedroom wall, with the sun shining through it, depicted a luminous European garden: jubilant daffodils on the left and right hugged a cluster of red and white Polish roses; cupped at the bottom, a carpet of violets; spread at the top, a spray of apple blossoms in a spring-blue sky. Zosia and Piotr, refugees from Poland, from Germany, from the camps that had offered their families no escape save up a chimney, had removed the captain's clear glass, which once enabled the tropical moon to shine onto his lover in her bed; they replaced it with Zosia's carefully cut pieces of yellow and crimson, green, white, and blue, leaded into place by Piotr's skillful hands. Now the sun shone almost every day through their European garden, a garden which, as Zosia once told Angelique, graced the family graves, which did not exist.

The captain and his crew had carted earth from the island to the fingertip, then spread it between the two houses at the edge of the northern cliff. In this bed of soil grew a broad patch of seagrape bushes, their pancake-shaped providing privacy to both homes.

As Angelique reached the top of the ramp, her fuzzy brown dog came bounding across the driveway toward her. Around his neck he wore a sun-faded, salt-crusted red bandana. Prancing beside her scooter with his bushy tail waving like a banner, he howled his welcome, "Ooooowwwwlllllllll!"

She parked at the edge of the loop near her house, turned off the motor and savored in her tiredness the delightful silence, then she leaned down to receive her hound's abundant kisses. "How yo' been, ol' pal?" She ruffled his ears. "Yo' kept the homestead safe from sea monsters?"

The dog wriggled out of her arms, ready for a romp on the beach.

"Not yet, Ulysses," she said wearily as she got off her scooter. "Ah got to check on Piotr."

First, however, a glass of cold papaya juice. She walked through an archway of purple-pink bougainvillea, then climbed a flight of weathered wooden steps up the stone side of her house, her legs aching with exhaustion, to a porch that jutted toward the island like an elevated dock; the porch was supported at its end by two poles, the frigate's mast and boom, the one twice as tall as the other, their tarnished brass cleats and pulleys still attached.

She leaned against the varnished railing of her sanctuary, (and of her salty dog's lookout,) facing both the cool breeze and the warm sun. The splash of waves against the rocky cliff a hundred feet below soothed her after a night of cranky patients and cumbersome paperwork.

The windsurfer caught her eye as it zigzagged past her house on its voyage out to sea. Several times she had noticed the pale figure wrestling with his yellow triangle, usually in the late afternoon after she had awakened from her day's sleep. She had never been on a windsurfer. She loved her sailboat too much to experiment with anything else.

Looking south toward the island, she scanned the two beaches, twin scallops of white sand divided by Candle Point. On the leeward beach, nestled among the palms, she spotted a sliver of red: the hull of her sloop. Its aluminum mast poked above the thatch and gleamed in the sun. Every weekend she pulled her fiberglass boat across the beach to the water, then she sailed with Ulysses on the sparkling blue waters of the Caribbean, leaving her troubles on the island far, far behind. Leaving, unfortunately, Nick behind as well. She smiled with sad humor: Funny Nick, sits on the beach like them waves gon' eat him.

Turning west, she gazed down the coast toward the distant green-gray hills. How different their two worlds: Nick's shadowy forest, where they occasionally went for walks together, and her own sunny realm, where he rarely came to visit. She wondered how much argument he would give her when she insisted, if they married, that they live here on Candle Point. Time for yo' to come out of hidin'. Time for yo' to get yo' feet wet. Because, Mistah Nick, our kids ain' growin' up in the shadows. Ah gon' raise a crew of sailors, and the sea gon' make them strong!

She looked again longingly at her little red sloop; but today was only Wednesday. She felt as if she'd been through a week of six Fridays.

Ulysses' claws clacked on the planks as he pranced beside her, hoping to inspire a trip to the beach. She scratched him behind his soft furry ears. "Soon, Ulysses, soon." But first, a glass of cold thick sweet papaya juice.

Then, her morning house call.

The oaken double-doors squeaked as she opened them. Sunshine pouring through the windows cast golden rectangles across the hardwood floor. Ulysses sat on the porch, ears drooping.

Piotr got out of bed every day at dawn to search for the Gestapo. Eighty-three years old, with white hair and a bushy white beard, he shuffled in pajamas from window to window and peered furtively out for soldiers in brown uniforms. He searched the bushes for lurking spies. He scanned the Caribbean for Nazi ships. To the west, his eyes darted over a cay for traces of an encampment. From his bedroom window, he scouted the isthmus that connected his home to the hills of St. Croix, where he trusted no one.

While he searched for the enemy, his wife stood at the stove, preparing breakfast. She wore a T-shirt emblazoned with the red-and-white Polish flag, and one word in red, SOLIDARNOŠČ. In her red shorts, red socks and white jogging shoes, she looked like a seventy-two-year-old marathon runner who would run and run and run until she collapsed into a wheelchair.

Zosia was trying to crack an egg on the edge of a skillet. But her bony fingers felt nothing, for she suffered from neuropathy of the extremities: the nerves of her hands and feet were dying. With numb fingers wrapped around the egg, she knocked the shell against the pan, knocked it harder, then harder still; the egg smashed and its jelly and broken yolk dribbled through her fingers, half into the skillet, half onto the stove. "Psiakrew!" she cursed.

Piotr called with a frightened whisper, "Zosia, a ship!"

She looked across the L-shaped counter separating the kitchen from the dining room. Her husband turned from the window, shuffled with urgency around the table and reached for his binoculars on a peg. He looked at her—his eyes filled with fear verging on panic—then he opened the door to the porch and shambled out.

With a sigh of exhaustion, she rinsed the egg from her fingers, reached for her cane and followed him out the door. He stared through the binoculars and muttered, "Neun neun acht." She glanced at the ship, a destroyer near the horizon. But she was far more interested in the clouds above it, ocher-orange wisps of cirrus in a gray-blue sky: perfect for pastel chalks.

He whispered anxiously, "Can you see its flag?" He handed her the glasses, though he held the strap so she would not drop them into the sea.

She hooked her cane over the railing, wrapped both hands as tightly as she could around the glasses, then leaned her elbows on the rail. Her hands trembled; the round field of vision jiggled as it moved along the horizon. Nevertheless, she located the familiar destroyer, bristling with twin radar towers, 998 painted on its bow. No matter how many times he sighted that ship, he never remembered it from one day to the next. She reassured him, "It's American, Piotr. Allied." She returned the binoculars to him.

He declared with relief, "One of ours." He stared through the binoculars at the friendly vessel. His hair hung in tangles after his restless night in bed. His breath, even outside in the breeze, stank of decay. She wondered how much longer he would fight to stay alive. They had promised each other in Berlin that no matter how wretched life became, they would struggle to keep on living. And so they had survived. Now, that promise again kept them going, though he grew weaker every day. She wondered too how much longer *she* would survive as she struggled to care for him, while she suffered the anguish of watching him slowly die. Old age, she thought, the early hearse of death.

Suddenly she smelled egg burning. She grabbed her cane. Thumping with it along the porch toward the house, she cursed, "Psiakrew!"

Husband and wife sat at the dining room table, eating breakfast. He gazed vacantly as he dug a spoon into the soft orange pulp of a papaya, lifted the spoon to his mouth, and chewed.

Unable to endure the silence any longer, she set down her slice of toast and called to him, "Piotr!"

He raised his eyes and slowly turned to look at her across the corner of the table, but only after a long moment did he focus on her. Recognizing her, he murmured, "Zzzzosha."

She suggested with enthusiasm, "Piotr, let's go on a picnic."

His eyes brightened faintly, though his words were slow. "White . . . wine and . . . camam . . . bert cheese."

She smiled at him. "We'll fill the basket brimming with food, and we'll take the tartan blanket."

A flush of life returned to his face. "Ja. We . . . hike to the . . . meadow."

Delighted with his renewed vitality, she elaborated, "I'll make your favorite potato salad, with chives from the garden."

He leaned toward her. "And I know . . . what I shall make." His eyes kindled with roguish affection. "I shall make . . *love* with you . . . on the blanket."

She raised her orange juice glass. "A toast to the picnic!"

He reached for his own glass, but his big hand knocked it over, spilling juice across the mahogany table. She stared with dismay at the orange puddle that streamed over the edge and splattered on the floor. However, undaunted, she held her own trembling glass with both hands to his lips, then toasted with exuberance, "Na zdrowie!"

He mumbled, "Nah . . . zzzdroviahh." The light in his eyes was fading.

Watching him sink back into his abyss, she called desperately, "Piotr,

I love you!"

He stared down at his papaya. His hand hunted for his spoon.

She set her glass of juice on the table, unable to drink her half of the toast to a picnic that would never be.

After breakfast, she needed to get him into bed before he fell asleep and toppled out of his chair. Bracing herself with both hands on the table, she stood up. "Piotr, let me wheel you to the bedroom."

He looked dully at the wheelchair by the table, then shook his head.

She tugged at his arm. "Please get into the wheelchair."

"Nien!" he roared with sudden energy. He would walk, he would not ride. Gripping the edge of the table with both hands, he struggled to push himself up.

To argue was useless; she reached for her cane, hooked over the back of a chair. Then she waited as he, groaning with the effort, bits of papaya and toast tumbling from his lap, managed to stand.

Together, he gripping her shoulder, her cane thumping between them, they shuffled across the living room, then followed the hallway to their bedroom. At the door, they stopped to rest. He turned his gaze slowly to look at her and wheezed, "Danke schön."

She nodded with silent affirmation that they would keep on fighting.

The couple shuffled to a rented hospital bed. They turned slowly until the bed was behind them, then he bent his knees and sat down heavily. Lying on the narrow mattress, he dragged one leg up onto the bed, then drew up the other. His head settled into his pillow. Within moments, he was asleep. She pulled up the blue sheet and tucked it beneath his beautiful white beard.

She tried to lift the safety gate. But she was too exhausted to heft its weight. Angelique would arrive soon; she could do it.

She returned to the living room, where she climbed a staircase: gripping its railing and thumping her cane, she progressed step by slow step up to her studio in the loft.

She would paint. How else to survive?

Looking out the eastern window, its bottom half obscured by unpruned seagrape bushes, she saw a cream-yellow sun peaking above Angelique's roof. And now she could hear the scooter buzzing up the road; her neighbor was home, and would shortly come to check on Piotr. Fine.

Turning to the loft's northern window, she glanced at the destroyer, disappearing to the west; then she studied the Caribbean's emergent blues and deepening greens. Pleased with the day's clear air, she perched on the stool in front of her bench and set to work.

Awkwardly, but patiently, she opened tubes of acrylic paint: she willed her thumb and forefinger to pinch the caps so she could unscrew them. She lay each rumpled tube on her palette, then leaned on the tube with her palm, squeezing out a blob of color: cerulean blue, violet, and aquamarine; olive, and emerald green; a blob of white, a squirt of canary yellow.

The rocks today? She peered down from the window at two arms of jagged rock that reached like tongs from the tip. Yes, the rocks. Then a squirt of burnt umber.

She chose a brush from the dozen standing bristles-up in a mayonnaise jar, then willed her fingers to wrap around its handle. She poked the trembling brush at the blob of cerulean, dabbed at the green, and began to mix her first color. Her eyes danced back and forth between the evolving hue, and the colors in the sea. She needed a hint of morning yellow. A touch of white to lighten. Finally she painted a stroke of turquoise across her pad, then peered out the window to compare. "Perfect!" she declared.

Her eyes focused with serene concentration as she mixed her second color: the indigo of the shadowed sides of the waves.

Piotr needed to get to the bathroom.

He nudged one foot to the edge of the mattress. Moved his other foot to the edge. Turning slowly on his back, he slid one leg over the side. Then the other leg. He never thought to question why the safety gate was down; the absence of the barricade simply made his bed normal again. He raised himself to his elbows. Pushed himself up until he sat. Dizzy, he sat for a long time without moving.

He managed to stand, then to shuffle across the bedroom to the bathroom, where he stood beside the toilet, bracing himself with one hand on its vertical tank. But his other hand alone could not untie the bow of his pajama bottoms. Urgently, angrily, he jerked at the loops, but only pulled the knot tighter. "Scheisse!" His knees buckled and he crashed with a triple thud of hip, shoulder and head onto the floor.

Zosia heard a strange bumping sound. Alarmed, she called down the staircase, "Piotr?" She reached for her cane. "Piotr?!" She descended the stairs as quickly as she could, then she thumped along the hallway. "Kochany, what's wrong?"

From the doorway, she saw with shock that he was not in his bed. Her eyes darted around the room until she discovered his white head sticking out from the bathroom door. "Piotr!" she shrieked as she hurried toward him. He moved his arms and legs like a crab that had been stepped on, its shell crushed but the animal inside still alive. Urine spread across the floor from his wet pajamas. She grabbed the doorknob, gripped the toilet seat and knelt beside him, then cradled his quivering head in her hands and shouted into his ear, "Piotr, I am *here. I am with you.*"

His convulsions grew stronger.

Helpless, frantic, she remembered Angelique's air horn. Yanking a towel from a rack, she stuffed it as a pillow beneath his head. Then she gripped the toilet seat and doorknob, raised herself to her feet and thumped across the bedroom to the night table, where she grabbed the air horn. Leaning her knees against the mattress, she dropped her cane on the bed, then pointed the horn's dusty chrome bell toward the latticed window facing Angelique's house. With the fingers of both hands, she tried to pull the trigger. It would not budge. "Psiakrew!" Gritting her teeth, she squeezed her numb knot of fingers with all her strength, willing them to gather an increment tighter. Suddenly the horn blared; her heart jumped as the piercing blast filled the stone-walled room.

She held the trigger as long as she could. When her fingers quit and the blast abruptly stopped, she dropped the horn on the bed, grabbed her cane and thumped back to her husband.

Slumped in her kitchen chair, Angelique jolted upright, set down her juice glass, dashed into the living room and grabbed her physician's bag. Ran down the steps and sprinted around the driveway to Honeggers' door. Throwing it open, she raced down the hall, then stood baffled when she found the bedroom empty.

From the bathroom, Zosia cried, "Help him!"

Rushing to the door, the nurse discovered the disaster on the floor. She knelt beside Zosia, lifted Piotr's eyelids open and examined his quivering irises, his unnaturally wide pupils. Then she opened her black bag, snapped on her stethoscope, slid its chrome disk under Piotr's pajama top and listened to his wildly fluttering heart. The Honeggers steadfastly refused to go to the hospital, and she knew both would be fortunate if this seizure were his coup de grace. She managed to stuff the corner of a towel between his gnashing teeth.

Zosia's face was pale and damp with sweat. She was panting. Angelique feared the old woman would collapse from shock. "Let's get you to bed."

Zosia disagreed sharply. "Help him first."

"No. First is you in bed." Knowing she could do little for Piotr, the nurse gripped her first-priority patient under the arms and hoisted Zosia to her feet.

Struggling to pull free, Zosia insisted, "Help *Piotr*!"

Angelique glanced around the bedroom for the wheelchair; it was not there. So, half-lifting, half-pulling, she drew the protesting woman across the room to the king-size bed, sat her on the mattress and ordered her, "Lie down, please."

Zosia pointed her twig-thin finger, "Go to *him*. Proszę, proszę, save Piotr!"

Angelique tossed the air horn out of the way, then lifted her seventy-nine-pound patient and laid her on her back. Scowling, she warned, "Zosia, you are not to give me trouble."

Zosia glared back, her wrinkled face hardened with defiance; but she lay still.

Angelique fetched a pink blanket from a closet and spread it over Zosia. She felt the pulse at the carotid artery in the neck: rapid, but not critical. "Lie quietly. I'm going to help Piotr."

She hurried to the bathroom, where she ran her skilled fingers over his skull, spine, and hips: nothing seemed to be broken. But better he was strapped in the bed than thrashing on the floor. She gripped his wrists and dragged the heavy man to the hospital bed; then she crouched, held him under the arms and hefted him up so that he sat on the mattress. She laid him lengthwise and raised the barricade into place. While she buckled the straps over his jerking chest and hips, she could not stop the tears running down her cheeks.

Zosia demanded angrily, "Bring me my cane."

Angelique shot a stern glance at her—and saw that Zosia was sitting up! She snapped, "You stay right there."

"Nogh. I will *be* with him." Zosia's eyes blazed with furious impatience. "I promised him that. Please bring me my cane."

Angelique hurried to secure the third strap over Piotr's knees. "Zosia, *please*. You must lie still. Keep that blanket over you."

Zosia threw off the blanket, swung her feet to the floor and started to stand without her cane.

Angelique rushed to the iron-willed woman before she fell. Knowing that to argue was useless, she braced Zosia from behind and helped her to stagger across the room to her husband.

Zosia gripped the top of the safety gate, then gasped, "A chair." The gate rattled as she teetered unsteadily. Angelique reached for the chair from Piotr's writing desk, placed it behind Zosia, then supported her as she sat down. Zosia reached between the chrome bars and gripped Piotr's spasmodic hand. "I'm right here," she shouted. "Kochany, I am *here*."

After the convulsions had passed, Piotr's quivering eyes became still; his jaw slackened; his brow unclenched; and he kept breathing.

Zosia held his hand. She had calmed; the blood returned to her face.

Angelique sat on her heels beside her. "He fights like a tiger."

Zosia's eyes shone with faint admiration. "Yagh. He is a tiger."

"Do you want me to call an ambulance?"

"Nogh. We promised each other we would finish together, here in our home."

"I know that. But I am asking, to be sure."

"We are sure." Zosia took a deep breath, gathering her strength. "We are fine now. We thank you."

The nurse unfastened the straps over Piotr, pulled off his wet pajamas, washed him, and dried him. She covered him with a fresh sheet and blanket, then she rebuckled the straps.

With a mop and bucket, she sopped up the urine on the bathroom floor, then cleaned the tiles with hot water and Clorox.

Returning to the bedroom, she hooked Zosia's cane over the safety gate, then sat again on her heels and said, "I'll take a nap on the couch in the living room. You call me if you need me."

Zosia shook her head. "Nogh. We are fine. You go now. We want to be alone."

"I will be on the couch."

Zosia's olive-black eyes hardened. "Please leave us alone in our home."

"Then . . . you must call me if you need me. By phone or with the horn. I will be in my house all day."

Zosia nodded, though from a great distance away. "Thank you,

Angelique. We both thank you so much." She stared through the chrome bars at her husband.

"You are both very welcome."

Angelique put the night table beside Zosia's chair and set the air horn on it. Then she picked up her black bag and left the room. She washed the breakfast dishes, sponged up spilled orange juice. Stepping out of the silent house, she pulled the heavy oaken door closed behind her.

Contrary to her daily routine, she did not walk with Ulysses down to the beach for a swim. She took a shower to wash away Piotr's clinging stench, then, desolate, she lay in her bed. Her eyes ached to let the tears pour out. She had been nurse and neighbor to the Honeggers for five years. But though she felt at the verge of bursting into sobs, the tears would not come.

She laid her arm over her eyes to block the sunshine seeping around the curtains, and tried to sleep.

Outside the bedroom window, waves pummeled the cliff.

She envisioned Zosia in the chair, reaching her arms through the bars, her thin fingers clutching Piotr's big yellow-white hand. She felt the devotion between those two, and she wondered if she and Nick would ever share such enduring love. Suddenly the dam burst and the sobs poured out. Overwhelmed with doubts that he would ever change, cursed with fear that the Navy would forever threaten her island, she cried silently for herself and all the years of solitude she had endured. To protect her children. Her poor unborn children, victims of the last war, victims of the next.

The thought rose briefly in her mind that she ought to pray for help, for strength, for solace and guidance and grace. But she did not fold her hands in prayer. Since Leroy had disappeared, the church had remained a mighty fortress for her parents; but whenever she herself tried to find her faith, the holy words seemed a taunting lie.

Ulysses nuzzled her cheek. Rolling to the edge of the bed, she buried her face in his soft fur and hugged him. "Ah sorry. Ah does be on call."

At least she had Ulysses, her steady uncomplicated friend.

She rolled with a groan onto her stomach, pulled the pillow over her head and waited for the oblivion of sleep.

CHAPTER SIX

The Garden

Before she went to the hospital that evening, Angelique visited her neighbors. Zosia still sat in the chair, holding Piotr's hand. He lay in a coma. Angelique listened with her stethoscope to his struggling heart. Then she looked up at the round window beneath the peak of the roof. The flowers were lit by a chandelier, their colors drab. She saw them as truly flowers over a grave.

She heated a bowl of soup and set it on the dining room table. But when she returned to the bedroom and tried to coax Zosia to come eat, Zosia showed no sign that she heard; she stared through the bars at her husband.

Angelique wrapped the pink blanket around her against the evening's chill. "Your dinner is on the table. Phone me at the hospital if you need me. Otherwise, I'll see you in the morning."

Zosia turned her head; her eyes looked like tunnels with fires burning deep inside. "Please, would you turn out the light?"

"Turn out the light?"

"Yagh. I do not want to see this sickroom anymore. I want to be with Piotr. Just us."

Angelique dimmed the chandelier.

Zosia frowned, unsatisfied. "Nogh. I want it out completely."

She clicked off the lamp. A glow from the nightlight in the bathroom suffused into the bedroom.

Zosia nodded. "We thank you."

Angelique said a silent good-bye to Piotr, then left the old couple alone.

During the night, Zosia sat with her cold hands wrapped around Piotr's feverish hand. The moon shone through the round window, casting a circle of blurred colors on the hardwood floor behind her. The cir-

45

cle crept across the floor as the moon traveled across the sky.

She heard the phone ringing down the hall in the living room. She turned her head toward the bedroom door, but she did not wonder who would be calling at this hour. Her ears heard the ringing, then heard silence; nothing more registered in her mind . . . until she noticed the luminous palette of colors on the floor. Gazing at it, she asked "Piotr, do you remember our garden in Switzerland?" She turned to her husband. "Shall we have a picnic out in our garden?"

For the first time in hours, she let go of his hand. She wrapped her fingers around the railing of the safety gate and pulled herself up; the blanket fell to the floor. Shuffling around his bed, she poked the rubber tip of her cane at the four footbrakes, releasing them. Then she gripped the railing at the head of the bed and leaned her weight toward the radiant garden. The bed rolled easily on its castor wheels. Walking backward step by slow, unsteady step, she pulled her husband until the upper half of his bed was lit by the circular patchwork of colors.

With his high forehead, his beloved face, his bushy white beard, tinged with rose and violet, yellow and blue, he looked like a Gothic saint in a cathedral window.

She hooked her cane around a leg of her chair, dragged it toward her, and sat. Then she reached through the bars to take his hand.

The faint gurgling of his breathing was silent.

She listened.

Silence.

"Piotr?" She stared at the rose-and white blanket over his chest: he lay motionless. "Nogh!" Outraged that he had been stolen from her, she shook the bars with a fury that rattled the whole bed. "Kochany! Don't leave me here alone!"

Gasping, she stopped to catch her breath. The pale blurred garden, creeping by increments across the bed, brushed his face with tatters of colors. When the dark edge of the circle touched his cheek, she staggered up and pulled the bed until he again lay safely among the flowers.

She drew her chair to the side of the bed and collapsed onto the seat. Reaching through the bars, she straightened his hair. Smoothed his beard. The dark scythe moved across his slack face. But she had no strength to rescue him again.

She pulled his heavy hand out through the bars and caressed it with her numb fingers.

*   *   *

The mahogany coffin, its wine-red lid gleaming in the sun, lay on the stern of a fishing trawler. Piotr's and Zosia's friends stood in a cluster in their dark mourning clothes on Christiansted wharf; most of them were elderly, black people, Hispanic, and white.

Angelique pushed Zosia in the wheelchair across the gangplank. The captain gripped the chair's armrests and lifted Zosia down to the deck. He wheeled her to the shade of a canopy behind the wheelhouse, then faced her toward the coffin. Angelique set the brake levers; the captain lashed the wheels to deck cleats. Angelique stood behind Zosia, her hands resting with reassurance on the widow's bony shoulders. Both women wore black, their faces steeled against the ordeal ahead.

The mourners boarded the vessel and sat on benches along both sides of the stern, facing the mahogany casket. The captain entered the pilot house; the mate cast off. The funeral boat chugged slowly across Christiansted harbor. It passed moored yachts, their halyards clinking musically against their metal masts as the sloops lazily rocked. The boat passed the hotel on Protestant Cay, where tourists along the beach were oiling themselves for a day of sunshine. It passed the walls of the old Danish fort, where vacationers manned the ramparts. The boat followed a channel through patches of rusty-orange coral reef. When it passed the last pair of bobbing green and black buoys and entered the open sea, the vessel began to roll. The coffin strained against the straps crisscrossed over it. Zosia sat in her swaying chair, her eyes fixed on the box that contained her husband. Angelique spread her feet wide and braced Zosia's shoulders. The captain throttled to cruising speed; the trawler etched a frothing wake across the turquoise water. The hills of St. Croix receded off the stern. The widow turned her gaze and stared at a green speck several miles up the coast: the copper roof of her empty home.

The boat headed due north. When it passed over the drop-off, the water turned from turquoise to pure blue. The captain waited until Buck Island, distant off his starboard, had passed well behind them, then he slowed his trawler and pointed its prow east-northeast, holding his position against the current and trade winds. Rollers washed along the hull; the trawler teeter-tottered ponderously, bow up and stern up, and rocked gently from side to side.

Angelique addressed the twenty mourners, sweating in their dark clothes beneath the hot sun. "Zosia would be grateful if any of you would like to say a few words."

Several people spoke from where they sat, remembering Piotr with affection and respect. Zosia stared at the casket and seemed not to hear.

There was no clergyman aboard. No prayer during this funeral at sea. Angelique knew that Piotr had been born a Jew in Germany. Zosia had been born a Catholic in Poland. She wondered, Where is God today? Perhaps with Zosia's family, beneath the rubble; perhaps with Piotr's family, in the ash heap; perhaps with Leroy, lost in a jungle. She was glad that no hypocrisy dishonored Piotr's funeral.

A fork-tailed tern appeared off the trawler's stern, looking for fish. The delicate white bird rose up and hovered, then glided down again as if riding on a wave of wind. With a slight angling of its wings, it sailed away over the rolling blue sea.

After the last friend had spoken, Angelique leaned down and asked Zosia, "Would you like to say something."

Zosia's voice was faint above the wash of the waves, "You may proceed."

Angelique motioned to the captain in the pilot house. The mate took the wheel as the captain came out and removed a section of the transom. Beyond the gap was a roller for letting out nets. He unfastened the straps over the coffin. Now the mate came out. On opposite sides of the casket, they gripped its brass railing, hauled the box toward the stern and set one end on the roller. As the mate hurried back to the pilot house, Zosia struggled to stand up from the wheelchair.

Astonished, Angelique cried, "Zosia, what are you doing?" She pushed down on Zosia's shoulders.

Zosia pushed and twisted up. "I want to be with him."

"Then I will wheel you beside him."

"I want to walk."

"You cannot walk on this rocking boat."

With violent strength, Zosia gripped the armrests and forced herself up. "I will *walk*."

The nurse knew the stubborn old woman would fight until she collapsed; with no choice but to acquiesce, she braced Zosia from behind as they shuffled across the rolling deck. The captain held Zosia's arm until the trio reached the coffin.

Spreading her hands on the lid, Zosia stared as if she could see through the polished red wood to her husband inside. "Piotr!" she wailed. "My Piotr! How I love you!" She bent over—Angelique steadied her—and kissed the lid. "Dowidzena, Kochany. I will be with you soon."

When she stood up, she seemed calm. She wrapped her hands over the transom and stared down at the water. Her voice a dry rasp, she whispered, "We are ready."

The captain rolled the coffin over the stern; it dropped with a great splash. Obscured for a moment in a cloud of bubbles, it reappeared six, seven, eight feet deep, sinking slowly, its maroon lid a luminous blur. The rectangle grew smaller and dimmer and darker as it descended into the blue abyss.

Zosia shrieked, "I come!" as she stepped toward the sea. Horrified, Angelique wrapped her arms around Zosia's thin chest and hugged her tightly. The captain gripped Angelique's shoulders to keep the two from falling overboard. Zosia fought with all her frenzied strength. "Nogh! I come!" A man with tears running down his wrinkled cheeks reached his arm as a barrier in front of Zosia. "Meh dear, meh dear," he comforted, "dis what we got to live wid now."

Angelique held her patient with more than a nurse's protectiveness: with love she had never expressed, she squeezed Zosia tightly against her aching heart.

Trapped, Zosia stared into the depths where her husband had vanished. The wind whisked tears from her face and strewed them on the sea.

Defeated, she gradually calmed. She stood quiet and dignified in her black dress. Angelique and the captain helped her to walk back across the empty deck to the wheelchair. She sat, her hands clutching the armrests as she stared at Piotr's markerless grave.

The captain replaced the section of the transom, then returned to the pilot house. The engine growled and the trawler swung toward Christiansted.

On the trip back, Angelique stood behind the wheelchair, her hands on Zosia's shoulders. She could still feel her arms wrapped around Zosia's thrashing chest. In her heart she felt the pain of Zosia's loneliness, the depth of her desperation. The nurse had protected and preserved her patient's life. But Zosia had a mind of her own, and Angelique knew well: The next time Zosia attempted to join Piotr, she would succeed.

CHAPTER SEVEN

Mermaid

When Zosia returned to Candle Point, she asked Angelique to wheel her out to the porch; there she stared toward the horizon where Piotr had been laid to rest. Angelique worked in the kitchen preparing lunch from the many dishes that the Honeggers' friends had brought to the house. Looking out the kitchen window, she watched as the mourners went out, one by one, to stand at Zosia's side. Some tried to talk with her, some said a quiet prayer. Zosia never noticed.

Inside, people gathered in front of Zosia's paintings and sculptures; they spoke quietly as they admired her work. Angelique served lunch, talked with people she knew, kept her eye on her patient. She liked taking care of others; she could forget about herself.

Late in the afternoon, Zosia's friends went back out on the porch, one by one, to say good-bye. She looked up now. "Thank you for coming." She took their hands.

"Ah gon' come by soon for a visit."

"Yes. Please come."

"If yo' need anyting, yo' just call me."

"Yes. Thank you."

"Ah know how yo' feel. Ah been alone seven years now. Both yo' Peter and meh Arthur, dey been good men."

After the last of the mourners had departed, leaving the house eerily empty, Angelique carried a small table out to the porch, and a chair for herself. She brought out two bowls of kalaloo soup and coaxed Zosia to swallow a few spoonfuls of the conch and crab stew. When the sun disappeared behind a bank of clouds hugging the western horizon, she fetched the pink blanket and wrapped it snugly around her patient. Zosia said nothing, sat with her hands in her lap, stared toward the spot where Piotr would spend his first night.

Angelique returned to the kitchen to wash the dishes. From the window, she watched Zosia unwrap the blanket, then struggle up from the wheelchair until she stood with her hands wrapped over the porch railing. Zosia stared down at the water below her. She lifted her foot to the bottom rail—

Angelique dashed out the door and to the end of the jutting porch, ready to grab Zosia. The widow seemed not to notice, though she lowered her foot from the rail. Angelique ached to take Zosia in her arms and hug her, to let her know she was not alone; but the two women had never shown such affection. So she merely touched Zosia's hand: it was colder than usual. "Zosia, you must come inside. You are chilled."

Zosia gripped the railing, her hands like two bird claws.

"Come inside. We're going to wax your sculpture." She tugged at Zosia's arm. "Please, your mermaid needs waxing."

Zosia looked at her with eyes like tunnels: the fires had burned out, leaving cold ashes. "I haven't the strength."

Torn between using physical force to march the stubborn woman inside, and taking the chance of leaving her alone for a minute or two, Angelique hurried into the house and—watching Zosia through the glass door—laid an old, faded green towel on the kitchen counter. Among the potted ferns in the living room stood Zosia's sculpture of a pregnant island girl. The mahogany figure, four feet tall from thighs to head, had not been waxed for years; the briny air that sifted through the house had turned its surface to a dull white. Angelique stepped into the jungle of ferns, wrapped her arms around the life-size torso and lifted. "Uuh!" she grunted, amazed at its weight. Glancing out the glass door—Zosia, intrigued, was staring back—she shuffled with her burden toward the kitchen counter. Twice she had to set it down and rest. Then she hefted the sculpture and shuffled a few feet further. When she reached the L-shaped counter, she took several deep breaths, tilted the torso across her arms and hoisted it up onto the towel. The pregnant girl lay on her back, chalky-white breasts and belly swelling upward.

Zosia turned the doorknob. The nurse hurried to her patient, who had neither wheelchair nor cane. As if drawn by a magnet, Zosia crossed the kitchen toward her sculpture. She rubbed her fingers over its curves like a blind person feeling the face of a long-lost friend. Then she turned to Angelique. "Proszę, will you get the sandpaper for me?"

Delighted, Angelique climbed the stairs to the loft. Following directions that Zosia called up in a weak but excited voice, she rummaged through drawers until she located sandpaper, both rough and fine; cotton rags; and a smudgy tin of furniture wax. Hooking one arm around the leg of a stool, she carried everything down to the counter.

Zosia perched on her stool and set to work. Both hands on a sheet of sandpaper, she rubbed the ripe female curves. Wine-red wood appeared in patches. Angelique watched with fascination as the grain emerged, curling around a breast, ringing the pregnant belly. Zosia's hands moved as smoothly as water over polished stones, her elbows poking the air. She looked up, her olive-black eyes bright for the first time in months. "I can feel!" she exclaimed. "When my hands are moving, I can feel!" She rubbed around and around the bulging belly. "Not like normal feeling, of course. But still, I can feel how ripe she is!"

She invited Angelique, "You try."

Angelique laid her hands over Zosia's, wove her strong dark fingers between Zosia's pale thin fingers, then the two women rubbed the belly together. Zosia grinned with joy, but Angelique wondered, Will Ah ever be as beautiful?

She quickly cast aside her self-pity, and looked with satisfaction at her busy patient. The sanding worked like a tonic. Zosia would sand and wax through the evening, and then Angelique could put her to bed.

Tired herself from the long day, she pulled her hands from Zosia's and said, "I think I'll lie down for a few minutes while you work."

Zosia looked up briefly. "Yagh, you take a little nap." With earnest devotion, she sanded the African lips: a serene red smile appeared on the white mask.

The windows had darkened with dusk.

Angelique brought the wheelchair and blanket in from the porch and set them beside Zosia's chair. Then she brought the cane from the bedroom and hooked it over the back of the wheelchair. "You have everything you need?"

The sculptress nodded vaguely as she worked the sandpaper over her figure's closed, dreaming eyes.

Angelique lay down on the living room couch by the jungle of ferns. Lifting her head, she looked with despair at her own breasts and flat belly beneath her black dress. Unwilling to think anymore, she dropped her head to the couch and covered her eyes with her arm. Lulled by the rasp and rub of Zosia's work, she slept.

"Incoming! Incoming!" shouted Nick.

She was on the pier. The fire department siren was wailing, warning, wailing, warning. Beside her floated the enormous black egg, targeted. Frantically she searched overhead for the incoming Soviet missile. She saw a distant glint, a needle racing straight at her. The crowd stampeded in panic. Where be Chester? She discovered the boy sitting on the curb, too intent on his fishing to notice the danger. Dashing to him, she lifted him in her arms.

But when she tried to run with him along the pier, toward Papa and Mama waiting for them in Frederiksted, her legs dragged in slooooow mooooootion. Chester complained he had a nibble, he'd lose his bait if—

"*Incoming!*" screamed Nick somewhere in the chaotic crowd.

Her legs frozen with terror, she spotted the silver missile hurtling down to stab the black egg. She hunched over Chester, hugged him with all her strength. "Lemme go," he protested, struggling to wriggle free.

Then just as she had always known it would happen, the fireball engulfed them. The inconceivable heat of the sun scorched her skin, seared rags of flesh, incinerated her bones to ashes in that endless instant of agony when she did not die but kept burning and burning until nothing was left but her inextinguishable scream. "Aaaaaaayyyyyyyyy!"

The explosion drove a wedge of fiery light into the earth, splitting it like a coconut; she heard the earth scream in anguish to the heavens.

"Angelique! Angelique! *Angeliiiiiiiique!*" Buffeted and battered by the shock waves, she shook so hard she—

—awoke and saw Zosia's frantic eyes. Angelique pressed her hands over Zosia's cheeks and asked, "Be the boy safe?"

"Angelique, you're all right! Stop screaming. You're here with me. You're *safe.*" Zosia tried to pull her up from the couch, tried to hug her; the cane trembled as she tottered at the edge of balance.

Even as her mind whirled, Angelique gripped Zosia's shoulders to brace her. "Ah knew the war been comin'!" she insisted. "They ain' never gon' fool me, Ah *knew.* Ah try to— But yo' ain' know Chester. He ain' meh own boy, but Ah try to . . ." Panting to get her breath, she couldn't figure how to explain so much she wanted to say. "All Ah wanted been to save Rosemary's son."

Baffled, Zosia stood with both hands wrapped over the crook of her cane. She suggested, "We sit down together and have a glass of cold juice." She took Angelique's hand and led her, thumping the cane, toward the dining room table.

But Angelique saw the polished red torso on the counter. It was beautiful, so beautiful. Though dazed and trembling, she whispered, "Zosia, I must see."

As the two women approached the sculpture, Angelique gazed, rapt, at the face, so filled with peace; the woman's long neck, framed by the rich folds of her hair; her breasts which might have lifted with her breathing; her belly, showing five and a half months, maybe six. With both reverence and anguish, she cupped her hand over the tumescent belly. Then she looked at Zosia and asked, "Why is it so easy for most people to have children?"

Zosia answered with faint bitterness, "For me it was not easy. For me it was impossible."

Angelique dropped her eyes, ashamed that she had burdened a childless widow with her own unhappiness.

But Zosia asked, her voice filled with concern, "Why is it not easy for you?"

Angelique apologized, "I'm sorry . . . . Shall I help you get ready for bed?"

Zosia scowled, "Please grant me the dignity of not always being the one cared for. Angelique, please let me care for you once in a while."

Determined to keep her professional life separate from her personal problems, Angelique lied, "But I don't need to be taken care of. I'm fine."

"Fine?" Zosia fumed, "Is this how it's going to be? You administer the pills, I swallow them. Yes, no, please, thank you. Good morning, good night. Phooey! You think I have no heart? You think I watch the care and devotion you gave Piotr, year after year, and feel nothing more than what I express in a paycheck? Angelique, I *know* you are unhappy and I want to know why." Her voice softened. "And the answer clearly has to do with children."

With a will of their own, the words came straight from Angelique's heart, "Because of Leroy. Because of Nick."

"Yagh." Zosia shook her head sadly. "Five years together, and what do we know of each other? Piotr's temperature, my poor palpitating pulse, and that you never missed paying your rent." She thumped her cane on the floor and declared, "To hell with cold juice. Shall we have some Beaujolais? And then I want to know about Leroy and Nick."

Her resistance broken, she felt grateful to have someone to talk with, someone who might understand her. "Yes, a glass of wine sounds wonderful." She escorted Zosia to a chair at the head of the table. Then she returned to the kitchen, opened a bottle of wine and filled two goblets.

"A candle," suggested Zosia. "A nice red candle."

She found one in a drawer, placed it in a candlestick on the table and lit it. The flame leaned in the sea breeze drifting through the house. She sat in a chair across the corner of the table from Zosia, and opposite Piotr's empty chair.

Zosia held her trembling glass with both hands as she sipped her wine. "Now, who are these two gentlemen in your life?"

Unsure where to begin, or how much to say, she remembered the aquarium. "Leroy loved the sea. And he loved his little sister, six years younger." She smiled with remembered happiness. "We had an aquarium filled with creatures that lived among the pilings under the pier. He would snorkel with a net, and I helped him by climbing the pier's ladder with the net to empty it into a bucket. Then home we paraded with our prizes. We would sit for hours in the living room, staring into that bright little underwater world. We had shrimp, striped like peppermint candy. And sea anemones sweeping their soft fingers. Best of all were the sea horses that hovered among the plants and wrapped their monkey tails around a stem." She could feel her brother's presence beside her, with his ready smile and his hundred-and-one facts that he was always willing to teach her. Then she remembered the perfumy intruders and she laughed. "But too often we shared our evenings with some dumb girlfriend, and her interest in snails was next to none."

Zosia frowned with mock commiseration.

Angelique sat up proudly in her chair. "Well, I had *my* boyfriend." She chuckled sadly. "Though he never noticed scrawny little me. Nick was Leroy's high school classmate, and my first heartthrob. When Leroy took me to the Friday night basketball games, I used to watch Nick with utter longing as he performed his magic on the court. Nick, an orphan from the Queen Louise Home, was always welcome at our dinner table because he had no family of his own. Nick, who stayed in school and graduated because Leroy stayed in school and graduated."

She paused, fortified herself with a little wine. "On graduation day, Nick was with us like part of the family. When I get out the old photos, there's Nick standing beside Leroy, a full head taller, and broader at the shoulders, with his cocky confident smile. And Leroy, always with his arm around Mama or Papa or me, or some girl, and always with his gentle smile."

This ain' gon' be easy, she thought, almost sorry she had started. But maybe Ah'm like Nick. Got to get it out, get it all out, one more time.

"Two days after graduation, both boys received their draft notices. That was in 1969, and they had a choice: to fight with the American Army in Vietnam, or to flee from St. Croix as draft dodgers. Papa had served with the Navy in World War Two, so he was proud that his son would put on the uniform. But Mama wanted her boy to keep out of America's undeclared war. She suggested that Leroy and Nick stay with her cousins on Martinique until the war was over. The boys themselves, they spurned the thought of running away from home. They spent hours on our verandah, swapping tales of adventure as they imagined it all would happen: their first time in an airplane, their first trip to the States, months of 'gettin' tough' in boot camp. A trip home to show off their muscles. And then another trip halfway around the world, with a stop in California, they heard, and maybe Hawaii too! A year in the Vietnam jungle—but what was that for two Crucians who had camped in the mahogany forest since they were kids? And when their job was done, the battles won, there'd be the Welcome Home Heroes parade through the streets of Frederiksted, followed by speeches and fireworks out on the pier. Leroy and Nick basked in each other's excitement. They would do it all together, like brothers forever."

She could feel her anger rising.

"Me, I thought it was a great adventure too. Until Leroy emptied the aquarium. Suddenly I realized he was leaving us. As I helped him carry the buckets, I couldn't talk. When I watched him carry that empty glass box up to the attic, I started to cry, twelve years old and inconsolable. He said he couldn't listen to me anymore and had to get out of the house.

"He came home an hour later with a scrapbook. 'Yo' meh secretary now,' he told me. 'Ah want yo' to put all meh letters, and Nick's letters too, nice and neat in this scrapbook, so we can read them when we come home. Can yo' do that for us?' I said of course I would, and how happy I was to have a job that connected me with them while they were gone. An important job. I was Secretary."

Reaching for her wine glass, she felt her hands shaking; shaking from the rage that would be with her for as long as she lived. She looked out the window for a long minute at the sea, silvered with moonlight.

"A week later, the Two Buccaneers were on the plane to boot camp. Home they came in the autumn, unbelievably handsome in their snappy uniforms. They revelled in a busy week of family dinners, picnics at the beach, a solemn talk with Papa—a talk with both boys together—and a final all-night party with old school pals." She couldn't help but smile, "I fell asleep on the couch, despite my jealousy at watching Nick dance with those big-breasted twits."

But her smile was brief. "They kissed Mama at the airport, shook hands with Papa, and said good-bye to me. I remember, vividly, the inseparable soldiers as they stood in line to board that plane . . . stood in line with a noisy crowd of suntanned tourists." Yes, she understood Nick's hatred; and as she recalled the last time she saw her brother, she shared, deeply, his bitterness.

"The letters arrived on a regular basis, one a week from each of them: polite postcards from Nick, and long detailed accounts from Leroy, describing the sights of San Francisco . . . then the brutality they encountered in Vietnam. Leroy was shocked—not angry, not rebellious, but shocked—and several times he wrote, 'So much more to say, but can't put it into words.'

"Reading their letters, I wondered why they should have to see such terrible things. I even began to wonder why such terrible things should ever happen. Faithfully, I pasted the letters into the scrapbook.

"Then weeks of silence. Mama and Papa almost crazy with worry. I myself lived in a strange drifting limbo, vaguely nervous, but empty of fear, for I couldn't imagine that anything could possibly happen to my big brother. Or to Nick.

"Finally a letter came from Nick, telling us—five days before a form letter arrived from the Army—that Leroy was missing in action, but that Nick was doing everything he could to find him.

"Nick. Who came back from the war with muscles on his arms and lines on his face. His first day on the island, he rang our doorbell. He stood on the verandah, wouldn't come in. He apologized to Mama and Papa because, as he said, 'Ah failed to protect yo' son.' His face stricken with bewildered despair, he said over and over, pleading with Papa and Mama to believe him though of course they did, that he had tried, and tried, and *tried*, to find Leroy.

"Papa reached out and shook Nick's limp hand, Mama invited him in for dinner, but Nick said no, he had to go. He turned away and disappeared down Queen Cross Street. Mama and Papa would have adopted him as one of the family. As their own son. But my brother's keeper vanished from St. Croix. Rumor had it he'd gone up to New York. Lived in Harlem. Drove a cab."

A clock ticked on a bookcase shelf. Outside the windows, waves washed with perpetual indifference over the rocks.

"And you?" asked Zosia, watching her intently. "What did you do?"

She sat back in her chair, hiding nothing tonight. "I hated." Though she knew the old Polish woman probably had strong feelings for her adopted country, she preferred truth over diplomacy. "I stood with my parents in the Frederiksted cemetery, in front of a white marble marker with Leroy's name on it. A marker, not a headstone. Because the body never came home. I wore a black dress Mama had sewn for me, and I carried a bouquet of yellow frangipani. Leroy's favorite flower. Papa struggled to read from the family Bible. Mama somehow through her sobbing managed to sing a hymn. But I didn't pray and I didn't sing. I hated. As I stared at that slab of white stone, I knew it was not the Vietnamese who took away my brother. No, it was the Americans. Who, I was sure, never understood the Vietnamese any more than they understood us Crucians. The Americans had snatched Leroy from his island, used him like a conscripted slave, then forgot him when he disappeared.

"My grief and my anger settled into a seething bitterness. A sour, sullen teenager, I brooded around the house. Refused to go to church, dropped out of the choir, despite Papa's scoldings and Mama's tears. I would have spat in God's face if he gave me the chance. I flipped the bird at every Yankee I saw, especially the sailors on the pier. I called them all the curse words I knew, and learned a bunch more when they laughed and cursed me back. Yes, I even got suspended from school for a month after I stood on a chair during history class and held a BIC lighter under the American flag and set it on fire. Mr. Adams grabbed me down and smacked my face. And right there in front of the class I slapped him back."

And Ah'd slap him again today. With pleasure.

She emptied her wine glass, took a deep breath to calm herself.

"Mama was a nurse, and from when I was a little girl, that's what I wanted to be too. So, somehow during those high school years, maybe because I finally realized that my bitterness only ended up hurting

Mama and Papa more than anyone else—certainly it never bothered the people who had killed my brother—I tucked that anger away, buried it deep, and set my mind on becoming a nurse so I could make my parents proud. So I could make them happy. So I could try to fill the emptiness Leroy left behind.

"Hard to believe, but I graduated from Central High with honors. Then three years at the nursing school on St. Thomas, and graduated with honors from there too. Papa said that except for his wedding, my college graduation was the happiest day of his life. It was certainly the happiest day in mine."

She refilled both glasses; the Beaujolais glowed a beautiful red in the candlelight.

Zosia was quiet for a long minute, staring at the flame. The clock ticked.

Then she looked at Angelique with eyes filled with an anguish years old, and a longing still keenly alive, and the old Pole said, "You haven't told me yet about the children."

Angelique felt a faint hope, for here was someone who understood that children were precious. She leaned forward in her chair. "Zosia, do you remember when the Navy fired a missile at St. Croix? On a Tuesday afternoon in July, 1981."

"Yagh, I remember too well. That missile taught Piotr and I that no matter where we tried to hide, the god of war would find us."

"I was at the hospital when the news swept through the wards. My stomach twisted into knots, because I kept thinking, They killed Leroy, and now they're going to kill the rest of us." Even now she could feel the panic fluttering inside her. "The Navy announced that the firing was an accident. The Harpoon hit the water before it struck our island, and now lay at the bottom of the sea. They assured us that the missile had not been nuclear. They called it 'conventional.' Conventional! What on earth is conventional about a missile able to kill ten thousand people in a flash?

"But soon the conventional was replaced with the unconventional, which became conventional. Because during the military build-up of the Eighties, while we were hitching our wagon to Star Wars, American destroyers traded in their Harpoons for Tomahawks. Aboard the ships docked today at Frederiksted Pier are Tomahawk nuclear cruise missiles, each with a warhead twelve times more powerful than the bomb that leveled Hiroshima. Right there where the boys are fishing.

Sometimes the Navy is docked on one side of the pier, while a luxury liner loaded with tourists is tied up on the other side. Great planning, don't you think?

"And did the Navy ever ask the good people of Frederiksted what we might think about their nuclear powder keg on our doorstep?" She sucked her teeth.

"But even if another accident never occurs, those missiles make my hometown a target. A small target, yes, a ship or two docked every week, and thus there is a very small chance that the Soviets, or the Chinese—or, who knows?, the Chileans, the Peruvians, the Iranians—might decide to bother with us. About as much chance that someone might attack Frederiksted, I think, as of my brother's dying in Vietnam.

"After that Harpoon came firing at us out of the blue on a Tuesday afternoon, I was terrified. Every time I thought about starting a family, my stomach twisted into knots. I imagined speaking to my unborn child, 'All right, come along for nine months, come into this world, lie in your crib, play in your playpen, but oh, baby, you don't know what the world's got planned for you." Anticipating Zosia's argument—for so many others had criticized her for her silliness, her cowardice, her refusal to bear children—she hurried to say, "Leroy never came home, not even in a box. So I can't pretend that wars don't happen. Or that war happens only to other people. And how can I possibly believe that the next war can never happen? Because the last one most definitely did."

Zosia nodded grimly. "Had my father known on his wedding day what was going to happen to his family in 1939, I doubt there would have been a little Zosienka."

She understands! marvelled Angelique. This woman understands me.

Zosia stared again at the flickering candle, her face etched with grief and love both, no doubt for her Papa.

Drawing her thoughts back to the present, Zosia asked, "How old are you?"

"Thirty-two. Fourteen when Leroy disappeared. Twenty-four when the Harpoon misfired at the island. Thirty-two now, and wondering what comes next: the end of my childbearing years, or the arrival of somebody's missile."

Zosia frowned with disapproval. "It sounds as if you've given up. If you hate those missiles at the pier, then you've got to fight to get rid of them."

"Fight? Ha!" She sneered, "I tried to fight. Listen, after that accident, I started to read. And I found an article that listed pages, and *pages*, of accidents involving nuclear weapons. There have been so many accidents, they have a special name: broken arrows. No explosions yet, fortunately. But dozens of bombs have rolled off trucks, fallen off planes, sunk to the bottom with ships. Zosia, we had only three space shuttles, yet the finest experts in the world could not keep one of them from exploding. How confident can I feel with sixty thousand nuclear warheads spread around the world, most of them supervised by soldiers? Does a nuke have to blow up in our faces before we believe that it can?" She fumed at the world she was forced to live in.

"So yes, I tried to fight. I taught an evening course at the University: Everything you never wanted to know about the bombs at Frederiksted Pier. I was desperate to warn people, to wake them up." Recalling her passionate efforts, she shook her head sadly. "Not many people came. 'That Harpoon been a freak accident,' they told me. 'We survived. Why worry? Say, what's on TV tonight?'" She added with disgust, "Even my own family refused to be bothered."

Zosia said quietly, as if repeating something she had long ago learned nobody wanted to hear, but which she, on behalf of those who could not speak, would repeat anyway, "Yes, those who best understand weapons are unable to vote. Unable to run for office. Unable even to sit over a cup of coffee while they explain the business of bayonets and machine guns and bombs."

Yes, thought Angelique, if Leroy could run for governor. If he could run for president.

With a sudden look of determination, Zosia asked, "May I come to your classes?"

"Oh, I don't teach them anymore." She shrugged with defeat. "I quit. Got tired of being Miss Gloom and Doom. And maybe they're right. Maybe one day all those people who never came to my classes will be parents, and grandparents, doting on their little bundles of joy, and I'll be a nervous old spinster, still searching the sky for the incoming missile that never comes."

"You quit?" Zosia scowled at her. "You gave up?"

Defending herself, she could only say, "No, not completely. Now I take care of one soldier. Now I take care of Nick."

Zosia seemed not to hear; she reached for her cane, hooked over the back of a chair, and thumped its rubber tip on the floor. "Ask Oppy what *he* said about those bombs."

"Oppy?"

"J. Robert Oppenheimer. The man who directed the Manhattan Project. He lived in this house once. And this was his cane."

Dubious, she asked for confirmation, "The man who built the atomic bomb lived in this house?"

Gripping the cane with both hands wrapped over its crook, Zosia thumped it again. "Oppy and Kitty came to St. Croix in July of 1954, after his trial. They found solitude and peace here in this house, and down on the beach. Occasionally, they visited our gallery in town. Then Piotr would lock the door with a sign outside, 'Closed for Inventory,' so we could talk. And they invited us to visit them here in their home. When they moved to St. John, which then was even more isolated than St. Croix, Piotr and I moved from Christiansted to Candle Point. In the bedroom closet, I found Oppy's cane. His health had improved with a steady dose of sunshine and papayas." She paused, remembering. "Eventually he and Kitty were brave enough, and forgiving enough, to go up to Princeton."

She rubbed her fingers over the crook of the cane. "J. Robert Oppenheimer was an honest man. When he saw that first mushroom cloud punching into the sky over the New Mexico desert, he did not gloat. Nogh. He recalled the words of an ancient Hindu poem, 'I am become Death, destroyer of worlds.' Oppy knew what he had created. During the years afterwards, he spoke his warnings for all the world to hear."

She thumped the cane a third time, angrily. "What he called Death, is now called the Peacekeeper. Or the Minuteman, conjuring up good ol' Paul Revere. Polaris, as normal as the North Star. Poseidon, Trident, Thor: noble as the gods of yore. Call a car a Cherokee, call a missile a Tomahawk." Her wrinkled face hardened with disgust. "Angelique, I love America as only a refugee can. But I must complain when weapons are marketed to the public like automobiles and patron saints." Zosia pointed her finger at Angelique with the stern command, "You teach that class."

Angelique stared down at her wine goblet; no, she could not go through such humiliation again. "I haven't the strength."

And once again, Zosia did not argue, did not criticize. She hooked the cane over the back of a chair, then she asked with interest, "Now you take care of Nick?"

"Yes. You want to know about children, so I must finish telling you about Nick. The man I love and fear, fear and love."

Zosia said, "I imagine him still in exile, standing in front of that long black marble monument in Washington, touching his fingers to Leroy's name."

Angelique asked with surprise, "How did you know?"

"Who else but Leroy can free him from his guilt? Ask the Jews, ask the Poles: to survive is one thing, to live again is quite another."

She understands Nick too. They should meet each other. It would do him good to talk with a white person he can't possibly hate.

"So Nick came back to the island?"

"Yes, a year and a half ago. I walked into a post-op room at the hospital and was stunned to discover him in the bed. Nick, fifteen years later. He was still so very handsome, though his hair had turned gray at the temples. Glad to see him, yet hesitant to say hello—I didn't know who he was anymore, didn't know if he wanted to remember Leroy, or be troubled by anyone from Leroy's family—I said nothing as I checked the sutures over his appendectomy. He didn't recognize me, but," she grinned, "he flirted with me from the moment he saw me. It's funny, but even after all that time, I was delighted. I kidded with him: told him to roll over, I had to take his temperature. He howled with protest, then roared with laughter. He was so warm, so full of fun, so happy.

"Then another nurse poked her head into the room and called my name, 'Angelique, 209 needs an aspirin.'

"Nick stared at me with shock, then he rolled his head on the pillow and looked at the wall, his face a wooden mask trying to cover the shame in his eyes.

"'Nick,' I said, standing beside his bed. 'Our family knows yo' did yo' best.'

"He didn't move. So I stood there . . . stood there long enough to let him know I meant what I said. That our family never blamed him in the slightest.

"Slowly he rolled his head toward me. If I had showed even a hint of scorn, he would have gotten out of that bed and fled the room. I told him, 'Yo' can't blame yo'self. That war been insane. Leroy disappeared, but that ain' yo' fault.' I touched his hand. 'Nick, we always been grateful for what yo' done for Leroy.'

"He stared at me, and I couldn't see anything in his face, he just stared at me. And then suddenly he smiled, the most beautiful warm

gentle smile, and he said, 'So now yo' a nurse. Leroy would be proud.'"
She paused, ever grateful for those lovely words.

"Well, after I finished my rounds, Nick and I talked through most of the night. I asked him why he came back to St. Croix. 'Homesick,' he said. "Whether Ah had a home or not, Ah been so desperate homesick.'

"We looked at each other. He was thirty-six, I was thirty. A couple of misfits. And so after his discharge from the hospital, we had dinner together. Went to a movie. Walked the beach under a beautiful moon.

"But he was bitter. Oh, he was bitter. And I'll admit, for a while I let him resurrect my own bitterness. He kindled the coals of my grief, stoked the flames of my rage, until my dormant fury at the loss of my brother blazed anew.

"Bitterness, however, is different from hate. Nick hated white people. Hated them, all of them, without exception. And there we differed. I had worked too many years at the hospital, where white doctors labored with as much dedication as black doctors, and where white patients suffered as much pain, and showed as much fortitude, as my own people. And certainly, Zosia, after knowing you and Piotr, I . . ." She shook her head adamantly. "No, I refuse to lump all whites together as a species to be despised."

Zosia offered no comment, passed no judgment.

"So we quarreled. Fought horribly. And quit seeing each other. Then longed for each other so much, we realized we were in love." She stopped her story, aching for the happy ending that did not exist.

But Zosia asked, "And now?"

"Now, he wants children. And I want children. But Zosia, I'm afraid. Afraid he'll poison our children with his hatred. And afraid of those missiles. Do you see? I'm caught between two wars, one that happened, one waiting to happen."

Zosia regarded her with olive-black eyes that knew of love, that knew of grief. "Yagh. You are trapped."

She reached across the corner of the table and took hold of Zosia's hands; they felt like bundles of twigs. Grateful for this night of shared secrets, she said, "At least you and I, we have each other."

The two women in their black dresses gazed at each other, their eyes shining with long-hidden affection.

Looking at her watch, Angelique exclaimed, "Five after twelve! Zosia, time to put you to bed."

"That I can do myself. You go home and get some sleep too."

Remembering Zosia's foot on the porch railing, Angelique offered, "I can sleep on the couch if you'd like."

Zosia waved her hand dismissively. "Nogh." Then she changed the subject. "You must bring that dog of yours for a visit. Piotr was afraid of him, but I want to get acquainted. Does he like cookies?"

She laughed. "Ulysses loves Oreos. We'll come for a visit tomorrow. You'll see how nicely he can take a cookie from your hand."

"Yagh. So, until tomorrow. But now I want a Polish kiss good night."

She stood and kissed both of Zosia's soft cheeks. "Good night, Zosia."

"Dobry noc, Angelique." Zosia kissed both her cheeks with lips dry but firmly planted.

Angelique rolled the wheelchair to the table. "We had a little wine, so better you travel with wheels than with your cane."

"Yagh. Best I ride in my chariot." Zosia stood, braced by her nurse, then shuffled her feet and sat on the wheelchair's leather seat. She swiveled so she faced the door. Looking up, she said, "Thank you. With all my heart, thank you for your help today, and for your kindness to Piotr."

"Zosia, with all my heart, you are welcome."

Crossing the living room, Angelique walked past the thicket of ferns; her hand on the brass door handle, she gazed at the lovely woman lying on the kitchen counter, dreaming Zosia's dream.

She stepped out and closed the heavy door behind her, then she followed the sidewalk through a dark tunnel under arching seagrape bushes. Dead leaves crackled beneath her feet. Patches of moonlight swept across her face.

Emerging onto the driveway, she faced the moon that shone over her house. Three days past full, one half was round, the other half like an egg. The moon beckoned her.

Ulysses came bounding across the driveway, his tail waving like a moonlit plume. She knelt and hugged him, whispered into his ear, "Yo' want to go for a *walk*?" The dog wriggled free, then raced toward the road.

She watched a black wave rolling toward the beach; it shone along its back with a liquid sheen of moonlight. The wave toppled into a mat of foam that rushed up the sand and wrapped around her bare feet, teasing her . . . then the bubbles rushed back to the sea.

Ulysses galloped up and down the beach, chasing a flock of ruddy turnstones. The birds skimmed back and forth over the water, unable to alight for more than a moment before the dog caught up with them and sent them twittering into the air.

At the far end of the beach, she unzipped her dress and let it fall around her feet; it lay like a black wreath on the bright sand. She stepped out of it, finished undressing, then waded into the warm sea. Diving into a wave, she frog-kicked close to the sand until she was well beyond the breakers. Then she patted her hands on the bottom and called, "Angelique!" Rolling over, she rose toward the tarnished moon dancing on the surface. She kissed the moon and popped into the upper world.

Floating on her back, sculling with her hands, she drifted in the current along the shore. Above her sparkled the stars of November. She kicked her feet until they pointed toward Orion the hunter with his belt and sword, striding into the sky above the hills of her island. Bounding behind him was Canis Major, the great hound, its eye the brightest star in the heavens.

The turnstones flew just above her on one of their sweeps, so close she could hear the feathery beat of their wings. She smiled, for her own hound was hard at the hunt.

As she drifted, her thoughts wandered: remembering back, far back, as far as she could remember in her life, she recalled the sunny day on the Frederiksted beach when Leroy first taught her to swim.

She looked up at the stars, and at the faint haze behind the stars, and then to somewhere beyond, where soldiers Missing In Action disappeared to. Where her brother maybe or maybe not was looking down at this world. "Leroy," she called, "why ain' yo' here teachin' meh children to swim?" She kicked her feet with a burst of anger. "Why, why, *why* won' they stop their wars and leave us alone?"

The moon shone over the peak of Zosia's house, lighting the end of her porch. She stood at the rail and stared down at black water lapping the rocks. Then she lifted her eyes and looked at the silver-gray sea near the horizon, just below the stars. "Piotr," she called, "can you wait a little longer? We struggled so hard in Berlin to stay alive. Now, I cannot help it, I keep struggling. Kochany, do you understand?"

Her trembling legs threatened to buckle. She looked behind her at the wheelchair, then bent her knees and dropped with a jolt onto the seat. Pulling the pink blanket around her black dress, she wondered how she could possibly endure staying alive.

CHAPTER EIGHT

Stranger in the House

At noon the following day, Angelique stood, her stomach knotted with dread, at Zosia's door. Though she had dressed herself in a cheerful sea-blue sarong and put a new red bandana on Ulysses, she feared she might find Zosia's battered body on the rocks below the porch. Holding a bag of Oreos in one hand, she raised her other hand with apprehension, and knocked.

"Come in," called Zosia's raspy voice. Angelique smiled with relief and swung open the door. Despite Zosia's haggard look, there she sat at the head of the table, where she had been writing a letter. The mahogany mermaid lay on the counter, still peacefully dreaming. With a nurse's professional calm, Angelique said, "Good morning, Zosia. I brought you a visitor."

The fuzzy brown dog followed her, cautiously, into the strange house. Zosia's eyes lit with interest. She held out a shaking hand. Ulysses sniffed her fingers.

Angelique slipped a cookie into Zosia's hand. "Ask him if he wants an O-R-E-O."

Zosia leaned closer to the wary dog. "Ooolysses, do you want an Oreo?"

His ears perked up. He immediately sat, sweeping the floor with his bushy tail. Zosia laughed, "I'll hire you to dust the floor." Pinching the brown-and-white cookie, she held it out to him. He took it from her gently, then gobbled it down, spilling crumbs on the floor. When he stood to lick them up, his tail swished exuberantly in the air. She joked, "I'll hire you to dust my sculptures!"

Angelique patted Ulysses' strong shoulders. "He wants to know if he can visit you while I'm sleeping during the day. He tells me he gets lonely all by himself."

Zosia worried, "He might bump into me and knock me down."

Angelique reassured her, "Ulysses is a gentleman. He'll be careful around you. And we can teach him to fetch your cane."

"Really?" Zosia reached for her cane and handed it to Angelique. "I don't mind a few teeth marks."

Angelique showed the cane to Ulysses. "Cane. *Cane*." Then she told him, "Stay." She went down the hall and laid the cane on the edge of Zosia's bed. The room felt empty without Piotr.

Returning to the dining room, she said to Zosia, "Tell him to fetch your *cane*."

Zosia spoke to the attentive hound, "Ooolysses, would you be so kind as to fetch my *cane*?"

He bounded down the hallway, then quickly returned, prancing, the cane in his mouth. He brought it directly to Zosia and sat in front of her chair, ears perked, tail sweeping.

Beaming with satisfaction, Zosia took her cane and declared, "For that, you deserve another Oreo."

Angelique handed Zosia the bag of cookies. "No more than two or three a day. We don't want him getting fat." Pleased that Zosia enjoyed her new friend, she went to the kitchen to prepare a lunch.

While she was looking in the refrigerator, lifting lids on the dishes that the funeral guests had brought, Zosia called over the counter, "Would you wheel me down to the beach this afternoon? I haven't been on the shore in almost a year."

Unwilling to dampen Zosia's spirits, but concerned that her patient might be weaker than she realized, the nurse cautioned, "Are you sure you're ready? We might wait a day or two."

"Nogh," said Zosia firmly. "The funeral was yesterday. Today we must try to live a normal day."

Angelique wheeled Zosia along the wet fringe of the beach, while Ulysses galloped back and forth. Zosia laughed with delight as he zoomed past her, kicking up sand and spray. Her sharp eyes followed a flock of pelicans flapping across the bay. But her attention was focused primarily on the water. She stared at the curling waves that broke with a rush of foam; studied the pastel greens in the shallows; gazed at blues flecked with whitecaps further out. Not once did she look toward the horizon, where Piotr spent his second day in the frigid dark depths.

Angelique spotted the yellow windsurfer as it came skimming toward the beach. The rider let go of his sail and fell gracefully backward with a splash. As he pulled his board onto the shore, she admired his shoulder muscles, his big chest, his trim legs. He carried an underwater camera on a strap around his neck.

Ulysses trotted up to him, curious, though cautious. The man knelt and held out his hand. "Hey there, Salty Dog. Where'd you get that fine red bandana?" Ulysses stepped forward, warily. The man scratched him behind the ears with an expert's touch; Ulysses wagged his soggy tail.

Zosia called to the stranger, "Allogh. How was your trip?"

He turned to her with a cordial smile. "Fine, except I had to come back." He pointed toward the open sea. "I love to be way out there on the Big Blue. Out beyond the drop-off, three, four miles from land, where it's just the waves, the wind, the sunshine, and me. Until after a while, I don't exist anymore, except to lean the sail into a gust of wind, or to steer the board over the rolling crest of a comber." He explained in more detail than Angelique would have thought normal between strangers, "I like to drop the sail, then put on a mask and snorkel so I can float on the surface, look straight down and see nothing else but that pure deep blue. And sunbeams reaching down, down, down . . . until they disappear into infinity. I like to stare into that ocean so deep, I forget it's me staring."

Angelique thought the man a little strange. It seemed his primary goal was not to exist.

Zosia, however, showed no reservation in pursuing her questions. "And what do you take pictures of out there?"

He glanced down at the camera on his chest. "I just bought this magic box, so it's all an experiment. What I *tried* to take pictures of is simply that blue. And hopefully, those pale yellow sunbeams as well."

Zosia leaned forward in her chair. "Why do you want pictures of that blue?"

"Why? Because that same pure blue must have been there millions of years ago. It's refreshing, to look at something that's still the way God created it. Puts the clutter and clamor and claptrap commotion of my own little existence into perspective."

There was something about his eyes that disturbed Angelique. She guessed he was a year or two older than she, but his gray-green eyes, catching the afternoon sunshine, seemed much older. There was youth in his strong, suntanned body, and his face was almost boyish; but his eyes must have seen something that aged him beyond his years. She asked, "What will you do with your picture of the blue?"

Again he spoke with an openness that she found surprising between strangers. "I'm going to put it on the bathroom mirror, so while I'm shaving in the morning, I can look at something that makes sense."

She was familiar with a certain type of continental that washed up on St. Croix: failures up north, they fled to the tropics, where they promised themselves they would start fresh; but almost inevitably they brought their problems with them. Many of them sat on a stool in a wharfside bar, telling each other their soppy life stories. But this one seemed to prefer neither alcoholic oblivion nor human companionship. He liked to stare down into God's blue abyss. Uninterested in his broken marriage, or failed business, or whatever it might be, she leaned her weight against the wheelchair and gave it a push.

But when the chair nudged forward, Zosia wrapped her fingers around its sandy wheels, trying to grip them. "Wait, please," she called up over her shoulder. Reluctantly, Angelique stopped pushing. Zosia asked the stranger, "When you develop the film, may I have a copy of your blue?"

"Certainly. I haven't finished the roll yet, so it might be another week or two. But, how shall I find you? Are you often on this beach?"

Zosia pointed across the bay toward the tip of Candle Point. "My house is on the left. You are most welcome to visit."

Angelique winced; feeling protective of Zosia, she did not like the idea of inviting this odd American to Candle Point.

With a friendly smile, he held out his hand to Zosia. "Then may I introduce myself. Karl Jacobsen."

Zosia readily shook his hand. "I'm very pleased to meet you. I am Zosia Honegger, and this is my friend Angelique Nielsen."

Angelique noticed his surprise at Zosia's name. Though he said cordially, "Angelique, it's my pleasure to meet you" as he shook her hand, he looked back at Zosia with sharpened attention. "*The* Zosia Honegger? The artist whose painting I recently bought at the Compass Rose Gallery?"

Beaming with pleasure, Zosia sat up in her chair. "Which one did you buy?"

His eyes shone with admiration as he spoke to the artist herself. "It's an underwater scene, with ragged, jagged, rust-colored coral in a pale turquoise lagoon. A dozen fish, all colors of the rainbow, are swimming through the reef." He wiggled one hand like a fish.

She nodded with recognition. "Yagh, Buck Island lagoon." She pointed at the green hump of an island several miles to the northwest. "There's a horseshoe reef around the headland, *teeming* with life." She shook her head sadly, "I haven't been out there for years."

He told her, as if trying to cheer her up, "I discovered your water-color at the Compass Rose the first week I was on St. Croix. And I was stunned by your sculptures too. But, well, they're a little out of my price range right now. Your painting, however, I bought that very day. Hung it on the wall over my desk, so while I'm writing reports in the evening, I can," he laughed, "I can take a break and go snorkeling with all your bright busy fish."

Despite his friendly manner, Angelique was suspicious. She wondered if this Jacobsen wasn't after another painting at a bargain price. Or perhaps even a sculpture. Soften up the old lady with flattery, pretend to be so appreciative of her work, then swap a cheap photograph for a valuable piece of art. She was ready to turn the wheelchair around and return to Candle Point, when Zosia asked him, "I wonder if you would be so kind as to bring the painting up to my house? It was at the Compass Rose for quite some time and," she thumped her fist with exasperation on the armrest, "Ooooh, how I would like to visit that reef."

He smiled at the idea. "Well, of course. It's up there in my cottage." He pointed at a house high on the hill behind the beach. "If you'll give me half an hour, I can take my windsurfer home, then walk out to your place with the watercolor."

Zosia looked over her shoulder at Angelique. "Are we doing anything this afternoon? Could we make a pot of peppermint tea?"

Angelique saw no alternative but to acquiesce. She forced her professional smile. "No, we don't have anything else planned."

"Wonderful," exclaimed Zosia, turning to Karl. "See you in half an hour."

"Fine. I look forward to it." He nodded to Angelique, then turned to his windsurfer and began rolling up its sail.

As she wheeled Zosia home, Angelique scolded, "I think you're very trusting. He seemed a little odd. I wouldn't have said anything about where you live."

Zosia looked over her shoulder. "I'd like a picture of that blue on my mirror. I want to think that those sunbeams reach all the way down to Piotr." Then she gazed out at Buck Island. "Besides, our odd friend will take me on a visit to the reef."

*　　*　　*

Angelique was heating a chicken curry casserole on the stove, for Zosia, suddenly hungry, had decided to invite Karl Jacobsen to a late lunch. They heard his knock at the door. Turning to answer it, Angelique glanced at the sculpture on the counter. Impulsively, she took a dish towel from a drawer and laid it over the figure. The naked woman was too private, and too precious, to be displayed to an intruder. The towel was not long enough to cover the whole woman, though it reached from her thighs to her neck, and that was sufficient. As Angelique crossed the living room toward the door, Zosia gave her a questioning look from her chair at the table, but Angelique took no time to explain.

Opening the door, she saw Jacobsen, freshly shaved, wearing a blue dress shirt and pressed slacks. He carried a rectangular package: the painting wrapped in a towel. With a shy smile, he asked, "Is this the place?"

Professionally polite, she replied, "Please come in."

"Thank you." He turned his attention to Zosia. "Hello, Mrs. Honegger. I've brought your underwater window."

Zosia's eyes brightened with excitement as he unwrapped the watercolor and set it on the table in front of her. "Ahhhhh," she sighed as she examined the details of her work. "The parrotfish were so greedy. They wanted to be painted with every color on my palette."

"These are parrotfish?" he asked, pointing to a pair hovering over a branch of elkhorn coral.

"Yagh. And these silver ones with the electric-blue stripe, those are crevalle jacks. Here's a school of sheepshead porgies. I called them Porgies and Besses."

He sat in the chair to Zosia's right; the two, vibrant teacher and fascinated student, hardly noticed as Angelique set the table for three. She had often set the table for three, and rankled slightly that Piotr had been so quickly replaced by this Jacobsen.

She was at the stove, brewing tea, when she heard him say, "Hello, Salty Dog." She saw that Ulysses was sitting between the two, enjoying their attention. Karl asked Zosia, "What's your dog's name?"

"His name is Ooolysses, but he's Angelique's dog."

"Oh." Karl looked over the counter at her. "Angelique, what kind of dog is he?"

She answered stiffly, "A very smart dog."

Zosia leaned toward Karl and said with a conspiratorial tone, "What he likes is O-R-E-Os." She pointed at the bag of cookies on the table.

Karl reached into the bag and rattled his hand loudly while Ulysses watched, ears cocked. Then he played Guess-which-hand-holds-the-cookie, thus admitting himself as one of Ulysses' friends.

Angelique turned her back to them and opened the oven to inspect the rolls.

She heard Zosia ask, "How long have you been on the island?"

"Only a month. I've been so darn busy at the boiler works, I haven't had a chance to do much snorkeling. Could have gone today, I s'pose, but I felt a little frazzled and just wanted to sail out there to the Big Blue."

"The boiler works?"

"The oil refinery. I'm a petroleum engineer." Angelique heard a faint sneer in his voice, "A monkey on a cracking tower."

Zosia asked, "Why do you work at the refinery if you dislike it so much?"

He sighed wearily. "Debts to pay. But I can't tell you how much I'd like to take off that hard hat and do something else. Something . . . that means something."

"What sort of something?"

Angelique glanced at Karl. He was not looking at Zosia; he stared into her painting. "I don't know." Then he added mysteriously, "I just don't want to put my hat on anybody else's chair."

He said nothing more. Silence filled the house; the clock ticked. Zosia probed no further. She turned to Angelique. "I can smell our peppermint tea."

During lunch, which Zosia ate with gusto, Angelique looked across the table at Karl and said casually, "Tomorrow is Sunday. Perhaps you would like to sail with me out to Buck Island. You could take some pictures of the reef for Zosia to paint from."

"Yagh!" agreed Zosia. "Good idea. And Karl, Angelique would be a splendid guide. She's best friends with every turtle out there."

Surprised, uncertain, but grateful, he said, "Yes, I would be delighted. It's always good to go with someone who knows the territory. What kind of sailboat do you have?"

"A fifteen-foot sloop." She gave him clear instructions. "Pack a lunch and meet me on the beach west of Candle Point at nine o'clock tomorrow morning."

"Sure. Thank you very much."

"You're welcome."

Zosia repeated, "Good idea! Karl, try to photograph a French angel-fish. They're as big and flat as a dinner plate, black as coal and flecked with gold."

He assured her, "I'll do my best." Then he turned to Angelique and said with the enthusiasm of one trying to make conversation, "There are turtles at the reef?"

She nodded. "Sometimes." She stood and took her plate to the sink.

She was washing the dishes when he finally said, "Well, I'd best be going. I do thank you both for a wonderful afternoon."

As he stood from the table, he looked across the counter at her and seemed about to say something, when he noticed the mahogany sculpture. He stepped toward the figure and gazed at her face. Then he turned to Zosia. "She's beautiful. I'm so," he searched for the word, "honored to have met you."

Pleased, Zosia stood from her chair and thumped with her cane to the counter. She tossed the towel aside, then patted the pregnant belly. Eyes sparkling with humor, she announced, "In three months, I'll be a grandmother!"

Karl reached his hand, tentatively, and stroked the woman's hair. He looked at the sculpture for so long, with such tenderness, that Angelique was certain he must be remembering another woman he had left, or lost. As his gaze traveled down the naked voluptuous body, she bristled with resentment at this stranger who altered the mahogany woman into someone from his own sorry little world. But she could say nothing, for beside him stood Zosia, the proud sculptress.

Suddenly he leaned down and kissed the pregnant belly. Angelique stared as his lips pressed against the polished red wood, then she turned away and glared out the kitchen window, furious.

She heard him say, "Mrs. Honegger, please keep your watercolor for a week or two. I'd like you to enjoy it until I can bring you some prints from the reef."

"But are you sure, Karl? You don't want it over your desk while you write those reports?"

"I'm sure." He chuckled. "Let's say it's on loan from my collection." Then he asked, "Angelique, does that fine hound of yours come sailing with us?"

She turned to face him. He stood at the door, his hand on the brass handle. "Yes. Ulysses loves the boat."

"I thought so." He looked down at Ulysses, curled on the floor beside Zosia's chair. "See you tomorrow, Pirate." With a wink to Zosia, he went out the door.

Zosia turned to her with a puzzled look.

Angelique explained, "I laid the towel over her to protect our privacy."

"Yagh, I can understand. A stranger in the house. But why did you invite him sailing? You didn't seem comfortable around him."

"To protect you. If you're going to invite this person into your home, I want to know who he is."

Raising her frail hand, Zosia seemed about to protest; she was no doubt ready to assert that she was no fool and could take care of herself. But her hand settled on her sculpture as she smiled gratefully across the counter at her friend. "Thank you. Thank you very much."

Angelique was just about to go to bed that evening when the phone rang. "Hello? . . . Nick! How yo' be? . . . Yes, Piotr died Wednesday night, and the funeral been Friday. Ah been with Zosia right t'rough. . . . Tomorrow? Ah sorry, Nick, but Ah gon' sailin' out to Buck Island with a photographer who gon' take pictures for Zosia to paint from. . . . Who he be? A mahn we met on the beach. Ain' nobody special . . . . Nick, do it matter? Ah doin' this as part of meh job. Zosia need to be paintin' to keep herself motivated, and this mahn gon' help with a few pictures of fish. If he be Crucian or not, that ain' important . . . . Yes, Ah miss yo' too, Nick. It *do* seem a long time ago on Maroon Ridge. What about Monday evenin'? . . . Yo' place? All right . . . . Yo' did! So yo' all set for classes. Oh, wonderful, Nick. Nicholas! Ah got to call yo' Nicholas now! . . . Ah love yo' too, Nicholas . . . . Yes. Yes. Good night."

She hung up with mixed feelings: though she was overjoyed that he had actually registered at the University, and that he sounded excited about his classes, she was irritated by the tone of suspicion in his voice. She was so tired, so utterly tired, of his dividing the world into 'us' and 'them.' She hoped that somehow, somebody at the University would shake some sense into him.

CHAPTER NINE

One of Yours

Angelique's voice was flat and mechanical as she gave Karl instructions. She so rarely looked in his direction that he almost backed out of the trip. But her sleek red fiberglass sailboat, tucked among the coconut palms, looked as if it could fly across the water.

Ulysses waited in the shade of a palm tree, attentive to her every move.

She snapped the halyards to the peaks of the sails, neatly coiled the lines, checked a turnbuckle, while Karl stood nearby, feeling useless and unwelcome. Then she called, with life in her voice, "All right, Ulysses, *hop* aboard." The dog bounded across the sand and jumped into the sloop, ready for the launching.

"Karl, you push at the bow. I pull at the stern." She inspected the sky while she spoke.

He acknowledged her instructions with a noncommittal, "Okay."

She gripped the stern while he pushed at the bow: the boat slid backwards down the slope into the sea. He stood waist deep in the water, holding the rope tied to the bow, while she climbed aboard and pulled arm over arm on a halyard: the flapping mainsail rose up the mast. The boom wagged impatiently and the sloop tugged at his arms. He dug his heels into the sand as if he held the reins of a restless horse.

When she hoisted the jib, he was pulled—doing a slow-motion moon walk—across the sandy bottom. Struggling to draw the boat to shallower water, he called, "Say, Angelique, I'm having a little trouble here. What should I—"

"Push the bow to port." She took her place by the tiller. "Then hop aboard."

Port? Which way is port? Annoyed and perplexed by her behavior, he shoved the bow out to sea. The flapping sails became silent; the red hull glided forward. Bellyflopping onto the pontoon gunnel before he was left behind, he crawled awkwardly aboard. He sat beside Angelique and, striving to be an appreciative guest, gave her a cordial smile. "Steady as she goes, Captain."

But she was busy sheeting in the mainsail.

Bitch, he thought sourly. She's probably one of those reverse racists, like that madman at Fitzroy's. So why did she invite me sailing? Hoping I'll drown? Fat chance, sweetheart.

She trimmed the sails to catch the full strength of the wind; but the wind was weak, blocked by Candle Point. The sloop glided smoothly but slowly across the flat water.

Toward the end of the peninsula, Angelique looked up over her shoulder and called, almost singing, "Zoooooooshaaaaaa." Ulysses, seated alertly beside the centerboard, lifted his muzzle and howled, "Yooooowwwlllll!"

The thin old woman stood at the end of her projecting porch, eighty feet above the water. She wore a red and white T-shirt, red shorts, and red stockings pulled up to her knees. Above her she waved a long red scarf that trailed on the wind like a torch. She looked to Karl like an emaciated Statue of Liberty.

"Bon voyage!" she called down with her scratchy voice.

Angelique called back, "Don't forget to eat lunch."

Karl waved. "Get those watercolors ready!"

When the sloop poked its nose into the wind beyond the tip of Candle Point, it took off like a galloping stallion.

With the mainsail sheet in one hand, an extender to the tiller in the other, her feet braced beneath a strap bolted to the sloop's deck, Angelique leaned back, arching until her shoulders neared the tops of the waves. "Lean out, Karl. I need your weight to balance the wind." Her puff of black curls sparkled with droplets of spray.

Determined to give her no cause for criticism, he too hooked his feet under the strap and leaned back over the rushing water. His stomach muscles were soon aching as the sloop jounced from wave to wave.

She arched as far back as she could, until . . . POOSH!, she caught a wave in her face. She emerged laughing, her eyes bright. Then she challenged him, "Your turn."

Glad to see that Miss Moody was cheering up, he took a deep breath, squeezed his eyes shut, leaned back a little further . . . a little further . . . POOSH! Spluttering, he sat up, grabbed the top of the centerboard, then blinked at her and laughed.

With a friendly nod, she commented, "Not bad."

She looked up at her pink telltales fluttering high on the shrouds, and sailed as close to the wind as she could.

Halfway to Buck Island, he gazed with fascination over the stern at the low green hills along the eastern half of St. Croix, and at the taller hills to the west. A narrow cloud extended over the length of the island where the ocean air rose up the slopes and condensed; above the western hills, rain fell in a gray veil.

Like a giant rusty horseshoe lying just beneath the surface, a coral reef wrapped around the headland of Buck Island. Red and black buoys marked an entrance through the coral wall: Angelique guided her sloop into a shimmering pastel-green lagoon. Then she zigzagged up a narrow channel toward the headland, tacking between the cactus-covered bluffs of the island, and the ragged inner edge of the reef. With each tack, Karl worked the lines to the jib, and Ulysses hopped over the centerboard to the uphill side.

"See those buoys ahead?" she asked.

Scattered across the broad lagoon between the headland and the top of the horseshoe were a dozen white balls. He answered, "Yup."

"Please, if you would climb out to the prow. When I bring us up to a buoy, grab its ring and secure us with the painter."

"The painter?"

"The bow line."

"Aye aye, Cap." He stepped past the aluminum mast and crawled forward on the deck.

As the sloop entered the field of buoys, she tillered into the wind: the sails luffed noisily while the hull glided toward the ball she had chosen.

He leaned down and grabbed its ring. "Easy as pie." Then he tied the painter to the ring with two half-hitches.

They worked together to lower the jib: she released its halyard, he gathered the sail into a neat bundle, and following her instructions, wrapped it with a line. She lowered and bundled the mainsail herself. He praised her, "You certainly can handle this boat."

She busied herself by coiling the lines so that everything was neat.

So he busied himself by getting his camera ready.

Ulysses stared up at the frigatebirds, tiny black bent-winged specks soaring on the updrafts over the island.

Sitting on opposite gunnels, they put on their masks and flippers. "Roodoo?" she tooted through her snorkel.

He noticed her eyes looking at him through the window of her mask: they were a beautiful dark brown as they caught the sun. He thought of taking a picture of her, but hesitated; he didn't want to be intrusive. He nodded that he was ready. "Roodoo."

At the same moment, in opposite directions, the two rolled backward into the lagoon.

He stared with wide-eyed wonder, for beneath the sloop drifted a shifting cloud of silver fish, their sides glinting with sunlight. Angelique swam through the school—the fish opened in front of her, closed behind her as they formed a temporary passage—then she flippered across the lagoon's sandy bottom toward the jagged wall of the reef. He lingered behind, hovering in the midst of the glittering fish as he did his best to catch them on film.

Kicking hard to catch up, he scanned the reef wall; though it was a hundred feet away, the water was so crystalline, he could see every coralhead and cave. He surfaced twice for air as they crossed the lagoon, and wondered how she could stay down so long.

At the edge of the reef, she finally rose for air, then looked back to be sure he was following. He gave her an underwater 'okay' sign. She led him through a fissure into the reef. Careful not to brush against the sharp edges of elkhorn, he followed along a meandering passageway. The moment he saw it, he recognized it: a French angelfish!, coal black with golden speckles, shimmying through the tangle of coral. Holding his breath, he found it in the viewfinder, drew closer, focused, CLICK. Exuberant, he thought, One copy for Zosia, one for me, and one for Mom and Pop!

The fissure opened into a bowl-shaped pocket, like a clearing in a jungle. Sunlight rippled across its sandy bottom. A cloud of blue tangs clustered around a coralhead, nibbling it clean of algae. With slow easy kicks of her flippers, Angelique circled the indigo fish. When the school billowed up like a giant droplet of ink, then swooped down on the next coralhead, she followed.

He thought, I'll bet Zosia would be delighted with a picture of Angelique. Focusing through the whirl of fish, he framed the mermaid, gracefully dolphin-kicking in her red nylon suit—now maroon underwater. CLICK. Hearing the camera, she glanced in his direction, but did not wave her hand to stop him.

As he snorkeled through this Caribbean jewel box, he took pictures of treasure after treasure. He examined a bulbous sphere of brain coral; tiny blue-and-orange beaugregories darted and hovered over the cerebral convolutions like sparks of thought. CLICK.

A butter-yellow tang inspected the inside of a basket sponge; so did he. CLICK.

A trumpetfish stood on its head among undulating gorgonians; so did he. CLICK.

Back on the surface, puffing for breath, he noticed that Angelique, face down at the bottom, remained motionless for well over a minute. Worried that she might have hyperventilated and then passed out—as he had been warned against in his YMCA snorkeling class—he kicked down as fast as he could and grabbed her arm to haul her to the surface. She stared at him with surprise. He realized she was fine, felt exceedingly embarrassed and let go of her arm.

She followed him to the surface, took out her snorkel and asked, baffled, "What's wrong?"

"I thought you were drowning."

"I was watching two shrimps mating."

"Oh. I'm sorry. I didn't mean to disturb you."

Her eyes softened and she giggled. "It's *them* you disturbed." She put her snorkle back in her mouth. "Woot foo tootooz."

"What?"

She took out her mouthpiece. "Watch for turtles."

The two dove to the bottom together. But he suddenly backpedaled his flippers, his heart thumping, for hovering in front of him was a ghostly pale squid, rippling its frilly fin. Though the squid was only a foot long, it regarded him with an unsettling saucer eye. Gathering his courage, he wiggled a finger at it. The squid curled back its tentacles, revealing dozens of tiny suckers, ready to grab him and suck off his flesh and devour him to his bones. He jerked his hand back. Angelique's laugh bubbled to the surface.

On opposite sides of the sloop, they pulled themselves out of the water, balancing the boat as they climbed aboard.

"Karl, you're a good snorkeler."

"But you, *you* must have gills."

She smiled, her eyes bright. "Shall we have lunch on the beach?"

"Sure. Having escaped the clutches of the giant squid, I'm ready to attack my peanut butter and jelly."

She hoisted the sails. He cast off from the buoy. Like a pair of old salts, they cruised down the narrow lagoon, jogged through the cut in the reef, then hooked around the lee of Buck Island toward a long, white, crescent-shaped beach.

The Sunday crowd had already arrived: yachts and fishing boats bobbed offshore. Angelique threaded through the anchored flotilla, dodging swimmers and dinghies, then raised her centerboard and rudder just as her bow bumped the sand. Ulysses leaped out and dashed down the beach toward two boys playing with a Frisbee. Karl climbed out and held the painter while Angelique dropped the sails. Together, digging their heels into the sand, they hauled the sloop out of the water.

Ulysses came bounding toward them with the yellow Frisbee in his mouth; the boys chased after him. One of them asked Karl, "Hey mistah, yo' dog mean?"

Angelique answered, "No, he ain' mean. He just want to play." She knelt and said to her dog, "Ulysses, *give* me dat Frisbee. *Give*." Ulysses sat and let her take the plastic disk, dented with toothmarks. She gave it to the smaller boy. "Yo' want he to play wid yo', or he botherin' yo'?"

"He can play wid us. Jus' so he ain' mean."

"Ah promise, he ain' mean. When he catch the Frisbee, yo' tell he *give*. Yo' make he sit and give it back."

"Tanks!" The boys ran off; Ulysses charged ahead of them.

Realizing that Angelique made the effort to speak American English with him, Karl felt grateful. However, not knowing whether islanders were sensitive about their dialect, he refrained from thanking her.

They sat on a bluff of sand and ate their lunches. A radio on a picnic table behind them filled the air with the bouncing rhythms of reggae. Children splashed in the shallows, athletes jogged along the shore. Tourists, some white, some pink, searched for shells. A strutting body-watcher wearing mirror sunglasses gave Angelique a bug-like stare. Karl almost laughed, but when she showed no reaction, he discretely remained silent.

The two spread their towels side by side. Angelique stretched out, closed her eyes, turned her head to face the sun and smiled serenely.

Leaning back on his elbows, he peeked at her trim brown legs, then at the swelling of her breasts under her red suit. He glanced at her pretty face. But he felt odd, looking so at a black woman.

The sparkling turquoise Caribbean stretched beyond his feet like a picture in a dream-vacation poster. A flock of windsurfers approached the island; their multicolored sails would have made a perfect photograph. Among them, he discovered a blonde in a pink bikini who balanced her tanned body against a flamingo-pink sail. Yeah! he thought, sitting up. Yo ho!

The windsurfers raced up to the beach. Like migrating butterflies reaching their destination, they laid down their wings to rest. He admired the tawny woman in pink as she pulled her board out of the waves. Nice muscles on her calves. Terrific ribs. When she dove into the water, then floated on her back with her pink breasts lifted above the surface, he regretted that he wasn't alone today.

He looked again at his companion. Her lips were slightly open; by her breathing, he could tell she was asleep. He wondered what it would be like to kiss such voluptuous lips. But he cast the thought away. You don't know a darn thing about black people, he told himself. So don't go poking your nose into trouble.

Turning again to the blonde, he was crushed to see that she was splashing water at some hunk, who was splashing her back. Wrinkling his nose with a moment of jealousy, he lay back on his towel. Never mind, he thought. There must be more than one Danish descendant on St. Croix.

The yellow Frisbee floated back and forth in the blue sky like a peripatetic sun.

He closed his eyes. Within moments he too was asleep.

Aboard the *Reef Queen,* a glass-bottomed tourist boat anchored near Buck Island, Nick gripped the rail opposite the beach as he gagged with dry heaves, his breakfast long since lost from seasickness. Too wretched to attempt the trip in a wobbly dinghy to the island's steady shore, too embarrassed to risk being seen by anyone who knew him, and especially, too helpless to confront Angelique and her 'photographer' with the words she deserved, he could only peer over his shoulder at the happy couple sleeping side by side—How long she know this whigger? How long she been lyin' to me?—until suddenly, moaning with misery, he had to bend once more over the rail to puke the bile out of his aching stomach. Traitor, he thought bitterly. Traitor!

On the way home, Angelique taught Karl how to sail wing-and-wing. With the wind blowing over the stern, she let the mainsail sweep out to starboard, the jib to port, so the two white triangles spread against a blazing sunset. "Now Karl, you sit across from me."

He shifted so he sat on the opposite gunnel. Their feet intermingled under the strap, cinnamon, white, cinnamon, white.

"Now lean back."

They arched over the water like two wings.

Beyond the bow, the sun looked to him like the mouth of a cannon firing gold doubloons across the sea.

"Lean further," she called. The two arched as far as they could, until . . . POOSH!, POOSH!, both dunked into the cool molten gold.

Laughing, they lifted their heads and looked across the boat at each other. Her eyes were bright, her smile radiant. Sitting up, he reached for his camera. "A picture for Zosia," he explained. "Do you mind?"

She did not answer, but surprised him with her playfulness as she bobbed her torso, rocking the sloop. Though his stomach muscles ached from the day at sea, he bobbed as well. Together they rocked the boat with a slow steady rhythm. When she rose in her red suit into the sky, wisps of scarlet clouds behind her, she smiled like a jubilant child on a teeter-totter. CLICK.

"Now let me have your camera," she said. They sat up and transferred the black box from his hand to hers. She wrapped its strap around her wrist. Camera in one hand, extender to the tiller in the other, she leaned back and looked at him through the viewfinder.

Again they rocked the balanced boat.

How much better this was, he thought, than floating face down, staring into the blue abyss, the graveyard—yes, he had to admit he had toyed with the idea—of his pointless life. He smiled with appreciation at his new-found friend.

CLICK.

As they neared Candle Bay, she hooked around the end of a barrier reef, then sailed toward a sandbar. "Are you a fisherman, Karl?"

"Sure am. What are we after?"

"Dinner for two."

After they had pulled the sloop onto a serpentine bar of sand, she opened the hatch to a hold in the bow, reached inside and drew out a snare with a loop of wire at one end. He frowned at the apparatus. "What on earth are we fishing for?"

She handed him a pair of gloves, crusty with salt. "Be brave, Karl."

"Angelique, I'll tell you right now, I do *not* eat eels."

She reached back into the hold, then handed him an old canvas knapsack. "Be careful the eels don't eat *you*." Donning her mask and flippers, she walked backward into the lagoon until she was waist deep, then she ducked under and disappeared.

He pulled on the stiff gloves. The smelly knapsack scratched his sunburned back. He had never caught anything larger than a ten-inch bluegill in the farm pond. The sun had set: the water, dimly lit by a fading glow in the sky, would soon turn black. Dusk was feeding time, when the lunkers rose from the depths and snatched a tidbit skittering across the surface. He put on his mask and flippers, backed into the water until his knees were wet, then paused as he recalled the gasping jaws of the giant moray eels in the Chicago aquarium.

"Karl," she called, "are you eating hot dogs tonight?"

"Aw right, aw right, I'm coming."

She waited for him to catch up, then they snorkeled together to the end of the reef, where she dove to the bottom, peered into caves, searched under ledges, while he floated at the surface, longing for the simplicity of the line and bobber.

Now she reached her snare into a cave, reached a little further, her flippers twitching . . . a little further, until her gloved hands were almost inside the hole. With a sudden tug, she yanked the wire. Even in the gloom he could see that she was shaken by whatever she had caught. She struggled against her prey, and she managed to back away from the cave. He grimaced with apprehension. She pulled out a flapping lobster, the loop of wire tight around its tail! As she rose toward the surface, she looked up at him, her eyes exuberant in the window of her mask.

"Hooroo!" he cheered.

She stuffed the madly snapping lobster into his backpack, where it hammered its shell against his spine, knocking his vertebrae until they bounced around inside his ribcage.

"Now," she formed the bent loop of wire back into a circle, "the monster."

"The monster?"

Down she dove. She peered into the same hole, then swam around the shadowy, grasping arms of coral and searched under a ledge. Slowly she eased her snare into the back of the cave . . . flicked and twitched her flippers, reaching deeper . . . then yanked the wire. Her whole body was shaken; she fought not to be dragged into the hole! He rushed down—but hesitated before gripping her arm, for she never looked up for help. He hovered nearby, expecting a huge tentacle to reach out and grab him.

Stirring up clouds of sand with her flippers, she tugged on the snare. It tugged back, fiercely. He had to rise for air, though he hurried down again. Finally she drew a thrashing two-foot lobster into open water.

"Woohoo!" he tooted with astonishment.

Her eyes triumphant, she rose with her prize to the surface.

When she reached for his backpack, he protested, "Hey, where's your bag?"

"Where's your snare?" She stuffed the enraged beast into his sack. Neither creature was comforted by the company of the other, and both now pounded his kidneys into pudding and scratched with knitting-needle feet to dig themselves free.

Swimming back toward the sandbar, he paddled swayback along the surface while she glided gracefully across the murky bottom. With growing admiration, he thought, Now there is one spunky woman.

When Angelique carried the knapsack into Zosia's house and showed her the freshly-caught lobsters, Zosia was thrilled. But when Angelique informed her of the plan to share dinner with her, Zosia immediately objected. "Nogh. You two have a picnic on the beach."

"But Zosia, we have more than enough for—"

"Absolutely not." She waved her hand that she would hear no argument. "Lobsters must be cooked over a driftwood fire and eaten by the shore. Piotr and I never ate lobster in the house. Use that old cauldron we kept in the bushes."

"Then please, you must come down and join us."

"I've had my soup, and I'm soon going to bed."

Acquiescing with only slight regret, Angelique telephoned Information to ask if there was a new listing under Jacobsen. Then she phoned Karl at his cottage, where he was changing into dry clothes, and told him of Zosia's refusal. They agreed to have a picnic dinner on the windward beach, where the breeze blew away the no-see-ums that came out in the evening.

As the first stars appeared in the lavender sky, the two seafarers searched the beach for sticks of driftwood. They carried Zosia's rusty three-legged cauldron out from the tantan bushes and set it on the sand. Angelique filled it with buckets of sea water while Karl built a teepee of driftwood between the iron legs. When he lit the fire, flames fluttered around the big-mouthed pot, lighting the black water inside with shimmers of red.

They took turns adding wood to the fire until the water was boiling. She told him, "We each put in our own lobster."

"Then of course, the monster is yours."

"No, Karl, he is yours. You earned him. You were excellent crew today."

Surprised at her compliment, he smiled. "Thanks." He still wondered, however, why she had been so cold toward him at Mrs. Honegger's house, and then again this morning while they had launched the boat. She's a strange one, he thought, still suspicious that maybe she had scorned him because he was white.

He put on his wet gloves, reached into the rucksack and gripped the huge lobster. Though it snapped, he clutched it manfully, tugged it out and held it up for her to see. Its knobby eyes twitched in the firelight.

"They're so beautiful," she said with pained regret.

He dropped the lobster into the pot: it thrashed wildly, splashing water over the rim. Steam hissed up from the fire as the creature sank lifeless to the bottom.

She put on her gloves, drew the second lobster from the sack. She admired it for a moment, then, reluctantly, she dropped it into the cauldron. While it convulsed, she winced.

He had seen many calves butchered back home on the farm; as long as no cruelty was involved, he felt no qualms.

Twenty minutes later, she reached into the cauldron with tongs, lifted out the lobsters and laid them on wooden plates. The two fishermen sat cross-legged, facing each other, the fire to one side, the Caribbean to the other. They sliced open the soft undersides of the tails: clouds of sweet-smelling steam misted their faces. Both dug their forks into the puffy white meat, then closed their eyes to savor the first bite.

"Mmmmm," they hummed together.

When he was too stuffed to poke and probe at the carcass any further, he lay back on his elbows and stretched his legs toward the water. He searched the sky, but failed to locate his old friends. "Where's the

North Star?"

She pointed at a star straight out from the beach, a short distance above the horizon.

"So low?" he marveled. "Gosh, I'm used to seeing it," he pointed up at a forty-five degree angle, "way up there."

Poking with a stick, she smoothed the embers of the fire into a neat orange circle. He was struck by the beauty of her dark face in the glow from the coals.

"Back home on the farm," he said, wanting to share with her something of his own world, "if we look from the front porch on a chilly November evening, the Big Dipper is pretty much horizontal, like a pot on the stove. My father jokes that the North Star, straight above it, is a piece of popcorn that just popped up." He paused for a moment, for he could clearly hear Pop's voice saying, 'Yassir, they forgot agin to put the lid on!'

"But on St. Croix, so close to the equator, the Dipper has disappeared beneath the horizon." He added with delight, "It's hidden behind the edge of the world."

"If you wait until midnight," she said quietly, "you'll see the Dipper rise out of the sea like a fish dancing on its tail."

"I like that. I like the way things are different down here."

She gazed at Buck Island, now a black hump against the heavens. On its peak, a navigation light blinked like a winking star.

Honoring her silence, he surveyed the beach. Ulysses lay curled nearby, his head lifted, ears cocked toward the water.

Palm thatch rattled dryly behind them in the breeze off the sea.

Feeling drowsy, he yawned. The tropical night was so warm, so soft.

She abruptly sat up; her face hardened into a scowl.

He turned to see what she was looking at. Just coming into view beyond Candle Point was a ship, several miles from shore, heading east. Its pinprick lights, with two vertical spikes, did not look to him like those of a passenger ship, nor of an oil tanker. "What ship is that?"

"One of yours."

"One of mine?"

"An American destroyer."

"But why do you say it's *my* ship?" He too sat up.

"You're an American taxpayer, yes?"

He countered, "And so are you, yes?"

She shook her head. "My taxes stay here in the Virgin Islands. Not one penny of my salary goes to your Pentagon."

"My Pentagon? I wouldn't say the Pentagon and I are any great friends."

She regarded him with accusation. "You helped to pay for that boat. Your signature is on the tailfin of every missile on board."

Stunned, and a little annoyed, he asked, "Any special reason why suddenly I'm the bad guy?"

She jabbed her stick at the coals, sending up a flurry of sparks. "You mentioned a farm."

"Yeah, a dairy farm in Illinois."

"With cows in a pasture?"

"Yes, we've got a hundred fifty head of Guernseys. Any crime in that?"

A kindling flame cast its light on her angry face. "So tell me, Karl Jacobsen, how many missiles do you have parked in your pasture?"

You may have your complaints, he thought, but first you sure as hell ought to find out to whom you're complaining. "None. Not a single one. The missiles are in silos out west."

She laid a twisted root on the fire. "Your farm is surrounded by cows. My island is surrounded by nautical nuclear missile launchers. Why am I so privileged?"

"I see. I pay my taxes, therefore I own the Navy. Do you have this conversation with every American you meet?"

She sneered, "You Americans have only two ways of looking beyond your borders: either between the blinders of investment and profit, or through the sights of a gun."

"*You* Americans. I hear an awful lot of you, you, you. Guilty until proven innocent, huh? I've got news for you: under the Stars and Stripes, it's the other way around."

She sucked her teeth.

Baffled—and balanced between explaining to her why she was so wrong, or just telling her to piss off—he stared out at the destroyer.

Yes, I paid for you, he admitted to himself. What choice does a guy have? Taxes, or jail. But that doesn't make me a warmonger.

He realized he had probably never before been this close to nuclear weapons. They were out there to keep the peace, he told himself. Still, he felt a little uneasy. As Pop had often repeated, 'A gun in the house serves for protection. But never forget, it's a danger too.'

When he had calmed sufficiently to resume their discussion, he looked at her and said, "Here we've had such a terrific day sailing together. And a wonderful banquet on the beach. Then suddenly you're ready to tear my head off. C'mon, Angelique, settle down for a moment and tell me without polemics why that ship upsets you so much. I'm willing to listen, you know."

"Why?" Her eyes blazed with a rage she clearly had no desire to control. "Because I lost my brother in your war. And that ship never lets me forget."

"My war?"

"The American war. In Vietnam."

He stood up. He'd had enough of her ignorant, self-righteous contempt. "Angelique," he snapped, "I'm very sorry you lost your brother in Vietnam. Believe me, I know how it hurts. Because I lost my brother in that war too."

Without bothering to say good-bye, he crossed the beach and stormed up the path through the tantan bushes to the road.

As she watched him disappear, her face prickled with shame.

Aboard the USS *Defender*, Spruance-class destroyer DD 998, on maneuvers seven nautical miles north of St. Croix, missile technician 2nd class Schwartz noticed during a routine check at his Armaments Monitoring Terminal that Tomahawk quadrapod three was not properly circuiting a simulated prepare-to-launch signal. Schwartz checked and rechecked quadrapod three, and determined that one missile of the four on the aft starboard launcher was not relaying the simulated launch signal. Missiles A, B, and D seemed fine; but C had a bug in it somewhere.

Because the armament carried a nuclear warhead, Schwartz immediately phoned his duty officer to report that pod C was not serviceable.

CHAPTER TEN

Brothers

Walking up the hill the next morning toward Karl's cottage, Angelique worried that he would be too angry to listen to her. He might slam the door in her face. But her conscience told her that she had done something terribly wrong and must try to make amends.

She walked up flagstone steps through a grove of banana trees to his bungalow; paused for a moment at the door, her stomach fluttering with nervousness; then raised her hand to knock—but the door swung open.

Surprised, Karl blinked at her. He wore green overalls and carried a green hard hat in one hand, a briefcase in the other: he was clearly on his way to work. His surprise quickly faded, replaced by a contemptuous scowl.

She wasted no time with a polite good morning, but told him, "Karl, I have come to apologize. I was unfair, and I fear I hurt you deeply."

He stared at her, with mistrust.

She added, "I blamed you, when I should have blamed your government."

Still he stared, though his gaze softened.

From her heart, she told him, "I am sorry you lost your brother in Vietnam."

He stepped back from the door, set his briefcase and hard hat on a table, then asked her, "Please, won't you come in and have a cup of coffee?"

Grateful for his civility, she nodded, "Yes, thank you. But I don't mean to delay you on your way to work."

He motioned to a wicker chair beside the table. "Have a seat. I'll get a couple of cups." He went into a kitchenette, divided from the living room by a counter.

As she sat in the chair, she saw that his window looked down the hill onto Candle Point. He could easily see her house, and Zosia's. Again she felt—though perhaps it was no fault of his own—that he intruded on her privacy.

She noticed, upright on the table, a framed photograph of a family standing ankle-deep in snow in front of a barn. A soldier in uniform, his young face capped with a green beret, stood in the middle of the group with one arm around a woman who was clearly his mother, and one arm around the shoulders of a teenager with a crew cut. She recognized the boy as Karl. But her attention was drawn back to the soldier's face, for he had neither the usual cocky confidence, nor the blank, lost look of most recruits. Instead, it was a look of worry as the soldier stared not at the camera, but beyond it.

She glanced at the rest of the family, father, two sisters, grandfather, grandmother; and she thought of the photograph of her own family on the living room wall, with two young men in uniform. How alike, she thought, except of course the people in this picture were white, and standing in snow.

"Cream? Sugar?" asked Karl as he set both on the table in front of her. "So you've met the family, huh?" He pointed at the soldier and said with a tone of reverence, "That's Joe." He opened his briefcase, took out a thermos and poured coffee into two earthenware mugs.

Then he sat in a squeaking wicker chair and looked at her. "How can I tell you, so you'll understand what you did last night?" He sipped his coffee.

Embarrassed, but ready to take her scolding, she picked up her mug and sipped her own coffee; it tasted rich, hot, wonderful.

"Joe wasn't drafted," Karl began. "He volunteered for Vietnam. The trouble with Joe was, he was so darn democratic. He had a scholarship at the U of Chicago, the first in our family ever to go to college, but during the fall semester of his junior year, he dropped out to enlist. Mom and Pop pleaded with him to finish his schooling first. But Joe said that every time he rode the Elevated through the slums, he got disgusted with himself. Because if a guy was in college, he was safe from the draft, but if he was too poor to pay tuition, then 'Wham bam, Uncle Sam sends that guy to Vietnam.' Joe told us over and over, 'It's not fair.' "

Karl gazed with admiration at his brother. "Democratic is what Joe was. He sent a letter from boot camp saying he'd signed up to be a Green Beret, 'the toughest job there is, so no one else gets stuck with a job tougher than mine.'"

He looked at her with sudden, unhidden grief—a grief she knew too well. "So he filled a vacancy in the ranks, and left a vacancy at home . . . that will never be filled. Firstborn son. Had Pop's good looks, Mom's humor. Pitched a fastball that burned a hole right through the bat. Voted by his high school class 'most likely to become President.' Telephone'd ring, and it'd be some girl calling *him*." He spoke with reverence, "Joseph Lars Jacobsen. May 14, 1951. April 9, 1972." Then his voice dropped to a trembling whisper, "Joe was only twenty-one."

She thought, Leroy been nineteen and a half.

As he took a long drink of his coffee, she saw a dramatic change in his eyes above the steaming cup: his anguish was replaced with a fierce glare of outrage. Bitterness empowered his words, "Joe was killed in a war that Congress neither declared nor stopped. Six years after that war ended, America was at war again. And again, Congress neither declared it, nor stopped it. Only this time, we paid somebody else to do our fighting." He thumped his fingers on his chest with self-reproach. "*I* paid for that war. My tax dollars bought the bayonets and bullets that ended up in somebody else's body." He did not hide his guilt, nor his disgust with himself. His passions were so strong, he was almost like a drunk pouring out his tale to any convenient listener. She still found this openness strange, yet she admired his honesty.

"That eight-year war in Nicaragua was a bargain. Not a single American got drafted. Nobody came back in a body bag." He sneered, "And best of all, no post-Vietnam guilt. When the war fizzled out, few people seemed to care about the Contras. But of course, that was the decade of Trivial Pursuits. The little country down south was littered with graves, but our Commander in Chief retired to Beverly Hills, while the rest of us watched the Superbowl."

She witnessed another swift transformation, for now he frowned with worry as he leaned toward her. "I was scared, Angelique. Scared for America. Scared for the country I love. Because any nation that can fight a proxy war for eight years and hardly care whether it wins or loses . . ." He shook his head, perplexed. "What kind of moral backbone does it have? And what the hell did Joe die for?" She was stunned by the ferocity of his anger. "Don't you see, that half-assed war in Nicaragua cheapened Joe's death. Because he seems to have died for a country that doesn't know what it's fighting for. Or care."

He stared at the photograph and brooded, his questions remaining unanswered.

She wanted to know, "Karl, how do you handle the bitterness?"

He raised his eyes and looked out the window; not down at her house, she noticed, but at the sea far beyond it. When he spoke, his shame and disgust had vanished. He was almost calm. "Bitterness looks back. I want to look forward. What good does it do to be bitter on Joe's behalf? He'd kick my butt and tell me to do something that means something."

"You said that at Zosia's house."

"Yeah," he turned to her, "but I don't know what. I float out there on the Big Blue, looking down at the world the way it was before life crawled out of the sea, and I wonder why we're still crawling. I try to figure out what a divorced, disillusioned ex-cow farmer can do. I'm educated in only one thing: how to turn crude oil into 'gayzoleen.' But I sure as hell don't know how to turn a sword into a plowshare."

"Can't you go back to school to learn something else?"

He shrugged, helpless. "Debts. I gotta stick with the job. I send a check home to Mom and Pop once a month. Like a lot of farmers in the Midwest, they're going through a tough time making payments to the bank. If I say good-bye to dear ol' Petrox, they say good-bye to that farm."

He refilled both cups from his thermos.

"Actually, the folks would be thrilled if I'd come home to help run the farm. We could add another fifty head, Pop says. But much as I hate being a monkey on a cracking tower, I hate milking them cows even more. Up at five day after ding-dong day, put on the rubber boots and plug that ol' suck machine to a hundred udders while you listen to the sumptuous symphony of cow plop." He laughed. "No, that is *not* the—" Abruptly he stopped.

And now like a drunk who had to tell all, he confessed to her, "No, Angelique, the real reason I'm still wearing that hard hat is because I'm a slob. Joe had conviction. I have . . . conventionality. Conventional Karl. The guy who never—"

The phone rang, startling them both. He walked to the kitchenette counter. "Hello? . . . Oh, hi Ed. Yeah, sorry I'm late. Had a long-distance call from Illinois just as I was leaving the house . . . . No, nothing too serious. Some personal business that needed clearing up. I'm on my way now. See you shortly." He hung up and let out a tired sigh. "Eat my shorts, Ed."

He turned to her. "I gotta go, but . . . What was your brother's name?"

She stood up. "Leroy. Leroy Beaumont Nielsen. December 3, 1951. June 20, 1971. He disappeared on the 20th, so that's the date we used on his marker."

"Disappeared?"

"Missing in action."

"I'm sorry. That must be even harder, I think. At least Joe . . . came home."

She felt a surge of gratitude, for he was one of the few who understood. "Yes, perhaps it is a little harder. It's as if he's still out there, alone."

For a moment, he looked as if he might reach out his hand and touch her; but he didn't. He said, "Angelique, I hope we have the opportunity for you to tell me about Leroy. I feel rude, having done all the talking."

"No, please, I'm the one who should apologize for making you late."

He scoffed, "Never mind that. If all the traffic jams of the world have one less barrel of oil to burn, so much the better." He led her to the door. "Can I give you a ride home in the jeep?"

"No, I don't mind walking."

"Then," he held out his hand, "thanks for a great day yesterday."

They shook hands. "You're welcome. I enjoyed it too."

As she walked home, she considered inviting Nick to Candle Point on Saturday, so he could meet Karl. Karl seemed tough enough to handle Nick, and it would do Nick good to meet a white man he couldn't hate.

CHAPTER ELEVEN

Suspicion

Determined to bring the two men together, with the hope that Karl might encourage Nick to turn around and face the future, Angelique rode her scooter that afternoon to Harbor View, a three-story housing project, one of a dozen identical boxes near Christiansted. In the parking lot lay several wrecked cars, their wheels and doors taken for parts. On the patch of weeds that posed as a lawn, a battered garbage bin stood with its door yawning open; a stench of rotting fish poured out. Rats scratched and scurried inside. As she did each time she visited this neighborhood, she chained her scooter to a stop-sign post; the sign itself was long gone.

Nick lived on the top floor, facing the sea. As she climbed the three flights, the stairwell fetid with a dozen different dinners, she counted the days since she had last seen him: almost a week, though it seemed much longer. After the sorrow of Piotr's death and funeral, and the difficulties of Zosia's first days as a widow—dark days interrupted by the one sunny day of sailing with Karl—she felt a vague distance between herself and her lover. A distance she wanted to eliminate tonight.

She knocked on his gray metal door.

He opened it and beamed his handsome smile. "Hey, Sugah! Come on in. This poor lonesome bachelor just be fryin' up a batch of johnny cakes."

Stepping into his apartment, she sniffed an enticing aroma from the kitchen. "Mmmm. Ah starvin'!"

"And Ah starvin' for *yo'*," he declared. He kissed her with a passion that swept the week away, taking her thoughts back to Maroon Ridge and the moon on his gorgeous gleaming body.

Then he told her, "Set yo'self down and relax. Ah need about five minutes before tings be ready." Disappearing through the kitchen door, he called back, "So good to see yo', Sugah. This been one long lonely week."

Too restless to sit, she stood at the window and surveyed the view. But Harbor View had no view, at least not of a harbor. Below his window was the garbage bin. Across the street stood a stone wall, bounding a sweep of lawn that must, she thought, take a man a full day to mow. The tennis court was empty. Beside it stood the cone-shaped ruins of a Danish sugar mill. At the far edge of the lawn were Sugar Beach Condominiums, blocking the view of the sea. Only at one end of the long terraced building could she glimpse a sliver of water.

This be the view Nick see every day. This be the view that help keep him bitter.

Turning from the window, she called to him, "So yo' signed up for classes!" She could hear him working at the stove.

"T'ree classes," he called back. "Tell yo' all about it at dinner."

She looked at the table, set with earthenware plates on placemats; two yellow candles were already lit. Nick always made her feel appreciated.

On the opposite side of the small living room stood his weight-lifting bench and a rack of barbells. The walls were covered with maps: street maps of Christiansted and Frederiksted, U.S. Geological Survey maps of the entire island, coastal navigation charts, his own hand-drawn sketches. He had a passion for maps. "Hey, Sugah," he called, "can yo' help me carry this feast out to the table?"

Relaxed and jovial through dinner, Nick talked about the courses for which he had registered: Caribbean History, Caribbean Literature, and Economics One. "Ah gon' take Economics Two this comin' summer. Ah gon' learn all the tricks, so Ah can provide for yo' and our happy, hungry kids."

Proud of him, beginning to believe that the miracle might actually happen, she asked, "Be there any courses in the evenin'? Maybe Ah could join yo'."

He could not have surprised her any more had he slapped her in the face, than when he grew silent, stared at her with a strange look, then announced, "Saw the two of yo' asleep on Buck Island yesterday. Looked ever so cozy."

Speechless, she realized that he had been spying on her. Because he suspected she was cheating on him. With a white man. Masking her shock, she asked, "What yo' doin' out at Buck Island?"

He replied nonchalantly, "Friend invited me out on the *Reef Queen*. Took a little cruise. Then Ah see yo' two on the beach, lyin' side by side," he sneered, "like ol' friends."

She demanded to know, "But *why* yo' out there?"

"Why *yo'* out there?" He snarled, "With him."

"But . . . Ah *told* yo' Ah takin' this mahn to Buck Island. He took pictures for Zosia." She protested, "Nick, why yo' treatin' me this way? Why yo' blamin' me when Ah ain' done a ting wrong?"

He grinned slyly. "Ah know this boy. Mistah Petrox live up on the hill, Sugarbird Lane, tidy little white bungalow." He leaned across the table and leered at her. "Why, how niccccce yo' two does be neighbors!"

Furious at his insinuation, she slapped her hand on the table. "What kind of shit yo' t'rowin' in meh face? Ah take a mahn sailin'—Ah even *tell* yo' Ah gon' take him sailin'—and now yo' jealous!" She asked, incredulous, "What be the matter with yo'? Nick, yo' talkin' to the woman who love yo'!"

Silent, brooding, he studied her.

"Nick, he lost a brother in Vietnam. Yo' ought to talk with him. He ain' one more ignorant, arrogant continental."

Nick sucked his teeth.

She almost shoved the table at him. It was all so absurd!

But softly, she said, "Babe, how can yo tink such tings of me? Ah yo' woman, now and forever. Yo' *know* that."

He stared at her as if struggling to believe her. "When Ah see yo' two sleepin' side by side on that beach, Ah . . . nearly went crazy. If Ah," he grinned sheepishly, "if Ah hadn't been so damn seasick . . ."

"But we just takin' a nap! On a public beach, with the whole Sunday crowd around us."

He reached across the table and squeezed her hand. "Ah sorry, Angelique. Please, can yo' forgive me? Ah just . . . Ah just love yo' so much."

Though her mind whirled with anger and love, doubts and hopes, she knew the best way to free herself from his crazy suspicion was to prove to him how much she loved him. And the best place to do that was in his bedroom. She purred flirtatiously, "If yo' got any doubts who this woman love, yo' might take her in yo' arms and see how she respond."

This time, he did not complain about the diaphragm. Even in his rough passion, there was a kindness, a gentleness about him, as if he were desperately glad to hold in his arms the woman he had feared he was in danger of losing.

CHAPTER TWELVE

Veterans, and Victims

During the week following the funeral, Zosia struggled to adjust to life without Piotr. The widow's mood swung up and down unpredictably; she would seem to be in good spirits at breakfast, then suddenly she would withdraw into a wordless depression. If Angelique tried to cheer her up, she only provoked Zosia's surprisingly sharp temper.

At night, Zosia could not sleep, or slept only fitfully, despite bedtime cups of Angelique's strong soursop tea. Haggard and irritable, Zosia demanded sleeping pills. Angelique refused; she knew what Zosia needed was not a drug, but to be active during the day so she could sleep at night.

Exhausted and exasperated, Zosia sat up in bed one morning and threw a tantrum. "You're depriving me of the medicine I need!" she shrieked. "I'll fire you! I'll get another nurse!" She raged, her whole body shaking, until she gasped for air.

Angelique acquiesced and bought a bottle of sleeping pills. Zosia slept soundly the next two nights. Her disposition improved. However, Angelique discovered that Zosia was taking pills during the days as well. Nurse and patient had another argument. Thereafter, Angelique kept the bottle in her black bag; she dispensed a half-pill each evening before she left for work.

Worst of all, Zosia refused to paint. After Piotr's death, she quit. When Angelique offered to bring the acrylics down from the loft to the dining room table, Zosia declared sourly, "I am done with all that." But the nurse knew that painting was the best medicine. So on Friday morning, a week after the funeral, she went up to the studio and brought down tubes of paint, brushes in a jar, a block of paper, and the palette. Zosia, in her chair, watched in morose silence while Angelique arranged everything neatly on the table in front of her. Angelique squirted several colors onto the palette. Zosia frowned at the blobs of paint, glanced out the window, then complained, "There's no sepia out there. Why have you put sepia on the palette? Sepia is not a sea color."

Angelique asked, "Which brush would you like to use?"

"To hell with the brushes!"

So Angelique selected a brush. Leaning over Zosia's shoulder, she placed it in Zosia's reluctant hand, wrapped her own hand around Zosia's, then told her, "All right, fussbudget, *you* choose the color."

Zosia jabbed the brush at a squirt of green, then smacked an ugly splotch on the paper.

Angelique groaned, "Piotr would be quite disgusted with you."

Zosia glowered out the window. "What does he know? He's down there where the water is black."

"So shall we paint him a picture? He'll be wanting to know what the sea looks like on a sunny morning. And he'll certainly want to know that you haven't given up your art. If you quit, you'll break his heart."

Zosia glared at the ragged smear of green. "Let go of my hand."

"But I want to help—"

"Let go of my hand!"

Sighing at the hopelessness of her task, Angelique unwrapped her hand from Zosia's; the brush tumbled to the table.

With awkward, impetuous fingers, Zosia tore the sheet of paper from the pad, wadded it as tightly as she could and threw it at the floor.

But then she struggled to pick up the brush. Once again, Angelique leaned over her shoulder and wrapped her hand around Zosia's.

Together, they rinsed the brush in a jar of water. They dabbed the bristles at a squirt of aquamarine on the palette. Then they painted a smooth stripe across the paper. Despite some clumsy movements, Angelique soon learned to follow Zosia's lead. She felt when the artist wanted to sweep with a long stroke, and when to touch the paper with short strokes. She especially enjoyed blending the colors into delicate hues.

Zosia's eyes focused with concentration; her face became serene. After half an hour, the two were working with fluent teamwork. Angelique witnessed the creation of a seascape with colors far more vibrant than those outside the window. "Zosia," she exclaimed, "I've never been a painter before. This is exciting!"

"Yagh," laughed Zosia, glancing up from her work. "I think you have talent!"

Confident that her patient was able now to continue on her own,

Angelique stood up and arched her stiff back. She said, "Bedtime for me." Zosia, absorbed in her work, seemed not to hear.

But when Angelique opened the door to leave, Zosia turned in her chair and called, "Where is that young man who brought my painting?" The watercolor of bright fishes stood on the table, leaning against a bowl. Zosia had not mentioned Karl all week. Overwhelmed by her grief, exhaustion and tantrums, the widow had even ignored her painting of the reef. But now she looked at Angelique with bright curiosity. "Karl. Wasn't that his name?"

Since her difficult dinner with Nick, Angelique had decided to avoid Karl as much as possible. He could of course visit Zosia with his photographs, but she herself would not invite him sailing, at least not until Nick started at the University and built up some confidence in himself.

"There was something about him I liked," continued Zosia. "When shall we see him again?"

Prompted by Zosia's interest, Angelique reconsidered. Was she going to spend the rest of her life avoiding certain people because of Nick? Was she forever condemned to live with his jealousy? And especially, was she going to live with the intolerable insult of his suspicion?

She stepped back from the open door. "Do you remember, Karl was going to take pictures of the reef for you."

"Yes! I had completely forgotten. Well, where is he? Shall we invite him for a glass of wine tonight? Are you busy?"

Yes, this evening she was busy. "Perhaps tomorrow, Saturday."

Zosia pouted with disappointment. "Why not today?"

"Because today is November eleventh. Veterans' Day. I'm meeting my parents at the cemetery in Frederiksted at six."

Sitting up solemnly in her chair, Zosia said, "Leroy."

"Yes. "

"Today is Veterans' Day?"

"Yes."

Zosia's pouting vanished. "Then there are many whom I must remember today. Veterans. And victims."

Angelique realized that Karl must be remembering too. Remembering a veteran, and a victim. She recalled his sympathy when she told him that Leroy was still missing. "Zosia, Karl told me that he too lost a brother in Vietnam."

Zosia nodded with understanding. "Yagh. I saw something in his face. He lost his brother." She considered for a moment, then asked, "Didn't he say he works at the refinery?"

"Yes. "

"I will telephone and invite him for a Veteran's Day toast on Saturday. What time is good for you?"

Angelique hesitated. If Karl spent Veterans' Day alone—if she denied him the comfort of joining two friends—then she would feel ashamed when she stood at Leroy's marker. She could ride her scooter from the cemetery back to Candle Point by eight o'clock. And she didn't have to be at the hospital until eleven. "Zosia, tonight at eight would be fine."

All day up on the cracking towers, Karl heard the bugle playing taps at Joe's funeral. Joe had been buried with military honors, and when that bugle played taps in the DeKalb cemetery, Karl, a sixteen-year-old kid gripping his father's hand, thought the whole world should stop to listen. Back at the farmhouse, in dazed shock, he thought it should be on the evening news: taps for Joe. But of course it wasn't. The reporter had read the number of casualties that week: how many Americans dead, how many Viet Cong dead.

Through the clamor of the day at the refinery, behind the roar of the boilers, the whine of his drill, and Ed calling up orders, he could hear the clear, sustained, respectful, wrenching notes of the bugle sounding taps.

So he was both surprised and grateful when Mrs. Honegger phoned him during his lunch hour in the refinery canteen, inviting him to a toast in honor of veterans. When he hung up, he thought, Thanks, Angelique. For she must have understood how he felt, and had spoken with Mrs. Honegger, and so prompted the invitation.

Driving home from work, he parked his jeep on King Street in Christiansted, then walked to Express Foto in Caravelle Arcade to pick up a pair of prints. He wanted to give Angelique her picture sailing wing-and-wing, but sometime over the weekend. Not today; today he was not in the mood for remembering high spirits at sea. Today was for Joe.

He inspected the photographs before he paid for them: the portraits of Angelique and himself were excellent, even better than they had looked on the slides. He wondered whether to put hers in a frame before he gave it to her; but decided that perhaps such a gift might seem too formal, too forward. Better just a snapshot between friends.

The photo of himself he would send up to Mom and Pop in a letter. Mom and Pop, at the cemetery today, the first time in years that he wasn't with them.

He stopped at the jeep to put the photos in the glove compartment, then he walked further up King Street to a church that he passed every afternoon on his way home from work. With its tall stone walls and sturdy bell tower, St. John's looked like a cathedral transplanted from damp England to the sunny tropics. He walked through a gate, crossed a courtyard to the back of the church, then looked down a hill at its cemetery. Expecting a lawn with rows of headstones, he was surprised to find stone coffins, unburied, lying atop the brown earth. But beside a few of the coffins stood small American flags, so he knew he had come to the right place.

Wandering through the cemetery, he discovered that many of the coffins were homemade. He paused at the foot of one dilapidated tomb, built with bricks that seemed to have been salvaged from a torn-down building. The mortar had oozed out from between the bricks and dribbled down the sides of the tomb. Vines now climbed up the masonry, then laced across the gray lid, gracing the grave with clusters of tiny pink flowers.

Nearby was another homemade coffin, even more odd: for it was simply a long mound of concrete, decorated with conch shells that had been pressed into the cement. The shells had faded to a dirty white, though deep inside their smooth lips, he could see faint blushes of their original pink.

He walked past several professionally built coffins, white marble boxes with names and dates engraved on their lids.

Then he approached a fresh grave: simply a mound of red-brown dirt. Atop the mound, perhaps over the heart, stood a rusty can filled with wilted yellow flowers.

Different from home, he thought, but the same as home. Rich folks, poor folks, all going through the same grief.

He scanned the cemetery until an American flag caught his eye. Its red, white and blue colors were bright: the flag was new. No doubt someone had come today and planted it on its little stick. He walked toward the flag, for he wanted to pay his respects to a soldier, it could be any soldier, who had done the same as Joe had done: a soldier who had given his life for his country.

The coffin was a box of gray stone; its massive lid was covered with trumpet-shaped hibiscus blossoms. A red bouquet lay by the head-stone. Beside it lay a bouquet of white, then a large cluster of yellow, and a small bunch of pink—placed there by a child? At the foot of the tomb lay another bouquet of bright red. Clearly the family had remembered the soldier's favorite flower, in all its colors. The blossoms were fresh, laid here perhaps an hour ago.

He read the headstone standing atop the end of the coffin,

Juan Gonzalez Jr.
Virgin Islands

PVT
U.S. Army
Vietnam
September 12, 1943
April 22, 1973

YOUR FAMILY REMEMBERS

He noticed something scratched into the bottom of the headstone, as if with a pocketknife. Looking closer, he read "y Maria." And Maria. Someone named Maria had added her name to let Juan know that she too remembers.

Where are the gravestones, he wondered, not just for the soldiers, but for the women whose love had to wither and die? Where are the memorials for the children whose fathers never came home? Remembering Angelique's anguished fury on the beach, he would have demanded to know, from Eisenhower, from Kennedy, from Johnson, and especially from Nixon who did worse than burn the flag—who pissed on it with his lies—he would have asked all those commanders in chief, Where are the brass plaques for the devastated sisters? Add *them* to the casualty figures.

A breeze rattled the seed pods dangling in a flamboyant tree. The flag stirred on its stick.

No doubt Joe's grave had a new flag beside it. Karl envisioned his mother in her navy blue dress, and his father in his Sunday suit with the old-fashioned wide lapels, as they laid a wreath of red roses against Joe's black marble headstone. A wave of sorrow washed over him. Staring down at the white stars in the field of blue curled around the stick, he whispered, "Joe, I'm with you today. I miss you, Joe. I know I oughta be used to it by now. But I . . . miss you like hell."

He waited until the threat of tears had passed. Then he said with dignity, "Joseph Lars Jacobsen, and Juan Gonzalez Junior, and Leroy . . ." He could not remember his, her, last name. But no matter. And though every year he tried to think of something else to say, something wiser, more meaningful, he finally said what he said every year, "Your nation pauses today to say, Thank You."

What Ah supposed to do, Leroy? Yo' heart never once beat with hatred. White and black never enter yo' head. But the mahn Ah love, he got the sickness. Can Ah trust him, Leroy? Or have they made him so sick, he ain' never gon' be well?

She stood at her brother's white marble marker. She wore a black dress and held a fragrant bouquet of pink frangipani, Leroy's favorite flower. Her father, a tall slender man with gray curls, dressed in his Sunday suit, read with a strong voice from the family Bible, "De Lord giveth, and de Lord taketh away. Blessed be de name of de Lord." Her mother held a bouquet of yellow ginger thomas as she bowed her head in prayer.

But Angelique did not pray. She knelt and laid her flowers on the empty ground. With her fingertip, she touched the engraved letters, L E R O Y. Please, Leroy, tell me. Can a woman love a mahn enough to make him well again?

But the white stone gave her no answer.

Finishing his third glass of wine, Karl gazed at the mahogany torso that stood now in a corner filled with ferns. Perhaps it was the wine, perhaps it was the eons since he'd slept with a woman, but for a moment he had the strongest desire to cup his hands over the sculpture's beckoning breasts. She had no arms; her legs ended at her ample thighs. And then he remembered another torso. Ashamed, he cast away his erotic daydreams.

Zosia sat at the head of the table, lost in her own thoughts, her gaunt face lit by a candle. She had spoken briefly about her husband— Karl was stunned, and saddened, to learn the man had died so recently— and now her eyes seemed to stare back to the first winter of the war in Berlin.

Angelique, seated across the table from him, had told about the time Leroy taught her to snorkel. He had showed her the seahorses under the pier. But now, as she gazed into Zosia's candlelit painting of parrotfish and coral, she too was in that distant time when love passed back and forth between two people as easily as shared laughter. Love that today had to be carried like heavy coins in a pocket, impossible to spend.

And he himself had told his favorite story about Joe skipping stones across the pond on summer evenings. Karl, he could hop one fairly well, but Joe! He'd curve them right or left, just you ask, leaving the prettiest curve of expanding rings. He could even hop a stone right out of the water onto the far bank. Pop joked that Joe chose the U. of Chicago so he'd have the whole of Lake Michigan to practice with. Skip a stone across to the Michigan side, hook one up to Milwaukee. Joe could do anything, you bet.

Yeah, but what could Karl do? Not damn much. That time with Tony, Tony the torso, I never even said hello. Never went back. Just sorta forgot. But no, I never did forget. Never will forget Tony. What I didn't do is, I didn't do a darn thing to help him. Just paid my taxes, bought Girl Scout cookies, and diddly-dorked away the years.

He looked again at the torso standing among the ferns. You two shoulda gotten together. Tony damn well deserved you. Karl reached for his glass, but realized how silly it would be to propose a toast to Tony if no one else knew who Tony was.

"Zosia," he said, interrupting her reverie, "Angelique." Both looked at him. "Today's the day we remember. And there's a certain vet who deserves remembering. If you don't mind, I'd like to tell you about Tony."

The two women stared at him as if still distant in their own thoughts.

"After Joe's funeral," he began, but then he stopped. He could hear that bugle, the long clear slow notes like a prayer sent heavenward to accompany the rising soul. Like the words of a final farewell, called to someone who never waved back.

Taps. After all the lies of war, the screams of war, the moans and shrieks and tears and the shocked, pointless, purposeless, fist-pounding question, Why, Why, *Why?* And the silence of no answer. After the murder and mayhem. After the fever had burned its course. Taps.

But the two women were waiting.

"After Joe's funeral, I heard at school that another guy from

DeKalb, a guy named Tony Montadori, was in Great Lakes Naval Hospital, recovering from wounds he'd received in Vietnam. I knew Tony vaguely—he'd played shortstop with Joe on the Little League team—so I thought I'd go visit him. To cheer him up, y'know. I knew that Joe would've made the trip. So I called Tony's home and spoke with his father. Mr. Montadori sounded grateful, and he gave me directions to the Navy base. It was north of Chicago, about two hours' drive from DeKalb. I was seventeen and I had my driver's license, and Pop said I could take the Chevy. This was just before Christmas, you see, the first Christmas without Joe, and I was trying to do something positive, because I was feeling pretty rotten."

He took a long drink of his fourth glass of wine. "I found the Navy base all right. I can remember that as I walked from the parking lot toward the hospital, the elms were covered with ice because there'd been a storm off Lake Michigan the night before. The branches were click-clacking against each other in the wind.

"Inside the hospital, up on the third floor, I was directed through a pair of swinging doors. I entered an enormous room with two aisles and at least a hundred beds. The aisle in front of me stretched across the ward, and it was lined on both sides with small American flags . . . like a street decorated for a parade. Each flag stood on a stick taped to the foot of the bed, so that every sailor knew what he had been fighting for, and why he had ended up in that bed."

He no longer heard the bugle, but now the pandemonium in that room. "The ward was filled with the noise of televisions and shouting men. I asked an orderly—I had to holler to make myself heard—if he knew where I could find Tony Montadori. He pointed down the aisle. 'Two-thirds the way down, on the left.' Feeling pretty self-conscious, because I was healthy, I could walk, and I hadn't done a darn thing for my country, I started down the aisle.

"Televisions hung from the ceiling over every bed. Most of them were on and they were cranked up loud, though there weren't three in a row tuned to the same channel. I glanced at one guy whose face was scar tissue; he was staring up at his screen. I couldn't see the screen. I could see only his dead-looking blue eyes—blank—staring at that television. And I could hear the buzzer and clanging bell of a quiz show, and some woman cheering and clapping because she'd won a trip for two to Hawaii."

He had been angry today in the cemetery, and now again he felt his rage mounting. "Over the racket of the televisions, the guys were shouting to each other from bed to bed. Hollering back and forth, one louder than the next. It was such a madhouse in there, that all of a sudden I wanted to get out. I nearly bolted out the door and escaped. But I didn't, because I'd come to visit Joe's friend, and I knew Joe would've stayed and said hello. Joe would never have bolted. So I kept walking down the aisle.

"I found Tony, having a bath. Two orderlies were sponge-bathing him. He needed help, you see, because Tony had no arms or legs. He was only a torso covered with lumpy yellow-white scar tissue. The one part of Tony that hadn't been burnt was his face. He had a handsome Italian face, and lots of curly black hair. I didn't introduce myself just then, of course. I stood near his bed, waiting until he was done with his bath.

"The orderlies scrubbed his bumpy chest. They rolled him over and scrubbed his back. Then they turned him over again and washed his hair. They did a good job, those two. They gave him a nice vigorous massage, and rinsed his hair well, and dried it with a towel and then with a hair blower. But they didn't say much, and Tony never said anything. He just let them do their job.

"When he was clean and dry, one orderly lifted him in his arms while the other changed the sheets. Then they laid him down and put a fresh jock strap on him, for as badly hurt as he was, he still had . . . well, there was part of him still there.

"The orderlies pulled the sheet up to his chin and moved on to the next bed. I thought that now I would introduce myself. But I hesitated. Because Tony just lay there, staring up at the ceiling. I didn't know if he wanted to be disturbed." Karl lingered for a moment on the memory of Tony's pale, handsome face gazing up from those bushy black curls. "He was so detached from the wild uproar around him, I suddenly wondered if he was deaf."

Angelique shifted in her chair. She watched him intently.

"Suddenly a voice called from the end of the ward, 'Gentlemen!' I saw a seaman in a white uniform standing by the swinging doors. He cupped his hands and shouted, 'Could we turn down those televisions, please?'"

Karl shook his head. "No one paid any attention to him.

" 'Gentlemen, this concerns the visitation today by a number of young ladies.'

"Then, *then*, the place went totally nuts. The TVs were drowned out by hoots and catcalls. Sailors pumped their fists in the air. The seaman raised his arms to quiet the ward, then reached for a microphone on the wall. Across the ceiling, speakers boomed with his voice, 'Gentle—,' but a piercing electronic squeal filled the room. He adjusted a dial on the wall. 'Gentlemen. Coming your way today are twenty-seven young ladies from the major stores in downtown Chicago.' The men bellowed and roared twice as loudly. 'These salesgirls bring Christmas gifts donated by Marshall Fields, Carson Pirie Scott, Montgomery Wards, Sears, and let's see . . .' He checked his clipboard.

"A sailor in the bed beside Tony's sang out, 'I know what I want! Roll me over, in the cloooover . . .'" Mindful of his audience, Karl stopped. "Well, best I not get too graphic. Anyway, the seaman at the microphone admonished his troops, 'Gentlemen, as members of the U.S. Armed Forces, I am sure you will conduct yourselves with all proper accord.'"

He sipped his wine, wishing it were whiskey.

"About a minute later, the women came in through the swinging doors. They were nicely dressed, each of them carrying a box wrapped with Christmas paper. But they huddled by the doors. Some whispered, most were silent, as they stared nervously at the room filled with wild men shouting at them.

"Slowly, the noise subsided. One by one the televisions were turned down, until the ward became almost silent, filled with expectation. One of the women, a brave one, walked out from the cluster to a nearby bed. She was a redhead. She said to the delighted sailor, 'Hi. I'm Ann.'

"The other women began to disperse through the room. There were only twenty-seven of them, and there must have been a hundred men. It seemed like poor planning, but the guys didn't mind. Five or six would call for one girl's attention while she stood in the middle of an aisle, and she would try to talk with all of them at once. Some men didn't say anything. They seemed glad just to stare at a pretty woman.

"I looked at Tony. He had rolled his head on his pillow so he could watch one of the women walking down the aisle in his direction. She had long blonde hair with perfectly cut bangs, and a nice pink sweater. Her face was frozen as she glanced from side to side, her shoulders lifted with fright. Several men called to her, but she walked past them. When Tony saw that she was going to walk past him too, he lifted his head and even his chest with surprisingly strong stomach muscles. The sheet fell to his waist. 'Hello,' he called to her. 'I'm Tony.'

"She stared at his armless torso and put her hand over her mouth. And dropped her gift on the floor—it was a long narrow box with ribbons, maybe a fishing rod—then she turned and shoved through the women behind her and ran up the aisle between all those flags toward the door. Tony stared at her. She cried out something, words I couldn't understand. But Tony understood. His eyes were dark points that saw into the whole rest of his life.

"She threw open those swinging doors and disappeared.

"Tony lay back down; then with a snapping motion, he jerked his shoulders so hard that he rose right up on the stubs of his thighs, and there he balanced in his jock strap. He looked like a Roman torso carved in marble, rough-hewn. He stared toward that door with an anguish I'll never forget.

"Then he threw his head to one side, toppling himself out of bed so that he crashed on the floor. Someone shouted 'Medic!' Tony arched his back and smashed his forehead against the floor as hard as he could. He banged his head again, and again. Blood splattered across the tiles. An orderly came dashing up the aisle. He wrapped his arms around the writhing torso, lifted Tony onto the bed and buckled the straps. Tony's face was covered with blood. He was shrieking incoherently. The orderly stuck a needle into his shoulder. Tony convulsed under the straps for another half-minute, screaming like someone burning alive.

"Finally he lost consciousness. The orderly pulled the bed on its wheels into the aisle, then pushed it, American flag flapping, opposite the direction the woman had run. He pushed Tony out through another set of swinging doors.

"The entire ward was dead silent. My heart was pounding. Then a sailor near me said, 'Aw, never mind, Mary-Beth. This place gets a little crazy. Where ya from, Mary-Beth?'

"Conversations began again. I'd been in that room for maybe fifteen minutes. I hadn't said a word to anyone. No one had noticed me. I hurried up the aisle and pushed out through the swinging doors. The blonde woman was in the lobby, crying in a chair. A couple of other women were sitting beside her, trying to comfort her. I dashed down the steps and found the front door and took in a huge breath of the cold December air."

Silence filled Zosia's dining room. The clock ticked the eternity of time that filled a life of suffering.

Zosia reached both thin hands for her glass, raised the trembling goblet—red wine shivered inside it—and toasted, "To veterans."

Angelique, her eyes ever on Karl, echoed softly, "To veterans."

He added, because it didn't matter what side they were on, nor when, nor even the phony reasons why, "To the veterans of every war."

The trio clinked their glasses: his suntanned hand, Angelique's cinnamon hand, and Zosia's bony white hands came together in the candle-light.

Missile technician 2nd class Schwartz, known to his shipmates as a "living fanatic" who wouldn't let loose of a problem until it was fixed, ran every computer check he had through pod C, yet he was unable to determine the location of the circuitry fault. After five days of frustration. he requested permission to open Tomahawk quadrapod three, pod C, so he could dig into the circuitry itself.

CHAPTER THIRTEEN

Recon Patrol

Nick figured that if the whigger went a-courtin', he'd do it on a Friday night. So he would take a look for himself inside the Yank's abode, and if he found so much as a trace of Angelique's presence, he would continue his recon patrol down the hill and out to the end of Candle Point.

He parked behind Chenay Beach, opened the tailgate, lifted the flap over the spare tire and took out a satchel. As he changed into his camouflage, he considered, fearing the worst, whether he really wanted to do this. Angelique was all he had in the world. He longed for only one thing more: to lie beside her on Maroon Ridge and gaze in the moonlight at her brown belly round with their child. If he caught her in bed tonight with Hard Hat . . . he wasn't sure what he would do.

But he had to know if he could trust her. And certainly, he knew he could never trust a whigger.

He pulled his black ski mask over his head and adjusted the eye holes. Then he put on the black gloves: whatever happened tonight, there would be no fingerprints. From the spare tire well, he lifted out his belt and sheathed machete. He enjoyed the feel of the webbing around his waist, and the weight of the blade at his hip.

Wading through guinea grass, he traversed the field behind the beach, then climbed the flank of the hill overlooking Candle Point. He scanned the houses near the top, houses he had inspected earlier, both by day and by night, when he had cruised through the neighborhood in his taxi. Spotting the cottage, pale white in the starlight, its windows black, he grinned. That boy ain' even know to leave a light on.

He crouched behind a hedge of ornamental cactus, held his breath, and listened to the rasp of locusts; to the rattle of seed pods in a woman's-tongue tree; to the rubbery rustle of banana leaves when a gust puffed up the hill; he listened to the sounds of the night, alert for the sounds of anything else. In the center of the little yard, the cottage was silent.

Charged with the old excitement, he drifted like a shadow to the back door. He tried the knob: locked. Peering through the door's window, he discerned two gray-white shapes: sink and toilet.

Slinking in the shadows, he reconnoitered the four sides of the cottage, checking windows and the front door: everything locked. No signs of an alarm, nor traces of a dog.

He returned to the back door. A master with his machete, he set its point on the glass, then tapped its wooden handle until a crack etched the pane with a tiny silent bolt of lightning. Moving the point, he tapped again, forming a second fracture. A third tap, and he was ready. Pressing the point against the center of a triangle of cracks, he gave the handle a sharp knock. The blade pierced the window; glass tinkled on the tiles inside.

He listened: locusts, seed pods . . . the bark of a distant dog. No stir in any of the neighboring houses. No lights flicking on. He withdrew his machete—careful not to grate steel against glass—from the window. With gloved hands, he broke off pieces of glass and laid them silently on the lawn. When the hole was large enough, he reached inside and—wary of the glass encircling his wrist—turned the inner knob. The door opened; the scent of bay rum wafted out. He withdrew his hand, then slowly pulled the door open.

Not a sound inside.

He stepped into the bathroom and closed the door behind him. Taking a penlight from his pocket, he circled its pencil-thin beam around the bowl of the sink: no second toothbrush, no hair brush. No sign of her soft curly hair.

Peering through the door into the next room, he saw the dark flat form of a double bed; he felt a stab of jealousy. Stepping into the room, he bent over the single pillow and sniffed the bedspread tucked around it, but found no traces of her scent. With the penlight, he searched the night table beside the bed, then he zigzagged the beam over a dresser top. Nothing.

Checking all the drawers, he found not so much as a hairpin.

In the closet: Hard Hat's shirts and trousers, several pairs of green Petrox overalls, but no pink nightgown. Triumphant, he nearly crowed, Yo' meh Sugah! Yo' meh one and only! But the good soldier remained silent.

From the door, he peered into the living room: its walls were covered with pale rectangles that proved to be, with one quick sweep of the flashlight, maps of the refinery! He nearly whooped at his good fortune as he examined a schematic layout of Petrox with color-coded towers and tanks. The second map illustrated pipelines, pumping stations, key valves, even tiny arrows indicating direction of oil flow. The next chart: electrical. Next: office and field telephone system. Never in all his missions in Nam had he captured such a trove of information about a possible target.

But it was a trove he could not touch. For he was walking the straight and narrow now. His Angelique, his ever-loving Angelique, didn't care a damn about this Yank. She loved her Nicholas. Yes, they would buy a house just outside of Frederiksted, at the edge of the rainforest. He'd build a playground in the front yard that every kid in the neighborhood would be welcome to use. And for his Sugah, he'd stretch a hammock between two flamboyant trees, so she could swing while the red petals fluttered down and landed on her. He'd bring her a glass of milk and watch her drink it. Then she'd look up at him with her bright eyes and tell him, 'Ah love yo', Nicholas. Yo' meh whole world.'

He continued his search through the cottage, no longer for signs of Angelique, but driven now by a curiosity to learn all he could about Yankee Doodle. He swept his light over a table and saw a coffee mug, a paperback, a photograph. He picked up the picture. There was the brother she had mentioned. From the lack of ribbons, he knew that Rambo Junior was just shipping out. The hero's still green, he thought. Yo' ain' smeared yo'self yet with lipstick and blood.

He set the picture down, picked up the book. *There* was a clue: *Sturdy Black Bridges: Visions of Black Women in Literature.* Obviously this boy had an interest in Angelique. Nick shook his head, incredulous. He t'ink he gon' understand her by readin' a book?

He continued the search in earnest. Nothing on the kitchen counter but a basket of papayas that filled the room with their fruity ripeness. Nothing on a sofa. In a bookcase, nature guides—*Ocean Birds of the World, Seashells, Caribbean Flora and Fauna*—and a pair of binoculars. Looking out the window at the lights on the end of Candle Point, he wondered how often this voyeur gazed down with the binocs at an unsuspecting Angelique.

At meh Sugah.

He searched a desktop, cluttered with papers. His wand of light crossed a snapshot leaning against a pencil can. Bending over, he saw it was a picture of Angelique, bright-eyed and laughing as she looked straight at the camera. The nipples of her breasts pressed against her swimming suit. Her trim thighs stretched toward the photographer. He swept the beam around the photo: sailboat, wisps of scarlet clouds, green hills in the background. His heart thumping, he focused the circle of light on her face. Rarely had he seen her look so happy.

Sweeping his beam over the desk, he found a yellow KODAK envelope, and inside it, the matching photo: the whigger himself on the opposite side of the sailboat. Smiling at the camera as if he owned the world.

These ain' no pictures of fish. She lie to me. She lie!

He remembered the pretty whores in Saigon, whom the money-laden Yanks used with no more thought than if they had simply taken a good crap.

Staring again at the lights of her house, he maintained the clarity of mind to realize that if he stormed down there, he might spend the rest of his life in prison. Or face the electric chair. Certainly, when he was done with her boyfriend, he would have lost Angelique forever.

So Ah just scare him away, teach the little lady a lesson, and end this episode.

Scare the whigger. How Ah gon' do that? Ah tap on that hard hat just enough to let him know that next time, Ah gon' be tappin' with a ax.

He strode into the kitchen and opened drawers until he found a steak knife. Then he crossed through the cottage to the bedroom and laid Doodle Dandy's photo on the pillow. Holding the penlight with his left hand, the beam trained on the Conqueror's grinning face, he stabbed the knife so its handle protruded like a wooden nose.

Take that as a warnin', boy.

To leave no doubt that both Pee Wee and Petrox were equally unwelcome, he stripped the walls of maps. Popping out thumb tacks with his machete, he folded each chart and stuffed it into a pouch, until his pockets bulged with treasure.

Can do, sir! Can do!

Working now with polished speed, he sorted through the papers on the desk—graphs, data, a hand-written report—and grabbed everything that looked important. He sorted through drawers, then dumped them upside-down in a heap on the floor.

One last time, he shone his light on Sugah's picture, still leaning against the pencil can. He ached to pick it up, to put it in the pocket over his heart; but at the same time, he refused even to touch it.

As he slipped out the bathroom door and glided across the yard, he could not shake from his mind that image of her radiantly happy face.

With Zosia's painting under his arm, Karl walked wearily up his front steps. He unlocked the door, flicked on the lights and—the walls were blank! Maps gone!

Heaps of papers on the floor! "What the . . . ?" Freezing in the doorway, he listened: but heard nothing inside. Frightened, increasingly outraged, he stepped back outside and shot a glance to the right: there stood the rake, leaning against the house. He set the painting by the door, grabbed the rake and held it at chest level, its steel fingers ready to jab and claw and bludgeon. Stalking into his cottage, he glanced toward the bedroom door, then toward the kitchen counter, and decided to check behind the counter first. Rake raised like a harpoon, he peered over the countertop: nobody there.

At the bedroom door, he flicked on the light, dropped to a crouch, rake ready, and peered into the cavity beneath his bed: nobody there.

But as he stood up, he noticed something on his pillow. Stepping closer, he discovered his picture with a knife stuck through it! Shocked, horrified, he knew he was dealing with a psychopath. Who hated Petrox. And who was handing out a death warning. Probably that crazy guy at Fitzroy's. Of course, that's who it was. Somehow he found the cottage . . . Saw the jeep at Fitzroy's, spotted it again in the Petrox parking lot, then tailed me home. Figured I might have some goodies inside. Well, you hit the jackpot, fella. You got every spigot and spout at Petrox. Now, what you gonna do next?

He whipped open the closet door: his tropical-weight shirts and slacks hung as usual on evenly spaced hangers, their normalcy reassuring.

He snapped on the bathroom light: the shower curtain had been pushed to one side, but no one hid behind it. Spotting a hole in the window by the doorknob, he appreciated the professionalism of whoever could fracture glass so neatly. With the rake poised to dig its teeth into the face of any attacker, he opened the door and peered out. His eyes traveled slowly along the hedge of cactus; he saw raised arms, heads peeking at him, notches where a rifle barrel might rest. Behind the hedge was a field of coal-black grass. A whole gang of psychos could be out there, watching me right now, and I'd never know it. They're waiting for me to step outside so they can slice me up and leave my head on a pole at the Petrox gate.

Retreating into the bathroom, he shut the door and pushed the locking button on the knob, then saw the hole and realized how stupid he was to lock the door. And how vulnerable he was. Always would be without a fence and an alarm system. Hell, it's as bad here as South Chicago.

Remembering his bare desk, he returned to the living room and discovered with shock and outrage anew that his report was missing! Six weeks of work, gone. His mind raced: some of the report was xeroxed and on file, but the vast bulk he had simply brought home every evening on his clipboard. Ed's gonna blow his stack. *Why* didn't I make copies? The Xerox copier stood in the corner of the air-conditioned office; he could easily have stopped there for a minute or two at the end of each day, and then filed the copies in the metal cabinet. Damn damn *damn!*

His mind seething with rage and regret, fear and bewilderment at this invasion of his home, he noticed the picture of Angelique leaning exactly as before against his pencil can, as if a tornado had stormed all around her but never touched her. He picked up the photo, looked at her playful smile, and felt relieved that he had a friend he could rely on. Call Angelique. Even before you call the police, call Angelique. She knows the island. If the natives are restless, she'll know why.

But then it dawned on him: She's the only one who knew the charts were here. She was in the cottage, when was it? . . . Monday morning. She had to notice the maps on the wall, maybe the papers on my desk. So are the two in cahoots? Is that why I was invited down to Zosia's tonight? And how about Zosia? She in this thing too? Fuming with suspicion, he dropped the photo face down on his desk.

But then he thought, She came up here to apologize, and if that was phony baloney, she's a darn good actress. And she and Zosia certainly seemed genuine tonight. Naw, this is that guy who's angry because Petrox bulldozed his mangrove swamp. In a way I don't blame him. But that's no excuse for a knife stuck through somebody's face in a photo. Voodoo, that's what it is. Except this guy doesn't mess around with pins.

He went back into the bedroom and stared at the fragment of a nightmare that refused to go away. He reached to pull out the knife, to wash it and put it back in the drawer; to tear up the picture and burn it—he could have another printed from the slide; to sew up the holes in the bedspread and pillowcase. But he decided to leave the evidence for the police. There might be fingerprints.

Okay, let's not waste any more time. Call the police. No, phone Angelique first. Still wielding the rake, he hurried to the kitchen counter, lifted the receiver, poised his finger over the pushbuttons, and realized he didn't know her number. Zosia of course would know, but she was in bed.

Then he could hear Angelique's words, the day she came to apologize,

LEROY BEAUMONT NIELSEN

Leaning the rake against the counter, he looked up Nielsen in the telephone book, and found dozens; under A: Albert, Albertine, Angelique! 'Rgrd midwife. 773-2745.'

He tapped the buttons. While her phone rang, he looked out the window at the lights of her house, clustered against the black sea. Zosia's house was dark.

"Angelique? Hi, this is Karl. Sorry to bother you. I know you're hurrying to get ready for work, but I've just discovered that someone has broken into the cottage . . . . Yeah, stole a lot of maps and charts and a report I was working on. But there's something else. He stuck a knife through a picture of me . . . . Yeah, on my pillow. Am I supposed to read some particular message from a knife stuck in a photograph? Does it mean, Yankee Go Home? . . . All right, sure, come on up. Tell me what you make of it. But wait. How do we know the guy isn't still outside the cottage? I'll drive down and fetch you in the jeep . . . . Are you sure? . . . Okay. Just be careful . . . . No, I haven't yet. Anyone there you recommend I call? . . . Braithwaite. Arnold Braithwaite, nine one five. Got it. Thanks. . . . All right. See you in a couple minutes. Thanks again."

Well, she sounded properly shocked.

When she arrived, her face filled with concern, he showed her the empty walls. Then he took her into the bedroom and watched her face when she saw the knife stuck into his picture. "Oh no!" she cried, grimacing and raising her hand to her mouth as she backed away. She stared at the knife with unequivocal revulsion.

"Who would do such a thing?" he asked.

She looked at him, frightened for him. "Someone who wants to scare you away."

"Obviously. But is he mad at specifically *me*, or at somebody who works for Petrox?"

"Karl, last year there were problems with strikers at the refinery. This looks like the work of somebody with a grudge."

"Strikers, huh? So what happens next? Flaming arrows through the windows?"

"Have you phoned the police?"

"Yup. Braithwaite's sending a car with detectives and a dog."

She asked, her sympathy apparently genuine, "What will you do?"

"You mean, will I leave the island? Will this kook scare me away? Nope. He's just one more reason for me to stop being a monkey on a cracking tower. Time to take up a new profession." He shook his head at the possibility of leaving. "I'm certainly not going to go running back to South Chicago. I just got here. I like St. Croix." He smiled faintly. "And I've already made two friends. So I mean to stay."

She looked at her watch. "Karl, I've got to go. I wish I could be with you until the police arrive, but my shift starts at eleven."

"You go right ahead. Thanks for coming. I feel much better after talking with you."

She suggested, "I think it's best we don't tell Zosia. She would be shaken for days."

He agreed. "We won't say a word."

At the door, she paused, then asked, "Wasn't that the picture I took of you?"

"Yeah. When we were sailing wing-and-wing."

"Didn't you take one of me?"

"It's there on my desk. I was going to give it to you later, but you can see it now if you like."

Again he watched her face as he handed her the photo. She seemed in a daze as she stared at it, though finally she said, "We were like two kids, rocking the boat and having fun." She looked at him with the same warmth and respect that he had seen an hour ago in the candle-light at Zosia's. "May I keep it?"

"It's for you. I'm glad you like it."

After she had gone, he was convinced that she knew nothing about his burglar. Her shock, her concern, her helpfulness, her friendship: they were all genuine. He felt profoundly comforted that she was trustworthy.

While he waited for the police, he went outside and brought in Zosia's picture. He unwrapped it and hung it on the bare wall over his bare desk, restoring a measure of normalcy to the room.

Then he phoned Ed, at home, and was greatly relieved that Ed was not angry at him, but at the 'criminal element' on the island.

When he hung up, he felt drained. He sat in a chair at the table to wait. His eyes came to rest on the portrait of his family. He picked it up and gazed at each familiar face: he heard his mother's voice, his father's laugh, felt Joe's firm grip on his shoulder, and he was back again at the good, safe, cow-smelling farm.

CHAPTER FOURTEEN

Get Out!

On Saturday morning, she rode from the hospital to Harbor View. She chained her scooter to the signpost, climbed three flights of stairs filled with the smells of coffee and toast, then followed the hallway to Nick's gray metal door. She rapped her knuckles five times, demanding an answer.

Not a sound from inside: he was pretending he was asleep. With her fist, she pounded five peremptory thumps. Silence: he was pretending he wasn't home.

Down the hall, a door opened and a scowling woman in pink curlers peeked out. Angelique leaned toward Nick's door and shouted, loudly enough for the entire floor to hear, "Nicholas! Yo' open this door or Ah comin' back with a shotgun and Ah gon' BLOW it open!"

Doors opened up and down the hallway, then slammed shut.

Nick's door opened a few inches, to the length of a brass security chain. Wearing black Vietnamese pajamas, his chin dark with stubble, he looked sleepily out the crack and forced a casual smile. "That yo', Sugah?"

She hissed, "Open this door or Ah comin' back with the policcccce."

He narrowed his eyes to a steel-hard stare. "One word to the police and that be the end of lover boy." He rattled the chain free, swung the door open and growled, "Get in here. Yo' got some explainin' to do."

Entering his apartment, she saw charts spread across the table. Now she had to believe that it was Nick who had stabbed that knife into Karl's picture. And on the pillow of Karl's bed: a vicious insult, despite her faithfulness to the man she loved. She glared at him. "Only a coward would use a knife."

He shut the door and refastened the chain, then he folded his arms across his chest and studied her for a long moment. "Nice photo of yo' on his desk. Yo' look awful happy with that whigger."

124

She winced at the word, and knew he would never change. Her hopes had been futile. Her heart breaking on the inside, her face hard on the outside, she announced her decision, "Ah refuse to let yo' poison meh children with yo' hate."

"Children?" he scoffed. "Yo' t'ink Ah gon' marry yo' now? Yo' who—"

"Me who ain' done a t'ing wrong!" she raged. "Ah ain' touch the mahn and he ain' touch me. But yo' got to t'reaten him with a knife!" She wanted to slap him, not to hurt him, but to wake him up. "Nick, the war be over. Stop seein' all of us as the enemy."

He finished his sentence, "—yo' who lied to me. Ah ain' find no picture of fish. Just yo' two grinnin' like yo' on a honeymoon."

"Ah ain' know what he do with the pictures he took at the reef. But Ah do know he took them for Zosia to paint from, exactly as Ah told yo'. And Ah also know that Ah do *not* like bein' called a liar." She cocked her head back. "Or a whore."

"Whore of a whigger."

"No! Ah loved yo', Nick. Ah been yo' woman, true blue. Yo' ain' got no right to t'row this shit in meh face."

"Get out." He stiffened as he stared at her, as if she was beneath his contempt.

Unable to stop the tears running down her cheeks, she tried to convince him, "Ah loved yo', Nick. Yo' got to believe, Ah loved yo' with all meh heart. And Ah never stopped tryin' to help yo' to—"

"Get out!" He grabbed her arm and shoved her, struggling but helpless, to the door. He rattled the chain loose while she protested through her sobs, "Nick, this ain' the way to finish. Nick, Ah *do* love yo', even after what yo' done. Please stop this craziness so we can—"

He yanked the door open and flung her into the hallway. As she struck the opposite wall, she heard his door slam shut with a bang as loud as the shot of a cannon.

CHAPTER FIFTEEN

Potato

"Angelique!"

She awoke from the oblivion of sleep; immediately a profound sadness gripped her, though she couldn't yet think why.

"Angelique!"

Blearily she looked at the clock by her bed: 10:05, Saturday morning. She had slept for only an hour since—since Nick threw her out. Remembering that brutal moment, she dropped her head back to the pillow. After a year and a half of the most passionate love she had ever known, or given, she was devastated by his cruelty. What she wanted now was to sleep, remote from the world, where nothing could touch her but dreams of the sea.

"*Angelique!*"

Cecil's voice. In her churning cloud of despair, a bud of happiness appeared, for he summoned her to the work she loved best. She dragged herself out of bed, wrapped a pink terrycloth robe around her and hurried through the house to the front porch, where she looked down at a shirtless young man on a sweating horse. He held up both hands, fingers spread wide as he announced, "Number ten!"

She called down, "When labor start?"

"Ah leave when her pains begin. Maybe a hour ago."

"Why yo' ain' phone me?"

He shrugged, "Because, of course, the phone them dead again."

She groaned with exasperation. "Cecil, Ah be right down."

She hurried into the house, tossed off her robe, stepped into her white nursing slacks, quickly buttoned her white blouse, and tied the laces of her white shoes with tight neat bows. A splash of water on her face; she squeezed a squirt of toothpaste onto her finger and cleaned her teeth as best she could while she raced through the house, grabbing her black bag by the door.

Dashing down the steps, she spat toothpaste into her aloe garden.

But when she sat on her scooter, it felt odd. Looking down at the rear tire, she saw it was flat. She remembered now: the scooter had felt a little wobbly on the way home from Nick's, but she had been too upset to bother with it. She spotted a two-inch acacia thorn sticking out from under the fender. "Pistarkle!"

"Never mind!" cried the impatient teenager. "Ride with me!"

With no time to waste, she handed him her bag. Then taking hold of his hip, she hauled herself up onto the saddleless horse. Sitting snugly behind Cecil, she took her bag with one hand while she wrapped her other arm around his chest. "Yo' grown!" she teased him, clawing her nails into his adolescent muscle. "Yo, *almost* a mahn now."

Kicking the horse with his heels, he declared proudly, "Eighteen last month. Too bad yo' such a old lady."

"Old lady?" Clamping her legs against the horse's heaving ribs, she protested, "T'irty-two ain' old. Too bad yo' only eighteen."

Bouncing with Cecil to the horse's hurried rhythm, she gazed dully at the sun glittering on the bay. The old lady, she thought with a spark of panic. She recognized the demons of depression, ready to pounce. Yo' tired, she warned herself. And yo' got a job to do. Ain' got time for the glooms.

An hour later, Cecil reined the horse off Salt River Road onto a lane through a grove of banana trees. She looked ahead over his shoulder at the house that grew longer before each of her visits. The center section had been built with bamboo from the rainforest. Additions had been constructed with salvaged sheets of plywood: some were painted with pastel greens, pinks, yellows, and blues, some were simply rain-weathered brown. The two end wings were built, as Albert Witherspoon maintained a steady climb toward prosperity despite the number of mouths to feed, with neatly cemented cinderblocks. Most of the roof was covered with tar-spackled corrugated tin, though the section over the original bamboo bungalow was thatched with grass. Behind the elongated mansion loomed the mangrove trees bordering Salt River.

The lane passed through a thriving vegetable garden. Three children stood up from their weeding. "Angelique!" they chirped, waving to her on the trotting horse.

"Thomas! Rebecca! Suzanna!" she called with affection, for she had received all three into her own hands as each child had come into the world. "How yo' be?"

Near the house stood deaf-mute Sabrina, Albert's sister, wearing a black hand-me-down dress. She held the hand of a boy about a year old, whom Sabrina had brought forth into Angelique's hands without a single cry. Sabrina endured her pains in silence, and never named the father.

Now she stood motionless, holding her son's hand while he chewed on a slice of bread. As crumbs dropped to the dirt, fuzzy peeping chicks ran out from under the hem of Sabrina's dress and pecked at the bread. Flexing their stubs of wings, they disappeared again between her black sneakers. Charles watched them with fascination, but his mother stared at Angelique with dark eyes that saw everything and revealed nothing.

"Hello, Sabrina," called Angelique from the slowing horse, though she knew she would receive no acknowledgement.

Albert appeared in the doorway, beaming a smile of welcome. "Angelique, yo' right on time." He laughed, "Yo' must know de way by now." He wore denim work clothes, and a blue bandana wrapped over his head like a cap.

"Albert, how she be?" Angelique asked as Cecil reined to a stop.

"As good as ever. She know her job too!"

She slid down from the lathered horse, hurried up bamboo steps to a bamboo floor-above-flood-level, then followed Albert down a hall-way that creaked beneath her feet. Albert opened the door to a room smelling of disinfectant. Edith lay on a narrow bed, her eyes clenched, face streaming with sweat while she groaned at the pain of her contrac-tions. The tiny woman's belly covered by a white sheet looked like a giant egg.

Setting her bag on a table, Angelique leaned down to her patient. "Edith, how yo' feel?"

The woman opened her exhausted eyes. "Hullo, dearie. Water broke a hour ago."

"How yo' pains?"

"Awful as ever."

"Otherwise good?"

Edith closed her eyes. "When Ah hear de baby holler, den Ah say tings be good."

Angelique turned to a second table and inspected bowls of hot water, a cake of soap, a stack of threadbare towels. From her bag she took out several sterilized packets. She washed her hands, face and arms, then washed her hands again. Tearing open the packets, she put on a green surgical gown; tucked her hair into a surgical cap; tied a mask over her mouth and nose. Glancing out the windows while she waited for the contractions to pass, she saw rows of yams and then rows of floppy-leaved banana trees in one direction, and the wild tangle of mangrove roots and black swamp bottom in the other.

She drew down the sheet, revealing a belly that seemed to double the size of the wiry woman. Leaning over her patient, the midwife laid her hands across the top of the abdomen. Gently pressing the stretched skin, she felt the angular buttocks of the child inside. She slid her hands down the belly's lateral edges: felt the bumps of elbows and knees with her right hand, and the smooth hard back with her left. The head could not be felt; it was already engaged in the birth canal. "Everyt'ing fine," she reassured the resting mother.

Edith showed a faint smile.

Albert, standing anxiously on the opposite side of the bed, told Angelique, "We baked de potato last night."

Weeks before the birth, the midwife repeated her simple instructions for preparing the linen: sterilize sheets and towels in the kitchen oven at 350 degrees for one hour; or, if the family had a charcoal-burning oven, hot and long enough to bake a large potato.

"Who eat the potato?" she asked as she wet a cotton swab with alcohol.

The patriarch beamed with pride. "Cecil. He find heself a girl and gon' marry in June." Albert chuckled, "So he need dat potato to give he strength."

Eighteen, she thought morosely. How easily they do it. Why can't Ah be as blithe? As she swabbed Edith from breasts to knees, she mocked herself, Nick ain' trust me, and Ah ain' trust them boys with their bombs. Maybe he and Ah, we both be fools.

She washed her hands again, drew on a pair of sterilized gloves, then examined Edith internally: the head was pushing through a well-dilated cervix. "Everyting fine," she called again to the mother, who bared her teeth as she moaned with mounting intensity.

Edith spread her arms and gripped the edges of the mattress. Albert knelt and took hold of her hand. As she filled the room with sharp panting cries, she clung to his callused fingers.

Angelique put on her stethoscope and slid its chrome disk over the damp, drum-tight skin until she located the fetal heartbeat. Timing the tiny pulse with her watch, she counted one twenty-two beats per minute, strong and regular. As the contractions tightened around the fetus, its pulse dropped to a hundred and five. But when the stress passed, the heartbeat returned to one twenty-one. Angelique called to Edith, "Yo' got a tough little fighter in there."

Edith clenched her teeth, her brow creased with pain.

Angelique listened for another minute, for she loved to hear the racing heart of a baby waiting to be born. Comin' down the pike, she thought. Comin' home with high unfettered hopes.

Twenty minutes later, in the stretched oval between Edith's thighs, a wet scalp appeared. "Crowning," announced the midwife. "Give a good push."

Gasping with pain, still clutching Albert's hand, Edith pushed.

The elongated head slowly emerged, face down. Angelique cradled the forehead in her hand. She felt with a finger in the birth channel for the umbilical cord; her heart jumped when she found the cord wrapped around the neck. Quickly she slid a finger under it and lifted it away from the throat. No damage yet, she hoped. Please, little one, give us a good howl.

Half a minute later, the chin popped out.

The protruding head slowly rotated, while inside the birth channel the body was turning.

The upper shoulder pushed out. She lifted the infant slightly: the lower shoulder emerged. She pulled gently: the whole body slid easily into her hands, the cord trailing safely behind.

Holding the infant girl by her ankles, she cleaned the mucus from her mouth. A reflex in the ribs filled the lungs with air, and then a powerful wail announced the newborn's health.

Albert whooped a cheer. Outside in the garden, Cecil and the children echoed their father with shouts and applause. Edith's puffy eyes shone with delight as she reached up and touched her baby's slimy cheek.

Angelique laid the child on a towel across Edith's abdomen. Then she inspected the umbilical cord, its spiral artery still pulsing. When the vine of life had emptied most of its blood into the child's body, she clamped the cord, and sliced the link with her scalpel.

Placing her hand over Edith's lower abdomen, she felt a quickening of the uterus: the lump of the afterbirth was passing downward. She glanced at the empty bowl on the table to be sure it was ready. Then she turned again to the child. While she cleaned the squalling infant, she hummed a lullaby. Soon she began to sing, for well she remembered the words of the very first song her mother had taught her.

Washed, dried, and wrapped in a new yellow towel, Elspeth Witherspoon nursed at her mother's breast. Albert, kneeling at the edge of the bed, cooed to his daughter and touched her soft, sucking cheek. Edith gazed at her baby girl with glowing satisfaction.

Then Edith rolled her head toward Angelique. "Tank yo', dearie."

The midwife was packing her bag. "Yo' most welcome. Remember now, no work for one week. Yo' stay out of that banana patch."

"Yes mum."

"Ah *mean* it."

"Yes mum."

Before she left the room, Angelique smiled at the yawning infant. Blessed is life, she thought. Blessed is life, sheltered beneath the skirts of the universe.

Albert escorted her along the creaking hallway to the door, where she blinked into the sunshine. Cecil leaped onto his horse, raised his hands once again over his head, fingers spread wide, and cheered, "Number ten!"

After he had brought her home, she changed into her black bikini and walked with Ulysses down to the beach for a swim, hoping the sea might lift her spirits.

The welcoming sea washed over her. Frog-kicking, then sweeping her arms through the clear, pure, silent, soothing water, kicking and sweeping, kicking and sweeping, she wanted never to surface. She passed over bright sand, over dark turtle grass. She ached to remain immersed, to swim even deeper, until she reached that pure abyssal blue where she could close her eyes and sleep.

But finally she had to arch toward the surface and take a huge breath of air. She rolled onto her back and sculled with her hands, resting. The midday sun shone straight overhead, warming her face. Lazily she kicked her feet.

Never! cried a mocking voice. Never!

The demons scrambled loose; she was too tired to stop them. They taunted her with their scornful prophesies: never would she lie on a bed and stare with wonder at the big brown egg of her belly. Never would she grip her husband's hand to feel his strength while she pushed their child toward life. Never would she hear the beautiful, miraculous cry of her *own* newborn child. Never! yelped the demons, jabbing her with sharp reminders of her indisputable failure. Never! Because she was a coward. Afraid, afraid, forever afraid.

No! she argued. Because I protect my babies from this murderous world.

Never! they cheered with delight. Never, never, never!

Whenever the demons pounced at night, she always tried to imagine Nick beside her, gazing at her, his eyes filled with love . . . But now that image was replaced by his last look of unforgiving rage. Hating her for allowing herself to feel happy in the company of a white man.

What he t'ink Ah gon' do? she fumed. Come crawlin' back to beg his forgiveness?

Sorry, Mistah Nick. This woman don' crawl.

Especially when she done nothin' wrong. Nothin'!

But what he did. Vividly she remembered the knife. No! she thought, reaffirming her decision. No more. He may have thrown me out, but Ah had already said good-bye.

Gradually her heart softened, and she said good-bye to him not in anger, but with compassion, and love. Nicholas, Ah always gon' love yo'. But Ah been the wrong woman for yo', Nick. Yo' need a woman who ain' Leroy's sister. A woman who can take yo' big strong hand and lead yo' where them ghosts can't follow.

She rolled her head slowly back and forth, dipping her face into the water. Then she lifted her face to the sun and savored its warmth.

An image surfaced in her mind, of Karl standing beside Zosia's counter, staring with such tenderness at the mahogany mermaid. And then he leaned over and so gently kissed the red belly.

That unexpected moment lingered in her thoughts as she floated. The demons vanished, forgotten.

And then another memory came to mind: the sound of a fetal heartbeat. That hopeful steady little flutter, like the wings of a sugarbird.

Sculling with her hands, kicking with her feet, she lifted her slightly rounded brown belly above the surface. Drifting beneath the warm sun, she baked like a potato.

With keen satisfaction, missile technician 2nd class Schwartz reported to his chief petty officer that he had located and repaired a wiring fault in pod C. After having performed all simulated prepare-to-launch signal checks, he certified that the Tomahawk cruise missile was now serviceable.

PART TWO

CHAPTER SIXTEEN

Sanctify

Rolling her head on the pillow, Angelique opened one eye and saw through the window the red glow of dawn. Fuzzily she focused on the clock: 5:50. Hadn't it been two in the afternoon when she had walked home from the beach after almost falling asleep in the sea? She hadn't bothered with lunch, had simply collapsed into bed. Then she had slept . . . sixteen hours! She lifted her head to see better out the small latticed window in the stone wall. A blood-red stripe lay across the horizon between the charcoal-gray sky and the silver-gray sea; she stared with astonishment, gratitude, and hunger, for though each dawn over the Caribbean was beautiful in its own way, the pure and vibrant red of that broad stripe, tapering at its ends into dark maroon, enabled her to soak the color in through her eyes, to savor it in her soul, as if the stripe of red poured a fresh transfusion into her tired blood.

The sun itself would soon peek above the sea. Hopping out of bed, she put on her pink terrycloth robe and hurried out to the back porch, the ten-by-fifteen-foot concrete lid of the cistern that gathered rainwater from her roof. Because she was usually on duty at the hospital, nearing the end of her all-night shift, dawn was generally no more than pale light beginning to filter through the curtained windows while she took a pulse, or probed with an I.V. needle for a patient's vein. But today was Sunday, wonderful Sunday, and as she stood at the waist-high stone wall atop the Candle Point cliff and inhaled great breaths of the salty breeze, she savored these uninterrupted moments before the birthing of the sun.

A tiny scarlet cap lifted above the horizon, the same red as the stripe into which it lifted, but fiercely radiant. A capillary of red stretched toward her across the sea. As the red orb slowly rose to its full width, the artery beneath it became an aorta; dawn's heartbeat of light was offered to the awakening world.

Words stirred in the back of her mind, buoyed on the drift of a melody. Basking in the sun's growing warmth on her face as the full crimson orb revealed itself, she began to sing,

"My Lord, what a mornin',
My Loooord, what a mornin',
My Loooooord, what a moooooornin'!
When that sun begin to shine!"

Her memory of the second verse had dimmed since she had quit the choir, so she sang the first verse again, letting her long-unused soprano ring with its full jubilant power.

Zosia awoke to her neighbor's singing. Rarely had she heard such a joyous sound from Angelique's house. She sat up in the dim light, worked her legs over the side of the bed, reached for her cane hooked over the headboard; then leaned with both hands on its crook as, shakily, she stood up. No time to dally. First thing was to take two fat chickens out of the freezer for a Sunday dinner for three. With a fresh red candle on the table.

Never mind the disparity between them, she thought as she thumped along the hallway toward the kitchen. The attraction between them is almost inevitable.

Carrying his folded yellow sail under one arm, his sleek blue board under the other, Karl walked barefoot across the cool sand toward the gently lapping waves.

He had worked all day Saturday at the Petrox office, he and Ed assembling what data they had to compensate for the stolen charts, and then, with no plans to meet either Angelique or Mrs. Honegger on Saturday evening, he went to bed early. The robbery, the knife, the wariness he felt minute by minute—would the weirdo in camouflage attack again?—had worn him out. And Ed's incessant chatter, jumping back and forth between "These dimwitted islanders don't know how good they got it, what with Petrox providing the first real paycheck these loafers have ever known," and his roster of football scores, both pro ball and Big Ten, from all the games up north, "Hey, didja hear, the Steelers pounded the Oilers, but *good*!", had frazzled him to the point where he was ready to scream. So when he finally dragged himself home to the cottage, he hadn't one smidgen of energy for an evening sail; he fell fully dressed onto his bed, and slept the sleep of the dead.

A rooster awoke him, crowing from somewhere in the neighbor-hood on the hill. Gotta write Mom and Pop about *that*, he grinned as he stretched in bed, his windows faint rectangles of light in the still-dark bedroom. 'Woke up this morning to the cackle of a gull-darn *rooster*! Sure made this farm boy glad!'

He sat up, swung his feet out of the bed and peeled off the damn green overalls. He'd get a jump on the day with a sail at dawn, is what he would do. Jazzed with excitement at the idea—he'd previously been windsurfing during regular daylight hours—he pulled on his salt-crusted blue bathing suit, grabbed the yellow sail on its wishbone boom from where it say in the banana patch, hefted his blue board with his other hand, (and shifted it until it just balanced in his grip,) then headed barefoot down the lane that wound through the neighborhood, travers-ing the hill to the beach.

Listening, he heard the soft cooing of a mourning dove, and the raspy chirp of a sugarbird, from the yellow-flowered ginger thomas trees along the lane; but the rooster seemed to have gone back to bed.

As he carried his sail and board through the palm trees at the upper edge of the beach, he saw that the bay was fairly flat, though scattered whitecaps flecked the Buck Island channel: the early morning breeze was light, just picking up. Then his eyes were drawn up the coast by a stunning crimson stripe that stretched across the eastern horizon, as if the good Lord had taken in His hand a huge celestial paintbrush and dipped its bristles into a jar of scarlet, and then had swept that brush just above the sleeping sea. He wondered if Zosia—she had asked him Friday night to call her Zosia—was awake to see this early morning miracle of color.

The broad stripe of red extended far to the north, but it was hidden to the south by the jumble of black hills at the eastern end of St. Croix. He could not tell whether or not the sun was up, for it was hidden be-hind the tip of the island, although . . . he looked across the bay toward Candle Point and saw that the outer two-thirds of the black rocky pen-insula was tinged red: by the rising sun.

Now he spotted Angelique, a tiny pink figure standing beside her house at the top of the glowing red-black cliff. He couldn't wave, for he held the windsurfer in both arms; nor did she wave to him.

Walking barefoot across the cool sand of the beach, he glanced at the circle of ashes where he and Angelique had feasted on their lob-sters, and where they had argued; he remembered the fierce bitterness in her eyes. How far they had come since that horrible night. And yet, he knew her rage toward America remained undiminished, no doubt ready to flare up again if provoked. Well, he couldn't live with that. Either she stopped loathing "you Americans," as if one and all they were nothing but a bunch of warmongers, or there wasn't much point in getting too serious with her. Joe hadn't fought that war because he hated some enemy; he had become a Green Beret so that a draftable kid in South Chicago, whose skin was the same color as Angelique's, wouldn't have to go in his place.

He waded into the lapping waves—he expected a chill, and marveled at how the Caribbean kept its warmth even through the night—then stood in water waist-deep and attached the wishbone boom to his floating board.

Well, they'd made progress on Veterans' Day, that was certain. Coming from Leroy's marker in a Frederiksted cemetery, listening with absolute attention to his story about Tony, and looking at him with her probing dark eyes in the candlelight as they raised their wine glasses with a toast, she had become, in a sad, quiet, painful way, more of a friend than any he had ever found up in Illinois.

So let's hoist the sail and sweep out for a visit.

He climbed up on the wobbly board. The breeze cool on his back, he drew up the sail and leaned his weight against the wind-filled yellow wing. Setting a course nearly tangent to the tip of Candle Point, he sailed across the gray-green bay. When suddenly he emerged from the island's shadow, horizontal red sunshine cast his own lifesize shadow onto the bellied orange sail.

Leaning tight to the wind, he cut his board through a smooth arc in the coppery water, a show of forceful skill, of determination. And of celebration, on the dawn of the finest Sabbath he had known in years.

As he neared the cliff below Angelique's house, he saw her standing behind a stone wall, looking down at him. She waved with a smile, then called down, her voice thin against the wind, "Ahoy! Where you bound for?"

Pouring enough wind out of his sail to slow himself, he called up, "Bound for Cathay to fetch rare silks and exotic spices. But I'd rather meet you back at the beach."

She cupped her hands and called, "Will you teach me to sail with one wing?"

"You bet. Got a good steady wind today. Perfect for learning."

"I'll be down in ten minutes with a thermos of coffee."

On Saturday afternoon, as Nick drove his taxi from Alexander Hamilton Airport toward the hotel at Grapetree Bay, he answered the usual first-time-on-the-island questions for the tourist in the back seat: about the weather, driving on the left, tidbits of history, where to find the best beaches. He never said much. He felt like a trucker hauling pigs to their pens. But a comment or two along the way usually boosted the tip. "Nineteen-seventeen," he called over the seat. "The United States bought the three Virgin Islands from Denmark for twenty-five million in gold bullion." He added, "No vote, no plebiscite. Nobody in Copenhagen or Washington bothered to ask the Crucians what *they* thought about the transaction."

The tourist leaned forward in his seat; in the rearview mirror, Nick could see a balding head and aviator sunglasses hovering at his shoulder. With a hushed voice, the Yank asked the same question that about one in five asked, "Say, you wouldn't know where I could score a little reefer, would you?"

Nick shook his head. "Ah ain' mess with no drugs."

Yankee Doodle slumped back with disappointment.

A few minutes later, driving on the loop around Great Salt Pond, Nick heard the question that one in ten asked, "Say, you know where I might find a little poon tonight?"

Glancing back over the seat, he asked with a conspiratorial tone out of the side of his mouth, "Yo' mean a little black ass?"

The tourist nodded, gratified to have found the right connection. "Yeah. Not too pricey, but good, you know what I mean. And clean. I don't want no case of the clap."

He purred, "Nice juicy black tail, with a coupla jugs t' suck on?"

"Yeah, terrific. Listen, there's fifty in it for ya if you'll bring her to the hotel at eight o'clock sharp. Don't bring her into the lobby. When you and I reach the hotel, we'll pick out a spot in the parking lot where we can meet."

He drawled, "Yo' want a reeeeeal black one, huh?"

"Yeah, but listen: not one of those great big huge-assed—"

Nick slammed on the brakes, throwing the whigger against the front seat as the taxi screeched to the side of the road. Pointing his finger at the shocked passenger who was picking himself up from the floor, he threatened, "If yo' ain' out of this taxi in two seconds, Ah gon' hang yo' balls from meh rearview mirror."

Eyes wide with terror, the man frantically fumbled at the door handle and jumped out of the car. He looked up and down the deserted back-country highway, then scanned the green hills that formed an amphitheater facing the sea. On the other side of the road, he discovered a vast black swamp and tangle-rooted mangroves; beyond the swamp, the blue sea stretched to the horizon. Though unsure which way to flee, he bent down to look in through the window—his sunglasses crooked, but the collar of his lime-green polo shirt still turned neatly up—and stammered, "Wh-whwh-what ab-b-bout my luggage?"

Nick exploded out of the car, slamming the door behind him.

The tourist dashed down the road. "Police!" he cried. Thirty yards away, winded, he looked back over his shoulder and saw that Nick was still by the car. He staggered to a halt, then stood there panting, unsure whether to continue running for his life, or to protest that he wanted his luggage.

Nick swung open the tailgate, yanked out a leather suitcase and tossed it into the middle of the hot asphalt road. He tossed two more heavy suitcases after it. Then he grabbed the last piece of luggage, an aluminum box marked FRAGILE—CAMERA EQUIPMENT. Cocking his arm—the arm that had launched a thousand grenades—he sent the shiny box arching high over the pavement. It crashed and bounced and tumbled into the ditch on the swamp side of the road.

Now he stepped toward the Yank, who shuffled backwards like a helpless ninny, his mouth twisted with a silent plea for mercy. Nick shouted the truth, the absolute truth after his fifteen years in the United States of America: "Ah ain' *never* come to yo' home town and ask for white poon."

"Police!"

He got back into his taxi, roared in reverse over the suitcases, and continued to gun the engine until he nearly ran over Mr. Hot Bucks, who sprinted in his Guccis toward the mudflats and mangroves.

"Help! I've been robbed!"

The sky above Great Salt Pond was suddenly filled with a flock of startled egrets flapping their broad white wings.

The following morning, minutes before sunrise, Nick stood atop a cliff at the easternmost tip of his island, facing the wind that blew across the ocean from Africa. During the summer months this wind carried dust from the Sahara, and thus the earth of Africa had long been mixed with the earth of St. Croix.

Nick stared at the blood-red streak that lay across the dark horizon, like the stripe on a man's back after a lash of the whip.

Dark waves came rolling toward him, pushed by the trade winds, and borne by the great river of the equatorial current.

He stared at the sun while it rose with an angry eye and lashed the backs of the waves with red.

The combers surged taller as they approached his island. They towered at the edge of balance, then crashed against the cliffs below his feet with explosions of red foam.

Seething with rage, he vowed that he would rid St. Croix of its pestilence. He would cleanse the island of vermin, until only African feet tread upon the sacred soil. The warrior would take up his weapons against the Navy, against Petrox, against the white man who claimed to possess anything his money could buy. Yes, Pfc. Nicholas Cruz, U.S. Army demolitions expert, would place a little surprise under each of the three hats.

But he would more than clean his island. He would sanctify it. The forest itself, he would set apart as a sacred place. He would lead his people as they relit the fire that had once burned in the village of the Maroons. Deep among the ancient mahogany trees, they would rekindle the flame of freedom.

True Crucians would live with dignity, their tables heaped with the fruit of their gardens and graced with the bounty of their fishing nets. Their schools, their shops, their beaches would be peopled by citizens who would never again allow one square foot of their land to be traded for the foreigners' bullion.

Yes, he would cleanse, and protect, and sanctify. And in this new life, he would at last have found his sacred purpose.

On Sunday evening, after Angelique and Karl, the both of them stuffed with Zosia's Crucian chicken and Polish potatoes, had finished washing and drying the dishes, Karl set up his new slide projector and screen in Zosia's living room. He took three chairs from the table and set them in a row to complete his theater. Then he returned to the kitchen, rummaged in the cupboards until he found Zosia's biggest pot, and popped a batch of popcorn.

Angelique noticed the label on the quart-sized jar:

POP'S POPCORN
WHITE OAK FARM   DEKALB, ILLINOIS

She asked, "Did you bring this jar down from the States?"

He nodded as he shook fluffy white popcorn into a trio of mahogany bowls. "Yup. This popcorn's from the buckle on the corn belt."

The three sat in their chairs, bowls in their laps, as he took his audience on a tour of the Buck Island lagoon. Angelique glanced with satisfaction at Zosia, her gaunt, wrinkled face tinted aquamarine by the light reflected from the screen as she examined every detail of the reef. "Ahhhh," sighed Zosia, her excitement tinged with regret, "I haven't mixed such an aqua in years."

Karl encouraged her, "I can make prints from any slides you select. Then you can go to work with your paints. I hope to turn my cottage into a Honegger gallery."

Angelique appreciated his interest in Zosia, and winced with shame when she recalled her initial suspicion.

Now he showed his picture of her dolphin-kicking gracefully with a school of blue tangs, bubbles trailing from her snorkel like a string of pearls.

"There's my mermaid!" exclaimed Zosia with delight.

Karl chuckled, "Mermaid is right. Zosia, she comes up for air about once an hour."

"Yagh, I suspected as much."

Angelique smiled at her underwater portrait, as few people knew her. How wonderful to have found a friend who loved the sea as much as she did.

But when he showed his picture of her sailing wing-and-wing, she heard Nick's sneering voice, Yo' look awful happy with that whigger.

And when Karl showed the twin picture of himself, she saw it on his pillow with the knife stabbed through it. Her stomach knotted with dread. What would Nick do, now that he was alone?

She glanced at Karl, his face animated as he described for Zosia that treasured moment when they were balanced aboard the sloop. She wondered for the hundredth time if she should warn Karl about Nick. But he would insist on calling the police. And if Nick was caught with the maps in his apartment, then convicted and sent to prison, wouldn't he become berserk with bitterness? No, she couldn't do that to the man she loved, even though she had left him.

Karl clicked to the next slide, his picture of golden sunbeams shooting deep into the blue abyss. He and Zosia became silent, lost in their own thoughts.

As she stared into the pure and peaceful ocean depths, Angelique made her decision: Leave Nick alone. Once he left Vietnam, he had never hurt a soul—at least not that she knew of. For Nick was ashamed of the killing he had done in the war. The ghosts still haunted him. Surely he would never kill again. He was bitter, but he was not vicious. That knife in the picture: was it really a threat, or was it an attempt, in the fury of his jealousy, to salvage his honor? A shaking of the fist to restore some measure of dignity.

Yes, leave him alone. Let him start his classes at the University. He deserved a new start in life. If anyone did, Nick deserved a second chance.

Certain of Nick's essential decency, she was sure of the rightness of her decision. The knot of dread diminished; she dipped her hand into her bowl of popcorn.

After she and Karl had said good night to Zosia, they walked together through the black tunnel under the seagrape bushes to the driveway, where he looked up at the stars. "You sure don't see them sparkle like that in South Chicago."

She did not look up, but studied his handsome face dusted with starlight. She was not ready yet to say good night. "Karl, are you musical?"

He looked at her with his ready smile. "Well, I once had a dismally undistinguished career as a trumpeter in the high school band. I was pretty good at the triple tonguing, ta-ca-ta, ta-ca-ta, until I got braces on my teeth. Then every time I tried to hit high C, I'd start to bleed. Hamburger Lips, they called me."

"Have you ever played a conga drum?"

"A conga drum? No, I've never even played the bongos."

"I will teach you."

She led him around the driveway and up her steps, inviting him into her house for the first time. In a corner of her living room stood two conga drums, long unused. She and Karl carried the tall drums out to her back porch and stood them on their tripod stands near the stone wall where she had stood this morning. With a wrench, she tightened the turnbuckles around the leather drumheads, tuning each conga until the larger drum acquired a clear deep pitch, and the smaller drum gave out a clear but higher pitch.

Then she stood behind the second drum, the night breeze cool on her face, and tapped a simple rhythm: ta-ba-bum, ta-ba-bum. She explained to Karl, his hands at his sides as he watched her, "When I was a girl, I was taught to bow my head and pray. But after I lost Leroy, there didn't seem to be anyone listening." Her hands beat the drum quietly but steadily. "Though the God of People had quit the job, no doubt in disgust, the God of Creation still sends his sun arching across my sky. Still makes his winds to blow, his waves to roll, his stars to sparkle. So when say my prayers, I say Thank You. But I no longer bow my head. I look up."

Lifting her face toward the bright stars, and faint stars, and mere dust of stars, she quickened the rhythm of her dancing hands. Her shoulders loosened while she played; she flexed her knees, swayed her hips in her sarong. Her drumming grew stronger, quicker, the range of her tones richer, until she filled the night with the ancient call of hands on leather that beckon the heavens to listen.

Her prayer rolled . . . and boomed . . . and broke like a wave . . . then quieted, until her fingertips beat a whirring whisper.

She glanced at Karl. "Have you nothing to say?"

First he watched her hands, then he watched his own hands as he tried to simulate her pattern: one and one-two, one and one-two, right hand, right hand, left. But his beat was stiff, out of time. He dropped his hands back to his sides. "You go ahead. I'll save my prayers for church."

She looked up again and telegraphed her simple steady beat to an ear beyond the stars, beyond the luminous dust, to an ear far beyond what any human eye could see. "Look up," she told Karl. "You must look up."

He scanned the sky; his eyes came to rest on the brightest star in the east, Capella, the rising queen of winter. He thumped hesitantly on his drum. His hands began to blend with hers; their beats became closer and closer, his tone several pitches lower, until suddenly the two drums merged with precision, their twin beats bouncing into the night.

She shifted to a more intricate rhythm. Though he stumbled, his hands soon blended with hers as if they had a will of their own.

Then he shifted to a new rhythm. She followed as a dancer follows her partner's lead.

Sometimes she led, sometimes he led, as if they were tossing a ball back and forth: here, catch *this*. Neither spoke. Their breathing became as deep and regular as the breathing of long distance runners striding in tandem on a long course. They never looked at each other; their eyes were locked on the stars.

Her drumming flowed into a drum-roll; he followed. Her hands beat faster, faster; his hands tried to keep up, merging and sundering in and out of synchrony. But gradually her powerful drumming outpaced his. Sweat streamed down her cheeks, dripped from her chin, splashed on her hands. Her arms ached, her swollen hands throbbed as she called to the keeper of the universe. Her serene smile hardened into a grimace at the effort of sending up her prayer. She drummed until she was certain she had shown the strength of her gratitude.

And then she stopped. Almost as quickly, Karl stopped. In the ringing silence, she heard a wave crash against the cliff below them, heard the spray fall into the sea.

She turned to Karl, his face gleaming with sweat, his eyes fixed on her with a mix of exultation and wonder. "Balanced," he marveled. "We were so perfectly balanced."

She had felt it too. Thank You, she thought, sending up a heartfelt addendum to her prayer.

On a Sunday night jet bound for Kennedy Airport, New York City, United States of America, Nicholas Cruz sat by a window on the right side of the plane. As he gazed out at the bright star that seemed to accompany him on his mission, he wondered where he could get ahold of a Stinger, a shoulder-borne, anti-aircraft, mini-missile launcher.

Then he would be ready not only to take out any target on land; with a Stinger, able to shoot down any planes flying over his island, he would dominate the sky as well.

CHAPTER SEVENTEEN

Sabrina's Stare

As the autumn rainy season waned, the days of November became so clear that from her porch, Angelique could see St. Thomas, a flat gray-green island, and St. John, a taller gray-green hump, on the northern horizon. The winds grew strong and steady, reliable for days at a stretch: the famed Christmas winds. This was her favorite time of year, when she could sail her little red sloop far out to sea with minimal threat of a sudden storm.

She and Karl spent Saturdays with Zosia, and sailed every Sunday afternoon. She would have launched on Sunday morning, but Karl went to church, a different church every week. "I'm trying to find the right one," he explained, but said nothing more. She didn't ask him what sort of church he was looking for. She had no interest in church. She spent her Sunday mornings reading, or making small repairs on her sloop. When he came down to the beach with his snorkel and lunch, they launched the boat, and neither said a word about church.

She taught Karl how to sail and discovered that he was a gifted student. Out on the Big Blue, she showed him how to take the sloop over the tallest of the combers; how to cut through a steep crest about to break; how to ride the boiling carpet of foam if the hull was caught in the surge. Karl listened carefully, paid close attention to how she handled the sheet and tiller. He learned to read the telltales, learned to read the sails. And learned to read the weather in the sky to the east.

Ulysses, seated beside the centerboard, stumbled during Karl's first tacks. As the hull leaned from one side to the other, the dog hopped over the centerboard as usual, but when he sat, the boat was still lurching, wallowing, suddenly heeling, so he had to dig his claws against the rough deck. Once he slid all the way sternwards until he was struggling for a footing in the tangles of the anchor line. But the hound did not panic. When the sloop finally steadied in its new direction, Ulysses returned to his spot by the centerboard; he gave Karl a dour, droop-eared look of reproach, then returned alertly to his watch for flying fish that often burst out of the water just ahead of the bow.

Angelique was about to leave for work on the first evening in December, when her phone rang. "Hello? . . . Mama! How yo' be? . . . Oh, Ah be fine. Busy. Too busy . . . . Ah know, Mama. Ah sorry. Ah ain' been to see yo' in weeks. But after the funeral, Ah been so taken up with Zosia. And had a couple of deliveries this week. Seems Ah hardly have time to eat these days . . . . Of course Ah'm eatin', Mama. Yo' ain' to worry about me."

And then her mother brought up the old argument, imploring her to sing in the church choir. "Dat be all yo' ol' mother want this Christmas, chile. Just to hear meh daughter sing one more time, before meh Maker call me home. Please, Darlin', yo, Papa would so like to hear yo' sing, too."

"*No*, Mama." She fumed that her mother was going to drag her through this nonsense again. "Ah refuse to even discuss it. Ah ain' *never* goin' back inside that church . . . . No, not even when Ah get married. Mama, Ah told yo' that before. Why yo' got to start with all this? . . . Listen, Ah got to go to work. Ah come by for a visit, but one word about that choir and Ah gone again . . . . Ah love yo' too, Mama. Bye."

Despite her exasperation as she rode her scooter to the hospital, she could not help but remember the powerful pipes of the church organ, slowly and majestically building a foundation for the choir. She had stood with the other children in the front row every Christmas Eve, her voice true but thin. Mama always sang the soprano solo in "O Holy Night". She sang those final upper register verses with such reverent joy.

A child of twelve, and thirteen, and fourteen, Angelique was of course expected to follow in her mother's footsteps.

Well, she'd sing Christmas carols with Mama and Papa and the family at home in Frederiksted on Christmas Day. But if God was expecting to hear her sing in His house of lies, He was going to be disappointed.

Karl noticed on his Monet calendar from the Art Institute of Chicago that December was one of those rare months with two full moons, one on December second, and one on New Year's Eve.

On the evening of the second of December, he and Angelique sailed out to the nearby sandbar with a picnic dinner. They sat on the serpentine hump of sand facing the copper-red sun as it descended toward a rumpled copper sea beyond the tip of Candle Point.

Zosia's dining room light was lit; she too was no doubt watching the sunset and waiting for the moon.

While peeling her mango, Angelique glanced over her shoulder toward the east.

"Karl, look!"

Exactly opposite the sun, a giant red-orange moon rose from the sea. The two picnickers shifted in the sand so they faced each other, legs crossed, able to look back and forth at the pair of heavenly orbs. "I feel as if we're sitting on the fulcrum of an enormous teeter-totter," he said, "with a couple of pumpkins balanced at the ends. And one pumpkin is just a little bit heavier."

The sun seemed to gain momentum as it sank, catapulting the moon upward into the lavender sky. After the huge molten ball had winked and disappeared, leaving wisps of crimson cirrus drifting across the western sky, the two sailors shifted again so they faced east. Karl wrapped his arm around Angelique as they watched the moon pass through a palette of colors: remembering Zosia's paints, Angelique described the moon as first a "radiant saffron"; then "a pale apricot"; and in the darkening violet sky, the shrinking ball glowed with the faintest tinge of "cream yellow." By the time the twosome finished their tuna sandwiches, the moon shone "ivory white."

Though she did not say so, Angelique saw something else: like a bride in a wedding gown, the moon cast a long white train across the sea.

Their brief sail out to the sandbar, no more than a quarter-mile offshore, was but the first part of their voyage tonight. Since the moon would serve as their navigation light while they headed out several miles onto the Big Black, the two sailors toasted the radiant disk by raising cups of cold mawbee from a thermos.

While Karl repacked the picnic basket and stowed it in a hold inside the bow, Angelique fastened a battery-operated green light to the starboard gunnel, a red light to the port gunnel, and a white light to the peak of the lowered mainsail. As she hoisted the sail—it luffed in the evening breeze—and secured its halyard to a cleat at the base of the mast, Ulysses, wet and gritty from chasing a lone tern around and around the sandbar, hopped soggily into the sloop. Gear stowed, lines ready, the sailors launched their sprightly vessel, sheeted jib and mainsail, tillered slowly through scattered coralheads into open water, then headed north; they leaned their weight against the bellied moonlit sails that pointed their twin peaks toward the emerging stars.

Sitting just forward of Angelique on the pontoon gunnel, Karl leaned back over the black water that raced beneath him. The sea air tonight was extremely clear, and looking straight ahead, he could discern the faint glow of the lights on the island of St. Thomas, forty miles away. Looking back past the moonlit wake off the stern, he watched St. Croix, a low long knobby black island speckled with lights, as it receded into the distance.

Occasionally he glanced over his shoulder to the east, where bright Capella kept watch. Should that star disappear, weather was approaching.

Ulysses sat with ears cocked bedside the centerboard, staring forward, waiting for the flying fish that would suddenly burst from the sea and sail ahead of the bow, their long lacy wings lit by the moon, until they flew down a dark trough and disappeared into a black wave.

As the sloop galloped swiftly across the gently rolling sea, heeling more steeply with an occasional gust, Karl noticed that Angelique was smiling at him, half of her lovely dark face lit by the moon, half of it more faintly lit by the glow from the sail. He felt, though perhaps he was mistaken, that she almost leaned her face toward him to kiss him.

But then she peered up at the telltales, black ribbons tousled by the wind; she sheeted in the mainsail slightly, gaining speed, and now stared past him at the smooth, moon-silvered, ocean-roving rollers beyond Buck Island.

One morning in mid-December, Angelique came home from her shift at the hospital and found Zosia still in bed. The widow stared at her with sunken, anguished eyes and admitted, "I don't know if I will survive this Christmas without him."

Zosia would not get out of bed, would not eat breakfast from the tray that Angelique brought to her. "We spent our first Christmas in that hell-hole in Berlin," she said with a broken whisper. "But our second Christmas we celebrated in Switzerland. That was Piotr's present to me, that we were still alive. And every Christmas afterwards, it seemed like a miracle: we were alive, and together. His family gone, my family gone, but somehow we always had each other." She rolled her head toward the stone wall. "Until now."

"Zosia, we'll decorate a Christmas tree in your living room. Karl and I will sing Christmas carols with you."

"Nogh," she replied, her voice as dry as ashes, "I want no tree."

After days of turmoil in her mind, during which generosity and bitterness struggled for the upper hand, Angelique decided to invite both Karl and Zosia to the church service on Christmas Eve. Zosia needed to get out of her house, to see something new and fresh. She would enjoy the decorations and the music, especially if Angelique sang in the choir. Mama and Papa would at long last be happy.

And what better place, from her parents' viewpoint, to meet Karl than in church?

When she phoned home, her mother praised the Lord.

"Mama, don' tink a sheep come back to the fold," she warned. "Just tell me what time choir practice be."

On a quiet Saturday afternoon, Angelique was in her kitchen buttering a piece of toast when she heard Cecil call from the bay below her window, "Angelique!" Looking down through the open glass louvers, she saw the Witherspoons in their seafaring dugout canoe, Cecil in the bow, Albert in the stern. Edith sat in front of her husband, a pink bundle in her lap. The other eight children, some paddling, some riding, sat between bunches of bananas. In the middle of the long canoe sat Sabrina, wearing her long simple black dress. Charles, naked, was wriggling in her lap, though the toddler could not go far with his mother's arms wrapped around him.

Angelique hurried out to her back porch and called down, "Hello! How be number ten?"

Edith held up her baby. "Already a sailor."

Angelique cupped her hands and called, "If yo' paddle around the point to the lee side, Ah meet yo' at the beach."

Then she hurried through her house, down the steps, and around the driveway to a freshly-trimmed tunnel through the seagrape bushes. Zosia and Karl were oiling the squeaky hinges of Zosia's front door. Angelique called up the sun-dappled passage, "Zosia, go out on your porch. You have visitors."

Zosia turned to her, eyebrows lifted with interest. "Who?"

"Go see."

Intrigued, Zosia thumped with her cane through her house and out the porch door; at the railing, she looked down with delight at the ever-bountiful family sitting in their carved log like peas in a pod. "Ahoy!" she hailed them. "Is your canoe long enough?"

"Just!" laughed Albert.

Angelique and Karl hurried down to the beach to welcome the Witherspoons ashore. Karl inspected the sleek, thirty-foot, ax-hewn vessel. He asked Cecil, "What kind of tree did you use?"

The teenager answered proudly, "Kapok. Dad and Ah worked seven months." He showed Karl his hand-carved ironwood paddle. "Heavy, but strong."

Albert shouldered a bunch of bananas for the midwife, Cecil shouldered a bunch for Zosia, and Edith carried Elspeth for Zosia to meet. Albert nodded toward a bunch still in the boat. "Angelique, please won' yo' take dem to de hospital and pass 'em out to de patients? We got more dan we can sell." He turned to Karl. "Where yo' work?"

"At the refinery right now, but I'm in the process of—"

"Take a bunch for de men. We got more dan we can sell."

The banana parade made its way along the narrow spine of Candle Point, children scampering noisily among the laden adults. Zosia, leaning on her cane at the top of the driveway, laughed as they approached. "You look like ants that found a picnic."

Sabrina and Charles stayed behind at the beach. In the shallows of the quiet bay, she taught her son to dog-paddle.

When the Witherspoons departed late that afternoon, the family waved to Angelique and Karl on the beach, then they faced forward and paddled out to sea. But Sabrina looked back from the canoe, and her dark eyes focused for a long moment on Angelique.

CHAPTER EIGHTEEN

Lady Liberty

Karl called the police several times after the break-in, but they had found no fingerprints, nor any other clues in his cottage. They hadn't found the stolen maps, hadn't found the papers. They were sorry, but they didn't have any leads.

Though the knife remained unsettling, he decided to dismiss the whole issue as one more signal that he ought to get out of the oil business.

And there was another reason to get out. He shuddered at the thought that he would still be no more than a monkey on a cracking tower by the time he became a father. To be trapped inside that refinery fence in order to feed a child. . . . No, he was not going to allow himself to be reduced to that.

Especially now, for he had found someone special. Someone extremely, extraordinarily, exquisitely special. Though he may have been a fool in much of what he'd done with his life, he had learned one thing over the years, and that was to recognize quality in people when he found it. Angelique was a girl with a golden heart.

He was not sure what to think about her being black, except he was certain that Joe would scold him for thinking that skin color made any difference. And besides, the longer he was with her, the less she was a black woman, or an island woman, or a West Indian, as more and more she became his intriguing new friend, lovely, spirited Angelique.

During a dinner at Zosia's, he glanced across the table at Angelique and saw her faint conspiratorial smile. He turned to Zosia at the head of the table and said nonchalantly, "Y'know, back home on the farm, we've got five acres planted with Christmas trees. It's one of those Cut-Your-Own-Tree operations. I'll bet if I phoned Pop and told him that what his homesick boy really wanted this Christmas was a home-grown

Christmas tree, why, he and Mom would go out and pick the queen of the lot. They'd wrap it up in burlap, put it under a tarp in the back of the pick-up and drive it out to O'Hare. A jet to Miami, a jet to St. Croix, and I'd pick it up at the airport."

Then he frowned, perplexed. "But all I've got to put it in is that little bitty cottage. The ceiling's hardly a foot above my head." He gazed for a long contemplative moment across the living room toward a tall dark empty corner near a bookcase. "Zosia, how'd you like a gorgeous Norwegian spruce, filling up your whole house with the smell of a northern forest?"

She turned her head slowly and stared with tired eyes at the empty space.

"They probably won't take a tree over eight feet long on the plane," he said, "but looks like you could have a fifteen footer in here if you wanted."

"Papa . . . always cut a spruce." She turned to him, her voice brightening as she explained, "I was only ten our last Christmas in Bydgoszcz. Then we moved to Berlin. But I will always remember going with Papa to cut the tree in the forest by the river. He always cut the most elegant spruce, pointed, he said, like hands in prayer. And always so big, it hardly fit into the back of the sleigh. He let me ride Gryka, our big draft horse, with silver bells on her harness, and we sang Christmas carols all the way home. I sang like a chicken then, and still do. But Papa, oh what a lovely baritone Papa had!"

Angelique declared, "Then we *must* have a tree this year. Karl, you must telephone your father and order a tree for us."

He thought for a moment, mulling over some difficulty, then he asked Zosia, "Do you have any ornaments?"

She scowled, insulted. "If we have ornaments?" She pointed with her bony, bent, shaking finger toward the hallway. "Second closet on the left."

On Christmas Eve, Karl, more than a little nervous, met Angelique's family.

Following a long string of red taillights on a country road leading to the middle of the island, Zosia in the jeep's front seat, Angelique in the back, he looked ahead at the stately white church, spotlighted in the night, a fortress of faith on the dark plain. He parked on the roadside, then pushed Zosia in her wheelchair the last hundred yards to Holy

Cross Episcopal Church, its front doors wide open, golden light pouring out onto the steps. Wheeling Zosia along the sidewalk, he looked up at a palm tree rattling its thatch against the stars. A palm tree on Christmas Eve, he marveled. And back home they've got a foot of snow.

Then he heard a boy's voice calling from the door of the church, loudly enough for half the congregation to hear, "Angelique comin' wid What's-he-name!"

Angelique's family was waiting just inside the door. Karl could not keep straight who was a brother and who was a brother-in-law, nor whose kids belonged to whom, but he did distinctly focus on Angelique's mother and father. Estelle and Nathaniel warmly welcomed him, and both shook his hand. Estelle wore a maroon choir robe, Nathaniel an old-fashioned suit. The large family walked with Karl and Angelique, who now wheeled Zosia, down the aisle in the crowded church to an empty pew near the front, which the family nearly filled from one end to the other. Zosia sat in her chair in the aisle; Angelique left to put on her choir robe. Karl sat at the end of the pew beside Zosia. Next to him in the pew sat Angelique's father. Karl let out a silent deep breath: so far, so good.

He inspected the large mural over the altar. A dozen contemporary people, brown, black, and white, in formal clothes and in work clothes, were gathered in the picture around a cross, their faces filled with dignity and reverence. He liked the church already. Maybe he had found the one he was looking for.

In front of the altar was a crèche with a dark-faced infant in the manger. One of the kings approaching on a camel was black. The straw in the manger was real straw.

The organ played "O Little Town of Bethlehem" in a minor, mystical key. No one sang yet; the music was a message to stragglers to come in and take a seat. Karl quickly inspected the old West Indian church: its sturdy walls were built of plaster-covered stone; wrought-iron chandeliers hung from rafters beneath a wooden roof; tropical fans spun slowly; tall open windows along both sides of the nave let in an occasional breath of cool night breeze, scented with the sweet, exotic perfume of frangipani.

And right now, he thought, with the two hour time difference, Pop is up in the bedroom shining his shoes, and Mom is in the sewing room pressing her dress. They'll be arriving at church about the time I'll be heading home. Hope Anne is with 'em. I sure hope they won't be alone.

The organ shifted into a major key and the congregation rose. He helped Zosia to stand, then he held a hymnal with her while the choir led the singing of "Joy to the World" as they marched up the aisle and assembled on the steps behind the organ. Angelique glanced with a smile at Zosia as she passed by in tandem with her mother; Estelle's extraordinary voice rang above the multitude of other voices with the clarity of a powerful angelic soprano.

As the two stood together in their maroon robes, Karl noticed how much Angelique and her mother looked alike. Estelle was heavier, her hair gray, but her face held a dignified beauty. He could see that Angelique too, in later years, would be a fine looking woman.

Her legs unsteady, Zosia sat down in her wheelchair. Karl sat down with her for the rest of the carol. The entire congregation sat down for the Call to Worship, spoken from the pulpit by a tall black minister. When the congregation once again stood up for another Christmas hymn, Zosia shook her head and said to Karl, "Never mind me. You stand up and sing with the others."

So he shared a hymnal with Nathaniel. Holding the left side of the book, he looked at the dark brown hand holding the right; the calloused fingers, and the careful way they gripped the page, reminded him of his own father's hand, the many times he and Pop had held a hymnal together. Karl blended his meandering tenor with Nathaniel's monotone bass.

Zosia held her own hymnal, though she did not use it; she listened to the Christmas songs, and those she knew she sang in Polish.

During the service, the choir sang both traditional and Calypso carols. When brightly dressed children marched in and assembled as the choir's front row, Karl spotted a boy with curly sandy hair and beautiful golden skin, clearly a child of mixed parents.

Near the end of the service, when the spell of Christmas had been fully cast upon the congregation, the organ rumbled with the majestic opening strains of "O Holy Night." Angelique stepped forward to sing the solo. Zosia gripped Karl's hand as slowly, shakily, she stood up. Above the deep pipes of the organ, above the reverent voices of the worshipers, above even the polished voices of the choir, Angelique's soaring, resplendent soprano filled the church to the rafters. The radiant joy on her face convinced him that despite her bitterness, she nevertheless possessed a spirit capable of hope.

*   *   *

On Christmas morning, Angelique and Karl stood as a duet on the driveway outside Zosia's bedroom window, singing "Deck the Halls," the soprano intoning with vibrant precision, the tenor warbling exuberantly in roughly the right key. Ulysses howled.

"Wesołych Świąt!" called out Zosia's scratchy voice. "Merry Christmas!"

While Angelique helped Zosia to get dressed, Karl plugged in the lights of the splendid Norwegian spruce Mom and Pop had selected, its thick branches laden with Zosia's motley collection of ornate European seraphim, simple Caribbean santas, American tinsel. Then he called down the hallway, "Ready when you are."

"Here we come!" called Zosia as she thumped along the hall in a long red gown, a big green bow tied to her cane, her eyes sparkling like a child's as she approached the tree. She sat in a chair, then gripped the crook of her cane with both hands and pointed it at a gift wrapped with Frosty the Snowman paper. "That's for you, Karl, from your girlfriend and me. We each chipped in a nickel."

He unwrapped the package and opened a shoe box filled with rolls of color film. "Thank you!" he said to the two women smiling at him.

"We want another slide show," said Zosia.

"With popcorn," said Angelique.

Then Angelique unwrapped a gallon can of red marine paint for her sloop, and a quart of varnish for the trim, from Karl and Zosia.

Karl helped Zosia to unwrap their gift for Ulysses: a new red bandana. He took off Ulysses' old crusty sun-faded rag and tied on the bright red triangle. They also decked the hound with the bowed and curliqued ribbons from each present they opened. Ulysses pranced, sweeping the tinsel with his bushy tail.

But the present of the day was from Karl and Angelique, to Zosia. With numb, trembling fingers, she tore the white tissue, then lifted the lid from a shoe box and stared, puzzled, at a yellow kitchen sponge cut into a dozen cubes.

"We want you to try a new technique," explained Angelique. "We think maybe you can hold a piece of sponge better than a brush." She glanced at Karl; they were unsure how Zosia would react to this acknowledgement of her growing disability.

He said brightly, "This is a store-bought sponge. It might be fun to try a real sponge. You could experiment with big pores, little pores, different patterns." He knelt beside her chair and lifted out a cube from the box. "What do you think about the size? Maybe you'll want some pieces a little bigger?"

She reached hesitantly into the shoe box and curled her fingers around a cube of sponge. She was able to squeeze it slightly, enough to pick it up and rub it across the lid of the box. Then she looked at Karl, and at Angelique, her eyes reflecting a gratitude not only for the gift, but for the honesty between the three of them. "Yagh. I will try."

After blueberry pancakes and eggnog—and three Oreos for Ulysses—Karl said, "I'd like to phone home. The folks'll be waiting to hear from me. I'll run up quickly to the cottage," he looked at his watch, "and I'll be back by eleven. Plenty of time to be in Frederiksted by one."

Zosia offered, "Use my phone."

He declined. "I'll scoot up to the cottage. It won't take long and then the billing will be easier. Besides, I've got to pick up a few presents for the Nielsens."

At his cottage, he talked for almost half an hour with Mom and Pop; they used both the kitchen and bedroom phones so all three could talk together. Hiding his homesickness, his voice ever cheerful, he told them, "Oh we're having a great time down here. Been doing a lot of sailing with a friend of mine. He's got a spiffy little red sailboat, and he's teaching me to sail. We go cruising way out on the Caribbean. . . . Girlfriend? Well, Pop, nothing too serious yet. I've met a couple of nice girls, but I don't want to get into anything permanent. Just got here, y'know. . . . Well, thanks again for the shirts and slacks. Tell the cows I miss 'em. And Merry Christmas!"

When he hung up, he felt rotten. But Mom and Pop had sounded so good. Why upset them? If Angelique and I make a commitment together, then fine, I'll be glad to tell the whole family. But that's a big If. And until then, there's certainly no use getting the folks worked up about a black girlfriend. Definitely no need to throw them for a loop on Christmas. Not when they're both in such good spirits.

Nevertheless, as he carried his gifts for Estelle and Nathaniel out to the jeep, then drove down to Candle Point to fetch Angelique and Zosia, he could not shake the feeling that he had been less than honest.

During Christmas dinner with the Nielsens, he noticed their dining room wallpaper, old faded rumpled blue paper with patterns of gold flowers, a lot like the funny old wallpaper in the dining room back home. He scanned the mahogany table with two extra leaves in it, much like the old cherry table at the farmhouse, laden with equally bountiful dinners, all the family gathered around.

"Karl, yo' ain' like okra?" asked Estelle, sitting beside him.

He had nearly gagged when he tried to eat the strange-looking vegetable which he had ignorantly heaped on his plate, for when he picked up a green pod on the tines of his fork, it trailed strings of mucus that looked just like dog drool. But he replied heartily, "I sure do like okra. I was just digging into your scrumptious ham first."

"Dat okra home-grown."

"Is that right? The tomatoes too?" He took a huge red tomato from a platter and began to slice it on his salad plate, thus relegating the okra to a later course.

She smiled proudly. "After dinner, Ah tek yo' out and show yo' meh garden."

"Great. Say, this tomato reminds me of our Beefhearts back home. Real sweet."

And then he heard the voice of the patriarch at the head of the table. "Karl, what sort of work yo' in?"

There was a lull in the talk around the table as everyone turned toward him. He looked down the full length of the table, for Estelle and Nathaniel sat at opposite ends, presiding over the entire family between them. He saw by the solemn look on Nathaniel's face that Angelique's father was not just making conversation.

He set down his fork. "Nathaniel, I've asked my foreman at Petrox, where I work as an electrical engineer, whether I might start working only four days a week, starting in January. He said he had to talk with the Home Office in New York, but that he would give me an answer shortly after Christmas. I'm so busy up on those towers, you see, they really need me *six* days a week. It's been a battle holding my schedule to five. But I want one day a week free, because I've decided to try to get something new going. It's always been in the back of my mind that one day I'd like to build a solar cooker."

He turned to Estelle, though he spoke for all his listeners to hear. "A few years ago I was browsing through a *National Geographic* and I saw a picture of a woman carrying firewood on her head. It was a striking photograph, because she and her bundle of sticks were silhouetted against a spectacular sunset. But the caption said she had to walk for miles each day to find enough wood."

Moving his eyes slowly from face to face around the table, he was grateful for the nod of encouragement from Angelique. "Another photo showed a stretch of eroded hillside where the trees had been cut for firewood. That article was about Haiti, but the same is true of course in many other places in the world.

"So what I would like to do is to build a solar cooker, which people could use to cook breakfast, lunch and an early dinner without chopping all their trees down." He held a fist high above the table. "Here's the sun." He placed his other hand like a tilted bowl on the table. "And here's the polished aluminum dish that catches the sunlight. The dish supports a smaller dish on a tripod, which reflects the sun's rays through a hole in the center of the bigger dish, so that a beam of intense light is focused on the cooking apparatus. Actually, you need to reflect the beam one more time, so it shines up from underneath and forms a circle of light exactly the diameter of the black underside of the cooking plate. Well, it'd be easier for you to see if I showed you the sketches. But you get the general idea. A solar cooker needs no fuel. The energy shines down from brother sun."

Nathaniel remained as still as a statue, staring at Karl.

Confidently, Karl continued, "But of course, all my tinkering will lead to nothing unless I can manufacture and sell these gizmos. So I'm glad to say that after some telephoning, I located an agency at the United Nations which might be interested in funding a pilot project. First I've got to build an experimental cooker and make it work, and *then* maybe they'll help to set up a small business here on St. Croix. My plan is to manufacture cookers that can be easily assembled with one wrench and one screwdriver, which would come with the kit. I'd like to build up a shop that employs fifty, a hundred, maybe two hundred people producing Crucian Cookers for export to countries around the world. Our company could hook up with the economics department at the University, and with the physics department, and . . . Well, there's no end to the possibilities. I just wish I could give it more than one day a week, but at this point," he shrugged, "I can't afford to let go of a steady paycheck. So to answer your question, Nathaniel: I'm in a state of transition right now, between careers. It's a gamble, but I think it's worth a try."

"Please call me Nat." The patriarch smiled.

Karl's spirit soared.

"Yagh," said Zosia with hearty approval. She reached with both hands for her glass of wine. "We have a toast. To Crucian Cookers!"

"To Crucian Cookers!" echoed Angelique, raising her glass.

"Yo' park a Cooker in meh backyard," said Estelle, "And Ah gon' boil up de first pot of goat stew."

He felt himself blushing as he raised his glass to acknowledge the words of encouragement from Angelique's entire family around the table. "Thank you. Thank you very much. And a toast to new friends on what has been for me a very special Christmas."

The trouble began after dinner, when he and Estelle were out in the backyard inspecting her garden.

"Chester!" shouted Angelique with a shocked voice.

He looked up from where he was crouching beside a cassava seedling. Angelique stood with her father by Nat's chicken coop, but she was staring aghast across the yard. Following her eyes, Karl saw Chester dashing across the lawn; the boy's face was smeared with brown and green camouflage paint. He wore a child's-size army camouflage outfit, complete with leafy twigs in the netting of his helmet. He disappeared behind a kapok tree, then peered around the trunk, aimed a space-age toy rifle at some enemy target and opened fire: instead of old-time caps, the rifle roared with a raucous electronic buzzer while its barrel flashed red. "Gotcha!" he shouted, then the boy-soldier raced again across the yard, avoiding enemy fire, and dove for cover behind an up-turned wheelbarrow.

"No!" shouted Angelique, running after the boy, who peeked over the top of the wheelbarrow with fear in his eyes as his aunt raged toward him. She cried, "What yo' doin' wearin' such clothes?" She grabbed him by the arm and yanked him to his feet, then snatched the gun from his hands and like a wild woman smashed it against a tree, beating it again and again until there was nothing left but shattered plastic pieces.

Then she turned to the confused, terrified boy, gripped the collar of his camouflage suit and ripped it open to the waist. Shrieking at him, "Don' yo' ever, *ever* wear a soldier's uniform again!", she pulled the suit from his shoulders, tugged it down from his arms, from his hips; the embarrassed boy stood in a pair of blue underwear in the middle of the yard while the stunned family stared at him. He looked to his mother, who was stomping angrily down the back steps.

"Don' yo' *touch* that boy!" shouted Rosemary, as enraged as a lioness rushing to protect her cub. She grabbed Angelique's arms from behind and heaved her aside, then stood between her son and his attacker. "Yo' leave him alone!"

Angelique glared at her sister. "Yo' give him that soldier suit?"

Rosemary answered with provoking conviction, "Cyril and Ah give it to him for Christmas."

Angelique's eyes widened with horrified disbelief. "What kind of trash be that to give a boy at Christmas?"

"Trash?!" snapped Rosemary. "Bein' a soldier be something to be proud of. It be *yo'* who ain' see no pride in bein' a patriot."

Fierce anger flashed in her eyes as Angelique retorted, "Ain' yo' know what a soldier be? He be a mahn dead for nothin'. Yo' want that for Chester?"

Rosemary grimaced with disgust. "Ah be *proud* of meh brother Leroy. He went like a mahn and he done his duty. He follow Papa's footsteps and defend freedom in the world. But yo'," she sucked her teeth, "yo' tink Leroy ain' been nothin' but a poor ignorant victim. Yo' do him the dishonor of tinkin' he ain' been nothin' but a boy snatched from Mama's apron strings. Yo' ain' never seen any good in what Leroy done. But Ah have. And Ah gon' teach meh one and only son to stand up and be a mahn too."

Chester tried to explain to his aunt, "Lots of kids wear Kommando Kamouflage." He pulled the suit back over his shoulders and snapped up the front.

Rosemary shook her finger in Angelique's face. "When the day come that yo' got children of yo' own, yo' raise them as yo' see fit. But other folks' children," she glared with fierce warning, "yo' ain' got no right to meddle with."

Nat intervened, stepping between his daughters. "Now girls, dis ain' what we want to talk about on Christmas Day. Dis be a day of good cheer and—"

"This is *exactly* the day we should talk about guns and soldiers," insisted Angelique. "Isn't Christmas about peace and brother—"

Estelle shouted with thundering finality, "Now yo' two stop it!"

They did. The sisters glowered at each other in silence. Then Rosemary grabbed Chester's hand and marched him into the house.

Angelique turned to her mother. "Mama, how can yo'—"

"Hush! Meh poor ol' heart cain't take any more fightin' in dis family."

*   *   *

As they were driving home through Christiansted, Zosia said to Karl, "Let's stop at the Comanche for some Christmas punch."

He nodded with agreement, for he too felt the tension in the car and did not want to take it with them back to Candle Point. He looked into the rearview mirror at Angelique, who sat silent and sullen. "How about you?" he asked her. "Want to stop at the Comanche for some Christmas punch?"

"A nice American toy rifle," she sneered. "A very nice American toy for a boy to have."

Before he could answer, Zosia snapped, "Nogh!" She turned around in her seat and scolded, "You are unfair."

"Unfair?" exploded Angelique. "Who was that running around the yard but a little GI Joe? A little American soldier-boy! Shooting everything in sight!"

"Yagh, I saw him. And it pained my heart. Because I saw boys marching once, thousands of boys with real rifles, in Berlin. Boys who would soon be men." She shook her finger at Angelique. "Men whom no one could stop, no one, until the Americans poured into Europe and stopped them for good."

"Sorry to interrupt," said Karl, "but we're coming to the parking lot at the wharf. What's the consensus? Do we stop or not?"

"Yagh," said Zosia decisively. "We have some punch and we talk about the Americans."

He found an empty space near the old Danish fort. He and Angelique helped Zosia into her wheelchair, Angelique too angry to speak, he warily keeping his mouth shut, while Zosia admired the Christmas lights strung in the rigging of some of the yachts in the harbor. Angelique pushed Zosia toward the boardwalk; he walked beside them, his heart sinking with despair, for his friendship with Angelique, and—he had hoped—something more than friendship, would clearly be destroyed by her unrelenting bitterness.

They rode in the Comanche's old-fashioned cage elevator to the second floor; Angelique pushed Zosia across the pedestrian bridge over Strand Street and into the crowded restaurant. They found a table where Zosia could sit in a wicker chair with a high round back; in her red gown, she looked like a queen in a throne. On the table burned a white candle encircled with a wreath of holly.

Several old friends rose from their tables and came to greet Zosia. They told her how well she looked, and clinked their goblets of punch with hers. Karl was glad to see Zosia in such good spirits, and resolved to get her out more often.

When quiet finally settled on their table, he glanced at Angelique; she would not meet his eyes, but tied her plastic straw into knots.

Zosia turned to Angelique and stated with whole-hearted gratitude, "One of the most *beautiful* sounds I have heard in my life was the low steady rumbling drone of the American bombers from Italy, flying over Switzerland on their way to Germany. They weren't supposed to fly over Swiss airspace, but they did, and every time they roared over Davos, Piotr and I hurried outside from our little hut and looked up. At first they flew over only at night, and we could not see them; we only heard their thunder and the thunder echoing off the mountains. But near the end of the war they were flying by day too, as brave as a flock of eagles. Angelique, I felt a thrill every time I heard them, because they were heading north to pound *hell* out of the Nazis." She thumped her fist on the table; the candle flame wavered. "Those were *Americans* up there in those planes, Angelique. Those were Americans, strong enough to finally punch Adolf in the nose. When the planes rumbled out of sight with their bombs, then rumbled back hours later, their bellies empty, I remembered Papa and his garden of red and white roses, and I remembered my grandmother, my Babsha, in the farmhouse kitchen in Bydgoszcz, and Angelique, I *loved* the sound of those American bombers."

Angelique met Zosia's eyes with a silent glare; though angry, she was willing to listen.

"But what I really want to tell you," continued Zosia, "is about the spring of 1946, when by a miracle that never stops being a miracle, Piotr and I arrived by plane in New York. In America! We had come aboard the first airplane with refugees to cross the Atlantic. But because we had not come by boat, we had missed sailing past the Statue of Liberty. Piotr and I of course wanted to see her, to . . . to know with our own eyes that she really existed. And to thank her."

Karl noticed that people at the tables nearby became quiet as first Zosia's friends, then others in the restaurant, turned to listen to the old woman with an accent as she spoke about coming to their country. Zosia never noticed her growing audience, for her attention was focused solely on Angelique and himself.

"We had been in New York for a week, had found an apartment in the Village, had looked for jobs, had met our first friends. Then on Saturday morning, a bright spring morning, the sky robin's-egg blue above those amazing buildings, Piotr and I walked down West Broadway from Washington Square to the Battery, where we took the ferry out to Liberty Island. I had bought my first pair of American saddle shoes for the trip. And I remember, I was wearing a blue blazer and a pleated white skirt, and a red scarf that fluttered in the wind while we stood on the bow and looked across the broad harbor at the tiny green figure we had dreamt about for seven years.

"As our ferry approached her, we stared up at a stern towering goddess, copper-green in the blue sky." Zosia raised her arm, holding an imaginary torch; now even the people seated on bar stools were listening. "We saw her torch of liberty, the beacon that had pierced even the dark pall of Hitler's war."

Lowering her arm, Zosia took hold of Angelique's hand. "But do you know, the Lady of the Harbor is also a magnificent piece of sculpture." Her eyes brightened with excitement. "From the boat, I examined her every detail. 'Can we really go inside her?' I asked Piotr, for we had been told that visitors could climb stairs inside the statue all the way up to windows in her crown. He smiled at me, his gray eyes always happiest when I was happy. He linked his arm with mine as together we crossed the gangplank to Liberty Island.

"Walking up the steps to the pedestal, I stared up, up, up at her copper robe. Then we stopped to read a poem on a plaque, and we knew we were welcome. Yagh, we had been tired and poor. Yagh, we had been wretched and homeless. We had been tossed by the storms of war." She turned from Angelique and stared for a long moment at the flickering orange flame of the Christmas candle. "We could remember the faces of many who did not stand there with us on that day in April. In America."

Glancing at Karl, she turned to Angelique and continued, "Piotr and I bought our tickets, then we started up those spiral metal stairs. As we climbed, I examined the inside of Liberty's robe. I studied the riveting, and the bands of iron that supported the seams of her drapery. When I had been an art student in Berlin, I had often sketched sculptures in the parks, but never had I seen a statue from the inside!

"Up and up we climbed, around and around, our feet ringing on the metal steps. I stared up the giant green tube of Liberty's arm, marveled at the ingenious steel armature. When finally we reached her head, I looked at the smooth insides of her cheeks, peered into the cave of her nose. I was stunned by the great size of her eyes. Her irises were a meter wide! When I reached up and touched the ripples of her hair, flowing like waves across the sea, I felt a shiver run through me." She smiled as she remembered that extraordinary moment.

"Yes, we looked out the windows in her crown at the blue-gray sweep of New York Bay. Following Liberty's gaze, we saw the funnel of the Verrazano Narrows: the Golden Door. On the other side of that passageway, what horrors we had endured! And then I heard a voice, my grandmother's voice, my Babsha's, saying as she had said at the end of every grace," . . . Zosia whispered, "Dzięki Ci Boże. Dear God, thank you." She clenched her jaw, her eyes glistening with tears.

"We watched the freighters and tugs steaming busily around the bay. We watched the ferry crossing from Staten Island toward the Battery. And then we started down. Now here is what I want to tell you about, Angelique. About going down that spiral staircase, around and down and around and down inside Liberty's robe." Zosia's olive-black eyes stared deeply into Angelique's. "Because I felt like an embryo, about to be born. Born into America, born into freedom, born into a new life.

Angelique admitted quietly, "Yes. I have been unfair."

Thank you, Zosia, thought Karl. Thank you so very much.

A hearty voice called from a nearby table, "Merry Christmas to you, Zosia! We're very glad you're here!" The speaker, a handsome seafaring man, stood and raised his glass to her; he had a shock of white hair, and his blue eyes shone with the warmth of years of friendship.

A chorus of toasts filled the restaurant. Zosia raised her trembling glass of punch with both hands and cheered to one and all, "Wesołych Świąt! Merry Christmas!"

As Angelique pushed Zosia in the wheelchair along the moon-dappled tunnel under the seagrape bushes, Karl, walking behind them, could see from her unsteady shuffle that she was drunk as a skunk.

She had been quiet in the back seat all the way home, quiet and pensive. Now as she pushed the wheelchair over the uneven flagstones, she suddenly spoke, "Zosia, I've decided to teach my weapons class again. The one that failed before. This time I want to change some—"

"Good!" exclaimed Zosia, thumping her fist on the armrest. She looked over her shoulder at Angelique; a patch of moonlight slid across her earnest face. "About time you stopped sulking and started doing."

"What's this?" Karl asked with interest. "You taking a course?"

Angelique stopped pushing the chair and turned to him. He was stunned by the look in her eyes, for she challenged him. To what, he didn't know. "I'm going to teach a course," she said. "As a nurse, I want to tell the public what is going to happen to them if we suffer a nuclear explosion on St. Croix."

Cautious at the mention of this touchy subject, and remembering her outburst at Chester and Rosemary, he was unsure what to say.

"Will we have a hospital?" she asked. "If we do, will it have electrical power? Will the generators function? Will we have water? Critical burn facilities for how many patients? Five, ten? Certainly not for ten thousand. I want to say to people, I've *got* to say to people, 'The day that mushroom stands high over yo' heads, don' bother comin' to the hospital with yo' burns and yo' blindness. We warnin' yo' right now: ain' no way for what few nurses and doctors still alive, with what few bandaids we still got left, to fix the damage *yo'* let happen. Save yo'selves the trip. Yo' might just as well lie down in yo' pain and die.'"

He said, "Angelique, can you back up a bit. What kind of course is this?"

"It's an evening course at the University, about war and racism. About peace and cooperation. About swords and ploughshares."

"Good. Sign me up."

She studied him as she tested him. "As a student?"

"More than that. Let me help you . . . . that is, if you need any help. I can be your teaching assistant."

"No. If you're going to help, then we're both teachers. Balanced."

Zosia watched them intently.

He agreed, "All right. Two teachers, team teaching."

The challenge in her eyes disappeared, replaced by a measure of respect.

Zosia offered, "I want to be your research librarian. I suggest you start the students with Hersey's *Hiroshima*. I've got a copy on the bookshelf above the phone."

"I started to read that book in high school," said Angelique, "but I couldn't finish it. It was too real. So, yes, we'll assign *Hiroshima* as the first text."

"I've never read it," he admitted. "Too busy reading chem and double E." He thought for a moment, about possibilities. "Angelique, since St. Croix is an American territory, I'll bet both the Christiansted and

University libraries can tap into a stateside network. We could order all kinds of books to be shipped down. Maybe some films too."

Now he saw that same look on her face that he had seen aboard her sloop far out to sea: a faint smile of determination as she rode up a rough wave. "Yes," she said, "the three of us. Let's *do* it."

Nick stood on the Battery, his woolen coat buttoned against a sleet storm as he stared out at the churning black water of New York Bay on Christmas night. Waves slapped against the seawall, tossing spray into the frigid air that stung his face.

He had walked countless blocks on this Christmas day, from Harlem at the northern end of Manhattan Island to the Battery at its southern tip. While around him the city had celebrated Christmas, (quietly in the morning as he walked the nearly deserted streets, jubilantly in the afternoon when people came out from their homes to try a new pair of skates on the pond in Central Park,) he had walked and walked and had not spoken to a soul. The festive displays in the store windows, the colored lights and greenery festooned from lamppost to lamppost, the Christmas music which he could faintly hear from the courtyard of Rockefeller Center as he walked past, only served to quicken the memory of Christmas in New York two years ago.

He had come home on the twenty-first from driving his uptown taxi, and found the apartment empty, her half of the closet empty, Andy's bedroom empty of books, of clothes, of posters on the wall. Devastated, he felt not even a moment's anger toward Denise; the fault was his own. He was clearly such an impossible, hateful person that they could not bear to be with him any longer, especially at Christmas.

Standing lost in the kitchen, he spotted a scrap of crumpled paper on the floor. He picked it up and opened it: Greyhound 271. Denise's handwriting. He phoned the bus terminal. "New York, Los Angeles," they told him. His heart pounding wildly, he asked, "What time that bus arrive in Los Angeles?" While at the same moment, he knew that they could get off at any of the dozen stops along the way. The ticket clerk at Port Authority told him, "December 24, two-thirty-five in the afternoon."

He phoned Kennedy Airport, made reservations, ignored a flight attendant who tried to flirt with him on the jet, then stood in the Los Angeles bus terminal on Christmas Eve, two-thirty-five in the afternoon, at arrivals Gate 15, and watched a parade of people get off Greyhound 271, full of smiles and hugs as they greeted family who welcomed them home for the holidays . . . until the bus was empty. Maybe, he thought with a sneer of self-contempt, they stopped to see the Grand Canyon.

He lived and ate at the bus station for two weeks, slept at the YMCA. Hard to see every person getting off every bus from New York. Hard to meet every bus arriving all hours of the night. He came as close as he'd come in his life to popping pills.

In mid-January, he visited a dozen high schools where Andy might have enrolled as a freshman. Hiding his embarrassment, he explained to principal after principal that he was the boy's father, that the boy's mother had disappeared with Andrew, that Andy was tall for his age and crazy about basketball and would surely have tried out for the team— Principal after principal shook his head. "No Andrew Cruz here. Sorry."

But of course Denise could have changed their names. After all, why be a Cruz? Why be a loser? Why not be an Aaron, or a Cosby, or a Chamberlain?

Standing now in wintry darkness at the southern tip of the island where he had tried to start a new life, his feet nearly frozen, his face wet with the sleet in the biting wind off the harbor, he wondered, Why all the people Ah love keep disappearin'?

The deep prolonged groan of a ship's horn rumbled against his chest; peering south through the storm, he could just faintly see the freighter's lights as it passed through the Verrazano Narrows.

Can't even send meh son Andy a Christmas card.

One step, just one more step, off the seawall and into that frigid black water, and the whole shameful shambles of his life would be over.

Not a soul in all the world would even know he was gone.

An yet, there had been a measure of success. This trip to New York had not been without some definite progress. He had located a dealer with contacts along the arms pipeline into Afghanistan, a pipeline that continued to function even though the superpowers had politely decided the war was over.

Yes, he'd found his Stinger.

But was he really going to do all that? Back in that other world, on that other island, where a university waited for him?

Stomping his feet, two blocks of ice, he remembered his happiness a year ago with Angelique: making love with her deep in the mahogany forest on Christmas morning, two passionate pagans, wild and free. And dinner in the afternoon at her parents' home, both Papa and Mama so welcoming, and Leroy never mentioned.

Maybe Ah should just go back and start classes in January. Let her see that Ah tryin' meh best to be the mahn she want me to be.

He turned his back to the storm and faced Manhattan; he looked up at the wall of skyscrapers, their scattered lit windows misted by sweeping clouds of sleet. College was the American way. But he would be enrolling as a thirty-eight-year-old freshman. His foot on the bottom rung, and those buildings were so tall.

The people who bought and bulldozed and sold pieces of his island worked in those buildings.

Turning again to face the pummeling icy wind, he decided, Let college be yo' camouflage.

CHAPTER NINETEEN

To the Sandbar

On the Monday after Christmas, while riding into work, Angelique stopped at the taxi stand in Christiansted and casually asked one of the drivers, "Nick Cruz been by this evenin'?"

Eyes glazed with boredom as he sat in his car waiting for a fare, the driver mumbled, "He off island."

"Where he go?" she asked.

The driver shrugged. "Somebody see him at the airport. Ain' nobody see him since."

"When was that? When did he leave?"

The man rolled his eyes, imposed upon. "Listen, sister, ask me to find any road on the island and yo' got it. Ask me about somebody's business . . . Me ain' know nothin'."

"T'anks."

As she rode away on her scooter, she couldn't help but feel a little hurt. He had left the island and never even said good-bye. Maybe Denise wrote to him. Maybe Andy. Yes, maybe Andy. Sent his father a Christmas card and Nick got on a plane to Los Angeles to find his son.

And never even said good-bye.

Well, Ah a free woman now.

She and Karl combed the Florence Williams Library in Christiansted, and the library at the University of the Virgin Islands; they carried armloads of books about weapons, history, and international relations out to his jeep. They reserved a classroom large enough for fifty students at the University, for Monday evenings through the spring semester. They decided to hold the first class on January 23rd; they had considered the 16th, Martin Luther King Day, as an appropriate date on which to begin, but then they reconsidered, for most people would be with their families on that holiday. The turnout for the first class would no doubt be better on the following Monday. They considered holding the final class on Memorial Day, but again decided that such a holiday was for families to be together.

As they blocked out a sixteen-week syllabus, the two co-teachers mulled over the course's overall theme, and finally decided that it should not deal primarily with war, but with peace. "Building the Peace," said Karl, "because peace has got to be more than just the absence of war, the same as a house is more than just the absence of a bomb crater. A house has got to be built and maintained by everyone living in it. Otherwise the roof starts to leak and the foundation begins to rot. Keep up the repairs, and add a wing here, a wing there, until there's room for everybody in the mansion of peace."

"Yes," she agreed. "This must be a course in carpentry."

On New Year's Eve the wind dropped to a dead calm; the sea lay as flat as a mirror reflecting the black sky and bright moon. Unable to sail, Angelique and Karl promised Zosia they would join her an hour before midnight, then they went for a walk on the beach. The pale scallop of sand stretched ahead of them, flanked by bushy black manchineel trees, and by the silver-shimmering bay.

Karl reached for Angelique's hand, and felt a surge of happiness when she wrapped her fingers comfortably around his.

At the end of the beach, a jagged wall of rock blocked their path. They could walk no further, but neither did they want to turn around and go back. They looked out at the sandbar, a white, moonlit hyphen on the black water.

"Shall we swim out?" she asked.

He gauged the distance: about a quarter-mile. If Candle Point and the beach formed two-thirds of a horseshoe, then the sandbar was the tip of the second prong. He asked uneasily, "Any monsters out there feeding at night?"

"Just the giant squid. It wraps one huge sucker over your head and plucks your skull off your shoulders so fast, you don't suffer at all."

"C'mon, I'm serious. Don't sharks feed at night?"

She reassured him, "They stay out beyond Buck Island, down in the deep water below the dropoff. Anyway, I'll be swimming beside you. We'll get eaten together."

"Terrific. Any currents?"

"Nothing you'll notice. The water flows west at about half a knot. I thought you told me you're a swimmer."

"I *am* a swimmer. It's just that I don't want to be bait too."

She untied the knot of her sarong and let the folds of yellow cloth fall to the sand. Naked, her dark skin softly aglow in the moonlight, she waded into the water until she was waist deep; then she dove with almost no splash and disappeared.

Acutely aware that his life was hopefully about to reach a major turning point, and that he was ready for it, he stripped off his T-shirt and shorts and waded into the warm sea. He swam butterfly with a strong dolphin kick, the old power and grace from his swimming team days returning to his limbs.

Frog-kicking across the blurry moonlit bottom, she dodged eerie black arms of coral, glided over a dark pasture of turtle grass, patted her hands on a pale patch of sand. When she heard his rhythmic 'kathum, kathum, kathum,' she rolled over and watched him stitching across the surface. There's my Viking, she thought happily. There's my Karl.

Then she couldn't resist. Springing off the bottom, she shot toward the surface, gripped his belly and back with her fingernails—her hands like two huge saber-toothed jaws—and SHOOK him!

"Yaaaarrrrg!" he cried, flailing frantically across the surface.

Helpless with laughter, she lay on her back and gasped for air. "Ho ho ho! Karl, you— Ho ho ho!"

"Angelique, that wasn't funny!"

"Karl, ho ho, say it again. 'Aaaaarrrg!' Ho ho ho!"

"Angelique," he scolded, treading water, "that was exceedingly immature."

"K-K-Karl, what was it like to be eaten? Hee hee hee!"

"Very funny. Now are we swimming out to the sandbar or what?"

"What what?"

"I don't know what. I'm just asking if we're swimming together like two grown-up adults, or if you're going to float there having an astonishingly thoughtless chuckle while I have a heart attack."

"Okay, Karl, we swim."

The two backstroked, side by side, their feet boiling a froth of moonlit foam, their arms arching overhead in tandem. He raised his head to watch her: her wet black breasts lifted one and then the other as she swept her arms; her belly skimmed the glimmering surface while her hips rocked with the rhythm of her kick. "You look like one of

Zosia's sculptures," he told her, "in wet ebony."

She smiled at him, her eyes bright. "And you of the big chest? Carved in sturdy oak."

When they neared the tiny island, the two rolled over and swam breaststroke, so they could avoid the sharp coralheads. They waded from the shallows onto a boomerang-shaped patch of glowing white sand, its crest a mere foot above the black lagoon. She faced the moon and shook the water from her hair.

Then she looked at him, her eyes inquiring.

He took her hand and kissed her, tentatively, and found that he was welcome. His heart pounded as her voluptuous lips pressed against his mouth with growing passion. She wrapped her arms around him and hugged him with all her strength, and then she pulled her lips away and whispered urgently in his ear, "Kaaarrrrrrl, lie on your back so I can face the moon."

He lay on the cool soft sand. She knelt over him, her luscious dark body luminous in the magical light as she gazed down at him and rubbed her hands over his chest.

But then she seemed to forget him. She looked up at the moon and stared as if in a trance while she rocked her hips. She arched her back, offering her bouncing breasts not to him but to the sky. Her face acquired an extraordinary beauty as she gazed in a state of elevated passion at the heavens. Her breathing quickened; her eyes widened; surges of pleasure trembled her body.

His eyes beheld only Angelique and the stars above her. But the moon was her lover, and he felt abandoned and cheated and angry. His hands clenched her hips as he demanded, "Angelique, look at me. *Look* at me."

She heard Karl calling her name. Looking down, she saw the hurt and hope in his eyes. And then the dam burst inside her: the backed-up river poured forth and flowed, free and wild at last. "Kaaarrrrrrrlllllll!" she cried, yet even now she hesitated to tell him, Ah love yo'.

He saw her staring at him with wide-eyed bliss; I love you, he thought; he shuddered and gave her seeds and seeds, as many seeds as all the stars.

CHAPTER TWENTY

The First Blow

The question in her mind was not, Could she imagine having children with Karl? With a white man? She loved him, and though she had qualms about her family, and his family—about whom she knew almost nothing—she felt that with Karl, her life had at last begun to move forward. The question that haunted her was the same question that had cursed her for years: Could she have children at all on an island that was both an arsenal and a target of the worst weapons the human race had ever created? Could she rock her cradle beside a nuclear time bomb?

Could she, through her course at the University, educate her people to the point where they *demanded* that the Navy leave St. Croix? No ships, no missiles, no radar, no sonar: Nothing military on their island.

But even if her people responded, how long before they petitioned Congress, demonstrated against the warships at the pier, published an appeal to the United Nations, asking simply that their island be allowed to live in peace? How long before Crucians, and any visitors to the island who wished to join them, threatened some form of civil disobedience: a transportation strike, an island-wide day of fasting on behalf of the children who never asked to be born in a war zone?

And how long before the Navy actually departed?

She was thirty-two now. She could not wait many more years before she had her children. The time bomb was ticking, but so was her biological clock.

She knew only—and oh how it made her smile inside, filled her with a glow of happiness—that Karl was the man for whom she would gladly toss her diaphragm into the sea.

Because he insisted on attending church every Sunday, she decided to continue singing with the choir. Zosia enjoyed the weekly outing, and Mama and Papa were delighted. Thus her life was rich with busy days and shared happiness when the first blow sent her staggering.

She and Karl were on the beach, preparing the sloop for launching. Before they slid the boat into the water, Karl turned to Ulysses, lying in the shade beneath a coconut palm; he called, "Hop in, Pirate."

But instead of bounding across the beach and leaping into the boat, Ulysses got up slowly, stiffly, then walked to the sloop and stood as if the gunnel were an obstacle. When he tried to jump over it, he got his front paws up on the red pontoon . . . and then he sank on his rear haunches as if his hind legs had lost their strength. There he remained, apparently helpless, drooping his head as if he expected to be scolded.

She realized immediately that something was extremely wrong. She knelt beside him and examined his hips. Then she helped him to stand beside the sloop and felt his hind legs: everything seemed normal, no swelling, no cuts, and he showed no sign of pain. She inspected his eyes, felt his nose. Everything was normal. But then she noticed the two rear feet were placed in the sand slightly wider than usual: Ulysses was bracing himself.

Karl said, "The other day when we were running along the shore, he seemed to wobble a little. I thought he had a thorn in one of his paws, but I couldn't find anything." He too knelt beside Ulysses. Ruffling the dog's ears, he reassured him, "It's all right, Pirate. You're a *good* dog."

Ulysses lifted his head in his old cocky manner, but made no effort to jump into the boat.

She straightened his salt-crusted red bandana. It was still dry. He had not dashed into the water today, chasing the birds; he had simply lain under the palm tree. "Karl, we must take him to the vet's."

"Exactly. I'll run up the hill and get the jeep. Want me to carry Ulysses to the road?"

"No. If he needs help, I will carry him."

Karl touched her arm. "I don't think there's anything to worry about. He's just off his oats a little, is all."

An hour later, Ulysses stood trembling on a stainless steel examination table while she held his shoulders and the veterinarian, a redheaded American in his sixties, worked his freckled fingers over the dog's hips. The doctor asked, "Can we roll him over on his back, please?"

Hiding her anxiety with a steady voice, she coaxed her frightened dog, "Roll over, Ulysses. Come on, Big Bear, roll over."

Slowly, his nails scratching the metal, the cowering dog lay down and then rolled over, his legs drawn tightly to his body. She dug her fingers into his soft fur and scratched his chest. "Good dog. Yo' a *good* dog."

When the doctor pulled one hind leg straight and rotated it in its socket, Ulysses yelped with fierce pain. His shriek knifed through her heart as she held Ulysses' head to keep him from snapping at the vet.

Dr. Johansen released the leg and massaged the dog's hip. "It's all right, old boy. We won't hurt you anymore." Then he asked her, "Does he have any German shepherd in him?"

She helped Ulysses to roll over and sit up. "I don't know. I found him when he was a puppy. Someone left him at the Tipperary dump."

Dr. Johansen shook his head grimly. "From his bone structure, I'd say he's half shepherd. I'd like to take some x-rays, but my initial diagnosis is a condition known as hip dysplasia, compounded by degenerative myelopathy. Shepherds are especially prone. The ball joint becomes encrusted with a calcium deposit that causes pain as it grinds against the socket. In some cases—perhaps this one—the nervous system is involved as well. The nerves in the hindquarters degenerate until the dog will have difficulty standing. The hip muscles atrophy. The condition progresses up the spine to the diaphragm, until the dog has trouble breathing."

Stunned, barely able to believe what she was hearing, she asked desperately, "Is there any cure? Is there some medication?"

With profound regret, the doctor shook his head, No. "We could surgically remove the crust on the ball joint, or the ball itself. Were that the only problem, I'd say his chances were good for several more years. But there's nothing we can do to retard the deterioration of the nerves. I'll be frank with you, Angelique. You'll soon have to walk behind him, supporting his hips while he urinates. In about two month's time, you'll have to make a decision."

Through the fog of shock, she whispered, "Two months?"

"I'm afraid so. Do you have any stairs at home?"

Unable to speak, she buried her face in Ulysses' soft fur.

Karl answered, "Yes, we've got some stairs."

"Best if you carry him up and down. Sling your arms under his chest and abdomen, so his legs hang free. He can walk as much as he wants, but steps will be difficult. We don't want him falling." Dr. Johansen lifted Ulysses' lip to examine his teeth. "He's not an old dog, is he?"

Her voice a trembling whisper, she answered, "He would have been six next summer."

"I'm sorry. This is usually an affliction of older dogs." The doctor reached into a pocket of his white lab coat and gave Ulysses a biscuit; the dog dropped it on the metal table. The doctor said, "Let's take some pictures."

The x-rays confirmed the disease as irreversible dysplasia. The doctor gave her a brown bottle filled with pills. "This is Prednisone, to reduce his pain. I'd like you to bring him back in two weeks for a check-up."

She rode home in the rear seat of the jeep with Ulysses lying across her lap, his head down, eyes closed, exhausted from his ordeal. She stroked him from his head to his hips. She did not mind that Karl heard her crying.

CHAPTER TWENTY-ONE

The Second Blow

The second blow came like a slap in her face, a very hard slap that opened her eyes.

She and Karl had spent the day at the beach with Ulysses. The dog trotted up and down the shore after flocks of peeping birds, but she could see that his hips swung slightly from side to side; if he turned too suddenly, he staggered to keep from falling. She sat on a bluff of sand, Karl beside her, both of them silently watching the irrefutable evidence of Ulysses' approaching death.

Tossing back and forth between grief and rage, she wondered, Why should such a bright, happy creature be struck down? Many times she had tried and failed to answer a similar question at the hospital, when distraught parents asked about the health of their child. Knowing how she felt now, she doubted she could endure the ordeal if it were her own human child who was dying.

Late in the afternoon, Karl suggested, "Let's go into town tonight and have dinner at the Chart House. I think it might be good for you to get away from Candle Point for awhile."

They left Ulysses with Zosia, who encouraged them to "spend a nice long evening together. Maybe see a movie after dinner."

Driving into Christiansted, she struggled to revive her spirits. If Karl was nice enough to invite her out, she didn't want to be such morbid company. She forced herself to look out the window; people were strolling along the sidewalks, a couple laughed on the corner by the post office. Then she remembered she ought to pick up Zosia's mail. "Karl, could you drop me off by the post office, please? Zosia was too kind to remind me."

He reached into his pocket and handed her his mailbox key. "Would you pick up mine too? I'll park at the wharf, then I'll come back to meet you."

As she walked down the post office hallway with its ranks of numbered boxes, she felt numb, too drained for either sadness or pleasure. She opened her own mailbox first and found a paycheck from the hospital, and a telephone bill.

In Zosia's box she found a bill from the pharmacy; an envelope—probably with a check—from the Compass Rose; and a square, brown, slightly battered envelope postmarked BYDGOSZCZ, 10 GRUDNIA. She looked at the feeble handwriting of Zosia's nursemaid, Stasha, now in her nineties, the only survivor from Zosia's girlhood on the family farm. Stasha always wrote in big letters UNITED STATES Virgin Islands, for though she might never be able to envision the tropical island that was Zosia's home, she did know with certainty that her beloved Zosieňka lived in America. The envelope no doubt contained a Christmas card, delayed by the slow Polish mail.

She looked at the number on Karl's key, found his box further down the hall, opened its little glass door and took out a postcard with a picture of a young, beardless Abraham Lincoln, his shirtsleeves rolled up as he held an ax poised in both hands, ready to swing. A red, white and blue banner at the bottom read,

ILLINOIS   LAND OF LINCOLN

Curious, she turned the card over to see who it was from: it was signed, "Pop." She glanced at the salutation: "Dear Karl,". Though she hesitated to invade his privacy, she felt compelled to understand his world up north, for it was so much a part of him. She read the large loopy handwriting:

> "Your Mom and I sure enjoyed your phone call on Christmas. Glad you're so happy down there. Your long descriptive letters are a big hit around the farm. Anne and Sal stop by regular to read them. Life here is about the same. Zeke, the hired hand, quit last week, so I've had to do all the nigger work myself."

She flushed hot as she stared at the words "nigger work." Then she read,

> "Ol' Man Winter treated us real nice with a white Christmas this year.
> Lots of love,
> Pop"

Staring at the words "nigger work," she grew furious at the bigoted, pig-headed American who was Karl's father. And then she realized what a fool she had been.

"Hi, Angel," called Karl as he strode down the hallway. "Guess what. There's a steel drum band playing on the boardwalk tonight. Any mail?"

She handed him his key and the postcard. "Something from home."

He glanced at the picture, turned the card over, then stuck it into his shirt pocket. "It's from Pop. I'll read it later. Let's go have a nice dinner."

"Read it now."

"Angelique, what's wrong?"

"Read it."

He took the card from his pocket and read its message. He frowned, then tried to apologize. "Angelique, I'm terribly sorry. But it's an old phrase, just a way of talking. Pop doesn't mean anything by it."

"Karl, I do not appreciate your father's racism."

"Pop? He's not prejudiced. Listen, that's just an expression he used. Okay, it's a lousy expression. But Pop'll shake the hand of any person, I promise you."

"Then he is oblivious, which is almost worse."

"Well, yeah, I guess he didn't think of what he was saying."

"Karl, I want nothing more to do with Pop." Her eyes flashed with accusation. "Nor with his son who defends him." Turning away, she hurried down the hall.

He argued as he followed her, "Hey wait, that rotten word came from him, not me. Angelique, why are you mad at me? You're being unfair. Angelique!"

She snapped over her shoulder, "I will take a taxi home. Enjoy your dinner."

"Angelique, please calm down for a moment."

When he followed her up the sidewalk, she began to run, her legs hampered by her sarong. He fortunately did not pursue her, for if he had touched her, if he had even come close, she probably would have screamed.

As he walked back to the parking lot, he fumed at her unfairness.

But as he got into the jeep and slipped the key into the ignition, he realized how close he had come to a far worse disaster. Pop could so easily have mentioned my sailing with a 'guy' on 'his' sailboat, and she would have known I'd hidden my black girlfriend with a lie. If I had told Mom and Pop at Christmas, Pop never would have used 'nigger' in his card. So really it's my fault, not his. Damn, I hurt her. And when she's already struggling with Ulysses.

He remembered standing beside her father in church, holding the hymnal together; and sharing dinner with her entire family, and he cringed with deepening shame.

By the time he reached the cottage, he had decided to phone home and do the job that needed to be done. Sitting at the glass-topped table, he pushed, his finger trembling, his heart thumping, the eleven buttons that would bounce his voice via satellite to the Land of Lincoln. As he listened to the familiar ring of the old farmhouse telephone, he looked out his window at the lights of the two houses at the end of Candle Point. Zosia's stained-glass window shone in the night like a distant jewel. Is she with Zosia now? he wondered. Then he heard his father's voice, gruff with irritation that anyone would call right at dinnertime, "Hello?"

"Hello, Pop. This is Karl. How are you? . . . Oh, I'm fine. Listen, is Mom there? Ask her if she'd get on the bedroom phone, would you? I've got some good news for you both."

While he waited, he picked up the family portrait on the table and studied the faces: his father stern, his mother strong.

"Hi, Mom. How are you? . . . Oh, I'm sorry to hear that. Are you drinking lots of orange juice? Staying in bed? . . . Well, for heaven's sake, Mom, get some rest. Those cows'll be the death of you . . . . Me? Oh, I'm doing just fine. The job's going well. We're even a little ahead of schedule. It's been rush rush rush, but when we're done, the refinery will be one of the most efficient in the whole world. But listen, ahh, what I'm calling you about is some good news. I've found a wonderful girlfriend. She's a registered nurse at the hospital. . . . Angelique. Angelique Nielsen. . . . Thirty-two, a coupla years younger than me. Very bright. Well-educated. She's a midwife as well as a nurse. . . . Pretty? Pop, she's a dazzler. I'll send a picture of the two of us, but, ahh, first there's something I want to explain to you. Angelique was born right here on St. Croix. She's an island woman and—"

His father interrupted, "Karl, you ain't got yourself some nigger woman? What, is this a joke?"

"Pop, these days they call themselves Blacks." He gripped the phone angrily. "I'm phoning to tell you both that I'm in love with a wonderful woman who happens to be black. I know it may take you a little while to get used to the idea. But I didn't want to be secretive about this. I wanted to share the news with you, the *good* news. Especially since you've been fussing at me for so long to find someone and— Marry her? Well, it's too early to be thinking about marriage. We're just getting to know each other and— Pop, I don't ever want to hear that word again! Not *ever*. She's a woman. She's a nurse. She's a Crucian. And she's one of the finest human beings I've ever met."

He listened to their heavy silence.

"I want to remind you, Pop, that you never heard Joe use that word. And he never let anybody else around him use it either. You remember that day he told Zeke to shut his mouth or get off the property? That was Joe."

Silence. Faintly, in the background, he could hear the farmers' weather report on the radio.

"Mom, you haven't said a word."

She was stunned, but not angry, as she asked one simple question, "Are you happy, son?"

"Yes, I'm happy. Happier than I've ever been in my life. Angelique is a wonderful, wonderful woman."

"Then, that's all we want for you, Karl. Whatever's best."

Atta girl, Mom. I knew I could count on you. "Thank you." Nothing more to say now; he'd given them the news, so best to get off the line. "Well, listen, you drink that orange juice. And hire one of the neighbor kids to do the milking for a few days. Get some *rest*, Mom. . . . Yup. Bye bye, now. I love you both."

When he hung up, he let out a long breath. Well, that's over. It wasn't too bad. No worse than predicted, anyway. Mom was terrific, and Pop'll come around. Just takes a little getting used to, is all.

Still holding the family portrait, he gazed at his brother in uniform. Sure wish you were home, Joe, to talk some sense into the ol' man.

He set the picture back on the table, then—bolstering his courage for Round Two—stepped out the door into the night, his eye on the round jewel at the end of Candle Point.

Zosia could tell the moment Angelique walked through the door that something was wrong. "You're back so soon?"

Her face was rigid with anger. "I have come to get Ulysses."

"Not before you sit down and tell me what happened."

"I do not wish to talk about it."

"No? Where is Karl?"

"That is no longer my business." Angelique knelt beside Ulysses and patted his shoulders. "How yo' be, ol' friend?"

Glad to see her, he wagged his tail weakly.

Zosia looked down from her chair. "So you two had a fight. What did you fight about?"

Angelique glared up and snapped, "Please! I said I don't want to talk about it. I respect your privacy, do I not?"

"Yes, and when you see me upset, you do something about it. Now allow me to return the favor. Sit your obstinate, miserable self down and tell me what happened." She slapped her hand on the table in front of Angelique's chair.

Invited to pour out her rage, Angelique sat and told Zosia about the postcard. "What infuriated me the most was that Karl *defended* his father. Suddenly my eyes opened and I saw inside this Karl Jacobsen. I had thought he was so special, so unlike other Americans. But oh, I was wrong. What a fool I've been!"

"Listen, I'm sure that if you explain—"

"Explain?! *Never* will I speak to him again!"

Zosia scowled. "You criticize him, but then you abandon him. No, I won't allow it. You must talk with him. I'm quite certain he'll—"

"Those Americans," she spat out the word, her eyes fiery with righteous anger, "are incapable of—"

Three loud knocks at the door made both women jump.

Zosia turned in her chair and called, "Come in."

Karl swung the door open and stepped into the house, his resolute eyes on Angelique. He reached into his pocket, took out the postcard and tore it in half. He tore it again, and again, then he crossed the room, opened the porch door and disappeared outside. When he returned, his hands were empty.

"Angelique, I have come to apologize from the bottom of my heart. I should have torn up that card the moment I read it. I want you to know that I just telephoned my father to say that I don't ever want to hear that word again."

She blinked with surprise. "You phoned your Pop?"

"Yes." He added sternly, "I told him I don't want anything to do with that attitude. You might be pleased to know that my mother immediately agreed with me."

His voice softened. "I told Pop that you were deeply hurt by that postcard. And Angelique, he asked me to extend his apology to you. He wants you to know that he's very sorry, and that he's learned an important lesson."

She sneered, "A pig's apology."

"Angelique!" scolded Zosia. "Karl and his father are two different men. But both are offering you an apology. *And* some understanding."

Still glaring at Karl, his face filled with remorse, Angelique realized she was angry because she was frightened: terrified that Pop would drive a wedge between herself and this man who made her so happy. If ever once she heard such a word from Karl, even suspected such a thought, she would leave him forever. And that, she never wanted to do.

"Karl . . . ,"

He took her hand, pulled her up from the chair, wrapped his arms around her and hugged her tightly. "Angelique," he whispered into her ear, his voice desperate, "there's nothing more clear to me in all the world than this: I love you. I've got a lot to learn, I know. But believe me, Angel, I'm trying. I *love* you."

Squeezing him with all her strength, grasping the man she had almost lost, she too said for the first time, "I love you. Karl, my Kaaarrrl, I love you so much."

In the background, Zosia declared, "Yagh! Now the sun can shine again."

CHAPTER TWENTY-TWO

Prove It To Me

The third blow came not from a bigoted pig up north, but from her own people, and it caused her to begin to lose her footing. The fourth blow sent her reeling; the last bit of solid ground on which she had stood, disappeared.

At eight-thirty on Monday evening, half an hour after the course should have started, she sat in a desk beside Karl in the otherwise empty classroom and admitted, "Nobody came."

"Well, we've just got to publicize it more," he reasoned. "One four-day ad in the papers wasn't enough. I think maybe you should give a pitch for the course to the staff at the hospital. And I've also thought about an announcement in church. Listen, I'll ring up the radio and see what a spot costs. We've got to invest a little, you know, if we want to make this thing work. And how about a personal letter to each of the representatives in the Virgin Islands legislature? Let's get some heavies into the classroom."

She stared at the blackboard, covered with a neat, ambitious outline of the sixteen-week course. "Nobody came."

"C'mon, Angelique, don't let it get you down. You think Orville and Wilbur got off the ground on their first try?" He began to gather the five handouts, fifty copies each, which they had placed on desks across the front of the room. "Tell you what. It's still early. I'll buy you a piña colada in town, then we'll map out a new strategy. Whatdya say?"

She sneered softly, "Well, they didn't come to our peace class, but they'll sure as hell come to the next war."

Her anger was brief. As they walked out of the classroom and down the stairs, past the library busy with people, and out to the parking lot, her mind raced. Hopelessness, she knew well enough. And days of total despair. So though the demons threatened to pounce, to yelp and to mock and to torment, her mind hastened, eluding their grasp, to that one bright new spot of hope in her life which had never existed before. Because despite the insanity and apathy of these bewildering creatures called people, if she could trust Karl—trust him to stand at her side no matter what—then he would give her the strength that might make children possible. They two could form a world, their courage together able to prevail over her presumption that her children were doomed.

They reached her scooter standing beside his jeep in the glow of a streetlamp. As he assured her in his cheerful, optimistic manner that "we'll whip this course into shape in no time," she felt compelled not to wait for their love to take its course. She had to ask him, to be certain of his allegiance, now and forever. Her children needed to know.

They stacked their armloads of books and handouts on the passenger seat. Then she studied him closely as she asked him, "Karl, what do you think about us? About our future?"

He stood so he squarely faced her. "Angelique, it's one thing to say you're in love. It's another to say you love someone. So I ask myself, How do I feel about you? Do I want to be with you a year from now? Five, ten, fifty years from now? Do I want to be with only you, and never with any other woman? Can I see myself as a father, and you as the mother, raising a bunch of kids? Do I see us together for better or worse? Through rich and poor, sickness and health? I think and I think and I think about that. And Angelique, the answer to every one of those questions is, Yes. Yes, I honor you and I cherish you. I want to love you and love you and love you . . . forever.

"Karl, are you sure you want children from a black woman?"

He did not hesitate. "Now you listen to me, Angelique Nielsen. I knew we'd have to talk about this sooner or later, so you hear me loud and clear. How could I love you and not love our children? You hold a baby in your arms as dark as . . . a baby as dark as this tropical night, and the only argument you'll get from me is I'll want to hold her in *my* arms. You want to braid her curly black hair with beads? Fine, I'll buy the beads. You want to give her an African name? Good. I happen to think that Dick, Jane and Sally are pretty boring. If you're worried that I'm not going to teach those kids how to swim, and how to read and write, then Angelique, you don't know me."

She took him another step: "Karl, have you thought about a wedding?"

He smiled with anticipation. "Of course. I imagine it in your parents' church, with my sister Anne at the organ. She plays for the church in DeKalb, and I tell you she can raise the roof with jubilant music. And I thought we could have the reception in the Botanical Gardens, with a steel drum band out on the lawn so everyone can dance surrounded by bright flowers. June is the month for weddings, so I thought . . ." Then he laughed. "But I haven't even asked you to marry me yet."

"Karl, how do I know your Pop won't insult my father? How do I know your family won't bring with them that same attitude I saw on that postcard?"

He was stunned. "Good heavens, Angelique, that's over and done with. There's no problem with my family."

"How can I trust them? You know my family fairly well, but what do I know about yours? Almost nothing, except you lost Joe, and your father is a little old-fashioned. Am I to accept on blind faith that everything will be just fine when the two families meet each other the week before the wedding?"

He scolded her, "Angelique, this is absurd!"

"Karl, I risk humiliating Mama and Papa."

"You've got no right to talk like that. I'll have you know, I come from a family of good, decent, fine, respectable people. People who believe in some good, solid, respectable principles, like equality, and honesty, and giving the other guy a fair chance. Which is something you're not doing right now. If anybody is prejudiced, it's *you*."

She denied the accusation, "No, I'm not prejudiced, I'm afraid."

He retorted angrily, "Your fears are absolutely unfounded."

"So you insist that your family must come to the wedding?"

"Absolutely. They would be terribly hurt if I got married without inviting them."

"All right. Then one last question. Can we have children without a wedding? Can we sign a civil certificate, with no family attending, and then have our children?"

"Well, seems a sneaky way of getting married. And then your family would be hurt too. Angelique, to start a new family before getting the old families together to celebrate, well, that's just not right. Mom and Pop would have a tough time understanding a civil certificate. They're kind of conservative about weddings and having children and stuff, and they would want me to do it right. Furthermore, I refuse to hurt them. They've been through enough with Joe, and they don't deserve to be hurt by their only other son. So why don't we do it right? Why hurt other people's feelings? Let's have a big happy wedding and—"

"*Other* people's feelings? What about my family? What about me?"

"Hey, that doesn't mean I care any less about you. I just want *both* families together, at a nice, normal wedding."

"Karl, you are so naive! You say, 'They're kind of conservative.' Please spare us all the embarrassment of discovering just how conservative they are."

"You want to know something, Miss High-and-Mighty? This conversation is entirely premature. Because I haven't yet asked you to marry me, and I'm darn glad I haven't. Because it isn't that dumb postcard that's prompted all this. No, it's that bitterness of yours, that *poison* inside you. You're like a cobra, ready to spit venom every darn chance you get. Well, Miss Fangs, that's not the kind of mother I want for my kids. My kids are going to be raised by a mother who can teach them fairness and decency and equality, not suspicion and bitterness and hate."

"Prove it to me."

"Prove what?"

"Prove to me that Mom and Pop are not going to insult my family."

"Why should I? I thought it was the law of the land that people are innocent until proven guilty. You with your sickness, you think Mom and Pop are up north wearing white sheets and burning crosses, lynching every darkie in DeKalb County. What they're really doing is milking a string of cows, paying their bills on time, going to church every Sunday but when a blizzard closes the road, buying Girl Scout cookies and Christmas cards and who knows what else every time a kid appears at their door. And kicking in to the United Way once a year with what little extra they've got. And you ask me to prove that they are good people?" He glared at her with disgust. "I never insulted your family. Never once. I don't know where you think you get the right to insult mine."

Devastated, her whole body shaking, she got on her scooter, kick-started the engine and roared away toward Centerline, toward her job at the hospital, and beyond that she didn't know.

CHAPTER TWENTY-THREE

Voyage

His roots were back on that farm. If he and she married, surely one day he would abandon her and the children so he could go running home to Mom and Pop: the prodigal son begging forgiveness. And what Ah supposed to say to meh children? To meh half-white, fatherless children?

Angelique stared at the clipboard with her shift duties listed; her mind registered none of it.

He'll go runnin' home. Of course, he'll go runnin' home. Home where they never have any wars. Fight their war in Vietnam, fight their war in Nicaragua. Anywhere but home. Oh no, we can't hurt the children at home!

"Miss Nielsen, yo' all right?"

She looked up and saw Edna Charles, the head nurse, examining her with professional eyes that missed nothing. "Yes, Ah . . . a little tired."

"Yo' more than a little tired." Edna frowned with grave concern. "Worried about yo' dog, ain' yo'?"

"Yes, a little."

"Yo' go home to bed. Yo' ain' up to workin' tonight. When be the last time yo' had a vacation?"

Home. Home to her dying Ulysses; home to a childless widow who hoped that her substitute daughter would give her a substitute grandchild; home to Pop Jr.

And then a possibility opened: Edna was setting her free, free to launch her sloop and sail far, far out on the night ocean, out where the world made sense. How far? To where? Never mind. Just to be at sea. Away, away, away. She would take her children sailing. "T'ank yo'. Maybe Ah do need a little rest."

Seems I'm more interested in having Daddy at the wedding than the

191

bride.

And admit it, she's right. No telling how Pop would react at the wedding.

Driving home, Karl saw that Zosia's round window was still lit. The ol' night owl, he thought. She's who you ought to talk with, to straighten out this mess.

Over cups of tea, he recapitulated as accurately as he could the conversation which had developed into such a horrible argument.

Zosia asked, "Is Angelique right about your father?"

He let out a long sigh and admitted the truth. "It isn't that Pop's an evil man. He certainly never wore a white sheet. It's just that his attitudes . . . well, have never been challenged. He lives isolated on that farm and thinks the way he thinks. But he's never gone out of his way to hurt anybody. He never would."

"Karl, his postcard set things wrong. I think your father needs to write a letter to Angelique, to set things right."

"Pop write a letter to Angelique?" He shook his head, dubious.

"Yagh. You write a letter to your mother and father and you tell them about her, and about your plans for marriage. Then you ask them both to write a letter to both of you, with their blessing."

"Their blessing? But I haven't even proposed marriage yet."

"Angelique is not going to accept your proposal until she has their blessing."

"Yes, you're right there."

"And I think you should enclose a picture of the two of you with your letter. Let them take a good look at her. Let them know you're absolutely serious."

He considered the idea. "I s'pose the best picture we could take would be after church: she'd have a nice dress on, and I'd look sharp in my coat and tie. But I'm warning you, Zosia, this letter with their blessing . . . it's a bit of a gamble."

"So we don't tell Angelique a word about it. As far as she knows, we're taking the picture so I can have a nice portrait of the two of you on my dresser."

He held out his hand. "Thanks for your help, Zosia."

The conspirators shook on their plan. "In June," she assured him, "the Polish delegation will keep her eye on Pop."

Ulysses suddenly howled with loud urgency. Startled, Karl and Zosia turned to the dog, seated on his withered haunches by the glass door to the porch. Looking out the window, Karl glimpsed the peak of a sail moving past the house. He sprang to the door and opened it, helped Ulysses to stand, then walked behind him, bracing his hips as the dog hurried out. On the black water beyond the porch Karl saw the unmistakable ghostly-white triangles of Angelique's jib and mainsail, back-lit by a half-moon, as the sloop headed out to sea. A gray figure— she was still in her white uniform—sat at the tiller. Confused, but certain that something was terribly wrong, he cupped his hands and called, "Angelique! Where are you going?"

The sloop glided toward open water; she sat with her back to him.

Zosia thumped with her cane to the end of the porch. Her voice high and frenzied, she cried, "Angelique, come home!"

The two listened for an answer. Ulysses kept howling, his muzzle raised to the sky, and Karl had to kneel to hush him. He heard the wind gusting around the corner of the house; heard water sloshing at the bottom of the cliff. But from the boat, silence.

Zosia told him, "She's never done this before."

"I don't like her out there alone. Not as upset as she is."

Zosia gripped his arm. "Go to Raphael."

"Raphael?"

"The captain of Piotr's funeral boat. He doesn't have a phone. But you can find him in Gallows Bay. That's where the fishermen live. Ask at any house."

"Are you all right here by yourself?"

"Yagh, you hurry."

He reassured her, "Listen, Zosia, don't you worry. She's probably just heading out to Buck Island. Needs a place to get away from it all. A moonlight stroll on the beach."

Then he hurried out of the house and sprinted through the seagrape tunnel to his jeep. As he raced toward Gallows Bay, the books about weapons and war bounced on the seat beside him.

Once she had sailed far enough from Candle Point that the voices of the three who loved her were blown away in the wind, she knew the rest of the voyage would be easy. No rage, no guilt, no fear; she shut the demons out of her mind as she fantasized that seated beside her on the gunnel were three young adventurers, out with their mother on a nighttime voyage.

The wind was brisk, stronger than usual at night and she wondered if she should reef the mainsail to lessen the danger of capsizing in a sudden gust. She surveyed the silver-black water ahead, spotted only scattered whitecaps, and decided against reefing. Instead she let out the sheet, pouring some of the wind from the sail. The heeling sloop stood more upright, though it raced nearly as fast as she had ever sailed. Pointing her bow toward the North Star, she felt the old exhilaration of piloting her craft in perfect weather.

To the northeast, the Big Dipper had fully risen out of the sea: the dolphin was dancing on its tail.

Peering over her shoulder, she cast a weather eye eastward: the stars were clear above the entire horizon. She recognized the crescent of Leo's mane, and the triangle of his haunches and tail, as the lion began its hunt across the January heavens.

Facing south over the stern, she admired the brightest star in the sky, the eye of the great hound. Her own crippled hound was— No, she would think no more of him.

To the southwest, Orion's belt. And the horns of the bull that seemed to toss the half-moon. Leaning down to peek under the boom, she could see, faintly, the tail of Pegasus, low on the misty western horizon.

Leaning back and looking straight overhead, she smiled up at Capella, the queen of winter, shining in resplendent majesty.

She felt cheered by her old friends. She would teach her children to know the stars, well enough that they could glimpse a patch of sky through a hole in the clouds and know exactly which direction they were sailing.

The captain turned once more toward the bow, tiller and sheet comfortably in her hands. She would watch through the night as the dolphin jumped over Polaris.

She should have noticed when the stars to windward disappeared behind a black shroud. Had the weather come from any other direction than east-northeast, she would have felt a change in the wind. But the front did not precede a slough of low pressure from the south, nor a high of cool weather from the north; this storm rode on the trade winds as it swept the water wild beneath it. She should have glanced behind her. But as she yawned, her eyes watering, she sailed more and more by automatic reflex.

A gust shook her sails and heeled the boat sharply; mechanically she let out the sheet. Now miles beyond Buck Island, she rode the giant rolling black swells: the sloop rose up their rounded backs until sky arched over water, then dropped into their deep troughs until water cupped under the sky: up and down, up and down, with the hypnotic gentleness of a cradle. A gust buffeted the sails, shaking the mast. Waiting until she lifted to the crest of the next wave, she looked groggily over her shoulder— She sat up with shock, for the whole eastern sky was black, flashing with thunderbolts. Moonlit whitecaps drove toward her like a stampede of white horses. "Meh great God!" she whispered, her hands gripping tightly the sheet and tiller.

Get the mainsail down! She could try to run with the wind on just the jib. Glancing back at St. Croix, a distant string of lights, she saw she had plenty of open water no matter which direction she blew. If she could keep from capsizing.

She nosed the sloop nearly straight into the blustering wind so the mainsail, flapping like a frenzied ghost, trailed over the hull. One hand on the tiller, she shifted forward, stretched her arm to the mast and uncleated the halyard. Steering the bucking boat as best she could—the stampede now five, six hundred yards away—she grabbed at the sail and struggled to haul it down the mast. As the wind rose, the sail thrashed so crazily it threatened, if it touched her, to lash the skin off her face.

Gusts bludgeoned the jib; the sloop swung broadside and rocked in the chop to the point of capsizing had she not abandoned the mainsail and thrown her weight onto the gunnel. No choice now but to run. She yanked the jib's sheet from its jam cleat, let out half a yard and re-cleated. Then tillered hard and swung her tail to the blast: the bellied jib pulled the sloop with reassuring steadiness. If, when the squall hit, the old dacron didn't explode into rags.

A third of the mainsail was still up on the mast and wrapped in a tangle in the rigging. The bottom portion, caught from behind, struggled against the boom that jumped and clunked on the deck. Pellets of cold rain stung her back as she clawed at the sail until finally her bruised fingers wrapped around its peak. But before she could get the mass tucked beneath the boom, the wind grabbed it from her hand: the sail sprang into the air, flailed like a crazed banshee, then as suddenly dropped limp into the sea. Where it would soon tangle in her rudder.

A desperate glance over the stern at the seething front: two hundred yards, half a minute at most. No choice but to cut away the mainsail, get free of it. She grabbed the knife from its sheath taped to the tiller. Stretching her arms from tiller to mast, heaving her weight to hold her balance in the hurtling vessel, she cut the halyard's cleated end. Clamped the blade between her teeth and yanked out the tack pin at the front of the boom. Took the blade from her teeth and cut the outhaul at the back of the boom. Sheathed the knife. Tugged the foot of the sail along its track in the boom. Or should she just throw the boom overboard, taking the sail with it? Rage rising in her, she refused to throw away her boom. Where the hell was her jib man? She tongue-lashed him with every sailor's curse she knew until finally she freed the sail and heaved it over the gunnel: it disappeared quickly behind, a drowning ghost, clear of the rudder. She dropped the boom into the hull. A brief moment of satisfaction: she had managed. Boat was trim.

By the roar behind her, she knew the squall was seconds away. Checked forward: jib straining as if it would break loose and flee. She knelt by the tiller, weight low. Tried to look back but the rain—

A fist of wind punched the jib. The stern heaved up and the hull convulsed as if it would shake into pieces. The mast tossed against its rigging. Her feet hooked under the strap, one hand clamped on the gunnel, one on the useless tiller to the airborne rudder, she looked down and saw the prow was submerged in boiling water. The sloop seemed about to pinwheel. But the stern dropped with a hard smack, the tiller clubbed her across the ribs. The aluminum mast bowed as if it would snap in half and the sloop shot forward like a tiny skiff bound by its harpoon line to a raging whale.

Wind shrieked through the rigging like a choir of demons. The centerboard vibrated, sending quivers through the hull. Water sloshed over the stern, but she saw before the moon was quenched that the drain was sucking valiantly. Rain pummeled her in horizontal sheets, and when she tasted salt, she knew the water had been whipped from the sea itself. Lightning exploded so close overhead, she was certain it must jab at her mast and fry her where she knelt in a growing pool of water. In those crackling moments, the black sea turned to white-spattered blue, and her hull—like a boat in a dream—shone bright red. Thunder crashed down with a battering roar. She could do nothing more than battle with the tiller to keep from broaching, while her heart pounded with stark terror.

The rigging screamed at a wavering pitch. If one shroud snapped, the mast would topple and the next wave would waterfall into the boat and bury it.

Knees banged on the deck, deck hammered against knees. Sloop like a runaway sled racing down a mountainside of rock.

But the jib held. The mast held. The drain guzzled. Despite the sodden, salty hair wrapped by the wind around her face, and her throbbing knees, and aching arm fighting with the tiller to hold the boat steady, she grinned, and wished her children could see their mother now.

And then her thoughts burst free, clear of the tangled webs cast upon her on shore; her mind soared with clarity and streamlined ease over the petty quandaries and shabby impediments. Pop? If Ah can handle Hurricane Beulah, Ah can damn well handle Pop. He ain' got no right to come between me and meh children.

And Zosia. Didn't Zosia fight every day? Didn't she have the option any time she wanted to join Piotr? And for what did she struggle? For sponge paintings of sunsets and fish? No, she achin' to cup her hand over meh fat belly. And here Ah be, riskin' the one t'ing keepin' her alive.

She felt a stab of guilt.

But she tossed it off, turned her thoughts to Karl. He ain' mind kids with dark skin and curly hair. He say so hisself. That mahn love me. He say so hisself. The boy, he love his family, but the mahn, he love me.

A comber broke over the stern: its warm water engulfed her and nearly swept her from the tiller. "Noooo!" she protested, determined that nothing would keep her from reaching home, even if she had to swim from a swamped boat.

But the sloop did not swamp; it plunged onward, heavy and awkward, its mast bent even further in the flashes of silver rain, while the drain gradually purged all but a few inches.

War, that was something else. Pop she'd slap in the face if she needed to, but impossible to slap away the ships at the pier. The radar, the sonar. The missiles from Moscow. Nevertheless, she could do better. She sucked her teeth at her pitiful collapse in the classroom. Gon' whip that course into shape. Gon' move into the auditorium and fill it to burstin'. Karl want senators from the legislature in the class. But he tinkin' small. Ah gon' *be* a senator. Yeah mahn, Ah gon' run for governor. May not win, but this candidate gon' tell the people loud and clear they deserve an island just as safe as a DeKalb cornfield.

Though her teeth chattered from the cold rain and whipping wind, her mind dwelled on the possibility of running for governor, and as that path opened before her, she felt a measure of hope, a determined hope she had not known since she received that devastating letter from Nick in Vietnam. Leroy, she thought, now yo' watch what yo' sister can do.

And Nick? Poor Nick. Meh battered and broken hero who never healed. Will yo' campaign for me, Nick? Will yo' knock on doors in Frederiksted? Will yo' invite me to speak in yo' high school history class? Will yo' shake Karl's hand? Will yo'? Will yo'? Ah wish Ah knew.

Ah believe in yo', Nick. Ah remember yo' magic on that basketball court. We used to say when the ball left Nick's fingers, it be headin' home to the hoop like a chicken to roost. Swoosh!

The furies in the rigging slowly diminished their cries. Thunder rumbled further to the west. Stinging drops became a finer rain falling from above. The mast straightened slightly. The sea darkened, no longer carpeted with froth, but streaked with horses' manes, as the squall settled into a downpour.

And Ulysses. There was no magic for Ulysses, no decision, no determination that could alter the senseless fate that awaited him. But it wouldn't be on that stainless steel table. The vet would understand. Ah gon' ask Red if he give me a hypodermic and whatever serum he use. Ah a nurse, he trust me. Ah take meh handsome hound down to the beach in the evening and build a driftwood fire. Grill some hamburger, hide tranquilizers in it and give Ulysses a feast. He fall asleep with me right there beside him, sea birds twitterin' in his dreams. Then Ah . . . No, maybe Karl . . . give him the shot. Karl can yo' do that for me?

When?

Ah tink meh prancin' pirate deserve a full moon. Next full moon in a week. Too soon, too soon. Then, full moon at the end of February. Six weeks, Red said. All right. A campfire and a picnic, and a moon for magic.

Her mind quieted; she felt an overwhelming sleepiness. Despite the puddle she knelt in, she ached to lie down on the deck and sleep. She wondered if the wind would yet allow her to hook south toward St. Croix. She would have to bring the jib across from port to starboard. She yawned at the thought of so much effort.

But it was either that or breakfast in Puerto Rico. She shifted forward, scuffing her knees—Could she ever wear these white hospital pants again?—until she was able to gather both jib sheets into her hand. She tillered enough to port that the wind threw the jib across, jolting the sloop. She set the sheet for a broad reach. Shifted aft, changed hands on the tiller—her fingers so cramped she could hardly let go—then brought her vessel perpendicular to the wind, homeward bound.

But how far west had she blown? Would she see the lights of St. Croix, or would she sail in the rain past the west end of the island? What if another squall hit? Did she have the strength to fight it? Did she have a choice?

Next time, she promised herself, Ah gon' bring meh jib mahn. She imagined his gentle eyes, his ready smile. She thought with sudden inspiration, He need a beard! Meh Viking need a big bushy—

A wave slapped the broadside boat, drenching her anew. Her whole body was shivering now, her teeth chattering so hard she had to clench them or it seemed they would batter themselves to pieces. Ooooooh, Ah gon' sleep when Ah get home. Ah gon' sleep till chicken dinner on Sunday.

The drizzle diminished to a mist. The wind punched only occasionally at her sail, and she knew she was nearing the edge of the storm. But she could see neither lights ahead of her, nor stars overhead. Not even a glow from the moon behind the clouds. An immense soggy blanket had been laid over the world.

She heard something. A distant beating whirr. She listened sharply as the sound grew louder. Then she spied a blinking light below the clouds, a quarter mile away, moving slowly across her bow. A helicopter! Searching for her? Then certainly she should help to make herself found. Her flare kit was in the hold, too far to reach with a hand on the tiller. Damn, Ah need meh jib mahn!

She brought her bow close to the wind; the jib snapped as if scolding her for interrupting its steady journey home. She scrambled forward, turned the toggles and removed the hatch, then felt with anxious fingers in the lightless cave until she found the round plastic cylinder of her flare kit. She scurried back to the tiller and fell off the wind to the south again, the petulant jib immediately quiet. The helicopter droned into the distance. Her leg over the tiller, she opened the canister, took out the pistol, loaded it, aimed toward the dim light blinking in the mist, and fired. A red meteor arched across the gray heavens.

The blinking light hovered, angled, came straight toward her! Beneath it, a spotlight shone down: a circle of steel-gray water swept across the sea toward her. Then the circle of light enveloped the red sloop so she seemed to sail on a stage. The helicopter hovered well above her, though the jib luffed in its downdraft. A voice called through an electronic megaphone, "—ited Stated Coast Guard. Do you wish to abandon ship? We can lower a basket to you."

No mahn! Mother Nielsen bringin' this ship to port, all hands safe. Squinting into the sun-bright beam, she waved that she was fine; then she swung her arm like a compass needle, asking for directions.

The strong male voice called down, "You are six nautical miles north of Hamm's Bluff lighthouse."

Only six! She could keep herself awake that long.

"Your present course will bring you west of Frederiksted. We'll radio for an escort."

Escort? If the damn Navy tink they gon' assist this poor helpless girl to shore, they—

"Do you need medical attention?"

She shook her head, then held up her hand with the 'okay' sign.

"Roger. Will follow until escort arrives."

The spotlight disappeared and the night engulfed her again. The helicopter rose several hundred feet and followed off her stern where its wind no longer disturbed her sail.

As she stared ahead into the gloom, she had a vague sense that she had been thinking about something nice before the Coast Guard, though she couldn't think what it was except it had something to do with Karl. Her drifting thoughts recalled her swim with him to the sandbar, his shy, cautious kiss. Her own hesitation at touching the lips of a white man.

An engine thrummed in the distance. A red light appeared, faint in the rainy night: the portside lamp of a vessel heading north on a course that would miss her. Her guardian angel swooped down, hovered over- head and lit the red sloop in a circle of daytime brightness.

Now she saw, peering into the darkness beyond the cone of light, a green lamp joining the red as the boat swung toward her.

A fishing boat, vaguely familiar, swung broadside and motored ten yards from her. Karl's face was in the cabin window!

He disappeared from the wheelhouse. She could see another man at the wheel, someone she knew but could not remember.

"Angelique!" called Karl's beautiful voice from the stern. "Are you all right?" The helicopter's beam spread until it encompassed both boats and she could see Karl, his face a fervent mix of worry and relief, his turquoise shirt the one he had worn in the classroom.

Her heart beat with joy. "Yes. I have so much to tell you."

"Raphael says you're about five-six miles out from the island. Do you want me to come aboard?"

"Now? I suppose you want to sit at the tiller and sail to the pier so you can tell tales about the typhoon you come through."

He was laughing. Then he called, "Angelique, I love you. No man ever loved a woman more."

"Karl," she called back. But she hesitated, unsure what to say, for he had to answer to her children first. Prove it to me: that they have priority over Pop.

"Where's your life jacket?" he asked, scolding her.

"It's . . ." It was in the hold, but she was too tired to say so.

The searchlight vanished. The beating whirr grew fainter. She waved her thanks as the blinking light swept west—perhaps to Puerto Rico.

Little of the rest of the trip was she aware of, except that a few of the brighter stars appeared, for a minute or two the hazy shape of Leo prowling south. The Hamm's Bluff lighthouse winked at her. And there was a cluster of houses on the coast. But the people must be sleeping, it was so late, so they were sleeping, how nice to be sleeping.

Keeping her eyes open, she gazed at the string of amber streetlights along the pier. Yo' fishin' tonight, Chess? Yo' ain' to be up so late. Rosemary got to watch yo' better.

She realized there were other boats around her, people shouting questions at her. A spotlight shone on her white uniform, the beam so bright it hurt her eyes. "Turn out yo' damn light!" It disappeared.

Her jib undulated lazily like a dancing ghost. In the lee of the island. Sloop wallowed in the calm water like a sleepy sloop.

Karl reached with a boathook for her painter. "Going to tow you to the beach, Angel. You've come as far as you can."

How smoothly the sloop glided. Staring dully at the jib, she decided it could stay up. With a surge of conscious thought, she whispered, "Thank you," bestowing her gratitude on that proud white flag of survival.

A destroyer was anchored near the end of the pier, its twin radar towers bristling into the night. She smiled with her secret. Make way for the governor. Next time, yo' boys gon' salute.

On the end of the pier stood a crowd; people waved and called her name. She heard Chester's voice and raised her heavy arm to wave back. The crowd moved along the pier as the trawler towed her toward the beach. Many in the throng hurried ahead to meet her at the shore.

One person she recognized as he waded into the water, his arms reaching toward her as the sloop glided the last few feet toward the sand. "Papa," she called, able to see his face by the lights on the pier, his eyes filled with anguish and love, tears gleaming down his cheeks. "Papa," she said again as his strong arms scooped her from the gunnel. And then, in the safest place in all the world, her Papa's arms, she slept.

PART THREE

CHAPTER TWENTY-FOUR

Children of the Sun

Karl carried Ulysses up the steps of Nielsens' yellow gingerbread verandah. Zosia thumped her cane beside him, one hand clutching his arm as she stared toward the door. Ulysses cocked his ears when the knob turned.

Angelique stepped out in a red sarong tied above her breasts, her arms and shoulders bare; she greeted them with a smile Karl would never forget. She wrapped her arms around Zosia, who dropped her cane. Karl set Ulysses down on the porch, picked up the cane, then waited his turn while Angelique knelt and hugged her unsteady dog, his bushy tail sweeping the air.

Now she stood and looked at him, her face a mix of churning emotions, her eyes steadfast and clear with love. "Karl," she whispered.

"My Angelique." They kissed, and he knew without questions and answers and lengthy explanations, all of which he had prepared, that she was his woman and he was her man. Forever.

Out the door came Estelle and Nat, their eyes on Karl, the man who had brought their daughter home. Last night, by the time he had come ashore, they had taken Angelique into the house, and he decided not to disturb them. But now Estelle squeezed him with a long hug of gratitude; and Nat shook his hand, and then held it, firmly gripped, as if unwilling to let go. Karl saw in their eyes that they knew they had come close to losing a second child—and that they credited him with her rescue. "Come in, come in," said Nat. "Yo' girl just woke up a hour ago."

While Estelle readied dinner in the kitchen, and Karl and Nat sat talking in the living room, Angelique led Zosia out the back door into the yard. Karl glanced from a window at the two friends sitting on a bench: Angelique wrapped her arm around Zosia's thin shoulders; the faces of the two women were close as they looked up, Zosia pointing, perhaps at the first evening star.

It wasn't until after dinner, when Angelique led Karl by the hand out the back door, that he finally had a chance to talk with her alone. "Angelique, if . . . if we have a wedding, then I want you to know that you can invite whomever you want, and not invite whomever you don't want. Yeah, their feelings will be hurt, but it's your feelings I care about."

She cocked her head with confidence. "Never mind about Pop. I can handle him. I want him to come. And your mother. The whole family."

"You do?"

"Yes. If there are problems, I think we all care enough to solve them."

He nodded with assurance. "I'm certain we all care enough."

Suddenly, half the battle was won. If the portrait of the two of them did the trick—and really, why shouldn't his parents, after a little thought perhaps, write back with their blessing—then he and Angelique would have the most beautiful wedding, with everyone there, getting to know each other, discovering that really, after all, folks were folks, and good folks at that.

The air smelled earthy; a breeze drifted into town from the damp mahogany forest. Something flapped overhead; he looked up and discovered a flock of egrets gliding over the roof of her house, their white wings spread against the stars. Like a flock of angels just off work, they landed overhead in the branches of a huge kapok tree.

He heard her say, flirtatiously, "But you haven't asked me yet."

He knew he did not deserve her, but that he would work in the years ahead to make his life worthy of such a woman. "My beloved Angelique, will you marry me?"

Beauty born of joy shone in her face. "Yes, Karl Jacobsen, with all my heart, I wish to marry you."

They kissed with such passion that had they been alone, they would have spread her sarong on the grass and let the fecund breath of the forest caress them as they lay in the warm darkness and loved. But Mama's song and Papa's laughter trailed out the window.

He knew his own mother and father would need some time. A month certainly, two to be safe. Nearly the end of January now. February, March. But Angelique would spend February with Ulysses. Why rush things? And let's give Zosia something to look forward to. He suggested, "June is the month for weddings."

She thought for a moment. "When is the full moon in June? You said you wanted the reception at the Botanical Gardens. Think of our guests dancing to a steel drum band with billows of flowers wrapped around us in the moonlight!"

He took out his wallet, found a little plastic calendar and held it so he could read it by the glow from a window. "Full moon on the twenty-fifth. But that's a Sunday. Saturday night would be just as bright. What do you think about Saturday the twenty-fourth of June as the date of your wedding?"

"Perfect."

He gazed at her, then shook his head. "No, I can't wait a whole five months to tell you. . . ." He put away his calendar, then reached for her hands. "Angelique, I honor you, and cherish you, in sickness and in health, through rich and through poor, until death do us part."

"Until death do us part?"

He promised, "Until the very end."

They pressed their lips with a kiss that promised many more kisses over many, many years.

Then she asked excitedly, "Shall we tell Mama and Papa?"

"No. First I must ask them for your hand in marriage."

She smiled, pleased. "You will?"

"As a show of respect."

When they entered the living room, holding hands, unable to repress their tattletale smiles, the conversation ceased. Zosia's sharp eyes looked back and forth between them.

With respect in his voice and dignity in his bearing, Karl addressed the parents of the woman he loved. "Estelle, and Nat, I would like to ask you for the hand of your daughter in marriage."

Nat stood up, the wicker rocking chair still in motion behind him as he reached out his hand. "Son, ain' no mahn on earth we rather have to join the family. Yo' have our most heartfelt blessin'."

"Amen," said Estelle, smiling at the verge of tears.

The two men shook: the hands that had held the hymnal in church now gripped together in silent promise of mutual support, mutual love.

"Hurrah!" cheered Zosia. "When's the wedding?"

Angelique announced, "June twenty-fourth."

"In church?" asked Estelle, worried.

Angelique hesitated; Karl stated firmly, "Yes, in your church."

"A toast!" proclaimed Nat. "Mama, ain' we got a bottle of Cruzan rum in dis household?"

Following the service on Sunday, Father Abrams held Karl's camera and took a picture of the entire family on the church steps. Karl and Angelique stood in the middle of the group, she in her choir robe, he in his coat and tie. Zosia kept grinning at them; Angelique, giggling, told Zosia to turn around and face the camera.

CLICK.

Then Nat took the camera while his daughter and future son-in-law stood in front of a sunlit bougainvillea bush. Karl held Angelique's hand; they smiled shyly.

"That's no good," complained Zosia. "You look as stiff as a couple of clothespins."

So he put his arm around her shoulder, she put her arm around his waist.

Then she whispered, "Tonight on the beach, nine o'clock, full moon. Is it a date?"

"A hot date?" he inquired.

"A hot date," she affirmed, her bright eyes full of promise.

He grinned, profoundly happy. "It's a date."

CLICK.

On the way to work Monday morning, he stopped in Christiansted to drop off the film for processing. Standing at the counter, he held the yellow film can on the palm of his hand as if it were a nugget of gold. "Ten dollars extra if you can have the prints ready by tomorrow morning at eight."

On Tuesday morning, he sorted quickly through the three-by-five prints—pictures of his cottage, of Angelique's stone house, Zosia's house, Ulysses wearing his bandana on the beach—until he came to the picture of the Nielsen family on the church steps. Good, good, great! Gosh, it's good of everyone. Look at Zosia, what an imp.

Then he turned to the next photograph: the portrait. "Perfect," he whispered with elation as he admired the bright-eyed beauty standing beside him. "Who could possibly disapprove of such a lovely woman?"

He hurried to the post office. He had his letter ready. He described her as a nurse, a member of the choir, a devoted daughter. He mentioned that her family too had lost a son in Vietnam. He concluded,

Angelique and I plan to marry in June, and we ask your blessing. I'll

phone you on Sunday evening, February 12th, so we can discuss plans. We'd like you to come down for at least a week before the wedding, so you can meet the Nielsens, and enjoy our tropical paradise.
Your loving son,
Karl

His hands were trembling as he folded both the portrait and the family photo into the letter. At the post office window, he laid the envelope on the counter. "Special delivery, registered mail, please." His heart thumped as he watched the postmaster affix the stamps, then cancel them with a BANG-BANG, and toss the letter into a gray sack. Stepping out the post office door into the sunshine, he thought, That phone call is either going to be terrific, or sheer disaster.

During her last month with Ulysses, Angelique wanted to be with him as much as possible. She changed her schedule from the night to the day shift; she wanted to be with her dog on the beach during the cool evenings for as late as they might like to be together, without her having to shower and dress and ride off to work. She wanted him to know, though he could no longer chase the birds, that every evening he could at least lie near the waves and sniff the wind, watch up and down the shore, and cock his ears at the occasional twittering of his old friends.

She needed those evenings, just the two of them, apart from the complications of daily life—and the inappropriate joy of wedding plans—so she could sing his name and run her hand through his fur; and in the simplicity of beach and sea and comforting stars, hold in her grief so that he could not guess that their time together was soon over.

She was doubly surprised, as she walked across the hospital parking lot, to discover Nick sitting on her scooter. She had not seen him since November, nearly three months ago. And how had he known she was working the day shift now? Was he spying on her again?

He greeted her with a cordial smile, but strange eyes. "Hello, Sugah."

She stopped several feet from him and stood stiffly, waiting for his explanation.

But he offered no explanation, no apology. He told her, as if it were excuse enough to take him back, "Ah miss yo', Sugah."

"Get off meh scooter, Nick." His station wagon was parked nearby.

"Angelique, yo' meh whole world."

It was fear that she saw in his eyes, the fright of a lost child; and a trace of desperation that she heard in his voice.

"No, Nick. Yo' t'row me out. But Ah already left when Ah see that knife. Ah see yo' never-endin' hate. And Ah see yo' shamin' me when Ah ain' but just met the mahn."

"Ah sorry, Sugah. Ah got so crazy angry. Please, Ah sorry. Can't we please try again?"

"Yo' left the island with no good-bye to me."

He dropped his eyes, a silent admission that he had deserted her.

Then he pleaded, "Angelique, Ah tryin' meh best. Ah takin' four courses at the University, and Ah just devourin' them books. Listen, if we could start again, maybe yo' could help me with meh first paper. Ah mean, Ah can write it all right, but if yo' could read t'rough it and fix the mistakes—"

She interrupted, "Ah loved yo', Nick. And in a way, Ah will always love yo'. But Ah ain' the right woman for yo'. Ah too close to Leroy. Yo' need a woman who can let yo' start fresh." He reached for her hand; she stepped back. "Ah hope yo' find her. And Ah know yo' can, if yo' set yo' sights on Nicholas the college graduate, Nicholas the teacher. Them kids at Central High be achin' for teachers who be strong, for teachers who love them with a big, big heart. That be yo', Nicholas Cruz. Oh, what a wonderful mahn yo' can be."

"Angelique, Ah sorry! Ah askin' yo' to forgive me. Ah promise, in the future, Ah gon' treat yo' the way yo' deserve."

"No, Nick. We ain' got any future. Except, Ah hope, as friends."

"Yo' . . . Yo' still with that white boy?"

Hearing him sneer, she wondered how she had ever lasted a year and a half with him. She ended his fantasies by stating the truth, "Ah love Karl."

He regarded her with sudden contempt, his suspicion confirmed. "So yo' been with the whigger all along. Ever since that first little nap on Buck Island."

"No!" But she did not want to argue about her integrity; she wanted him to know—so he could believe he had been worthy of it—that she had loved him. "How can yo' possibly t'ink Ah suddenly change from yo' lovin' woman to somebody else? Ah ain' change at all. Ah loved yo' and loved yo' and *loved* yo'. Then Ah spent one day happy as a kid out sailin', and yo' take a notion yo' got to destroy everytin' beautiful we share together. Why, Nick, why?"

His face frozen, he stood up from her scooter, swung his leg over the seat and stepped away. Never had she seen his pain and rage as intense as in the eyes that hated her now. "Don' blame Karl," she warned. "He ain' responsible for what happen in yo' life. Nick, he lost his brother in Vietnam. Ah tried to tell yo' that once, but yo' ain' listen. Ah tellin' yo' now: Karl feel the pain too. So Nick, don' blame Karl."

She put her bag in the luggage basket, sat on her scooter and kick-started the engine. Then she tried one last time to console him, "Nick, yo' always in meh heart."

As she rode away, her stomach knotted with dread. She wondered if he would hurt Leroy's little sister. Or the man she had chosen to be the father of her children.

If he ever tried, he'd find himself faced with a mother lion.

Petrox refused to give Karl one day a week off, so he was forced to experiment with his Crucian Cooker on Saturdays. He had a big row with Ed, but Ed kept fending off by saying, "Hey, don't blame me, blame the guys at the home office." So Karl phoned New York and argued with an assistant director of personnel, who told him if he didn't want the job, "full-time, no ifs, ands or buts, there's plenty of double-E's fresh out of college who do."

Making the best of it, he set up shop in the old carriage house beneath Angelique's apartment. He uncrated a pair of shiny aluminum dishes, one of them five feet in diameter, one ten inches, which he had ordered from a professor at Cornell who was glad to find a co-researcher in the sunny tropics. As he assembled the prototype in the driveway, the sun shining off the big dish was so intense that he had to wear extra-dark sunglasses, and coat his chest and arms and face and poor pink peeling nose with a heavy dose of coconut oil sunscreen.

Ulysses lay curled in the shade in the garage. Earlier Karl had given him a bath—for the dog had tried to lift his leg and tumbled and peed on himself—then had brushed his coat, so Ulysses was especially fluffy.

"What's your preference, sir?" asked Karl while he tightened a nut. "T-bone, porterhouse or a nice tenderloin? T-bone it is. And how would you like your order prepared, sir? Rare, medium, or well-done? Tartar! Listen, fella, there's no point in my putting this thingamabob together if you don't want you steak cooked at least a little bit. Tell you what, how about a poached pelican?"

*   *   *

As Angelique crossed the driveway on her way to Zosia's house, she paused to watch Karl in a bathing suit, his muscular body gleaming with suntan oil and sweat, as he fitted the smaller mirror onto a tripod attached to the larger dish. Intrigued by the apparatus, she asked, "How are you doing?"

The dark sunglasses glanced at her. "Fine, if the first thing I cook isn't myself."

"Why don't you work in the garage?"

"Because," he tipped his head back and looked straight up at the blazing sun overhead, "that's my business partner up there, and I'm getting to know just how powerful he is. Ninety-three million miles away, takes eight minutes for a beam of light to reach us, and yet the transportation cost anywhere on earth is absolutely zero. He's doing his job. Now it's up to me to figure out what to do with this bowl of sunshine."

"Do you need any help?"

"Just keep your eye on that wolf in the garage. He's hoping I'll turn into a strip of bacon."

Feeling strangely restless, she continued with her basket of clean laundry to Zosia's. Entering the house, she was shocked to find Zosia sitting on a step half-way up the stairs to her studio. She was wheezing badly, pumping her shoulders for breath.

"Zosia! What are you doing up there?"

"I'm . . ." Puffing so hard, she could barely talk. "I'm climbing the Alps." Then she pushed with her arms and legs and lifted her bottom to the next step.

Angelique hurried up to her. "But why?" She and Karl had brought Zosia's painting supplies down to the living room so she would stay off those stairs.

Zosia gasped, "I'm out of . . . Vandyke brown . . . . I think I have a . . . tube in one . . . of the drawers." She lifted herself up another step.

"But I can get it for you."

"Nogh!" Zosia snapped with angry defiance. "I climb . . . these steps myself."

Though Angelique argued with her, Zosia would not allow her to climb past to fetch the tube of paint. Her red shorts caked with dust, the artist persevered, pushing herself up another step.

The bride-to-be thought, Nearly five months to the wedding. And then at least another nine months. What right do we have to ask her to wait those extra five months? We're stealing five months of her time with that child, while she's struggling with every bit of fight she's got just to survive until the baby's born.

Angelique knew her timetable as well as any woman: she'd gotten her last period on the day she found Pop's postcard. That was a Saturday, today was a Saturday, two weeks exactly. Now she knew why she felt so restless. She was ripe.

When she returned to the sunshine in the driveway, she told Karl about Zosia on the stairs. He smiled with admiration. "She's a case. And did she find the brown paint?"

"Of course. It was behind an old rag in the back of a drawer. She said she had to have it for the brown in the young pelicans."

"Right. She showed me the other day out on her porch, the adults have yellow heads, but the juveniles—"

"Karl, she's getting worse. Fast."

Struck by the seriousness of what she was saying, he asked, "Will she make it to the wedding?"

"Yes, I think so. She's already planning to wear red and white frangipani in her hair. But it's not the wedding I'm thinking about. It's the baby."

He took off his sunglasses, but he did not meet her eyes; he stared down at the pavement. Finally he looked up and asked, "Shall we reschedule the wedding to an earlier date?"

"Or," she studied him closely, "have a child four months after the wedding."

He walked into the garage and set his glasses and wrench on a workbench. She warned him, "Both of us must have no regrets. No second thoughts because of our families."

He turned to her, fifteen feet between them. "Zosia, your parents, my parents, yes. But what do *you* want?"

What she wanted, she had realized only minutes ago, with absolute certainty. "Karl, I was fourteen when Leroy disappeared. Today I am thirty-two. For eighteen years, more than half my life, I've been angry and bitter and afraid. I've been a victim of that war for almost as long as Leroy was alive on this earth. But now I've met another victim, who sat with me in that empty classroom and promised to help me fill it. And," she pointed into the glare of the curved mirror that cast its heat onto her body and made her sweat, "who wants to help people do something better than cut down their last tree." She paused, to let him know how much her love was based on respect. Then she told him, "So I don't want to wait any longer."

She watched him walk toward her; saw his green eyes lit by the sunshine; felt his hand on her cheek. He said, "I don't want to wait any longer."

"Certain?"

"Certain."

He picked her up in her sea-blue sarong and carried her up the steps and through her house to the back porch. He brought out the mattress and lay it in the hot sunshine. She untied the knot of her sarong and shook out the cloth so that it settled in a blue billow over the mattress. He slipped off his bathing suit.

This time, she thought with joy, no diaphragm.

She felt as if her breasts would melt into his hands, that her thighs would melt around his muscular leg, that her fingers would dig molten furrows across his slippery back. She rubbed her breasts against him, until they were covered with coconut oil and sweat from his chest. The blue sarong stuck to them, wrapped around them as they entwined; they tossed the cloth off and stretched their limbs in and out of each other's grip. He teased her until she was turning inside out, chasing him with her hips, grappling with him with her legs and holding him prisoner until she almost had him. Then he escaped, but caressed her with his knowing hand until she lifted her hips toward the blazing sun for release, for release.

The sun shone through his tussled halo of blond hair. The sun warmed his strong shoulders, his powerful back. And then the sun seemed to pierce her loins with a good strong hot beam. She rode on that beam of sunshine, let it call forth the tiny creature whom it would bless.

They dozed, side by side, his lips still touching her cheek, in the beneficent heat of the midday sun.

When she awoke, the cool seagrape shadows had spread across them. Karl slept heavily beside her. She worked her fingers into his sun-bleached hair, kissed his temple. She could not say how she knew, but she knew for certain.

She gazed up into the deep blue heavens. Leroy, yo' want to know a secret? She whispered the news, her brother the first to know. "Ah'm carryin' a chile."

CHAPTER TWENTY-FIVE

Debate

When Karl phoned home on Lincoln's Birthday, he hoped to receive his parents' blessing. He did not. His mother wept, his father exploded with rage. "Is this some joke?" roared Pop. "Your wanting to marry a nigger girl?"

Karl was too devastated to speak. His mind had been optimistically brimming with the details of wedding plans, plane reservations, hotel rooms for aunts and uncles and cousins, formal suits and bathing suits. As his father's ugly words sledge-hammered his dream into shattered ruins, he was unable to muster any sort of argument.

His mouth dry, his hands shaking, his heart pounding with despair and reciprocal rage, he stared out his window at Angelique's house, her lights on, her open front door a golden rectangle. Abruptly he told his father and mother, "All right then. You just lost a son."

He hung up.

Several hours passed that evening—he phoned Angelique, then Zosia, to say he wasn't feeling well, a touch of the flu, so he wouldn't be coming down for dinner—before he was calm enough to compose a letter that he would mail in the morning.

Above the fruited plain

Dear Mom and Dad,

I couldn't help but overhear your phone conversation with Karl, and I thought that despite the great distance, I should try to get in touch with you. Maybe it's easier to understand things from up here, looking down at the entire continent, rather than just at the cornfields and pastureland of the farm. Time is different here too. It's not Monday morning milking time, or Saturday chores in town. As we view the land from sea to shining

215

sea, so we mark time in terms of centuries. And we regard people not as friends and neighbors inside DeKalb County, but as
peoples: tribes and races and entire civilizations that march
past in a parade far more fascinating than those little flag-
waving shindigs you have marching up Lincoln Highway on
Memorial Day.

And of course I'm no longer bothered with what the neighbors might think about some scandal in the family. No, I spend
my time hobnobbing with people whose minds travel much
broader horizons. Really I'm quite fortunate, given the company I'm able to keep up here. Seems it's an American tradition
that so many who had something to say, got shot. Just the other
day I was listening in on a conversation between old Abe, who
doesn't look so old and tired any more, now that the pressure's
off, and a much younger man—only thirty-nine when he had to
say good-bye—named Martin. The two were sitting on the top
rail of a fence, enjoying the sunshine and just talkin' as folks
do. Abe was asking questions about life in the South, how it
was coming along. And Martin, who had such difficulties in
Illinois—you remember, Mom and Dad, I'm sure, the riots in
Cicero, that quiet little northside suburb, where Martin's head
was bloodied by a rock—well, Martin was asking Abe to explain those folks in Illinois.

When they came to a pause in the conversation, I took the
opportunity to mention Karl's situation, and Angelique's, by
way of asking for some advice. I repeated for them, as best I
could remember, your words on the phone to Karl. It was a sad
moment then, for I saw the old weariness return to Abe's face,
and I was sorry I'd interrupted his tranquility. Martin too
seemed deeply affected, though he didn't look saddened as
much as sickened. Maybe he was worried about his wife and
four children, still down there, a long, long way from Paradise.
Well, I apologized for bringing the matter up, and would have
let the whole thing drop, except that wouldn't do Karl and
Angelique much good. Nor all the rest of you, still fighting
your wars while God Almighty himself, all-knowing as He
may be, shakes his hoary head, puzzled, wondering why on
earth you people keep brutalizing each other.

Abe spoke up first. He asked if the youth and the lass truly

loved each other. I said they did. He was still for a long
moment, maybe harking back to his own courting days with
Ann, a stroll together on an April evening when the sweet
warm air was filled with hope . . . . Well, I can only conjecture,
but for a moment there seemed to be a fond look in his eye, as
if, yes, Abe knew what it was to be a young man in love.

Then he looked up at me and he asked, Did my brother have
the consent of the young woman's parents? I said he did. I told
him about church every Sunday morning, and about the family
dinners on Sunday afternoon.

That's when Martin reached out and touched my arm and
asked, Did they have the blessing of the church? I said they
planned to stand before the altar in June, performing the holy
sacrament of marriage. "And do they wish to live in peace?" he
asked. He gave me a stern look, for I'm still wearing my uniform, you see, with the bullet hole in the chest. I said, "Yes,
they wish no one any harm." "That's not enough!" he retorted,
impatient with me. "It's not enough just to mean others no
harm. A dream is nothing but an empty wish, unless you *build*
that dream." I said—maybe my remark was a little presumptu-
ous, given what these two men had tried to do, given the work
they'd left unfinished—I said I wished I were back down there,
helping to build. But of course that's just empty talk.

Abe took off his stovepipe hat and let the celestial winds
blow through his hair. "Tell the good people on that farm in
Illinois," he said, "that heaven is integrated. If this is where
they want to come when their candle grows short and the flame
is finally snuffed, then they had better be ready for the circum-
stances here. Otherwise," his lean, craggy face looked downward, past the fruited plain, to that fiery territory below, "they
can dwell where brotherhood is a forgotten word."

Martin said, "Amen."

Yours truly,
Joe

Angelique arranged an informational meeting at the hospital for the
staff, where she explained her medical concerns in the case of a military disaster on St. Croix, outlined the course she proposed to teach,
and invited nurses and doctors to present their views to the public. Karl

placed ads in both newspapers, and talked with the guys at work. Angelique spoke with Father Abrams, who made an announcement from the pulpit. Karl contacted the Naval office and invited any servicemen in port on Monday evening, February 13, to attend. Angelique taped a thirty-second community news bulletin, which WSTX aired daily. Zosia phoned old friends and encouraged them to attend. To save Ed the embarrassment of refusing to give him a day off, Karl called in sick, then visited the four high schools on the island, where he talked with principals and teachers, and addressed several highly responsive classes. Angelique talked with people at the University. She wrote a letter to every member of the Virgin Islands Legislature; Karl addressed the envelopes; Zosia paid for the stamps.

On Monday evening, eight o'clock, the classroom was packed. Angelique distributed a syllabus listing books to be covered during the four-month course. Karl handed out fact sheets. But the two co-teachers did not get far with their lesson plan, for a debate broke out between those in the room who "appreciated the security of Uncle Sam's big stick," and those who felt threatened by "the hidden arsenal at our doorstep." The argument became heated, but Karl managed to maintain order with his calm voice, strict neutrality in his brief summation of each argument, and his insistence that everyone have his chance to speak. Angelique was impressed by his ability to referee in front of such a passionate crowd. After two hours, the only agreement reached was that nearly everyone wanted to come back next week to continue the discussion.

When the last of the students and sailors, parishioners and professors and housewives and surgeons and senators had left the classroom, the two teachers collapsed, utterly exhausted, into a couple of empty desks. They looked across the room at Zosia in her wheelchair, backed against a bookcase. Though fifty people had spoken tonight, Zosia had not said a word. She sat up now as proud as a queen, her eyes filled with admiration as she stared at the two of them. "Yagh!" she said with vigor. "That's the America I like to see."

On Saturday the eighteenth, and on Sunday, Monday, Tuesday, and Wednesday, Angelique did something she had never done before in her life: she missed her period.

When her test at the hospital—she swore the gynecologist to absolute secrecy—reported positive, she could wait no longer. Using the

public phone booth in the lobby, where none of the nurses would overhear, she dialed the number at Petrox.

Karl was up on a cracking tower scaffold, drilling into the outer
sheath so he could mount a thermocouple sensor. As he drew out the
spinning bit, clearing the hole of tiny curlicues of steel, he heard a
shout, "Hey, Jacobsen! Phone call, ol' buddy!"

He looked down fifty feet and saw Ed Ashley holding a mobile
telephone. The first thing he thought was a cow had kicked Mom or
Pop, and Sal was phoning to tell him somebody was in the hospital. He
called down anxiously, "Who is it?"

"Woman named Nielsen. Says it's urgent."

Had Zosia fallen and broken her hip? Had Ulysses died? Was
Angelique hurt—crashed on her scooter? "Ed, I'm harnessed in up here.
Let me drop you the basket." He set down the drill, then quickly lowered a wire tool basket on a rope. Ed set the heavy phone in the basket;
Karl hauled up the line arm over arm. He took one of his ear plugs out,
lifted his hard hat to make room for the phone, cupped his hand over
his other ear to block out the roar of the pipes as best he could, then
shouted into the mouthpiece, "Angelique, is everything all right?"

"Happy Father's Day."

"No, it's . . ." He was about to say Washington's Birthday, when he
realized what she was telling him. "Really? It's true? Then, Happy
Mother's Day."

He was in a daze; he heard the rapture in her voice. "Yes," he
agreed, "we'll keep it a secret." A precious egg, hidden from the world.
"Right, we'll wait for the right time to tell her." Time enough, time
enough, no rush. "You feel all right?" He felt a sudden powerful need
to protect her. "Starting tomorrow, you drive the jeep and I ride the
scooter."

She told him she loved him.

"Yes, I love you too."

Then she was gone. And the refinery was round him again.

He lowered the phone down to Ed. "Everything's fine," he called.
"That was a neighbor, with a little good news. Ed, I'll have this thermocouple installed by lunchtime."

Ed hollered up with his Texas twang, "All right, ol' buddy." Then
he laughed. "Bah doggies, I thought it was some gal's mother invitin'
you to a shotgun wedding!"

Karl smiled and waved his thanks.

Before he started drilling again, he stared between the distillation towers at a stretch of blue ocean. Through the stink and the roar, he growled, "Dammit, Pop, is that any way to treat a grandson?"

CHAPTER TWENTY-SIX

The Nest and the Grave

Angelique parked the jeep behind the beach, then turned to Ulysses curled on the passenger seat, his freshly brushed fur lit by the full moon through the windshield. With forced cheerfulness, she asked, "Ulysses, yo' want to go to the *beach*?" He lifted himself with his forelegs to look out the window. She tousled his soft, twitching ears. "The beach, Ulysses." He nudged her arm with his nose: he wanted to get out.

When she opened her door, stepped out and walked around the front of the jeep, she felt her movements were not real; she was following the script of some insane play. As she opened the passenger door, she sang, as much to calm herself as to comfort her dog, "Uuuuuuuuu-lyyyyyyyyseeeeeeeeees." With one arm slung beneath his strong chest, one under his atrophied hindquarters, she lifted him from the seat, then carried him to the beach. Under the coconut palms, the sand was dark with ragged shadows. She felt like Death, bringing the unsuspecting victim to the chopping block.

She carried him beyond the palms, to where the sand was radiant with moonlight.

A wave lifted a gleaming stripe along its crest, then splashed milk-white foam on the shore.

Clouds drifted in stately solemnity over the sea, their flat bottoms dark, their billows blue-white, their bulbous crowns luminous beneath the moon.

She grew increasingly angry, because the night was so soft, so beautiful, so perfect, and so all the more absurd. She and Ulysses should be running along the shore, chasing the turnstones. They should be swimming in the shimmering water. They should be—

But she did not want anger to clutter a time that ought to be pure and peaceful. With an abrupt decision, she banished her rage. And in

221

its place, she felt a sudden gratitude. Yes, the night was perfect, honoring Ulysses with a final magnificent evening. As she carried him, she squeezed him against her heart. "Ulysses, we gon' build a beeyoooooti-ful campfire."

She put him down beside a stack of driftwood she had collected that afternoon. The sticks looked now like a pile of bones. Ulysses sat with his ears perked toward the sea. She asked with a whisper full of suspense, "What yo' see out there? Sea monsters lurkin' in the bay? Yo' keep guard!"

Down the shore stood a cluster of Australian pines, tall and shaggy against the stars. "Ah be right back. Yo' stay. Yo' *stay*." As she walked toward the pines, she often glanced back, for even these last days when his legs quickly collapsed, he would try to follow her, dragging his hindquarters. But tonight he was more interested in watching for birds.

Crouching beneath the boughs, she gathered handfuls of fallen needles. Then she returned to Ulysses and shaped the needles into a hollow mound on the sand. Over this tinder she built a teepee of twigs. When she lit a match, the needles sparked and popped. The orange flame flickered up into the twigs. The smoke smelled sweet. She added larger sticks, one by one, until the campfire blazed, warming her face. Despite Act Two, she was determined that Act One was going to be a celebration.

Sitting with her legs crossed, she straightened his salty, tattered bandana, Karl's gift, and wondered if she should have washed it for tonight. No, Ah want this night to be as normal as possible.

While she tended the fire, and he sat facing the water, she told him stories. About the time when they camped together on the sandbar and she had forgot to pack his dog food in the sloop. "And yo'," she giggled, "yo' had to eat tuna-noodle casserole for dinner. Yo' looked at me like Ah must be crazy to eat such stuff. Ha! "

She recalled their hike through the mahogany forest with Nick, when a downpour soaked them, but afterward rays of sunshine beamed through holes in the jungle canopy, spotlighting the green dripping trees with patches of gold. "Ah ain' never forget that day."

She scratched his chest and told him about the summer they snuck through mangrove trees toward the mud flats at Great Salt Pond. Hundreds of egrets and stilts, herons and avocets were wading in the shallows. "Yo' stayed right by meh side, silent as a tiger. But ooooooooh yo' saw them birds! Ah whispered, 'Okay,' and yo' took off like yo' been shot from a cannon. Yo' galloped, blacker and blacker with mud, until yo' filled the whole sky with them big beautiful birds, sweepin' back and forth in crisscrossin' flocks. Oooooh, yo' been in heaven then!" She blew on his ears, tickling him. He gave her a quick kiss, then continued his sharp-eyed survey of the shoreline. "When there ain' been a single bird left on the ground, yo' come runnin' back to me with yo' tongue hangin' out. But yo' wasn't any dog *Ah* knew. Meh dog been brown, but yo', meh friend, been the blackest creature Ah ever seen! Drippin' with muck. We had to swim in the bay for an hour before yo' come clean. But even then," she brushed her cheek against his soft fur, "it been weeks before yo' stopped stinkin' like that ol' mud flat."

The fire collapsed with a dry crunch; a fountain of sparks joined the stars. Just above the palm thatch, Orion leaned forward as he sprinted across the sky. At his heels leaped his hound with the bright eye. But the constellation was not Orion any more; there was herself running along the shore, and the hunter's sword a stick she was about to throw. Yo' ain' need a marker, Ulysses. Yo' got one already, gon' last me all meh life.

She raked the coals into a circle, placed four conch shells around the periphery and set a wire grill on top of them. Then from her picnic basket she took out a steak, and laid it on the grill over the coals. Ulysses stretched his nose toward the sizzling meat. She asked with an excited voice, "Yo' hungry, Bear. Yo' want yo' *dinner?*" He stared at the feast with eager eyes.

When the sirloin was cooked on both sides, she laid it on a driftwood board and cut it into ten pieces. With the tip of her knife, she slit a pocket in each juicy morsel. Then, her fingers trembling, she reached into the basket, took out a small envelope, and inserted a tranquilizer inside each chunk of warm meat.

Ulysses took the chunks gently from her fingers and gobbled them down. But he spat out two of the pills. Feeling like a traitor, she picked the capsules out of the sand, rinsed them with water from a thermos, then held his lower jaw, placed the pills on the back of his tongue, held his muzzle closed and stroked his throat until he swallowed them.

She filled his bowl with water. He drank thirstily.

A breeze quickened over the beach. The circle of coals glowed brightly. Stroking her dog from his head to his bony hips, she sang his name, "Uuuuulyyyyyysseeeeeeeeeeeees." She wanted him to fall asleep in a peaceful world where everything was the way it was supposed to be. "Uuuulyyyysseeeeeeees."

His head wobbled unsteadily as he gazed with half-closed eyes at the coals.

Karl's dark form emerged from the shadows.

No! she thought desperately. She stopped singing, dug her fingers into Ulysses' fur. She wanted to reach up and grab the swinging pendulum of the moon and cast it into the sea; but she knew the Second Act had begun.

He sat beside her. "How are you?"

She leaned against him. "Not so good."

He scratched Ulysses behind the ears. "Hi, ol' pal. How's our Pirate?"

The dog stared blearily at him and lifted the tip of his tail in greeting.

Karl asked her, "Do you want to take a walk for a little while?"

She would clutch at the stars to keep the sky from turning. She would cap her hands over the rising sun. "Not yet."

Ulysses laid his muzzle on his paws and closed his eyes.

Her body rocked back and forth with a slow rhythm as she petted him and sang his name, her voice as faint as the glow of the coals, as soft as the breeze through the palm fronds, as pure as the moonlight on the beach, "Uuuuuuulyyyyyyyyyysseeeeeeeeeeees."

"Thud," came a sound from the water's edge.

Startled, she peered toward the sea, but saw nothing unusual. She wondered if a log had washed up and were bumping the shore.

"Thud."

Ulysses lifted his unsteady head and stared toward the water.

"Thud."

He barked, his voice the high thin cough of an old dog. Then he pushed himself up on his front legs and twisted toward the water, growling.

Cautiously, Angelique stood up. Something black and dome-shaped, like a giant beetle, was emerging from the sea onto the bright sand. It reached forward with two long pointed flippers and dropped them—"thud"—on the beach. With a thrill, she whispered to Karl, "It's a turtle!"

He marveled in a hushed voice, "She must be six feet long."

"She's a leatherback."

Ulysses barked again. Angelique knelt and hushed him, "Shshshsh. She won't hurt us. We ain' want to scare her away." Silent, ears cocked, he stared at the strange creature.

The turtle gasped as she dragged her enormous bulk up the slope. Her flippers, ten feet wide from wingtip to wingtip, left a rippled trail.

Forty feet from the water, she rested.

Then with her rear flippers, she began to dig.

Ulysses pulled against Angelique's arms. He wanted a closer look. She knew that once the nesting process had begun, the turtle would no longer retreat. She braced Ulysses' hips as he staggered forward. He peered warily at the turtle's head, twice the size of his own. The leatherback ignored him. Ulysses led Angelique in a half-circle around the silent, ponderous sea monster, until he stood behind it and stared at the movement of the rear legs. He stretched his nose low to the ground, sniffing.

One flipper, and then the other, scooped up the damp sand and pushed it into piles beside the hole. The flippers moved like giant black hands working in slow motion. When the leatherback had formed a nest a foot wide and three feet deep, she spread her flippers like fans over the top.

She let out a breath as if wind were rushing from a deep cave. Her head slowly bobbed. A clear mucus, rinsing sand from her eyes, trailed like heavy tears down her cheeks. From her jaws burst another enormous breath.

Ulysses stared with keen attention. Angelique lowered his hips so that he sat.

Then she and Karl stepped closer. Peering down between the two protective flippers, they glimpsed her treasure: a cluster of white eggs as big as tennis balls. Karl put his arm around Angelique.

Entranced, she studied the five knobby ridges running down the turtle's back. She admired the carapace jutting protectively over the tiny tail: like the ridges and armor of a dinosaur. She watched the turtle do what turtles had done on this beach beneath a million bright moons. She heard the great breaths bursting into the night, and remembered the gasps of her patients, laboring mothers pushing their children closer and closer to life.

Now one flipper reached to the side and dragged a load of sand back into the nest. The flipper reached into the hole and pressed the sand down. Then it fanned once more over the top.

The opposite flipper scraped a second load of sand into the nest and carefully pressed it down.

Ulysses lay down to watch; his eyelids began to droop.

Angelique sat beside him, his last sleepy minutes filled with fascination. She gazed at the turtle, then up at the bone-white moon. Though she had no drum to send her prayer, she thought, T'ank yo'. T'ank yo'.

The leatherback filled her nest with sand, then swept her rear flippers back and forth like two brooms, obscuring the site. She reached her front flippers forward—"thud"—and tossed two great loads of sand into the air. Suddenly covered with grit, Angelique blinked, and laughed out loud. She brushed off Ulysses' face, then lifted him away from the spray the turtle kept throwing behind her.

Dragging herself in a U-shaped path, up the beach, along it, then back toward the water, the turtle cast sand over a large area until her nest was completely hidden.

As she hauled herself toward the sea, Ulysses tried to follow. Angelique walked behind him, bracing his hips.

At the water's edge, a mat of foam washed over the turtle's face. She paused, her head rinsed clean, her back still spattered with sand.

The next wave wrapped around her with bright bubbles. She reached forward—"splash"—and nudged a few inches as the water swept away.

The third wave carried her several feet, swiveled her slightly, then set her down again. She pushed against the soft wet sand.

The trio huddled behind her, watching her departure.

A surge of water carried her out to sea. She swept her long wings and sailed weightlessly, her head etching a silver wake across the black surface.

Ulysses waded after her until he was chest deep. Angelique supported him against the slap and pull of the waves. She wanted to dive in herself, to swim close behind the leatherback. But she held her feeble dog.

The turtle ducked her head and disappeared beneath the shimmering surface. Though Angelique stared for a long minute, scanning back and forth over the bay, the turtle was gone.

Ulysses tried to turn toward shore, but he floundered. Angelique slung her arms beneath him and carried him, his fur dripping, back to the circle of coals and ash. His drugged eyes half-closed, he watched as she added twigs and blew on the coals until she had built up a small flame. He lowered his muzzle to his paws and closed his eyes. Within a minute, he lay unconscious, his head turned slightly on its side.

Karl walked to the jeep and returned with her black bag in one hand, a folded bed sheet and a spade in the other.

Following the relentless script, she opened the bag and took out the hypodermic needle, then a glass vial with a skull and crossbones on it. Not daring to pause in the role she was playing, she stuck the needle into the vial's rubber cap and drew back the plunger, drawing the clear moonlit fluid into the hypo's calibrated tube. Struggling to maintain her professional calm, she turned to Karl and asked, "Do you still want to do it?"

He took the hypodermic from her. "Why don't you go down to the water."

She buried her face in Ulysses' soft fur. "Good-bye, my wonderful friend. Thank you for five and a half precious years." She could no longer hold back the tears. She dug her fingers into his coat. "Ulysses, we . . ."

She looked up at Karl's anguished face in the firelight. "I want to hold him," she said. "I want to be here."

She watched as he pushed the needle into Ulysses' shoulder. His thumb pressed the plunger.

Ulysses' eyes opened wide. Awakened by a surge of feeling, he raised his head and stared hard at the light of the flames.

Then his head slowly lowered, and lay beside his paws on the sand.

Karl drew out the needle. Angelique pulled the limp dog into her lap and hugged him while she cried with blind, wrenching shrieks.

When she looked up, Karl was gone. Her black bag was gone, and the picnic basket was gone. She gazed numbly across the dark bay. Zosia's round window, filled with fragments of color, shone in the night. Zosia and Karl would be waiting for her.

But the script was not finished. She looked down at Ulysses: his head drooped from her lap. His tongue hung out of his mouth. She tucked it back inside his teeth. Then she laid his body beside the circle of ashes.

She stood, opened the sheet and spread it on the sand. Picked up Ulysses, his forelegs dangling now as his rear legs had dangled before. Placed him on the radiant white cloth. Folded one corner up, one corner down. Tied the other two corners together, lifted the loop over her head and stood with Ulysses slung in a hammock across her chest. She reached for the spade.

As she walked along the water's edge toward the far end of the beach, she hugged his warmth against her.

Fringing the last thirty yards of beach was a flat bank covered with grass, well above the reach of storm waves. She stumbled with her burden up the bluff, then waded through knee-deep grass. Lifted the heavy loop over her head and set Ulysses down. Opened the sheet so the moon could shine on him while she dug.

Stepping on the spade with her bare feet, she shoved its blade through thick roots, outlining the grave. Lifted out chunks of sod and tossed them aside. Dug down several feet; piled the loose damp sand beside the hole.

When the job was done, she crouched beside Ulysses and ruffled his ears. Tried to sing, "Uuuuuulyy—" But her voice cracked. She forced out the hoarse words, "Ah come visit yo'."

She straightened his wet bandana. Patted his strong shoulder. Folded one corner of the sheet up, one corner neatly down. Straddled her legs over the grave and lowered him to the bottom. She turned her eyes away as she shoveled in the first load of sand. Only when he was covered could she watch her work.

She did not replace the chunks of sod, but returned to the beach several times for shovelfuls of dry white sand. On the last trip, she stuck the spade into the beach, scooped up two handfuls of sand, walked back through the parted grass and let the sand sift through her fingers like fine white sugar.

She knelt, and imagined Ulysses' shoulder as she patted the grave. The imprint of her hand showed clearly in the moonlight.

CHAPTER TWENTY-SEVEN

Rainbow Sail

Nick stood outside the door to the classroom, torn between an almost overwhelming desire to hear what Angelique and the other Crucians had to say about 'weapons and war,' and his inability to see Angelique with another man, especially a man who, as she herself had told him, she loved.

With the resentment of a neglected expert, he brooded, Ah could tell them people about war. But it was more than that. He was drawn to be with people who thought about war, people who recognized the existence of a soldier's ordeal and sacrifice . . . people he could really talk with.

But to see Angelique with . . . He imagined her, on the other side of that wooden door, standing at the front of the classroom with the whigger at her side, *both* of them teachers, and Nick still years from being a teacher. No, he couldn't endure that. But he could stand here at the door every Monday night, so he could listen, listen to the voices of people who cared about war, about soldiers, about the loneliness that never ended.

"Hi, Nick."

He turned and saw Valerie, the girl who had glanced his way in their Caribbean History class. "Hey, Valerie. Yo' . . . ah . . . on yo' way to the library?"

"Ah already stare at them books till meh eyes swimmin'. What yo' doin'?" She glanced at the poster beside the door, MONDAY NIGHT SEMINAR: WEAPONS AND WAR 8 pm. With unhidden disdain, she asked, "Yo' want to learn about war?"

Before he could answer—before he could formulate in a sentence or two why it wasn't to learn, but to teach—she continued, "If everybody just realize that life be made for havin' a good time," she flashed her eyes at him to let him know just what she meant by 'a good time,' "there wouldn't be no silly wars."

He understood that he could either try to describe to her the war that destroyed his life two decades ago, when she'd just been born, or he could accept the invitation of one of the best-looking girls at the University to have a good time. "Say, Ah been at the books too long mehself. How about a beer together at Fitzroy's Hot Spot?"

"Fitzroy's?!" She sucked her teeth. "That ain' but a ol' roadside chicken joint. How about a Remy Martin at the Blue Lagoon?"

Inwardly he cringed, for the Blue Lagoon was a disco in Christiansted that mimicked the flashing lights and loud music of a nightclub in Manhattan. But he hadn't been with a woman for months, since he had held Angelique in the grass on Maroon Ridge; because angry as he was at her, he couldn't think of being with anyone else. But maybe what he needed was to stop standing like a fool at a closed door, and to start living again. "Yeah," he smiled, "the Blue Lagoon sounds perfect."

He endured nonstop music so loud it was almost impossible to hear each other's voices; he endured the continental slang of the very self-impressed Crucian D J; he endured the embarrassment of gyrating on the dance floor in the midst of people half his age; he grit his teeth and endured the outrageous sexual simulations on the dance floor between sailors in white uniforms and Crucian girls in weird disco-glitter outfits; he tried to ignore the frivolous, bland, drunken, drug-dazed, confident white faces that loomed around him in the flashing arc-light, while he smiled at Valerie and bought her drinks until her hand slipped into his and began squeezing his fingers one by one.

At her apartment, she was so quick to undress, he felt rushed, though at the same time he was so hot to have her he worried he would come before they'd even gotten started. "Oh Nicky," she moaned into his ear as she wriggled her young body against him.

He needn't have worried; for as she writhed beneath him on her black satin sheets, the sound of late-night traffic outside her window, she cried, "Nicky, Nicky, Nicky, yo' soooo goooooooood." And he felt nothing; utterly numb. While he drove her wild with his seemingly indefatigable manhood, Pfc. Nicholas Cruz wondered, in a remote but very clear corner of his mind, what the people in that classroom had said tonight about war.

The setting sun shone through Zosia's glass door; it painted a red stripe across her hardwood floor and up the opposite stone wall. Angelique and Karl stood at the door, gazing out. The shadows of their legs stretched long and thin across the floor and up the wall; the shadows of their torsos touched at the shoulders. Zosia slumped in her chair at the end of the table, staring at her hands folded in her lap.

Karl marveled loudly enough for Zosia to hear, "I've seen sunsets spread like a blanket afire over the Illinois prairie, but I've *never* seen a blazing sky reflected on a blazing ocean." He turned to her, "Zosia, don't you want to come watch?"

She seemed not to hear him.

He almost said, 'Shall I take a picture for you to paint from?', but her silence was so deep, her isolation so absolute, that he too fell silent.

Angelique saw the gaunt hollows in Zosia's face; the paper-thin skin laid over the skull beneath; the coma-like stare she knew well from elderly patients after they had given up. The days following Ulysses' death had been quiet on Candle Point, for there was no happy welcoming friend on the front porch, no exuberant terror-of-the-turnstones splashing up and down the beach, no furry gentleman prancing into Zosia's house. Angelique whispered to Karl, "I think we should tell her."

"Me too. Time for the bambino to cast her magic."

They sat in their chairs on opposite sides of Zosia. Angelique asked her, "Zosia, can you keep a secret?"

The old woman seemed deaf, sightless, to everything around her.

Karl told her, "You're the *first* person to know. But you've got to promise you won't tell anyone else."

She sat like a sculpture carved in white marble to such a thinness, that the stone seemed ready to shatter.

Without further delay, Angelique announced, "Zosia, I'm four weeks pregnant."

The olive-black eyes turned to her and stared, expressionless.

Angelique waited, and finally was about to repeat the news to be sure Zosia understood, when the raspy voice asked, "Is it true?"

"Yes. You're going to have a grandchild."

Twig-thin hands lifted from Zosia's lap and reached across the corners of the table for Angelique's hand, and Karl's. No joy appeared in her eyes, no exuberance, but a brave happiness which had struggled with despair for much of her lifetime, and which now seemed to have won a brief victory. "Congratulations."

Then, as if awakening, she gave Angelique an impish look and said, "Stand up and unwrap your sarong."

Puzzled, Angelique asked, "Whatever for?"

Zosia waved her hands impatiently. "Come on. Stand up. The sculptress needs to see her model before you start to swell up."

Angelique stood and ceremoniously opened the folds of her coral-orange sarong as if she were opening the curtains to a stage.

With both reverence and sharp-eyed fascination, the sculptress inspected the trim brown belly. She wrapped her cool fingers around the hips and spanned the abdomen with her thumbs, taking the measure of a torso she could not feel and would never sculpt.

While she worked, she asked, "Karl, do you want a boy or a girl?"

He replied eagerly, "What I want is a whole bunch of little girls, full of noise and commotion, each of them as pretty as her mother."

"A whole bunch," repeated Zosia with satisfaction as she pressed her palms, one above the other, against Angelique's belly. "Have you chosen any names?"

"We haven't really had time yet to consider—"

Angelique interrupted, "If he is a boy, his name will be Leroy Joseph."

Karl stared at her, stunned, and honored.

"And if she is a girl, her name will be Estelle Zosia."

Now Zosia looked up, speechless.

Angelique placed her hands over Zosia's. "She will be named after the two strongest women I know. Our children," she looked at Karl, "are going to be very special."

After the parents-to-be had gone home, Zosia stood at the railing of her porch and stared at the black water near the horizon. "Kochany, can you wait? Soon there will be a child in the house!" Torn between devotion to her husband, and her newly awakened hope, she assured him, "Piotr, I love you so much. But I must keep going another eight months."

Returning to Candle Point after Sunday dinner at the Nielsens, where the trio had kept their secret with conspiratorial delight, Karl accompanied Angelique and Zosia to Zosia's front door, then he said, "I'll be right back."

Without further explanation, he hopped into his jeep, drove to his cottage, grabbed the two blue sacks he had bought a month ago, then drove back to Zosia's, where his girlfriends were now ready for a little festivity.

He set the sacks beside Zosia's chair, turned on all the lights in the dining room and living room, then he said to Angelique, "Happy Valentine's Day, a little late."

Surprised, intrigued, she loosened the drawstring in the neck of the first sack and pulled out . . . a new jib! The sail was bright white, with re-enforced stitching along its seams.

"It's guaranteed to Force 12 on the Beaufort scale," he told her. "The mast'll blow away, but the sail will still be standing."

When Angelique opened the second sack, she stood stunned, for the bundle she pulled out was red.

He suggested, "Spread it across the floor."

She unfolded the big triangle across Zosia's living room floor and discovered a rainbow sail: a stripe of red at the bottom, bright as the red of her sloop, then stripes of orange, yellow, green, and blue. A triangle of purple capped the peak. "Oh, Karl, it's beautiful!"

Zosia's intent stare moved stripe by stripe. "Winsor red. Cadmium orange. Chrome lemon. Viridian. Cobalt blue. And a dab of French ultramarine mixed with indigo." She grinned at Angelique. "You must tack back and forth below my porch so I can paint you."

"Of course," said Karl. "All the great square-riggers had their portraits painted. Angelique's sloop should be no exception."

March was a month unlike any Angelique or Karl had ever known.

The two parents-to-be were pruning sea lilies in pots on Angelique's back porch when a single dark cloud came marching down the channel between St. Croix and Buck Island, trailing a veil of rain. The two quickly undressed, threw their clothes into the house, then stood at the wall to watch the miniature storm approach. The sun behind them lit a rainbow across the dark front of rain: the bright arch grew taller as it floated like the mouth of a tunnel toward the house. Wind gusted up the cliff, wet with mist. The two braced themselves, squeezed their eyes shut. Pelted by huge cool drops, buffeted by the wind, they whooped and shivered.

At dusk, they sat on the mattress while they watched a night-blooming lily slowly open. Slits appeared along its white tube; the two inhaled a delicate perfume. The slender petals parted at the tip, revealing the lily's male parts, tiny anthers covered with orange pollen. As minutes passed, the petals curled outward, forming a trumpet. Angelique felt no impatience, no boredom, as she stared in a state of prolonged rapture: she was watching life unfold. She inspected the deeper female part, a sticky green knob that waited for a night-roving bee to come visit. She coaxed Karl to sniff the lily; then giggled, for his nose and cheeks were painted like a clown's with tiny stripes of orange. She touched her fingertip to his nose, then touched the little green knob, dusting it with a blush of magic.

They watched until the flower had completely opened, a pale white spider in the starlight. Then she and her bee made love.

Nestled in his arm, she nuzzled against his cheek, bristly with stubble. "I think the jib man would look nice with a big bushy beard."

"A beard? I tried it once in college. I warn you, for the first two weeks I'll look like a derelict bum. Going to smoke old stogies I find on the sidewalk."

"But then the bum will become a Viking!"

"The Viking and the Mermaid. Sounds like a perfect combination."

Something flapped above them. Staring up, she saw nothing but stars; near the zenith were the inseparable twins of Gemini. Watching carefully, she noticed that some of the stars were blinking. But there was no cloud. Suddenly she spotted a frigatebird, or at least its shape: long thin bent wings and a forked tail silhouetted against the silver haze. The huge bird floated like a pterodactyl on the cushion of wind blowing up the cliff. "Karl," she whispered, "do you see it?"

He searched overhead. "See what?"

"A frigatebird. About ten feet above the wall."

"No, I don't see anyth— Oh yeah! I was looking right past it."

She searched carefully . . . and discovered a second bird, higher up. And a third. Gradually a flock assembled, facing the east wind. Once she even saw, or thought she saw, a hooked beak. Karl's arm squeezed her as they watched in awed silence.

The lowest bird rose on the wind and disappeared into the night. Another bird wheeled out to sea. One by one the others vanished, leaving behind the unblinking stars. Now she could hear, faint in the distance, the chugging motor of a boat passing Candle Point. "They were waiting for the fisherman. They'll follow him to Gallows Bay while he cleans his catch."

He said softly, "A flock of black angels."

"Then let's hope they were guardian angels." She snuggled again in his arm.

During the rainy nights of March, Karl became as adept as Angelique at waking from a deep sleep on the back porch at the first gust of wind. Without a moment's delay, they sat up and peered over the wall at a patch of black cloud in the starry sky. Was it far enough north, or south, to miss them? Could they just pull up a heavy blanket against the mist along the squall's fringe?

But if the dark menace were due east, they knew they were doomed. Sometimes with sleepy annoyance, sometimes with a dramatic thrill, Karl announced, "It's gonna get us!" Then up they jumped, she grabbed the blanket and sheets, he hefted the mattress, and they dashed for the house before the rain hit. Dropping everything on the living room floor, they returned to the open door and peered out, safe and dry as the rain streaked past.

He often took the opportunity to make popcorn. By the time he was adding butter and salt, the squall was over and Angelique had swept the puddles from the porch. They laid the bed back under the stars, then sat with the wooden bowl between them, filled with a pale white mountain of popcorn. She ate a few handfuls while he devoured the rest. He tossed the unpopped kernels over the wall.

At dawn they were awakened by the chatter of a pair of oyster-catchers feeding at the bottom of the cliff. Karl and Angelique knelt on the mattress and peered groggily over the wall, saw a copper sun staring back at them over the sea. Looking straight down, they watched two black-and-white birds on the rocks at the edge of the waves. Probing and pecking and pulling with their long orange beaks at snails and limpets and crabs, the oyster-catchers rejoiced with frequent cheers of "Kweeeeeeeep! . . . Kweeeeeeeeep!", as if every morsel they discovered were the most scrumptious they had ever tasted.

Karl declared, "They like the popcorn best."

Every afternoon after work, the two lovers swam in the bay. They dove to the bottom, patted their hands on the sand and called each other's names, one blurry syllable and three blurry syllables. Two clouds of bubbles danced toward the surface.

She reached for his hand; he wove his fingers with hers. Pulling together in underwater slow-motion, they kissed. "I love you," he called, his bubbles washing over her face. "I love you," she bubbled back.

Hungry for air, they rose toward the amber sun wobbling on the surface.

They hoisted the rainbow sail. Riding the oceanic rollers, she taught him all the Calypso tunes she knew. Their voices wove with increasingly polished two-part precision. Their repertoire expanded with each voyage, and they added to the traditional verses with new ones of their own. She wore the bottom half of her black string bikini, her breasts, swelling with pregnancy, bared to the sun, her belly of trim muscles showing no sign yet of the miracle inside. But the little one was already gaining her sea legs as she sailed in a rainbow-winged cradle.

Much further out to sea, missile technician 2nd class Schwartz noticed the faint flicker of a red warning light. Ding dang, he thought, ol' pod C again. Immediately he ran a full circuitry check, but found nothing amiss. And the warning light, after its brief flicker, never flashed again.

He reported the incident to his superior and requested permission to open pod C so he could recheck its wiring. But Chief Petty Officer Richards told him, "Hell, no. Tear that thing apart again when all systems check out? You'll do more damage than good. The trouble isn't pod C, Schwartz, the trouble is *you*: you're just a technician, glued to the dials, but what you really want to be is an engineer, fiddling with the tinker-toys inside. Why don't you put in a request to go back to school? Get yourself a degree and be a fucking officer."

So Schwartz did not open pod C to dig into its wiring. But he kept a sharp eye on that warning light, and he wondered, Why, why, *why* had it flashed?

CHAPTER TWENTY-EIGHT

To the Pier

Nick paced. The phone in one hand, the receiver at his ear, he walked back and forth in front of his window as he listened to a phone in Brooklyn ring and ring and ring. He had called a dozen times, no answer, no answer, and he wondered now if he was going to have to waste a week and a thousand dollars on another trip to New York. As he paced, he looked across the street: beyond the stone wall, a Crucian slouched on a sit-down lawn mower as he cut a straight swath across the huge Sugar Beach lawn; then the islander turned his mower around and cut another swath in the opposite direction, while whiggers dashed and pranced on the tennis court.

Suddenly a gruff voice barked in his ear, "Hello?"

"Fix? Cruz here. Hey mahn, how yo' be? . . . Well, been t'ree months now and Ah ain' hear from yo'. We still set for the t'irteenth of April? . . . May! Hey mahn, what the shit? Yo' got a down payment and the date been the dark of the moon of April . . . What do Ah care about Afghanistan peace talks? Ah ordered munitions, not Have-A-Nice-Day buttons . . . . Seventeen! What yo' tryin' to pull, mahn? A deal's a deal. We agreed on— Damn! Sure Ah want the stuff. But Ah ain' no fat cat, Fix. Ah runnin' a one-mahn operation. This island gon' be a part of Africa, Fix. Ah thought yo' understood why— All right, all right. Ah lookin' at meh calendar. Dark of the moon in May does be on the twelfth, a Friday . . . . Oh no. No way, mahn. Yo' want an extra two grand, yo' got it in May. Salt River Bay. Payment upon delivery. Stinger and sticks . . . . No more screw-ups, Fix. Or Black Rambo gon' be knockin' on yo' door, hear?"

He hung up, and slammed his fist on the table. May! That moved everything to June. Then he remembered: June, 1971. The month Leroy disappeared. He flipped the page on his calendar: new moon on the tenth, a Saturday night. Perfect. Leroy, we gon' honor yo' anniversary on the dark of the moon in June. Boom BOOM! on the dark of the moon in June. Yo' and me, we gon' clean out the trash and sanctify with fire. Just like ol' times. Can do, sir! Can do!

But how was he supposed to come up with an extra two thousand dollars in six weeks?

All right, he'd stoop to the bottom.

He drove from Harbor View to Alexander Hamilton Airport, parked in a far corner of the lot. Spotted Garfield by the luggage belt, nodded him aside. "Ah change meh mind. Cut me in."

Garfield patted his big belly and grinned: another salesman, another twenty percent. "Now yo' talkin'."

They walked out to the parking lot, spent ten minutes in Garfield's taxi-van.

"Ah sellin' only to whites," said Nick with finality. "Ain' never gon' sell to a brother. Never."

Garfield shrugged, "Aw right aw right. Turkeys get off the planes every day. Make yo' payments on time, yo' got no argument from me."

Nick walked casually from Garfield's van to his own taxi. Wrapped the stash in a beach towel, slid it under the seat, beside his Colt. Then he drove to the pick-up curb.

He met American flight 978 from New York. Standing near the luggage belt, he surveyed the crowd, picked out a lone, middle-aged, well-dressed man with bags under his eyes: a Success Story who looked as if he might enjoy one of life's expensive pleasures. Yeah mahn, t'ings go better with coke!

With a warm West Indian smile, Nick stepped forward. "Help yo' with yo' luggage, sir?"

Easter came and went without a card from home, and Karl sent no card north. Neither did he phone. He was determined to hold firm: either his parents wrote or phoned to him, or they would never hear from him again. Maybe he would send them a Christmas card. Wishing them happy holidays and announcing the birth of their grandchild. Maybe.

But while he was angry, he was also haunted by an unshakeable sadness, for his parents were ruining their own happiness. Several times he almost grabbed the phone to call them, to explain, to reprimand, to coax; but no, he refused to risk the chance, the very strong chance, that once again they would insult Angelique. For her sake, he couldn't bear to hear it; and for theirs, because it demeaned them so.

But was it really both of them? After all, his mother had cried on the phone. Pop had done all the talking. So he didn't really know how she felt. But at any rate, she hadn't sent an Easter card, hadn't phoned on her own, hadn't done a darn thing but . . . lose her son.

Since the evening after the storm, when Angelique had said she wanted his parents to come to the wedding, neither he nor she had mentioned them again. She and Estelle and Nat politely proceeded with plans for June as if his family did not exist, and he was profoundly embarrassed because he was unable to reserve even two places for Mom and Pop at the rehearsal dinner.

When he asked Zosia for advice, she only shook her head. "To *have* a child," she said, "and then to abandon him . . ." Her voice trailed off in disbelief.

He decided to admit to Angelique that she was right in her first appraisal of Pop; time to stop pretending, time to face the truth, time to cut the apron strings.

And especially, time to end this prolonged insult to the Nielsens.

In bed on Angelique's back porch, he rubbed her back, massaged her shoulders, lovingly carressed the dimples of her lower back for much longer than usual—for he feared her angry outburst, and hated to besmirch her happiness—until finally he was able to force out the words, "Angelique, I . . . I doubt my parents will come to the wedding. I'm sorry. And I can't tell you how sorry I am for how your parents will feel. It stinks. I'm so damn angry, I . . . I just don't know what to say except I'm terribly, terribly sorry."

She did not even lift her cheek from the pillow. "Well, then we know: they're not coming. For me, they no longer exist. And do not worry about Mama and Papa. The blame is not on them."

"I feel so ashamed."

"Don't. You have done nothing wrong."

"I tried to talk some sense into them, but—"

"Karl, stop. For me, they no longer exist."

"All right. But I never thought it would come to this."

During the following weeks, though he wrestled with anger and a slowly growing grief, he never mentioned them again.

He found that working on the Crucian Cooker helped to occupy his mind. He tinkered with the apparatus until he was able to telephone Professor Van der Voort at Cornell to announce that he had successfully roasted a filet of tuna. Dr. Van der Voort offered to fly down to St. Croix "sometime after examinations in June. Ithaca, New York is the town where God wrings out his socks, and I'd like to try the rig with something more than a sunlamp."

"Great," said Karl. "July would be best. I'll be getting married in June."

"You don't say! Congratulations!"

The two researchers arranged to meet at the airport on Monday, July 10, for a week of intense work together.

But that was the easy part.

Talking with Ed one day at Petrox, he learned that the refinery provided substantial sums to various schools on the island, and that one project was a machine shop where apprentices could develop their skills. "Hey, ol' buddy, it's part of our 'good neighbor' policy," boasted Ed. "We do one hell of a lot more for this island than provide jobs." Ed suggested that Karl knock off at three so he could visit the shop.

Karl found a dozen boys working at an assortment of lathes and cutters. He spoke with Luther Stewart, the shop foreman, and met some of the students. By the end of the afternoon, he had engendered enough interest in his Crucian Cooker that when he returned to Candle Point, he disassembled the apparatus and loaded it into his jeep, so he could take it to the shop the following afternoon.

Ed asked to come along. He helped Karl to reassemble the cooker in the shop's sunny parking lot. Then Ed surprised the boys by presenting them with a twenty-pound package of hamburger meat. "Ain't as good as Texas longhorn," he apologized, "but, bah doggies, it'll shore do for a barbeque." The boys helped Karl with his "solarizing," as he called the cooking process. As they ate their burgers—Ed had also brought plenty of buns and ketchup—Karl and Ed and Luther discussed the details of a small-scale manufacturing enterprise, to begin in September with the new school year, initially backed by Petrox until the business could pay for itself. Pending, of course, that Karl found sufficient customer demand for the cooker by September. Luther and his students were keen on the project, and there were handshakes all around.

But that, too, was the easy part.

Karl spent endless hours on the phone, ringing offices at the United Nations, the Peace Corps, World Bank, Department of Commerce, Department of Agriculture, U.S.A.I.D., trying to drum up support for a pilot program in some corner of the world where there was a shortage of firewood. He struggled with his rusty high school French as he spoke with officials in Haiti. He rang up pan-Caribbean offices on Jamaica, Trinidad, Barbados. He tried to find officials on Puerto Rico who could understand—or make the effort to understand—English, then he recruited Raphael in Gallows Bay to come with him to the telephone office in Christiansted, where Raphael spoke to recalcitrant bureaucrats in Spanish.

But progress was slow. Budgets were tight and people wanted proven results before they would invest in something new. Department chiefs were "out of the office right now," and rarely returned his calls. Secretaries informed him that Mr. So-and-So was in Zimbabwe, Hungary, Thailand.

He groaned with frustration.

Zosia blossomed with newfound zest. She spent her days painting flowers as she remembered them from her grandmother's farm in Bydgoszcz. "We're going to take down all those old pictures," she announced, sweeping her hand toward her walls. "Estelle Zosieňka is going to want fresh flowers." Fervently she painted her father's white and red roses; the wild violets in the woods behind the barn; blue irises from the shore of the duck pond; white and yellow water lilies; orange tiger lilies in the meadow by the spring; buttercups from the pasture; daffodils that lined the path to her Babka's farmhouse door.

As her walls filled with jubilant bursts of color, Karl declared, "This isn't a gallery. It's a greenhouse!"

One Saturday morning in April, Karl and Angelique drove into Christiansted and back again, then called from the driveway through Zosia's lattice window, "Close your eyes!" They carried a large object covered with a white sheet into her house, and ignored her questions as they carried their surprise down her hallway to her bedroom. They returned to the dining room, where Karl explained mysteriously, "We have one at Angelique's house, and now you have one at yours."

Brimming with excitement, Zosia looked around for her cane. "Where's my pogo stick?"

Angelique and Karl walked beside her down the hall; they paused at the door, where Zosia pointed at the covered object standing beside her bed, her finger trembling like a twig in the wind. "What *is* it?"

Angelique suggested, "Why don't you pull off the sheet?"

The trio stepped into the bedroom; Angelique and Karl braced Zosia while she grabbed hold of the cloth and pulled it away: she unveiled a mahogany cradle on rockers. With astonishment, she asked Angelique, "In my house too?"

Angelique nudged the cradle so it rocked beside the bed. "We want you to practice your Polish lullabies for when the three of us come to visit."

After Sunday dinner at the Nielsens', Angelique suggested that everyone take a walk down to the Frederiksted pier. But by the time she and Karl finished the dishes, her father was asleep in his chair; Rosemary and Cyril said they had to get home to finish painting the kitchen; Nat Junior wanted to wash his car; Suzanne had a report to write for work; and Mama, showing Zosia around her garden, decided she'd better get busy picking the caterpillars off the tomatoes. "Or we ain' gon' have nothin' next Sunday dinner," she laughed, "but caterpillar stew." Zosia, leaning down on her cane, tried to pinch her fingertips together to pick off one of the wriggling pests.

Karl stood in the middle of a patch of thriving melons. "Estelle, you'd win a dozen blue ribbons at the county fair. What's your secret?"

She handed him a fat purple eggplant. "Meh son, Ah gon' teach yo' de old ways." She whispered, guarding her secret from all but a chosen few, "Dishwater, coffee grounds, and fish head mulch."

So there were only four in the group on the after-dinner promenade to the pier. Zosia rode in her wheelchair as Karl pushed her up Hospital Street, then left on Custom House Street, and right on King Street, or Kongens Gade, as the old Danish sign still read. Though there was little traffic, the streets were nevertheless busy with people out strolling and talking, and Angelique often traded a cheerful greeting. Chester, who had changed out of his Sunday school clothes and now wore cut-offs and a T-shirt with a picture of Martin Luther King Jr. on his chest, raced up and down the street on roller skates, terrifying the dogs that panted lethargically in the middle of the street.

Karl was fascinated by the Victorian-Caribbean architecture of the houses: their porches, shutters and eaves were trimmed with gingerbread, and painted with the pastel colors of salt water taffy. But most of the homes had been painted decades ago, and their chipping facades and sagging porches gave them the air of weather-beaten aristocracy. The seaport had clearly seen better days.

He noticed that many of the people in Frederiksted wore their hair in Rastafarian dreadlocks. Some of the people in the street returned his shy "Hello" with a nod or a smile; some gave him a deadpan stare. He felt conspicuous in this village of blacks, and he was glad he was pushing Zosia, and not walking with Angelique as a couple. She was no longer at his side, and he glanced back to find her: she was talking with a cluster of men who lounged against a pick-up truck. She was laughing and they were laughing with her. He felt a jolt of jealousy. As he turned around and continued to push Zosia—who called ahead to Chester, "Let's see a figure eight!"—he realized it was not he who had grounds to be jealous, but of course, the men of Frederiksted.

"Karl," he heard her call.

He looked back over his shoulder. She waved to him to come.

He stopped pushing the chair. Surely these men scorned an outsider who tried to steal one of their women. Despite his apprehension, he leaned down to Zosia and said calmly, "Angelique is calling. May I turn you around?"

Her eyes sparkled with delight. "Did you see? Chester can do a figure eight on one foot!"

He turned Zosia around and pushed her toward Angelique; though he maintained a cordial smile on his face, his heart was thumping, for Angelique was one of the most beautiful women on the island, and who was he? A foreigner, a honky, a fool who presumed to claim the town's princess.

"Karl," she said, "Ah want yo' to meet Victor. He workin' at the University Agricultural Research Station, raisin' African bass. Jus' the t'ing for yo' Crucian cooker. Ah t'ink yo' ought to visit Victor's ponds and check out the possibilities."

With a surge of gratitude to Angelique for her loyalty, he extended his hand to the man standing beside her. "Hello, Victor. Karl Jacobsen. Nice to meet you."

Victor wore blue denim overalls, just the kind that still hung in Karl's closet in DeKalb. His dreadlocks reached to his shoulders; his eyes were sleepy, perhaps skeptical; his handshake was limp. He said, "Check."

Angelique introduced Victor to Zosia. "Victor, this meh neighbor Ah tell yo' so much about, Zosia Honegger. Zosia, this meh good friend Victor. He live two doors away from Mama and Papa."

"No more," Victor corrected her. "Live in de forest now." He shook

Zosia's hand, his eyes still sleepy.

"That's no handshake!" complained Zosia. "Shall we do it right?"

Angelique laughed. "C'mon, Victor. Zosia come to this island 'fore yo' been born. Give the woman a clasp!"

Bowing slightly, a smile breaking out on his face, Victor again offered his hand. Zosia, moving her twig-like fingers as best she could, matched him through an intricate sequence of grips. Their handshake finished with two fists, one large and black, one small and white, coming together and touching knuckles. "Yagh," declared Zosia with approval. "Much better."

Now one by one, all the men stepped forward for their turn to shake hands with her. With quiet grace, they spoke their names. Pleased with the attention of so many men, Zosia sat tall in her wheelchair like a queen on her throne. "Gerard. Sam. Lenny. Eduardo. How wonderful to meet you!"

Angelique turned to Karl, whom everybody seemed to have forgotten. "Karl, maybe we could visit Victor at the Ag Station on Saturday."

"Fine. Saturday's a good day for you, Victor?"

Victor nodded sleepily. "Check."

"Shall we say, around ten in the morning?"

A nod.

"Terrific. Well then, I look forward to seeing your African bass." Karl almost added that he was a bass fisherman himself, that he and Pop had stocked the farm pond with bluegills, but Victor turned to say something to Eduardo in such heavy Crucian dialect that Karl caught only a couple of words.

"Hey, ain' we goin' to the pier?" called Chester, restless on his skates.

Angelique hooked her arm through Karl's as he pushed Zosia down the street; Chester whirled around them, enclosing them in one of the loops of his figure eights. Karl said quietly to Angelique, "Thanks for the introduction, but are you sure Victor really wants me to visit?"

"Of course. Victor is interested in meeting anyone who will help him to help this island to feed itself."

"Hmm." He said nothing more. He'd visit Victor's ponds and see what happened. After all, he mused sadly, a limp handshake is probably more than Victor would have gotten from Pop.

They approached a grassy park below a wall of the Danish fortress that had once guarded the harbor. Zosia asked, "Could we stop here for a few minutes?"

"Sure." He tipped back her chair, lifting its front wheels over the curb onto one of the sidewalks that criss-crossed the park, then he pushed her to an unoccupied bench facing a bandstand. "How's this?"

She nodded with satisfaction. "After we cut the tops off the pilings, Piotr and I had lunch in this park."

"You cut the tops off the pilings?"

But she was watching a group of girls, still wearing their Sunday dresses, as they sang and giggled on a bandstand's round stage.

He sat on the end of the bench beside her, as he had sat that morning on the end of the pew beside her, except now he could stretch out his feet. "Ahhhhhhh."

Angelique sat beside him, leaned her head on his shoulder and closed her eyes. "Mmmmm."

Chester skated, clackety-clack, clackety-clack, on the uneven sidewalks.

Angelique began to hum the tune the girls were singing.

Karl remembered the summer concerts back home, when everybody brought a picnic basket and a blanket to Tilden Park and stretched out on the lawn in front of the band shell. He could almost taste Mom's barbequed chicken; he and Joe had washed down her hot sauce with mugs of root beer. And the nice thing too was that all the musicians were friends and neighbors from DeKalb. The conductor was a razzle-dazzle trumpeter, and what Karl especially liked was when Mr. Bishop put down his baton and played that trumpet with such brassy exuberance—the way Karl wished he could play. Closing his eyes now, he could hear the band's rousing rendition of Seventy-Six Trombones Led the Big Parade, With a Hundred and Ten Cornets Right Behind . . . And now he could hear the soft sweet strains of Good Night, My Someone, Good Night, My Love . . . But best of all was on the Fourth of July, when they lit off the fireworks at the end of the concert. Then everybody lay back on their blankets and looked up through the giant shaving-brush elms at those fiery phosphorescent powder-puffs. The flare-red sizzlers that floated down on parachutes. The cannon shots that made everybody jump! And then at the end of the show, they lit a fireworks American flag by the band shell and the band played the "Star-Spangled Banner" with Mr. Bishop hitting the high notes. Everybody stood up and sang with their hands over their hearts, and it was a tremendous thing to hear the voices of your whole town beneath the stars while Ol' Glory was spitting red, white and blue sparks. After the final ringing crescendo, when your skin prickled with pride, everyone applauded and the people in cars honked their horns.

Yeah, but it wasn't the same when Joe wasn't there anymore. That spark-spitting flag seemed kinda theatrical, kinda empty. He couldn't trust it anymore.

He remembered, after Joe's funeral in April, an April almost twenty years ago, he and Mom and Pop drove back to the farmhouse. To the empty farmhouse. They stood in the living room, Pop holding the flag that had been draped over the coffin, folded now into a neat triangle. They just stood there, dazed and silent, while the grandfather clock counted loud, slow seconds that threatened to stretch to eternity. They had a choice; or at least Pop and Mom had a choice, and he, a boy of sixteen, would follow. Either they believed in their country, and that the war—despite its cruelty—was fought to defend freedom around the world. Or they believed that Joe's death was a senseless waste. So they went back outside, took down the old faded flag from the pole, then he helped Pop to unfold the triangle. Pop ran up Old Glory, bright and new, waving her colors among the pale green buds of the maples.

Yes, he put his hand over his heart that Fourth of July in the park. But it was a mechanical gesture. Because so many of his friends at school, and so many on television and in the newspapers, kept saying that the war was wrong. Not for his country, not for the flag, but only for Joe, did he still put his hand over his heart.

Then came that half-assed butchery in Nicaragua, The War of the Contras, the war that America ignored, the war that stopped on the day Ol' Jellybean retired to Beverly Hills. Stopped as simple and easy as changing the draperies in the White House. That's when he no longer put his hand over his heart. Because that charade insulted every American who had ever put on a uniform.

Yup, I stood next to Pop last summer on the Fourth of July with my arms folded across my chest. Hiding my fists. Pop noticed, of course. Wanted to slap me right there during the Anthem. That's partly why he's so angry now. Thinks Angelique is just my way of getting back at him for his bone-headed belief in napalming the Commies.

Her head still on his shoulder, Angelique began to sing; the girls on the bandstand looked toward her and smiled that someone was singing along with them.

Chester clattered up to the bench. "Hey, ain' we goin' out on the pier?"

"Oooooh," sighed Angelique. "Chess, yo' don' ever sit still?"

The boy grinned at Zosia. "Yo' got wheels. Le's go!"

She scoffed, "I'm too fast for you."

"Nawwww," he laughed. "Ah can beat yo' goin' backwards."

"All right," she said, accepting his challange, "we'll race to the end of the pier. But I'm sooooo fast, that to be fair, I've got to give you a one minute head start. On your mark, get set—"

"What about them?" he asked, pointing at Karl and Angelique. "They just gon' sit here and . . ." He made loud kissing noises, then convulsed with uproarious snickers.

His mind aching with tangled thoughts of Joe and Pop, of unfinished wars and unrelenting bitterness, Karl stood up. "All right, Mister Chester. Let's go see if anybody's caught a fish."

He pushed Zosia across Strand Street, then through the pier's steelbarred gate, open to pedestrians and taxis. Chester glided backwards, spreading his skates and drawing them together in an hourglass pattern, while he told Zosia about the giant eel he had once caught. "It tek t'ree of us to pull up that moray. Five feet long, t'ick as a mahn's leg! And Ah tell yo', it ain' got teeth, it got fangs!" Chester snapped his jaws at Zosia, who howled with appropriate horror.

Both Karl and Angelique looked beyond the quarter-mile pier, beyond the parade of Sunday strollers: a destroyer was anchored offshore, its gray prow pointing toward the island, its radar towers bristling into the sky. She squeezed his hand on the grip of the wheelchair; he glanced at her, saw a strange look in her eyes, and then he noticed her other hand laid over the waist of her peach-colored dress.

Chester accelerated backwards, then spun around and zigzagged through the crowd. He looped around a parked bicycle, zoomed past a couple pushing a baby buggy as if they were obstacles in a race course. Zosia laughed and called, "Be careful you don't skate right off the end!"

Despite his distrust of all things military, Karl tried to be fair. He suggested to Angelique, "What about asking some of the crew to visit our class tomorrow evening? Maybe the captain himself would come. It'd be an excellent opportunity for people on St. Croix to ask him questions. And to give him equal time, a chance to have his say."

Her eyes never left the ship.

He continued, "When we head back into town, I'm going to stop at the pier office to see if we can send an invitation out to the Navy."

"Yes," she said, an edge of anger in her voice, "I'd like to ask the captain how he feels about being a father."

A dark spot appeared in the sky behind the destroyer. They watched it grow larger, heard the beating whirr of its rotors. The helicopter hovered over the ship, then descended and disappeared behind the radar towers, apparently to a pad on the stern.

The destroyer began to move in an arc to the north. As it swung broadside to the pier, Karl read the giant white numbers on its prow, 998. The warship's two towers, laden with complex arrays of antennas, pointed up like prongs of a fork at the afternoon sun. Its red, white and blue flag flapped lazily at the stern.

Angelique sneered, "Looks like Mistah Cap ain' got time to talk with us."

They could see the helicopter now, sitting like a wasp on the stern deck. She pointed, and he nodded with recognition: behind the guns on both the bow and the stern were rectangular containers, like big refrigerator boxes, which they never would have noticed had they not seen them close-up in a photograph in a magazine. Inside each container were four Tomahawk missiles, ready to fire from their launchers. Each Tomahawk carried twelve times the firepower of the Big Boy that leveled Hiroshima. "Sixteen Tomahawks," she said grimly.

"Seems so, though next time let's bring a pair of binoculars."

She sucked her teeth. "A hundred ninety-two Hiroshimas, keepin' meh baby safe."

Zosia too watched the vessel's squared stern as the ship steamed north. Then she looked up at Angelique and admonished, "Don't blame the captain. No doubt he would tell you he has devoted his life, a lonely life far from home, to protecting his children. And yours." She turned to Karl. "That captain probably feels more than most Americans the weight of responsibility on his shoulders. But he alone can't negotiate those Tomahawks out of existence. He would need a lot of help. So perhaps the captain would tell you, if you invite him to your class, that when the founding fathers wrote, 'We the People,' they meant it."

Karl looked down into Zosia's gaunt Polish face, saw the determination in her olive-black eyes, and thought, You are the reason I will never lose faith in America.

Nick was driving his taxi past the park toward the pier where he would meet the Norwegian cruise ship *Vista Fjord* in a couple of hours—he would while away the time by talking with friends out for a walk on the pier—when from the corner of his eye he spotted Angelique sitting on a park bench with her head on Hard Hat's shoulder.

He almost slammed on the brakes and strode into the park, but he didn't trust himself. His fists, even if he stopped short of manslaughter, would bring the police; best to lay low this close to June. However, neither did he drive onto the pier, but turned and followed Strand Street a short distance and parked, for he had no destination now. He had only the obvious truth: he would never have her back, no matter how hard he worked at the University. The decision was his, student, or guerrilla, right up to the dark of the moon in June. But what was the point in fooling himself? Leroy, gone; Denise, gone; Andy, gone; and clearly, Angelique, gone. He reached for his wallet in his back pocket, took out the photo she had given him, in her graduation cap and gown the day she became a nurse; Papa had taken that picture. Her bright eyes, her confident smile: how many times had he gazed at her and imagined those same bright eyes, but beneath a bridal veil.

He reached with trembling hands out the car window and tore the photograph into shreds.

He did not know what to do next. He stared through the windshield at the water lapping the beach, at people walking along the pier. Friends? Few would notice if he disappeared from the island. From the planet.

He stared at the destroyer pointed like an arrowhead at his island. He had been all right, and well on his way toward a good life, until the day his draft notice turned a Crucian high school basketball star into an American soldier.

Big White Sam, all he ever lost been the war. But Ah lost every-t'ing Ah ever loved.

Now he watched Angelique walking beside her Yankee Doodle as they pushed a wheelchair along the pier. Watched Chester skate ahead of them. Looked again at the white shirt and blond hair of the man who had ignored the knife stuck through his picture. Ignored it with the white man's confidence that nothing could ever hurt him.

Then he knew what to do. He would extend his options on the dark of the moon in June. He drove along Strand Street, up Queen Cross Street to its intersection with Hospital Street, turned and drove slowly past the green Jeep Cherokee parked in front of Leroy's house.

Drove to the airport, rented a Jeep Cherokee from Avis. Drove up Fountain Valley, crossed through the mahogany forest on Scenic Road, turned off and parked, well hidden, on Maroon Ridge. Took out the owner's manual from the glove compartment, lifted the hood, bent over and examined the ignition system wiring.

He'd phone Fix this evening. The rest was easy: the jeep was often parked in front of the cottage while Big Squirt was down courting and sporting with the Traitor Lady.

Traitor Lady, collapsed with grief, would no doubt send the police after Nick Cruz.

But car bombs leave no fingerprints.

And the police would be far too busy trying to figure out what revolutionary army had blown up a dozen strategic targets.

He lowered the hood, put the manual back into the glove compartment. Can do, sir! Can do.

Then he walked into the forest, the sacred forest, for he felt compelled to do something he had not done since he had prayed, desperately, on the night Leroy had disappeared in Vietnam. Clearly, he had prayed then to the wrong god. Now, he did not kneel, but stood. He did not know the ancient African words, did not even know to Whom he prayed, but he knew that in this forest the Spirit of His People surely dwelled.

A sunbeam shone down through the canopy onto a mahogany trunk. On that patch of gold he fastened his eyes as he called up, "Ah take the oath of a warrior that meh people shall be avenged with the blood of a white mahn."

His heart no longer ached; jealousy and pain and rage departed. No anticipated mission in Vietnam had ever filled him with such eagerness, such peace.

CHAPTER TWENTY-NINE

Flint and Steel

Maybe it was because Karl had to work that night on emergency electrical repairs at Petrox, leaving her alone in the bed on the back porch. Maybe it was because she had buried herself in books on weapons and war for three months now. Maybe it was because for two months, she had carried a child. Or maybe the ship with its refrigerator boxes had unsettled her more than she realized. She could not sleep, or half-slept, then jolted awake as if from a dream she could not remember, though she felt a lingering sense of dread; sitting up, she discovered that beneath the sheet, she was damp with sweat.

She almost went into the house to phone her mother, just to hear Mama's voice. But her parents were asleep by now, and she would only worry them if she woke them up—as if she were still a little girl—to tell them she'd had a nightmare.

She lay back down and let the stars comfort her. Vega was rising, an omen of spring. She closed her eyes, imagined that she was out sailing with Karl. The wind was brisk, the sunshine bright on the rainbow sail. She and her bearded Viking were headed out for a day on the Big Blue, to ride the rollers. So that later, back on land, when she and he made love, she would still feel the rising and falling waves coursing through her.

But the destroyer was nearby. Following her sloop. Frantic, she scanned the horizon to find it, saw empty sea.

Something was wrong. Horribly wrong. Nick was— Where was Nick?

She was inside a factory, people in white coats assembling components, bright lights, harsh lights. Amarillo, Texas. Black hands working from the sleeves of a white lab coat, someone hunched over a work bench at the Pantex Plant.

And war begat war. And war begat war begat war.

Putting something inside a metal cylinder, hands working skill-fully, each move practiced and precise. One hand reaches into a pocket. Bulging pocket. And something from that pocket goes into the cylinder. Agile fingers. Agile magic. Sent the ball to the hoop like a hen home to roost.

Begets war, and war begets war and more and more.

Pantex weapons fabrication plant, of course. Karl had marked the map in class. "Our Tomahawks," he pointed at Florida, "are manufactured in Titusville, but the warhead itself is assembled here," tapping the Texas panhandle, "in Amarillo."

Black hands move to the next canister and tinker with tools. Hand into the pocket, at each cylinder goes the hand into the pocket, and then he cradles something in his palm. . . . She leans forward to look: a flint arrowhead. An old Indian arrowhead. A pocket full of them.

And that begat a war about this and that begat a war about this and that at Pantex, where quickly the arrowhead is inserted and soldered and circuited with precision. One per bomb. One per bomb. One per bomb.

He looked up at her and she froze: Nick in a white lab coat, Nick got a job, got a good job, knows the trade, the demolitions trade, ain' drivin' that taxi no more. His hands still working, he smiled at her. "Flint and steel, Sugah. Flint and steel. Oh ain' them bastards gon' pay!"

Horrified, she drew back. Wanted to tell somebody. Arrowheads.

Karl, we've got to tell the class that . . . begat. And God begat light.

Forced herself back out on her sloop, where the sun shone on Karl's rainbow sail. She always thought of it as *his* sail, though he had given it to her. His Valentine's gift. He was leaning out, feet hooked under the strap, shoulders almost touching the waves. Patted his muscular stomach. "Like steel!" he boasted. "Listen." He knocked with his knuckles. "Clank, clank!"

Riding high on a roller, she cast a weather eye to the east. That long low gray shape on the horizon pretended it was not following. She knew better, had known for years. The visible ship merely a shark's fin of the beast beneath. Begat of man, by God not begotten.

"Karl, would you like to take the tiller today? I'm tired. I'm tired of things I'm too tired to think about."

But he was pointing at something so bright she could not see what it was. Unearthly bright. Puzzled—an instant while she was puzzled—

she looked at his face and his beard was on fire!

Then it hit, exactly as she had always known it would. Roar of sky torn open, wall of hurricane wind. Boat heaved up and hurled. "Karl!" she cried, dazzle-blinded by light only Jehovah could see in the beginning.

Swimming, somehow swimming, she heard him ask, "How's Elly? Keep an eye on Elly. Poor little kid doesn't deserve . . ." A wave washed over her.

When she struggled up into the air again, his voice was gone. "Karl!" she shrieked, frantic. "Where are you?"

And then she had him, by will she insisted that she *had* to have him in her arms, for he had no arms. Blown away by the explosion. His torso black, charred. "Well," he joked, "we don't have to worry any more about a mixed marriage."

She tried to will him to the emergency room, tried with all her strength to envision him on the table under the lamps, Dr. Schroeder in a white coat leaning over Karl. But she couldn't. She could not drag him out of the sea, his body heavy, limp in the rising and falling surge. "Karl, try to kick."

Felt something with her fingers. In his chest, inside his charred chest, buried in his heart. She pulled it out and felt with her thumb the pointed end of a stone. The arrowhead.

Begat war begat war begat war.

All she could do was scream to fill her ears so that no more did she hear the rising rumbling titanic roar that towered over her island.

Somewhere, she heard a phone ringing.

Staggering up from the bed, she dashed into the house, desperate to hear his voice. She grabbed the phone. "Karl?"

"Are you all right?" The scratchy voice was not Karl's. "Angelique, what is the matter?"

"Zosia, I . . ."

"You come. You come over here right now."

Still confused, Karl, Zosia, Mama, somehow all three on the phone, she started to cry and hung up. Hurried in her nightgown down the steps, around the driveway, up the dark sidewalk—her bare feet shuffled through crackling seagrape leaves—to the door. Opened it, closed it and locked it, rushed along the hallway toward the light in Zosia's bedroom. Saw Zosia sitting up in bed, saw the trembling hands reaching toward her. In her hurry, she bumped the cradle and set it rocking. Climbed into the bed, felt the thin arms wrap around her, heard the raspy voice repeat over and over with profoundest love, "Angelique, Angelique, my Angelique." She was awake enough now to know she had been dreaming, that Karl was safe at Petrox, and that her child, protected this night by a Pole who knew how to survive, would live.

CHAPTER THIRTY

The Arms Cache

During her Monday morning rounds, she made a decision, or really, reaffirmed a decision she had made on the night of the storm, a decision she had since neglected, for she considered such an undertaking, when viewed by the light of day, to be so unrealistic that she could only laugh at her presumption.

But as she shook down a thermometer, the terror of her nightmare still vivid, she remembered that decision. And as she took a pulse, counting those little bumps under her fingers while her watch swept around sixty seconds, she reaffirmed that decision. Though she needed a step in between. First, she would run for a seat on the legislature, and then, once she had built a foundation of respect among the voters, then she would run for governor.

So when her shift was over at three, she drove Karl's jeep—for he refused to let her ride the scooter any longer—to Government House in Christiansted and spent forty-five minutes with the registrar, learning how to submit her papers as a candidate for senator in the next election.

Then she drove to Karl's cottage, where the scooter was parked at the bottom of the steps. She let herself in, found him still asleep after his night at Petrox; there he was, still alive, breathing peacefully with that light gruff snore which until this moment had always irritated her. She looked at her watch—a quarter to five—and decided he would have to wake up soon anyway to have time enough to eat dinner and to drive together to the University, where their class began at eight. She leaned over him and kissed his lips until he awoke and, realizing what was happening, wrapped his arms around her and pulled her into the bed.

She told him about part of her nightmare: about sailing, the explosion, and his death; but of course not about Nick. He frowned with concern, and grumbled that he would never again spend a night away from

256

her, "even if Ed has a fit."

Then she told him about her decision. His reaction to her plans was far stronger. He sat up in bed, regarded her with admiration and offered to be her campaign manager. He was full of ideas: suggestions for her platform, for sources of financial support, for a carefully scheduled campaign strategy.

She laughed, "But Karl, the election isn't for another year and a half."

She appreciated his enthusiasm, but realized that he, ever the optimist, would never know the fear that haunted her. He would never, in his guts, confront the weapons that together they fought against. The monster in the cave was for him an abstraction, whereas she knew, with fierce intuition, that one day that monster could emerge, breathing fire, to devastate the village.

Unless the villagers bricked up the mouth of the cave.

Optimist and realist, they would work together. Lifting her T-shirt over her head, closing her eyes with a surge of pleasure as he massaged her breasts, she felt ready to burst with so much love for the man who last night at sea had died in her arms.

On Saturday morning they drove to the Agricultural Experiment Station at the University, where they found Victor working beside one of his ponds. He wore rubber boots, denim overalls, and an oversized knit hat, with red, green and gold stripes; the hat rose above his head like a turban. Victor swept his net through the murky water and lifted out several flip-flopping fish. He wet his hand in the pond, reached into the net and grabbed a ten-inch specimen to show his visitors. "Tilapia. Poor mahn's protein."

Karl inspected what looked like an Illinois rock bass. "Angelique tells me this species comes originally from ponds in Africa."

"Check." Victor winked at Angelique. "Home cookin'."

"Could they be raised in Haiti, for example?"

"Check." Victor tossed the bass back into the pond, then shook his net empty.

"And how about the quality of the meat? Pretty tasty?"

Victor spoke with conviction, "Tilapia live in the Sea of Galilee. Before Peter become a fisher of men, he been a fisher of tilapia. And when Christ feed the five t'ousand with loaves and fishes, it been tilapia them people eat. Ah ain' see why Crucians got to set traps in the fished-out reefs, when they can feast on food the Messiah Heself set on the table."

Karl told Victor about his Crucian Cooker, a solar stove that needed no wood, no charcoal, no electricity. He and Angelique offered to buy three dozen tilapia if Victor would bring them to the Nielsen house next Sunday for a neighborhood picnic. Karl and Victor could experiment as they fried tilapia in the yard in front of the house, where the neighbors could watch, and learn.

Victor nodded with ineffusive agreement. "Check."

Karl warned Victor that he was having trouble finding governmental backing for the project. "Can't seem to find anyone who recognizes the potential."

Victor lifted off his voluminous hat: matted ropes of hair fell to his shoulders. He tossed his head like a lion shaking its mane. "Yo' keep ringin' them phones. When the Lord see yo' be wantin' to feed He people, He gon' find the right person to answer that phone. Ain' no problem with that."

So Karl kept phoning. On the last day in April, a Sunday evening, he located a Quaker woman in Philadelphia who had just returned from Ethiopia, and who was eager to come to St. Croix on July 10 to meet with Karl, Van der Voort, Stewart, Ed, and Victor.

When Karl hung up, he whooped with a cheer of triumph. Then he looked at his brother in the family photograph on the table. "Whatdya think, Joe! I'm finally doing something with my life. Finally."

Though they were busy on Monday evenings at the University, Angelique and Karl tried to be on the beach at dusk during the other six evenings of the last week in April and the first week in May; they stood with flashlights near the spot where the turtle had laid her eggs. "The hatchlings dig their way up until they feel the warmth of the sand," she explained, "then they stop and wait, or the sun would bake them before they reached the water. So the best time to see them is when the sand starts to feel cool on your bare feet."

Evening after evening she and Karl walked down to the beach after dinner, and stayed until they had to beam circles of light across the sand, but they discovered no baby turtles. Then they walked to the far end of the beach and climbed the grassy bluff, stood by the patch of bare sand and greeted Ulysses. She always knelt and patted the sand. On the night of April's full moon, she cried as she swept her hand again and again across the sand, smoothing his fur; no sobs of grief, for that had passed, but tears of loneliness without him, tears of remembrance of that beautiful final night they had shared, and even tears of happiness as she imagined him sitting alert in her sloop, ever on the lookout for flying fish that burst out of the water ahead of the bow.

And then, on Tuesday the second of May, twenty minutes after sunset, Karl spotted five tiny black noses poking up from the sand. "There they are!" he exclaimed.

"Turn off your flashlight," she said as she knelt with him in the cool sand beside the nest. "The light disorients them. They have to see the glow of the sky on the water, so they know which way to crawl."

The sand-covered heads emerged, eyes closed. Shoulders pushed up, then flippers lifted free and pressed down so hard they bent and twisted, as the hatchlings corkscrewed in slow motion the last increments of their two-foot climb through heavy sand, without food, without water, and with little air. The turtles moved as if in a coma: a nudge, then a rest, another nudge, a long rest, so that nearly half an hour passed before a three-inch miniature adult, its eyes now open, its motions more rapid, began to crawl toward the sea.

By the faint glow of the stars, she and Karl watched that first pioneer cross forty feet of rippled beach, crawl down the slope of hard wet sand and—without benefit of food or training from a parent, without a weeks-long stay in a nest before it took to its wings, without even a peep or a howl to the heavens that it was alive—crept headlong into the ocean. The ocean picked it up in a wave, whirled it in a surge of foaming water and cast it back on the beach. Undeterred, the turtle pushed with its front flippers, each nearly as long as the body itself, leaving tiny paired tracks in the sand, toward the universe that had so peremptorily rejected it moments ago; and this time it was accepted, or at least swallowed, by the wave that boiled around it. For the little turtle . . . disappeared.

She and Karl watched a multitude of turtles emerge from the sand; she chased away a ghost crab that threatened to attack the fan-shaped parade. Then she had a sudden thought, and asked Karl, "Shall we swim with them? I've got a diver's light at my house. We could follow them for awhile."

He looked out at the vast black ocean. "Sure, but . . . let's stick together."

So she hurried to her house on Candle Point while he hurried up to his cottage. She thought to tell Zosia about the hatch, to help her into the wheelchair and roll her down to the beach; but surely the turtles would be gone by the time Zosia got there. No, best to tell her later over a glass of wine.

She met Karl as the last of the baby turtles were trundling toward the sea. Without speaking a word, they put on their masks and flippers, waded backwards into the water, then floated beyond the breaking waves. She shone her underwater flashlight back and forth, sending out a long thin gray cone of light, until the beam found a tiny turtle flapping its sturdy wings. She and Karl followed the voyager; they had to kick their flippers steadily to keep up. The baby turtle swam in the spotlight like a lone performer on a dark stage, propelling itself with its fore-flippers, while using its hind-flippers as rudders. The turtle swam with a definite pattern: it rose for a brief breath of air, then dove and swam horizontally about two feet below the surface for twenty or thirty feet; then it rose for air, dove and again swam well below the surface, thus hiding itself from birds that might pass overhead.

Aware that the embryo inside her was about three and a half inches long, roughly the length of the turtle swimming ahead of her, the mother-to-be took her child-to-be on a journey, to show her child the courage of the newborn turtle, an infant that guided them into a world which it must, without choice, call home.

She followed the little turtle until, lifting her mask out of the water and looking back over her shoulder, she saw the lights of Candle Point were well behind her. She felt as she always felt when she had sailed far, far out on the ocean: she didn't want to turn around, but knew that at some point, she had to. She stopped kicking—Karl paused beside her—and they watched the turtle as it flapped its wings toward the Equatorial Current of the Caribbean and eventually the Gulf Stream of the great Atlantic. It swam down the tunnel of her light until, with the indomitable faith of a tiny angel carrying some supremely important message, the leatherback vanished from sight.

She looked at Karl, his face hidden inside his dark mask; he reached out and squeezed her arm to tell her, That was extraordinary.

Then she clicked off her light and dove straight down through the black water, holding one hand extended ahead of her until she touched the sandy bottom she could not see. She did not pat her hands and call her name. She made no sound, no bubbles. She merely floated in that infinite saltwater abyss that stretched around the globe, so vast that half was lit with sunlight while the other half flowed and churned and brooded in darkness. And there, weightless in a warm bath, her heart thumping in her ears, she let her little one know that they were now where life uncountable eons ago had begun, and where today, with the necessary courage, it continued.

The following Monday evening after class, she was returning books to the University library when her eyes were drawn to a familiar person sitting at one of the carrels with his back to her: Nick, writing intently in his notebook, a coffee mug filled with pens beside him, the shelf in front of him piled with books. She felt a surge of affection for him, and pride; and she almost walked over to ask him how his courses were going.

But she didn't. Karl was going to meet her in the lobby. If she was late, he might come in looking for her, and she wanted to avoid the possibility of a confrontation. She remembered the pain and rage in Nick's eyes the last time she had seen him in the hospital parking lot. Even here in the tranquility of the library, she felt uneasy. If Nick were to turn around and see her with Karl, no telling what he might say, or do.

And yet, she trusted his essential decency. Deep inside, he was a good man, if only that goodness could be freed. Yo' can be such a wonderful mahn, Nick. Yo' keep workin'. Yo' gon' be that dedicated teacher them kids need.

She admired his broad shoulders stretching his shirt, and remembered with a pang of longing his passionate strength in the moonlight on Maroon Ridge. No, she would not interrupt his work. Let him pursue his dream undisturbed by the ache of a lost love, or the pain of jealousy. Let him pursue his dream.

She sent him a silent kiss, then hurried out the door to the lobby.

She loved to wake up in the middle of the night and rub her hand over Karl's strong chest; to brush her fingers through his ever-bushier beard; to touch his lips, tracing his sleeping mouth until he woke and smiled at her. Then she placed his hand on her belly and laid her hand over his. "Hi, father," she whispered. Sleepily he answered, "Hi, mother."

She imagined the bambino beneath their hands: a restless person four inches long, with an oversized head full of mysterious dreams, and a hummingbird's heart pumping a mix of African and Norwegian blood, West Indian blood and American blood, through a body with outer limbs and inner organs fully formed, floating in the tiny ocean inside her.

When the dry season arrived in May and the nighttime squalls no longer interrupted her sleep, she discovered that she missed the bowls of popcorn. Occasionally her craving became so great, she would get up and pop herself a potful, then return to the bed and devour the entire bowl of delicious salty buttery popcorn.

But one night, the big mayonnaise jar of popcorn that Karl had brought down from his cottage was empty. She tried eating a cracker. She tried a cookie. She tried a stalk of celery. But what she wanted was popcorn. She went back to bed and tried to sleep. Finally, too fidgety to lie awake alone any longer, she shook Karl until she woke him.

"Hunnh?" he moaned groggily, opening his eyes a slit.

"Karl, we're out of popcorn."

"Popcorn?" He closed his eyes; in a moment he was asleep again.

She poked him with her finger. "Karl, we've got to remember to buy popcorn tomorrow."

"Uuuuffff." He lifted his head and peered at her with bleary dis-gruntlement. "You ate almost a whole chicken at Zosia's, two baked potatoes, a jumbo portion of spinach, *and* a bowl of tutti-frutti with chocolate sauce. And now you want popcorn?"

"We'll stop at Pueblo on the way home from work, okay?"

Groaning, he sat up, then informed her, "Okay, but it won't be as good as what you're used to. You've been eating the world's finest pop-corn. And that was the last of what I brought down from Illinois."

"You brought it with you?"

"Yup. That was POP'S POPCORN, DeKalb County Fair Blue Rib-bon Winner. You wait till you taste the difference. You'll be going from champagne to table wine."

Thoroughly annoyed, she lay down and pulled up the sheet. "Never mind."

"Angelique, we'll stop at Pueblo tomorrow and pick up a bag of Pops-A-Lot, then we'll use plenty of butter and salt."

"Thank you. Good night." She tried to forget her silly craving for popcorn.

On the dark of the moon in May, Nick wrote the final draft of his term paper for Caribbean History. The essay was not due until Monday, but he wanted to finish it tonight before he ventured out on a long-awaited mission to Salt River Bay.

CHRISTOPHER COLUMBUS VISITS ST. CROIX

Columbus discovered St. Croix during his second voyage, in 1493. At dawn on November 14th, he sighted a green hump on the western horizon. Carib Indians aboard his flagship, whom he had captured on islands further south, called this new island "Cibuquiera." But Columbus ignored them and called it Santa Cruz, the Holy Cross.

As the admiral of an armada of seventeen ships, he was bound for the island of Hispaniola, where he intended to establish Spain's first colony in the New World. But what sort of men were these, who would stake their claim under the flag of civilization? We shall see.

While the flotilla sailed along the north shore of Santa Cruz, Columbus searched for a river where he could put in for fresh water. He passed a large bay, now the harbor of Christiansted, but found no clear entrance through the reef. Further on, he sighted a smaller bay that looked like the mouth of a river, and here he discovered an adequate gap in the coral. So he ordered the fleet to drop anchor at what today we call Salt River Bay. On the western shore stood huts of a village. Columbus ordered a rowboat launched with twenty-five armed men and an empty water barrel.

The party landed on shore, searched through the deserted village, then filled their barrel with water. As they rowed back across the bay, they spotted a canoe paddled by seven Indians: four men, two women and a boy. We know from the log of Dr. Diego Alvarez Chanca, a surgeon on the flagship, that the Indians stopped paddling and stared with "mouths open" at the seventeen tall-masted ships. Perhaps they thought the vessels had sailed down from heaven. But they were mistaken. These ships had brought devils from hell.

Columbus took every opportunity to capture a few more Indians, for gold had proven scarce on these islands, and he needed something to show the good king and queen when he returned to Spain. So the men in the rowboat, in order to please their admiral, pulled at full speed toward the canoe. The terrified Indians tried to escape, but they were driven against the reef. In desperation, they tried to defend themselves. "The Indians with great courage took up their bows, the women as well as the men," wrote Dr. Chanca, "and I say with great courage because they were no more than four men and two women, and ours were more than twenty-five, of whom they wounded two." The Europeans launched a volley of crossbow arrows, then rammed the canoe, throwing the Indians into the sea. The islanders continued to fight, but they were subdued by the Spaniards' heavy arms and brought aboard the rowboat. The victorious conquistadores took their prisoners to the flagship and presented them to their grateful captain.

But one of the Caribs had been so badly wounded that his intestines were hanging out. Dr. Chanca declared the man was beyond saving, so the crew tossed him overboard. However, holding his intestines with one hand, this warrior swam toward shore. The Spaniards pursued him with their rowboat, captured him, bound him with ropes and again threw him into the sea. Determined to survive, the Carib managed to loosen the ropes and swim free. This time the white man did the job properly: archers filled the swimmer with crossbow arrows. The Christians watched with satisfaction as his body floated limp in the waves.

Columbus named the eastern point flanking the bay *Cabo de las Flechas*, Cape of the Arrows. Then he sailed north toward the island he could see on the horizon. But what of the six captured Indians aboard his flagship?

An Italian named Michele de Cuneo, a boyhood friend of Christopher's, had been in the rowboat and had captured one of the two women. He wrote in his journal that she was "a very beautiful Carib girl." He asked Columbus for permission to keep the girl as his slave. The great admiral assented to this enslavement.

But what sort of slave did Cuneo intend her to be? He tells us in his own words:

"Having taken her into my cabin, she being naked according to their custom, I conceived a desire to take pleasure. I wanted to put my desire into execution, but she did not want it and treated me with her finger nails in such a manner that I wished I had never begun. But seeing that (to tell you the end of it all), I took a rope and thrashed her well, for which she raised such unheard of screams that you would not have believed your ears. Finally we came to an agreement in such manner that I can tell you that she seemed to have been brought up in a school for harlots."

In summary, the results of the first encounter between the people who once lived on this island, and the plunderers who came from across the sea, were:

unprovoked aggression

kidnapping,

murder,

enslavement,

battery,

and rape.

In modern terminology, Columbus and his crew would be labeled "terrorists."

These events took place in 1493. The butchery continued on the North American continent for 400 years, until four days after Christmas, 1890, when the "Indian problem" was finally solved at Wounded Knee.

In Central and South America, despite the white man's unrelenting efforts, the Indian problem still has not disappeared.

But what of Cibuquiero/Santa Cruz? The plundering continues. The 1980 census showed that 31% of West Indian families on St. Croix lived below the American poverty level. In 1984, according to the Virgin Islands Daily News, over one third of the people in the Virgin Islands needed food stamps. Consistently, most commercial enterprises are owned by whites. The outlook for the future is so grim that many high school students drop out before graduation. The crime rate per capita ranks with America's worst cities.

In conclusion, it is clear that the Americans have transformed our West Indian island into:

a white man's paradise,

and a black man's dead end.

He felt a degree of satisfaction as he held the finished pages in his hands. Here was excellent material for a lecture when he became a teacher. Here was the truth about that day 500 years ago when the whiggers first arrived with their weapons.

He tapped the pages on the table to straighten them, then fastened them with a paper clip.

He felt a degree of satisfaction. But nothing compared to what he hoped he would feel by the end of this night.

And nothing, certainly, compared with the exultation he anticipated on the dark of the moon in June: the night when Nicholas Cruz would free his people.

His lights off, he drove past the brass plaque commemorating the COLUMBUS LANDING SITE; parked with his tailgate toward the bay. Wearing camouflage and rubber boots, he walked where once the huts of the Carib village had stood. He and Leroy had spent an entire Saturday digging into a nearby mound: they unearthed dozens of pot shards, and Leroy was thrilled when he found a carved Zumi god. Ever generous, he gave it to the museum in Christiansted.

Standing on the shore, Nick looked out at Salt River Bay, where five centuries ago the rowboat had approached. Now, scanning the dark water, he spotted the stationary shape of a fishing boat large enough to make the crossing from Puerto Rico. He held up a cigarette lighter and flicked it twice; a spark appeared twice on the boat.

He put on his ski mask and gloves as a man rowed toward him in a dinghy. He handed the masked rower a roll of money.

The man paddled a short distance from shore, then leaned over, hands hidden while he counted the bills in the glow of a flashlight.

Nick eyed the wooden crates at both ends of the little boat.

The man stuffed the bills into a pocket, then rowed back. He laid his oars as a ramp from the stern to the beach, stood in the wobbly craft and slid a crate toward Nick's waiting hands. Though his days in Nam were twenty years ago, the shape and weight of the crate were so familiar, he felt reunited with an old friend. His blood tingled with that same exhilaration he had savored on nights before a mission. Just like ol' times, he thought. Good to feel alive.

After delivering four crates, the man rowed back to the fishing boat for another load. Nick carried the explosives to his station wagon, where he opened each box to verify its contents. "Little sweethearts!"

he cooed to the well-packed sticks of dynamite. "Ain' we gon' have a party!"

The dinghy returned with an aluminum case and five long wooden crates. At his tailgate, fingers trembling with excitement, Nick nearly sang with joy at the sight of his Stinger anti-aircraft guided missile launcher, and five ready-to-deploy missile-rounds in their launch tubes. Oh Leroy, Leroy, ain' we gon' make them bastards pay!

The dinghy made eight trips. The taxi was filled after five; he would have to make two runs to the mahogany forest tonight. He hid the extra boxes among the spidery roots of the mangroves; covered them with a camouflage tarp. Keeping a mental tally, he knew as he took the last crate into his hands that he had everything: timers, detonators, ignition wiring, and the good stuff. The boom boom stuff. Boom! BOOM!! On the dark of the moon in June.

He whispered, "Gracias."

"De nada."

"Tell Fix, t'anks."

The man nodded, then rowed away across the dark water of Salt River Bay.

As he drove into the hills, his mind raced with plans. Sonar first. Radar. Petrox. Casa Columbus. Incoming-outgoing jets. And finally, the icing on the cake, Hard Hat himself. Just yo' wait, Leroy. Ah gon' set yo' little sister free from her foolishness.

Roaring past a picnic table, he looked down at the lights of the refinery on the coast far below and growled with pleasure as he imagined a mile-long fireball rising above it, fueled by dozens of oil tanks. Yes, when the clock struck midnight on June tenth, he would be sitting comfortably at that picnic table with a glass of iced rum punch.

The treetops formed a tunnel over the road and blocked even the glow of starlight. He pulled to the shoulder, set a jack in place by the left front wheel, then took off the hubcap and laid it on the ground beside a spanner. Should anyone drive by—unlikely at 0130 hours on an early Saturday morning—the jack would explain his small difficulty.

He hefted the crates out of the car and hid them a short distance into the forest. Then he debated: bury these crates, or pick up the second load? He foresaw no problem either way, but decided to secure his first batch before he returned for the second. So for the next hour, he hauled his booty to a spot fifty yards into the forest: the crates fit snugly into grave-shaped holes he had prepared. He liked to think—though he could never be sure—that on this site the huts of the Maroon Village had once stood, and that the spirits of his people would guard his treasure. He covered the crates with dirt, leaves, bits of fallen vines.

By 0235 hours he was driving down out of the hills.

At 0520 hours, he set the last crate of the second load into its nest and covered it with dirt. Though his back ached and his fatigues were soaked with sweat, he longed to fill the forest with a wild whoop of triumph. For here at his feet, beneath a nondescript layer of leaves, was a munitions cache sufficient to throw the island into utter chaos.

But of course the good soldier remained silent.

CHAPTER THIRTY-ONE

Mother's Day

For the first time in twenty-five years, maybe thirty—Karl couldn't remember how young he had been when Joe helped him to make the first card with colored paper and crayons—he did not send his mother a Mother's Day greeting. On the Saturday before that special Sunday, he drove into town to buy roses for Angelique, and for Estelle and Zosia; but he had not sent his mother so much as a store-bought card. He was not happy with that decision. As he drove back to his cottage, the jeep filled with the scent of roses, he felt more than sadness; he was crushed by a devastation he had not known since Joe's funeral.

He slept poorly that night on Angelique's porch, woke up before dawn, never bothered to look over the wall at the rising sun. He tried to go back to sleep; tried to think about sailing; wondered if a cup of coffee—or two—would help to perk up his spirits. But he hadn't the motivation to drag himself out of bed.

Looking at his mermaid asleep beside him, who would soon awaken to celebrate her first Mother's Day, he wondered how he could possibly summon, or simulate, the appropriate joy. He felt more like bursting into tears.

Then he realized: he didn't want this divided family haunting his marriage. He would soon be her husband; but he was still his mother's son, and always would be. So whatever needed fixing, he'd better fix it. For Angelique, for his mother, he cast aside his stubbornness and made the decision: All right then, I'll phone home. I'll talk with her.

Immediately he felt better, for the stalemate was over: whether success or disaster, at least he would call. When? He certainly didn't want his mother feeling lousy all day. Why not call her now? Moving carefully so not to wake Angelique, he reached to his pile of clothes, took his watch from his pants pocket: 7:40. Two hours difference: 5:40. She'd be in the kitchen heating cornbread and coffee. Pop would be out in the barn already. Perfect.

He slipped out of bed, grabbed his clothes, then paused for a moment to gaze at his bride-to-be and to promise, Whatever it takes, there's going to be peace in this family before the twenty-fourth of June. He dressed inside the house, hurried down the steps and did not drive—he wanted time to think—but walked along the peninsula toward his cottage on the hill.

One moment he winced with guilt that he had hurt his mother these three months. And the next moment he was angry at her for hurting Angelique. Around and around his mind went again, but at last his feet were moving forward.

He entered the cottage and stared at the telephone. Make a cup of coffee? Plan what he would say a little better? Maybe write out a few notes, outline his argument, jot down key phrases he didn't want to forget. He sat in the chair. Looked to Joe for reassurance. Reached for the phone; his finger dialed the number. He envisioned her spooning coffee into the old kettle; her strong blue eyes, her short gray hair. He heard the old farm telephone, its funny rattling double ring, and then he heard her say, "White Oak Farm. Sally speaking."

He couldn't utter a word.

"Hello?"

His dry voice croaked, "Happy Mother's Day, Mom."

"Why, thank you. Just a second. Let me get your father."

She laid the phone down (on the wooden counter by the flour and coffee and sugar and salt canisters) and he heard her call (out the window with red-and-white checkered curtains blowing in the May breeze), "Ole! Karl's on the phone."

Then she was back on the line. "Karl, how are you?"

His heart was thumping. "Well, I . . . I'm not sure. I, ah, I'm sorry I didn't send you a card. There's been a lot on my mind lately and—"

She interrupted, "Karl, losing Joseph I was able to handle. The good Lord knows how, but we survived. Losing you," her voice cracked, "No, I can't bear it. We're a-comin' to your wedding, Karl, if you'll—" Now she was crying. "If you'll have us."

"Mom, of course I will. We *both* will. Angelique's been wanting to meetcha. We—"

" Karl?" There was his father's gruff voice, as always half trying to say hello, half hollering like he was herding cows into the barn. "Howerya doin', Son?"

"Well, I, I was just telling Mom that we hope you'll both be coming to our wedding." He braced himself; now it was either wedding bells or a broadside of cannons.

"Karl, I'll tell ye as straight as the wind blows, yer mother and I have had a time of it. They been days these last God-awful months when forty-four years of marriage purty near fell apart. And I'll admit, I don't claim to be any more good-hearted or enlightened or God-fearin' than I been three months ago. Because Karl, this marriage of yourn is hard for me to swallow. But I'll tell ye one thing I've learned . . ." He paused, and Karl could tell from his breathing that the tough old man was trying not to cry on the phone. "I love yer mother too much to let this come between us, Karl. And I love *you* too much too, boy, to be losin' ye. And maybe, maybe in that old oaken knothole heart of mine, I think there's maybe even a little love for that island gal of yourn."

There were the words Karl needed to hear; that was all the apology he knew he'd get, but it was all he needed. "Pop, do Angelique and I have your blessing?"

"Son, if ye were here, we'd kill the fatted calf."

"Well," Karl laughed, "why don't you two leave those darn cows at home and get yourselves on a plane in June and come down and meet one of the finest families you'll ever have the pleasure to know."

His mother nearly sang, "We'd be proud t'meet them, Karl. And we're very, very glad to be coming to your wedding."

"Good, Mom. I'm glad to hear that." Then he asked, his voice just a touch stern, "Pop, can I count on you? Handshakes all around?"

The gruff voice, chastened, assured him, "Handshakes all around."

"Thanks, Pop." He looked out the window at Angelique's house on Candle Point. "Listen, Mom, Pop, I wonder if you would do me a favor. I'd appreciate it if you both would write a letter to both of us, Angelique and I, saying, well, saying that you give us your blessing. That you're happy we're going to get married. Could you say that in writing, so I can show it to her? She's, ahhh, she's had a few misgivings and I think a letter would help."

"We certainly will," said his mother. "We'll write a fine letter this very morning."

"Son, it'll be in the ol' galvinized mailbox tomorrow, red flag up."

"Thanks. You might mention that photo I sent you. I mean, if you said something about how pretty Angelique is, that would clear the air, you know what I mean?"

"Karl, to tell ye straight, I chucked that photo into the stove. But I do recall yer gal had real purty bright eyes."

"Angelique is her name, Pop. And yes, she has beautiful bright eyes."

"Angel-eek. A lotta them people down there got foreign names?"

Karl laughed again. "There's some down here who might think Ole Oystein is a bit far-fetched."

His mother interrupted, "This call's a-costin' you, Karl. Send us a letter with all the details, when you want us to come and what we ought to bring. And how many of us you want to come."

"How many? We want *all* of you to come. Anne's family, and Solveig's family, and Uncle Odd. Aunt Amanda. I want to see the whole gang get on that plane."

His father chuckled. "Yer Ma's gonna look good in a grass skirt!"

"That's Hawaii, Pop. They don't wear grass skirts in the Caribbean. We'll find a nice sarong for you, Mom."

"All right, my baby boy." Her voice was filled with love. "Thanks so much for calling."

"You're welcome. Happy Mother's Day. Bye, Pop."

"So long, Son. Ye done a good thing to call us. Been three months since yer Ma had a night's sleep."

"Well, sleep well tonight. And see you in June."

When he hung up, he was limp with relief. Hooray, he thought, they're coming. He closed his eyes and sent up a simple prayer, Thank you, thank you, thank you, thank you, thank you.

Then he picked up the picture and looked at his mother, and his father, and at his brother. "Whatdya think, Joe? Peace in the family." But his heart was not entirely glad. "Sure wish you could be with us, Joe. You'd be my best man."

Finally he stood and took the three bouquets from the refrigerator. He would awaken his princess with a kiss, and roses, and the good news.

As he walked in the morning sunshine along the peninsula, the waves laughing against the rocks, he thought with conviction, They're good people up north. Americans *are* good people. They may be foot-shufflers, but at least they're shuffling in the right direction.

PART FOUR

CHAPTER THIRTY-TWO

A Tiny Speeding Locomotive

As he paced the halls of the airport with brooding restlessness, Nick looked at his watch: fifteen minutes before the late-afternoon flight from Miami. A rowdy college-age crowd at the check-in counter sang "Put de lime in de co-co-nut and drink it all up" with an uproarious imitation of his Crucian dialect. Seething, he muttered aloud, his voice unheard in the clamor, "Goddamn bunch of savages."

He brooded along the hallway, past the newsstand with its girlie magazines—all the smiling little bimbos were white, just like Santa Claus and Christ. Past an old Crucian woman oblivious to the world-travelers swirling around her as she mopped the floor, her tired eyes on the tiles. Past the Welcome Wagon with its ranks of paper cups filled with free rum-and-Coke for the new arrivals. Until his feet brought him to the luggage belt. He glanced at the gray New Arrivals door where the herd would soon come through.

Someday, he would see Ackerman walk through that door. Twenty years older, his blond butch-cut gone a little gray, his steel-belted stomach no doubt now a beer gut, his blue eyes fish-cold until they lit with a sneer at the first nigger who offered to carry his bags to a taxi. Oh, how he ached to see that sneer of disdain one more time. He'd even bow his head a little, shuffle his feet, baiting the trap as he led Ackerman to the taxi where the Colt lay hidden under the seat.

Sometimes, while he stood waiting for the next plane, he thought that Andy might come through that door, tired of his mother's bitterness, tired of her California lovers, determined to find his father and start fresh. When Andy scanned the crowd and recognized his father, he'd break into a smile and come running into the waiting arms that would hug that boy! Yeah, a year's coaching on the ol' b-ball court and Andrew Cruz would be the star of the Central team. Pan-Caribbean champion!

He'd introduce Andy to Angelique, and she'd see what a stable, loving father Nicholas could be. Yeah, she'd realize what a mistake she had made, and she'd dump Hard Hat, and then she'd invite Nick and Andy to meet her parents—she had told them so much about the remarkable boy—and of course Papa and Mama would be so glad to see Nick again, he was almost like a son. And on Memorial Day, a year from today, with his ring on Angelique's finger, and her ring on his finger, the whole family would stand together at Leroy's marker and lay a wreath of flowers. Honoring the son, the brother, the uncle . . . and the friend whose spirit had stood with them as best man at the wedding. And maybe by then, Angelique might be carrying a little brother for Andy! He felt a glow of deep peacefulness as he contemplated a family . . . something as simple and miraculous as a family of his own.

Once in a while—not often, because the pain after such thoughts was almost unendurable—but once in a while, he faced the gray New Arrivals door and imagined Leroy walking through it, thin and worn from prison camp, limping perhaps, but alive. Leroy's eyes would search the crowd for a familiar face. And Nick's voice would ring out, "Leroy, brother!" Oh Lord, the hug he would give that man! Pick him up in his arms, he would, and welcome him HOME. He'd drive Leroy to the Nielsen house, and he'd stand back a little on the verandah while Leroy knocked on the door: back far enough that Mama and Papa would see Leroy first, but close enough that they would know that Nick had brought their son home.

Oh yes, yes, if one day Leroy walked through that door . . .

Hard Hat in green Petrox overalls knocked on the gray door, opened it and peered through, then stepped into the sunshine and closed the door behind him.

Nick's dreams vanished.

The college-boy chorus at the far end of the corridor was singing, "Hey mistah tallyman, tally me banana! Daylight come and I wanna go hooooome!"

In too much of a hurry to stand in line at the check-in counter, and in no mood anyway to listen to the rum-soaked revelry of a bunch of yuppy-guppies, Karl walked along the airport hallway in hopes of finding a baggage attendant who could answer his question. All day up on the cracking tower, he had heard that bugle playing taps. The "emergency" phone call from Ed had turned out to be not much of an emergency—just another Monday shift at the boiler works—and he had chafed at having to work on a day supposedly dedicated to the memory and honor of soldiers who had fallen. Memorial Day was a day on which a person might even entertain a few reflections on the wars that swallowed people with appalling regularity; and now he chafed again at the Good-Time-Charlies waiting to board the flight back to Miami, for clearly they weren't bothered by any bugles.

He glanced around the arrivals wing, saw no baggage attendants, so he decided to try the door marked

NEW ARRIVALS   NO ADMITTANCE

Outside, he spotted an attendant lounging against a luggage cart. "'Scuse me, do you have a wheelchair for a passenger getting off a plane? My aunt is coming down in June and she's got a couple of bum knees."

"Yeah mahn, we take care of her." The attendant took a pad from his pocket. "When she comin'?"

"Saturday, June 17. She's originating at O'Hare, changing planes in Miami, arriving here at 5:35 p.m. Name's Barrington, Eleanor Barrington."

The man nodded. "Yo' want us to wheel her down the steps from the plane?"

"She can handle the steps, I think. It's the long walk from the plane to the terminal I'm worried about. She'll be pretty stiff after sitting all day."

"Yo' ain' to worry. Ah be there mehself."

Karl handed him a folded five-dollar bill. "Thanks. I appreciate your help."

As he pushed open the door and headed toward a telephone, he could still hear running through his mind—despite the distant laughter, and the loudspeaker announcement overhead—the clear, slow, dignified, heartbreaking tones of a bugle playing taps. Taps for Joe.

Nick saw the whigger come hurrying through the door. He followed him down the hallway, then stood nearby, an ear cocked, when the Bearded Boy stopped at a telephone, fed it a quarter and dialed.

"Hello, mother, how are you?"

Mother?

"Listen, I'll be a little late getting home. What time are we meeting your parents?"

Mama. Papa. Ah been almost like a son to them . . .

"Good. I can be at Candle Point by," he looked at his watch, "quarter to seven. If we roll by seven, we can be at the cemetery by eight."

The cemetery. She takin' a Yank to Leroy's marker!

"Fine. We can meet Mama and Papa at the Twining Vine by nine o'clock."

Leroy, she shamin' yo'!

"How's the bambino? . . . Well, lie down then and take a nap. You keep pushing yourself. You've got to rest for two now, you know. You're the midwife, but you won't follow your own advice."

No. No! He refused to believe it.

"All right, mother. I love you." Hard Hat sent a kiss through the phone, then hung up and hurried out to the parking lot.

No! He would see her, he would see Angelique with his own eyes, before he could believe that she had let a whigger filthify her.

"How do I look?" Zosia asked with excitement. She sat up proudly in her chair while Angelique finished braiding red and white ribbons into her bun. "Do I look like a proper maid of honor?"

Angelique laughed, "Zosia, the wedding's not for another four weeks." She tied a bow, then flicked the trailing ribbons.

"Yagh, but tonight is my rehearsal. How do I look?"

Angelique stepped back to inspect Zosia's red gown; she straightened its lacy white collar. "Tonight you are the queen of Poland! Let me get a mirror."

"Nogh! Absolutely not. Let me imagine that the old lady looks terrific." Zosia plucked at her puffy sleeves. "I must look my best for Karl's banquet."

For the past week, Angelique had been puzzled by the excited secrecy between Karl and Zosia. "What *are* you two up to?" She adjusted the dress over Zosia's shoulders; Zosia had last worn the gown when she was twenty pounds heavier.

"Never mind. And enough of this fussing over me." Zosia took hold of Angelique's hands and gently pushed her back from the chair. "Let me look at *you*." Angelique wore a sea-blue sarong she had bought especially for Karl's dinner. Zosia's eyes shone with approval. "Ahhh, tonight you are a West Indian princess."

Then she pointed to Angelque's waist. "Let's see if she's grown."

"But I showed you this morning! You can't see any change so

soon."

Zosia insisted, "Let's have a look."

Angelique opened the folds of her blue sarong, baring her slightly rounded cinnamon belly.

With keen eyes, Zosia inspected Angelique's abdomen; she worked her index fingers and thumbs like pairs of calipers. "Yagh," she asserted, "Elly Zosieńka has grown."

Angelique could see no difference in her slight but lovely bulge since this morning's examination. "Zosia, she couldn't possibly have—"

"The curve is an increment fuller," Zosia declared with the certitude of an expert. "The volume is distinctly bigger." She cupped her cool hands over the ripening belly.

Angelique placed her hands over Zosia's. "Every day I grow to your touch. What a magical sculptress you are!"

"How big is she now?"

"At sixteen weeks, Elly Zosieńka is a little person six inches tall. But her legs are folded, so she's just under four inches from her bald head to her rump. As you grip your cane, so her hand would grip a matchstick. She wiggles and kicks, though I can't feel her yet. Zosia, she weighs less than five ounces, and she would lie very comfortably in your hand."

"A little elf," grinned Zosia with delight.

BEE-BEEP! called the jeep's horn from the driveway.

"Ho!" Zosia cheered. "Our coach and six has arrived."

Angelique closed her sarong and straightened its folds, then looked expectantly toward the door. Her bearded Viking prince swung it open and strode in, wearing his white tropical suit and the turquoise tie she had given him. He gazed at her, his eyes filled with love. Then he smiled at Zosia. "Two gorgeous women. Oh, I'm a lucky man tonight!"

"We're all set," Zosia said as she lifted her cane from the back of a chair. "And tonight I'm going to walk."

Angelique placed her hand on Zosia's shoulder, keeping her in place; Zosia looked up with irritation, ready to refuse the wheelchair, no matter what her nurse said. But Angelique was not thinking of the wheelchair. She said, "Wait. I have a surprise for both of you."

She reached into her black leather bag on the table and took out a Doptone ultrasonic stethoscope: a small green instrument attached by a curlicue cord to a black cubical speaker. She set the speaker on the table and turned it on: it filled the room with a low electronic hum. "We won't be able to hear the elf with a regular stethoscope for another four weeks. But we can help her with a little amplification." While Karl and Zosia watched with interest, she opened her blue sarong, rubbed a clear jelly on her cinnamon belly, then placed the Doptone over the spot where she herself had listened that afternoon.

Suddenly the room was filled with the racing flutter of a tiny speeding locomotive. Her trained ears read the heartbeat at a healthy 160 per minute. "There she is!" she called to Zosia through the rhythmic swish. "Now you're listening to your granddaughter."

Zosia stared at Angelique's belly. She did not smile, she did not look up with astonishment. She said nothing, and Angelique wondered what was wrong. But then Zosia closed her eyes, her lips trembled as they lifted into a smile, and tears trickled down her wrinkled cheeks. "I only wish Piotr could hear."

Kneeling behind a stone coffin, Nick peered across its lid at the trio that approached on a path through the cemetery. Angelique held a candle as she walked, her face lit by its flickering glow. An old white woman walked between her and Hard Hat, holding their arms. Hard Hat shone a flashlight on the ground in front of the old woman's feet. As they walked toward Leroy's marble marker, Nick stared at Angelique's belly; she wore a sarong and he could see nothing unusual.

They stood before the pale white marker. The whigger turned off his flashlight, then he held a candle to Angelique's. He gave it to the old woman. Now he lit a candle for himself. Three faces illuminated by three flames stared down at Leroy's marker.

"Today," said Karl quietly, "is for remembering, for honoring, for setting everything else aside while we pause to say, Thank you, to those who will never enjoy the blessings they fought for."

His thoughts returned to the DeKalb cemetery, where this afternoon his family had surely leaned a wreath of red roses against Joe's black headstone. And though there was no flag by Leroy's marker, there was certainly one by Joe's, a brand new flag with bright colors. Pop would set it in place, then give it his snappy World War Two salute.

I miss ya, Joe. Damn, I miss ya. But I'll tell ya something. Last week, Angelique and I signed fifty-one certificates for the people who stuck with us through sixteen weeks of that course. I don't take any credit for it, Joe. I'd a done nothing without Angelique and Zosia. I just thought you'd like to know: there's fifty-one folks who'll think a little harder the next time they pay their taxes, and the next time they fill out that ballot.

Got a kid coming, Joe. If he's a boy, Angelique wants to name him after Leroy and you. Boy or girl, I sure hope the kid's got your heart, Joe.

Zosia had spent most of Memorial Day looking back. But now, sitting in a dark cemetery and gripping her candle, its flame wavering, she tried, for the two young friends standing beside her—for the three—to look ahead toward the future. "I leave to your child my paintbrush," she said to Angelique "And my old mallet and chisel." She turned and looked up at Karl. "And I leave to your child Piotr's pen. Let Elly Zosieňka choose."

She paused, looking down at the pale white marker, then she added, "May your child live in a world that looks back on this century of war as the final chapter of man's madness, . . . and at the beginning of the millennium as the opening verse of a renaissance, a renaissance built upon a foundation of peace."

Karl leaned down and kissed her cheek. Angelique kissed her other cheek. A Polish kiss.

Angelique looked down at the three bouquets that Mama and Papa, Rosemary and Cyril and Chester, and Nat Junior and Suzanne and their five children had already placed at the marker. She knelt and leaned her wreath of frangipani against the stone: his favorite flowers, which she had woven into a ring herself, a frail, ephemeral token of her enduring love. She held her candle near his name,

LEROY BEAUMONT NIELSEN

Then she stood with one hand pressed over her belly. "Ah promise yo' one ting, Leroy . . . If he a boy, when he grow up, Leroy Joseph ain' never, never," her voice rose with anger, "ain' never gon' be a soldier."

Nick watched the three turn away and disappear into the darkness, Angelique's candle visible until she passed through the cemetery gate.

He had thought that if it was true, he would slap the whore across her face, then beat the whigger to the ground, beat him just short of killing him. But now he knew it was true. And he hadn't done anything.

He had stared at her hand—her beautiful hand he had once held, had once loved—laid over her belly, and he was crushed by the thought that once again he had failed Leroy, because he had failed to protect Leroy's little sister.

And Ah failed yo' too, Mama. Failed yo', Papa.

Ain' never done nothin' meh whole life but fail. Failed meh wife. Failed meh son.

Sure as hell failed Angelique.

Ah ain' even brought any flowers for Leroy.

Standing up behind the coffin, he was too ashamed to approach any closer to Leroy's marker. He turned and walked slowly in the darkness toward another gate, wishing, as he had wished a thousand times, that it had been he and not Leroy who never returned from that trail into the sawgrass.

As he drove toward Maroon Ridge, his refuge, his sanctuary, the sacred cliff, the sacred forest, the one spot on all the earth where he felt any measure of peace, he wondered if he shouldn't just take his Colt and end it all.

But he also wondered, as he brooded on this new and intolerable filth on his island, if he possessed the patience to wait another twelve days until the dark of the moon in June.

CHAPTER THIRTY-THREE

The Banquet

Angelique paused by the jeep in the Twining Vine Restaurant parking lot, a clearing in the mahogany forest just west of Maroon Ridge, while she gazed into the dark jungle and thought about Nick. Had he been up on the cliff recently, or was he too busy in the library? And . . . had he found another woman to squeeze in his arms and drive wild with his loving, up there in the sea breeze and moonlight?

She hoped so.

Her eyes were drawn to the flight of a solitary lightning bug. Its blinking pale-green light drifted like the tip of a fairy's wand among the branches and vines.

"Hey slowpoke, you coming?" called Karl as he walked with Zosia through a stone gate that led toward the restaurant.

"Yes, I'll be right with you," she called back, though she could not force herself to hurry as she walked among the parked cars. For she had come here with great reluctance. Looking ahead through a row of dark mahogany trees, she saw the spotlighted stone walls of an old Danish greathouse, a two-story mansion recently renovated into a restaurant overlooking the sea. There the white master had lived; "rich as a planter" had been the phrase in those days, as in his sugar cane fields he had worked a Leroy, a Nicholas, an Angelique to death. She glanced up through frilly black mahogany boughs at the lit windows upstairs. How many African concubines had been taken to those rooms, and how many unwanted children conceived, children then tossed out the door before they were even born?

Following at a silent distance behind Karl and Zosia as they walked slowly, Zosia with her cane, along a fern-fringed path, she looked ahead toward an outdoor patio, lit by the flickering orange flames of tiki torches. The restaurant was virtually full; Karl had been right to make reservations. A mix of people, black and white, were seated around two dozen tables, each elegantly set with linen and blue-and-white Danish china. Candles burned in curving glass chimneys. Sprays of hibiscus, frangipani, and ginger thomas decorated the centers of the tables—the same red, pink, and yellow flowers that had decorated graves in the cemetery.

A Crucian waiter in a white coat descended the steps from the greathouse to the patio with a laden mahogany tray. Gracefully circling one of the tables, he served planters' punch in tall glasses to his appreciative Crucian clientele. Then he hastened across the patio, deftly weaving among the other tables, toward the tall, imposing greathouse. He scurried up the steps and disappeared through a large door to the kitchen inside.

She would have preferred a different setting for tonight's Memorial Day banquet, without the stone palace that once belonged to bullwhip aristocracy. But Karl had chosen the restaurant because it was on the island's northwest corner, close to Frederiksted and so a convenient drive for her parents. And someone at Petrox had recommended the Twining Vine's 'spectacular view of the sea.' She appreciated Karl's concern for Mama and Papa, and did not want to spoil his evening, so she kept her grumblings to herself.

She caught up with Karl and Zosia as they paused at the edge of the patio to admire the restaurant. Though they both turned to her with a smile of anticipation, she said nothing; better silence than false words of shared excitement. Instead, she looked up and around at the extraordinary setting. The forest loomed tall on both sides of the patio, and towered behind the greathouse, like a black curtain wrapped around a stage, open to the sea. High overhead, the stars peered down as a distant, mute audience.

She spotted her parents standing at a stone wall along the outer edge of the patio, Papa's arm around Mama as they looked out at the water. With a surge of love for them both on this difficult day, she called, "Hey, yo' two lovebirds!"

They turned and smiled at the approaching trio. Following greetings, handshakes and kisses, Papa said, "Mama and Ah been watchin' de dolphin jump."

"The dolphin are jumping?" asked Karl as the five stood together along the wall, facing the panorama of black ocean and bright stars.

Papa pointed at the Big Dipper, arching upside-down, the stars of its handle trailing over the North Star. "Dolphin gon' stand on he nose tonight."

"Oh, *that* dolphin," laughed Karl. "He's an old friend of ours."

"Karl," said Angelique, slipping her arm through her father's, "to you that fish is a mere acquaintance. Papa introduced *me* to the dolphin when I was only three."

"Dat's right," affirmed her father. "When de dolphin been only a minnow."

"There it is!" exclaimed Zosia, pointing to the northwest.

Angelique searched the darkness, saw nothing.

"There's what?" asked Karl.

"Keep watching," said Zosia in a hushed, excited voice.

In a faint blink of light, a cluster of pale rectangular patches appeared, perhaps a mile offshore.

"What on earth was that?" asked Karl.

"Keep watching."

In another faint flash, the rectangular patches reappeared, briefly; beneath them was a pale stripe.

"It's an old-time square-rigger!" said Karl, sharing Zosia's excitement. "But what was that light? Looks like somebody's in another boat, taking flash pictures."

Another blink of light illuminated five tiers of sails, towering above a ghostly white hull that was cutting north.

"Dat be de *Danmark*," explained Papa, "an old Danish clipper, now a trainin' ship. Comes every year wid cadets from Denmark to call on de islands. De boys been in town, nice kids, practicin' dey English. Tonight dey under sail for St. Thomas. De boys tell me dey passin' all t'rough de islands, den up to Miami, and New York, and den all de way 'cross to Copenhagen. Whooeeee, what a fine trip for de lads!"

Angelique sucked her teeth. "The master come back to snoop around the old plantation."

"Now Angel," scolded her father, "dey is just boys learnin' 'bout de sea. Yo' can't blame dem for what happen here long ago."

She could have asked Papa how many slaves that ship had once brought to the island, but she turned her back to the water—and to controversy—and kept quiet.

"But what makes that flash?" asked Karl. "It seems so regular, about every fifteen seconds."

Zosia pointed east. "Hamm's Bluff lighthouse is just up the coast."

"Of course. Amazing what a powerful light it beams out."

Angelique listened to the Rastafarian band warming up in a corner of the patio.

MIGHTY JAMES & THE MASTERS

read the logo on the bass drum in red, green and gold. Two centuries ago, mandolins and cellos had played stately quadrilles on this patio; now electric guitars ran though licks of reggae while conga drums stirred the night with their bouncing beat.

Hard enough to come from the cemetery on Memorial Day to a greathouse restaurant. Harder still to listen to dance music. She felt that her parents' smiles were a little forced, hiding the sadness they too felt today. She wondered once again why Karl had invited them out to dinner on this particular night.

"Well," she heard him say, "anybody hungry?" He led the group toward the tables.

After everyone had ordered dinner, Angelique noticed Karl and Zosia exchanging glances across the table, he with a nervous look, she with encouragement. He stared down for a long moment at his fruit salad. Then he reached into his jacket, pulled out an envelope and laid it on the table between his plate and hers, so that Angelique could read by the light of the candle,

> Miss Angelique Nielsen
> Mr. Karl Jacobsen
> Box 3684, Christiansted
> St. Croix
> United States Virgin Islands 00820

Curious, she looked at the return address,

> Sally and Ole Jacobsen
> White Oak Farm
> 1181 Lincoln Highway
> DeKalb—

Shocked, and angry, she glared at Karl. Why was he suddenly bringing his parents into Mama's and Papa's world? Hadn't they been insulted enough?

He whispered anxiously, "It's all right. I promise you, it's a fine letter."

She relaxed, slightly. Zosia caught her eye and gave her a nod of reassurance.

Karl asked, loudly enough for everyone at the table to hear, "Angelique, do you remember the picture Papa took of the two of us after church? The photograph that Zosia has on her dresser now?"

She nodded, wary. "Yes?"

"Sweetheart, I sent that photo to my folks a while ago. It's on their mantel, over the fireplace."

Am I supposed to be grateful, she fumed, that the old racist pig finally condescended to— But she cut off that thought, refused to follow it any further. She would let Karl have his say.

Zosia clearly knew what was going on, for there she sat in her red and white gown, her eyes sparkling with a secret happiness.

Karl became solemn as he looked across the table at Mama, and at Papa. "Today is Memorial Day." He turned to Angelique. "On this day of devotion, and dedication, I would like to honor your brother, and to honor my brother, by letting them know that two very different families from two corners of the world will soon be coming together." He paused, for a moment too filled with emotion to speak. "I think Leroy and Joe would be glad to know that . . . two very different families have built a bridge."

From the envelope he drew out a letter, then he held it so she could read the big, awkward, loopy script while he read aloud,

"My father writes,

> White Oak Farm
> May the 14th

> Dear Angelique and Karl,
> We were thrilled to receive your portrait. Your Mom and I both agree that Angelique looks like a very fine woman, with a bright twinkle in her eye. Karl, that's exactly what first attracted me to your mother, you know.
> We greatly look forward to the privilege of meeting Angelique's family. You have said so many nice things about them.
> You and Angelique have our most heartfelt blessing."

The letter was shaking in Karl's hands. Angelique now read the small, neat, schoolgirl's penmanship as Karl, somewhat embarrassed, read aloud,

"And my mother writes,

> Hi, my baby boy.
> The sun shined extra bright on the morning your picture arrived.

288 • *Children of the Sun*

We had hoped so much when you went down to your island that it would be good for you and you might find your way to a little happiness there. We know you were so glum in Chicago. We're very excited to meet Angelique, as well as her side of our soon-to-be-extended family.

Karl, you certainly look healthy and proud and very handsome in your picture. You remind me of your father when I first met him, the old devil.

Angelique, we wish you both deep and lasting happiness.

All our love,
Mom
Pop."

Karl handed her the letter.

She could hardly believe what was written there on the page. She glanced at Zosia and saw her nod of confirmation: it was true.

Then she looked at Mama and Papa and saw in their smiles that all was forgiven, that they too gave their blessing.

She reached for Karl's hand. "I think Joe and Leroy would feel . . . heartened tonight. Encouraged that, yes, people *can* move forward." She squeezed his hand. "Thank you."

Zosia cheered, "A toast to the bride and groom!"

Her hand was trembling so much when she tried to lift her glass that Angelique had to wrap one hand around Zosia's, while she raised her own glass with her other hand.

"Bądźcie szczęśliwi!" proclaimed Zosia. "May happiness settle upon you like the petals of the apple tree. And may your union ripen with a treeful of fruit!"

"Here, here!" boomed Papa's voice. "Ah waitin' for de day when meh tomboy make me a grandpa again."

As the five clinked their glasses around the table, Angelique noticed that Mama was looking at her with that all-knowing motherly look of hers. Angelique knew her mother had guessed and immediately she averted her eyes. Was Mama angry? Disappointed? Was the wedding ruined for her?

She helped Zosia to drink her wine.

Zosia grinned exuberantly. "Yagh. Tonight the bridesmaid will celebrate."

They set Zosia's glass down, then, still avoiding her mother's look, Angelique took a sip of her juice. Had she been mistaken, to hurry with

Chapter 33 • 289

a baby for Zosia's sake while she hurt her mother? Couldn't they have waited? Zosia seemed so healthy, so filled with vitality tonight.

She felt the nudge of her mother's foot under the table. She glanced up, and was profoundly relieved when Mama winked at her with proud approval.

At 2200 hours, the USS *Defender*, Spruance-class destroyer DD 998, headed north from Frederiksted and hooked around the northwest corner of St. Croix. The *Defender* had received orders to steam northeast toward the Anegada Passage, a channel through the chain of Caribbean islands, and so to the open waters of the Atlantic. Bound for the Norwegian Sea north of the polar circle, the destroyer would join vessels of several nations for NATO exercises in the waters between Norway and Iceland. A fleet of submarines, a fleet of surface ships, and squadrons of aircraft were to rehearse a tri-level blockade across the major channel serving the Soviet port at Murmansk. Such a blockade would protect the sea lanes of the Atlantic from Soviet interference in time of crisis. Or war.

As the *Defender* left Frederiksted, Captain Henry Fremont gave the order for battle drill: the vessel's weapons systems would proceed through all steps short of firing.

Missile technician 2nd class Schwartz, seated at his Armaments Monitoring Terminal, kept a sharp eye on the starboard Tomahawk quadropod warning light. Since that first flicker on April 1, the light had flashed twice more while he was on duty; other missile technicians, however, had not noticed any irregular activity. Schwartz, the living fanatic who wouldn't let loose of a problem until it was fixed, had twice run all computer checks through pod C, had twice reported the flickering to his chief petty officer, and had twice requested permission to investigate an intermittent fault in the wiring.

Based on the error-free computer checks, Chief Petty Officer Richards denied permission to open Tomahawk quadropod three, pod C. He repeated, tiredly, "Don't fix what ain't broke."

Overruled, Schwartz did as he was told. But he felt more than a little nervous during the battle drill as he brought his cruise missiles through all stages short of firing.

Dessert was a grand occasion. The waiter brought five papaya halves, their hollowed-out centers filled with vanilla-walnut ice cream.

"Please don' touch yo' spoons yet," he said, then over each papaya he poured a libation of brandy. The five banqueters murmured with approval. Holding a foot-long match like a magic wand, the waiter touched its flame to each dessert, creating over each papaya a crown of blue diaphanous flames. The five gazed with delight at the spectacle, then smiled at each other, their faces lit with a mercurial glow.

From the corner of the patio came a slow, enticing reggae beat, Mighty James' invitation to the dance floor.

When they had finished their Papaya Flambeau, Papa took Mama's hand, then asked the others, "Yo' mind if Ah sneak off wid meh hot date?" The two sashayed toward the deck near the wall.

Zosia waved her hand at Angelique and Karl. "You two don't have to keep the old lady company. Let's see a little boogie-woogie."

As Karl led Angelique to the dance floor, he whispered in her ear, "Guess what? You're glowing."

"I'm what?"

"You're glowing. I've always heard that pregnant women have a special glow, and now I see it. You have the most beautiful radiance in your face."

"It isn't me," she told him. "It's the little one glowing inside me. Elly Zosieňka is very happy to be able to come into a world with four loving grandparents." She snuggled into Karl's arms, her face nestled against his soft beard.

She waltzed with her Papa, surprised at how graceful he was as they twirled and laughed and basked in each other's unspoken love.

Karl taught Mama to polka, while the band played a calypso version of the lively hop-step, and Zosia clapped and coached.

Then Mama, puffing for breath, took Angelique aside. They stood shoulder to shoulder at the stone wall. A late-rising oval moon, still partially hidden in the lacy black treetops, cast its shimmering glow on the gently rolling sea.

Angelique noticed an elongated cluster of pinprick lights near the horizon, like a tiny constellation at the bottom of the sky. Recognizing the destroyer's twin towers, she thought, There goes the new master, out snooping around the old plantation.

"Angelique, honey."

Still apprehensive, she turned to her mother and asked nervously, "Yo' ain' angry? Mama, we done it for Zosia. She . . . maybe ain' got so much time left."

"Ah know Zosia ain' well. Yo' and Karl, Ah can't say yo' ain' done right." Mama brushed the hair back from Angelique's face, as she had done when Angelique was a little girl. "How many weeks yo' be now?"

"Sixteen. Ah just beginnin' to show."

Mama looked up with a reverent smile. "Ah t'ank de good Lord for dese sixteen weeks. He been workin' a miracle."

Angelique heard the familiar "thump, thump, thump" of Zosia's cane. She turned and saw her friend approaching with Karl on one side and Papa on the other. Zosia stepped regally in her red gown. "Make way for the queen!"

The five banqueters gathered along the wall and gazed at the dolphin that stood now on its nose.

Nick stared down at the heave of black water against the cliff, the crash and surge of pale foam. There where the sea had once been red. No, he would not fail his people. This warrior would not fail their spirits who still lived in the forest.

He would sanctify his island. He would disinfect it of five hundred years of vermin. He would cleanse and sanctify his island with the sanitizing heat of fire.

Lifting his gaze, he stared out at the destroyer. Gon' blind yo' eyes, Big Sam. Gon' deafen yo' ears. Yeah mahn, gon' stuff a stick of dynamite right up Big Sam's ass.

Can do, sir! Can do!

And before the job was done, on the dark of the moon in June, he would also clean his island of a whigger, a whore, and a half-breed bastard.

Papa pointed at the dolphin. "If yo' watch reeeeal careful, yo' can see him wiggle he tail. He belly full of flyin' fish, see, and—"

Among the destroyer's pinprick lights, an orange spark flashed. Angelique stared in stunned silence at the ship; seconds later, she heard a sharp BOOM!, followed by the faint but growing roar of a jet engine.

As the accelerating blast grew louder, her hands unconsciously covered her belly. It's happening, she thought with both certainty and horror. It's happening.

"My god," cried Zosia, "we're at war!" She dropped to the ground behind the stone wall with her thin arms wrapped over her head. "Piotr, take cover!"

Bewildered, the other four crouched behind the wall. Angelique lifted Zosia into her lap, then peered over the ledge toward the approaching thunder.

Suddenly she saw it: in the sweeping beam from the lighthouse, a missile glinted for an instant like a needle shot across the heavens. No! Please, no!

It disappeared, though it roared for seconds more across the stars . . . then she heard it ripping through trees as it crashed into the mahogany forest, no further than a mile away. Please, please, please, not now!

In frozen silence, she clenched her teeth and waited for the world to end in a flash that would incinerate her child to ashes.

But the missile did not explode. No flames appeared in the dark hills. She looked again at the destroyer: the miniature constellation remained unchanged.

"Piotr!" Zosia shrieked, her eyes wild as she searched the ground around her, "Are you all right? Answer me! Kochany!"

The nurse hugged her patient. "It missed us. Zosia, Zosia, it missed us."

Zosia stared at her with horror and confusion. "Why are they attacking St. Croix?"

"I don't know. I don't know." She could hear Zosia's shallow rapid breathing. She reached for Zosia's wrist and felt her racing pulse.

Papa asked, with fear she had never heard in his voice, "What been dat?"

Karl answered, "It must have been a Tomahawk. That's the missile those ships carry. "

Mama cried, "Why in heaven's name dey fire a rocket at us?"

Karl stood up. He reasoned, "It had to be fired by accident. A Tomahawk is too powerful for any target on this little island."

"How powerful?" asked Papa, still on his knees.

Karl stared east toward the hills where the cruise missile had crashed. "Clearly the warhead was never activated. The missile's launching mechanism misfired, but the warhead's a separate thing altogether. If it didn't explode by now, it can't."

Tears of fright trickled down Angelique's cheeks. "If it fired by accident," she insisted angrily, "it can explode by accident."

Zosia frantically searched the sky. "Are there planes? Kochany, do you hear planes?"

Karl knelt and held Zosia's face in his hands as he reassured her, "Zosia, I promise you, nothing more is going to happen. It was an *accident*."

Angelique told him, "Carry her to the jeep while I look for a blanket. She's in shock. Lay her on the back seat." She turned to Papa. "Steady her head while Karl carries her. Don't let her choke."

She relinquished Zosia into Karl's arms, then she ran across the patio toward the stone mansion. Though the mother-to-be expected the bomb to explode at any moment—How far would the fireball reach? The flash, shock wave, radioactivity?—the nurse focused on a blanket for a victim of shock. Zigzagging among the abandoned tables, she was nearly knocked down by frenzied people dashing toward the parking lot.

In the lobby, a white man in a lime-green coat and pink bow tie was clapping his hands for attention as he shouted to his cooks and waiters, "Please, people, stay on your jobs. I'm going to call the police." Some were staying and some were bolting out the door. Angelique asked a cook, gaping with open-mouthed indecision at the chaos around him, "Where Ah can find a blanket?" The man seemed not to hear. She saw a staircase. Lifting the skirt of her blue sarong, she ran up the steps two at a time. She tried several doors along the hallway: a messy bedroom, a child sitting on the floor, playing with a toy castle—the boy looked up with annoyance; a maid smoking a cigarette as she watched TV, canned laughter burst from the room—the maid stared at her with surprise; until finally she found a linen closet with shelves of towels, sheets, boxes of laundry soap . . . *there* were blankets, neatly folded, blue flannel with white trim.

She grabbed two, raced down the stairs and out the door and across the patio and along the sidewalk—running now straight toward the missile, coiled like a cobra and ready to strike—to the parking lot where cars were jammed, blocking each other, horns blaring. Drivers shouted curses as they jockeyed to escape through the sole exit: a colonial arch built of brick and coral, mortared with sugar molasses two centuries ago. She threaded through the pandemonium. Coughing from clouds of dust and exhaust that churned in the interweaving beams of headlights, she saw Karl at the jeep, passing Zosia head-first through the side door to Papa, who had opened the tailgate and was reaching over the back seat to brace her. Mama stood with Zosia's cane.

Angelique climbed into the back beside Papa, leaned over the seat and spread one blanket beneath Zosia while Karl and Papa held her in the air. Zosia, wheezing now as she panted, her eyes closed, her face pale in the jeep's dome light, began to mutter in Polish. Karl and Papa laid her on the blanket; Angelique spread the second blanket over her. Ah should have brought a pillow, she thought with self-rebuke; she folded the bottom blanket into a U-shaped cushion around Zosia's head. "Zosia, we're going home now. We're going home. Breathe deeply. Can you breathe deeply?"

Zosia opened her eyes; disoriented, terrified, she slowly focused on Angelique.

"Zosia, slow down. Try to breathe deeply. We're going home to your paintings. To your sculptures. Home to your mermaid." She held Zosia's wrist and felt her pulse, gradually slowing. Zosia's breathing became deep wheezing gasps.

Suddenly Zosia drew her arm out from under the blanket and laid her clammy hand against Angelique's cheek. "Get away from it," she warned, her dark eyes deadly earnest. "Get as far away from it as you can."

"Yes, we're going home now. Home to Candle Point."

She and Papa climbed out of the back of the jeep and shut the tailgate. The cars around them gradually unjammed and poured out of the lot.

"I think what we should do," said Karl, "is we *all* should go to Candle Point. If that thing does explode, though I don't see how it possibly can, but if it does, we'll be a good ten miles away. And upwind. Those stone houses on Candle Point have been through a dozen hurricanes. There's food for several days, enough for the whole family. We can fill bottles with water in case the power should go out. Get candles ready and all that."

"Got to phone Rosemary," said Papa. "Got to phone Little Nat. Mama, we got to get our family safe."

"Right," said Karl. "Tell everyone to head east to Candle Point and we'll—"

"We goin' to church," declared Mama. "Meh family gon' be safe in de house of de Lord. Yo' come too, Karl. We find a bed for Zosia in de rectory. And den we pray for de people on dis island."

Zosia screamed inside the jeep with her thin ferocious voice, "Get away from it!"

"We're going home," Angelique called to her. She knew she could never dissuade her parents from their faith in the church. She guessed Holy Cross must be four, maybe five miles from where the missile had crashed; surely they would be safe there, even from a nuclear blast. She told Papa, "Zosia need a doctor. We gon' stop at the hospital on the way home. Ah phone yo' at church."

He did not argue; neither did Mama. He said, "Soon as we get to church, we call yo'."

"We got further to drive," she reminded him, "so give us time to reach home."

She climbed into the jeep's passenger seat, reached back and found Zosia's hand under the blanket. Zosia gripped her with both hands and squeezed with surprising strength, her face etched with frantic terror.

Karl started the engine, then called over the seat, "Don't you worry, Zosia, everything's going to be just fine." His voice filled with confidence, he told Angelique, "And don't you worry, Mother. The Navy just did us a big favor. You can bet that when we teach our course next September, we'll have to use the auditorium to seat an overflow crowd. Because our guest speaker for the first class is going to be the captain of that destroyer."

They drove down out of the forest and onto the coastal road leading to Frederiksted, following close behind Mama and Papa in their little orange VW bug. Angelique looked out the back window: the destroyer's lights had changed to a slim vertical constellation, densely packed. "The ship has either turned toward the island, or it's heading away." It's happening. It's happening. It's happening.

Karl observed optimistically, "At least it stopped firing missiles."

When he saw the orange spark of artillery fire, Nick dropped instinctively into the guinea grass; when he heard the BOOM!, he scrambled with Nam-reflexes behind the nearest big rock. "Incoming! Incoming!" he shouted, his hands grabbing mystified at his head, for where was his helmet?

As the missile roared toward his island, he heard with well-trained ears that it was not a Rooskie SAM . . . and that it was heading east of him, toward the heart of the forest. "Leroy, get *down!*"

Ripping through trees, the projectile crashed near the peak of Maroon Ridge.

Eyes clenched, he held his breath, grit his teeth . . . It failed to detonate!

His heart thumping against the ground, his mind clearing, he nearly cheered, The Navy fired a dud!

But why were the Americans attacking?

Or were they firing dummy missiles at his island for target practice?

Was it a misfire?

He peered over the rock: no secondary firing, no aircraft, not even a pop from the deck guns.

Cautiously, he stood up. If it was a misfire, then he wanted to know: Did the missile carry a warhead? He felt a shiver of excitement. "Big Sam, Ah tink yo' just made a major contribution to the arms cache."

Springing to life, he sprinted up the ridge toward his taxi to fetch the Colt. No doubt someone would soon come looking for the missile. The Navy would surely send a chopper from the ship. Time to unearth the Stinger! Then to find the missile, hold off any guests, check out the warhead. And calculate his options.

Swinging open the taxi's door, he grabbed the Colt under the seat, and a box of cartridges. Opening the tailgate, he took out a rucksack of tools and checked to be sure it contained a pair of heavy-duty tin snips for cutting through cyclone fences . . . or into the fuselage of a maverick missile. He dressed in camouflage, strapped on the holster, dropped extra shells into a pouch.

As the warrior ran along a moon-dappled path through the forest toward the peak of the ridge, he hoped with all his heart, Tonight's the night! Tonight's the night! Tonight's the holy, sanctifyin' night!

CHAPTER THIRTY-FOUR

Stinger

In his cabin writing the *Defender's* monthly status report, Captain Henry Fremont heard the blast of a missile fired from his ship. He jumped up, overturning his chair, threw open the door and listened with horror to the thunder of a jet engine as one of his Tomahawks raced over the sea toward a blinking lighthouse on St. Croix! My God! He laid his arm over his eyes and turned his face away.

But there was no flash, no thunderclap. The diminishing roar simply stopped. He glanced toward the island: the lighthouse blinked; scattered lights along the coast shone exactly as before; to the east, the moon floated serenely. He let out a long breath. Thank dear God there's no mushroom over that island.

The captain first ordered an immediate check of the status of all Tomahawks on board.

Second, he ordered the *Defender's* helicopter to search for the missile, at sea, and if necessary on land in the vicinity of the lighthouse. Within minutes, an SH-3 Sea King chopper lifted from its pad on the destroyer's afterdeck and followed the missile's flight path. From an altitude of 200 feet, its spotlight lit a bright silver circle on the rolling black water.

Third, he reported the broken arrow to Roosevelt Roads Naval Station on Puerto Rico.

And fourth, he ordered the *Defender* to steam to a position of safety ten miles offshore.

Standing on the bridge as the destroyer swung sharply to the north, Captain Fremont comforted himself with the thought, Be glad of one thing: that Tomahawk's just a baby. It's only a cruise missile. You didn't launch an ICBM, a big mother. This one is just a baby.

Stationary high above the western hemisphere, a Soviet geostatic satellite detected, with its infrared sensors, the launching of a missile. The satellite relayed time, location, and flight path to the Early Warning Headquarters in Moscow.

Corporal Boris Petrov perked up at his console when a bit of unordinary data appeared on his monitor, indicating activity in the Caribbean. His screen traced the flight of what appeared to be a surface-launched missile, fired—strangely—outside of the American test range at Vieques, Puerto Rico. Either the missile's flight had been extremely brief, or it had evaded Soviet tracking. Petrov noted the time, 0446 hours on Tuesday morning, 30 May; then he picked up the phone and notified his duty officer.

After a day of parades and speeches on St. Thomas, Governor Adam Harper was wearily putting on his pajamas when the telephone rang. His wife, already in bed reading *The Life and Times of Marcus Garvey*, answered it while he headed barefoot to the bathroom to brush his teeth.

She called, "Adam, Public Safety on St. Croix. They say it's urgent."

"They *always* say it's urgent," he growled as he covered the bristles of his brush with a green squirt of Peppermint Plus. "Tell them to hold. Tell them Ah'm on another phone to Washington." In irritated protest against this intrusion of his bedtime tranquility, he scrubbed his molars with prolonged and vigorous diligence.

Finally he padded grumbling back to the bedroom and picked up the phone. "Harper here."

He listened for a moment, then groaned with impatience. "Has anyone verified these reports? . . . Well, has anybody found the damn t'ing? . . . Yeah, yeah, sounds like that UFO scare last August. Send a patrol car up Scenic Drive t'rough the rainforest. If yo' find any little green monsters, call me back. G'night."

He crawled into bed and laid his arm over his eyes against the glow of Twila's reading lamp. "Ahhhhhhh," he sighed.

"What was the problem, dear?"

"The Martians have landed again on St. Croix. But this time they crash-landed."

He was nearly asleep when the phone rang. "Ohhhh," he moaned, vexed that no one on St. Croix ever seemed able to wipe their noses without ringing up Daddy. "Twila, tell 'em Ah'm—"

"Ah am *not* yo' answerin' service."

He grabbed the phone and snapped, "Harper here."

Then he sat bolt upright, turned to the nightstand and scribbled on a pad,

TOMAHAWK CRUISE MISSILE

NO DANGER

NAVY SEARCH UNDERWAY

"All right. Ah'll phone Rosy Roads. Keep in touch." He pulled open a drawer and flipped through his address book to R.

Peering over her paperback, Twila asked, "Serious?"

"The Navy took another pot shot at St. Croix."

"Again?"

"This time they hit it." He pushed the buttons on his Touch-Tone.

A male monotone answered, "GoodeveningRooseveltRoadsNaval-Station."

"Good evening. This is Governor Harper on St. Thomas. Ah want to know what sort of weapon yo' people just shot at St. Croix. And *why.*"

"Thankyou. Willyouholdplease."

Harper glanced at the clock on the nightstand: nine fifty-five. His day had started with an American Legion pancake breakfast at seven a.m.

"Yes, Governor, this is Lieutenant Brodie. May I help you?"

"I want information on the sort of weapon yo' fired at St. Croix, as well as, goddamn it, an explanation."

"Yes, we have a report that the USS *Defender* sustained an accidental firing of a Tomahawk cruise missile. Unfortunately in the path of the missile's trajectory was the island of St. Croix, and thus the device now lies harmless either offshore or somewhere on your soil. Retrieval operations are under way. The device will be removed shortly."

"Exactly what sort of weapon is this? Do Ah have a nuke on meh island?"

"That information remains classified, sir."

"Classified? Don' give me that shit. How can Ah handle this emergency if Ah don' know what Ah'm dealin' with?"

"We can neither confirm nor deny the nature of the warhead."

"So what sort of precautions should Ah take until yo' remove it? How large an area should Ah evacuate?"

"I will forward your request for further information to the appropriate personnel. At what number may we reach you, please?"

"Forward my request? Ah need to know *now*! How can Ah mobilize meh police if Ah don' know how big a bomb Ah've got here?"

"We appreciate your concern, Governor. But there is absolutely no need to mobilize. The Navy should effect a retrieval within the hour. I will get back to you with all pertinent information as it is made known to me."

"Listen, people *live* in that rainforest. Do Ah pull them back one mile, two miles?"

"Governor, by the time those people awaken in the morning, the device will be long gone. We would like to request that the area be sealed off to any sightseers and especially to members of the press. News of such an incident might be detrimental to your tourist trade, wouldn't it, Governor?"

"Talk straight with me, Brodie. What happens if it does explode? How big is the blast?"

"Governor, I assure you, the possibility of detonation does not exist. The warhead was not activated. You have my word on that."

"And that is all yo' will tell me?"

"At this point in time, yes."

"Thanks for nothin', Navy.

"Good night, sir."

The governor hung up, then pounded his fist on the table.

Twila climbed out of bed. "Ah'll put the coffee on."

"Tanks."

He flipped through his address book to the name of the Virgin Islands representative in Washington, then he punched the buttons of his Touch-Tone. The line hummed faintly as he was connected via satellite to Area Code 202 . . . He heard a hearty voice, "Hello, this is Representative Roscoe Saint-George. Ah am sorry that Ah am not home right now, but if yo' will leave yo' name, telephone number and a message at the sound of the beep, Ah will return yo' call as soon as possible. Tank yo' for yo' interest in the Virgin Islands, America's Paradise."

"Beep. "

Governor Harper grit his teeth with exasperation. Then he barked, "Roscoe, call Harper. *Now*."

He thought for a moment, reached for the pad and scribbled a public announcement, ordering the evacuation of the western half of St. Croix north of Centerline Highway, including Frederiksted. Roughly a quarter of the island's population would have to relocate either along the southern shore or east of La Reine Shopping Center. There would be commotion and complications, and perhaps hell to pay afterwards for the unnecessary inconvenience to fifteen thousand people, but he would take that responsibility upon his shoulders. Better some flak, than to risk the lives of his people.

The announcement formulated, he phoned WSTX radio on St. Croix, then WSVI-TV.

He phoned the National Guard headquarters in Christiansted with instructions to facilitate the evacuation, and to set up emergency camps on the south shore and east end.

Finally he phoned the police with instructions for coordination with the Guard. "I want all officers on alert. Today's a holiday. Can yo' round them up?"

"A t'ree-minute blast on the siren will do it, sir."

"Right-o. Where's the chopper?"

"On St. Thomas."

"Alert a pilot, will yo'? Ah'll be at Truman Airport in fifteen minutes. Ah'm comin' over."

The Soviet submarine *Mikhailovsky*, on a surveillance tour of the Caribbean, was alerted by Moscow of unusual activity near the American island of St. Croix. A Typhoon-class ballistic missile carrier, at 557 feet in length one of the largest submarines ever built, this underwater nuclear arsenal carried twenty SS-N-20 missiles, each able to distribute its seven multiple warheads to a range of 4,800 miles. The submarine was thus able to strike targets anywhere on the North American continent within minutes, without moving an inch from its present position eighty nautical miles south of Puerto Rico. However, to facilitate tracking of NATO vessels in the vicinity of St. Croix, the *Mikhailovsky* proceeded at top speed toward the deep waters off the northern coast of the island.

Determined to get his hands on the warhead before the Navy did, Nick raced to the arms cache. He swept leaves and dirt from the lids of the aluminum case and one crate, then hefted the Stinger components out of the ground. Carrying the two like suitcases, he hurried as fast as he could manage along the jungle trail toward the beating whirr of a helicopter that zigzagged up and down the sloping coastline. Yo' keep lookin', chop-chop. Yo' gon' show Nick just where that rocket-bomb be.

He heard the wail of the siren at Police Headquarters, far below on the plain: the undulating alarm pierced the night as if the island itself were screaming.

Now he could see the helicopter's spotlight where it shone down into the forest, forming a green cone in the thrashing branches. His sharp ears told him the bird was stationary. He plunged ahead, his heart pounding with the old thrill as he closed in on his target.

And then he froze, his prey in sight: there on the forest floor in the center of a circle of light lay the wreckage of Uncle Sam's missile. It was bigger than he expected, over twenty feet long, maybe two feet in diameter, its blue fuselage torn open with a long gash from the battered white nosecone to the crumpled red tail fins. He nearly whooped a war cry. Instead he whispered, "Hello, sweetheart."

He looked up through the mahogany trees flailing in the chopper's wash: the bay door was open and men in white helmets and orange life vests were pointing down at the missile. He set the case and crate behind a bush, then stalked in the darkness around the spotlight's periphery as he searched through the branches for a clear shot. For twenty years he had brooded on the waste of his battles in Nam, where he had fought the wrong enemy. Now he would begin to correct the error of his ways. He raised the Colt with both hands, sighted along its barrel at an orange vest, then sent Big Sam a greeting card: PANG! His target shrieked and collapsed in the bay door. Nick inhaled the sweet-smelling powder. "Gotcha."

The other men vanished from the door. The chopper veered away and climbed at full throttle, arching toward the sea.

Bye-bye, Sam. Bring me a whole bucketload of Ackermans when yo' come back.

He stepped through the undergrowth toward the long dark cylinder lit by speckles of moonlight. Touching its torn aluminum skin, he spoke softly, nervously, to the power caged inside, "Don' blow, baby. Not yet. Ah gon' let yo' loose, but not quite yet."

He beamed his penlight through the gash and saw a complicated mass of microcircuitry. That's yo' guidance system, sweetheart, but it looks like yo' brains is a bit scrambled.

Hunting further along the jagged laceration, he shone his wand of light on a heavy cylindrical casing, one end broken open by the crash. Probing with his beam, he recognized a detonator. Though this particular mechanism was unfamiliar to him, it was clearly the hammer. And inside the heavy canister? It was the wrong shape, and too small, to contain conventional explosives in a missile this size. He felt a prickle slowly crawl up his back, for he knew he was staring the devil in the eye. "Sheeeeeeeeeyit! Nick got hisself a nuke!"

He examined the remainder of the missile as far as the gash permitted him to peer inside: fuel tanks, wing mechanics, the smashed innards of a jet turbofan engine. Returning to that strange cylinder, blunt-nosed and flat-ended like a two-foot Colt cartridge, he could not believe his good fortune. "No doubt about it. Yo' is meh little pinch of stardust."

Stardust that he would use, for how better to chase away the white man than to beat him at his own game?

He shone the light on his watch: 1017 hours. He had maybe half an hour before the chopper returned from the ship with troops. A midnight massacre! Just like ol' times. Can do!

First, get the Stinger ready where he had a clear shot over the water.

Second, a trip to the cache for a few sticks of the detonator's little helper.

Third, go to work on the warhead, with his ears cocked for the chopper.

But he hesitated.

Is this what Ah really want to do? he wondered. How much better if the missile had crashed in the refinery than here in the sacred forest.

Could he move the warhead? It would weigh several hundred pounds. He'd never get ten feet with it. Whatever he did, he would have to do it here.

No guarantee that he could set the nuclear warhead to detonate. At the very least, he could greet the retrieval team with a dynamite surprise that would reduce their ranks considerably. But if luck were with him, the jolt he would give that cylinder would trigger the genie inside. And he would win the quickest war in history, because Sam would never know who the enemy was, and never again would the whiggers trust St. Croix.

He considered further: What if he did not sacrifice the forest? Wouldn't the Yanks soon clear-cut it with chain saws to make room for their condos? Here where Maroons had toiled in their gardens and brought forth crops to sustain the village through generations of freedom: wouldn't bulldozers soon ravage this shrine? This very spot where he now stood, this holy earth: wouldn't Yankee Doodle Dandy turn it

into a putting green? Scenic trails for golf carts. Wooden walkways
threading through a few mahoganies left standing. Cyclone fences, NO
TRESPASSING signs. DELIVERIES AROUND BACK.

No.

He would do at least one thing right in his life. He would finish the
accident that had only half-happened. He would scar this forested corner of his island, for a few years. Hadn't the Japanese rebuilt Hiroshima
and Nagasaki on their former sites? Here on St. Croix, mahoganies
could be replanted. And a new nation—a pure nation—would be born.

He thought further: to make his message most clear, tonight he
would also visit the three hats. Sonar and radar: he'd pull their plugs.
Petrox: he'd blow it off the map. Fun-in-the-Sun: if that Stinger was all
it was cracked up to be, he'd welcome the next jet from Miami with
fireworks. That should drop the bottom out of the real estate boom.

BOOM! BOOM! BOOM!, as a promise, unmistakable and irrevo-
cable, that should the whiggers ever try to return, the band of guerrillas,
the gang of crazies, the ring of terrorists, never captured . . . would attack again.

Resolved to bring his people their freedom, he grabbed the handles
of the aluminum case and wooden crate and hurried to establish an artillery post on the cliff.

Angelique reminded her parents, "Yo' phone me from church."

Papa kissed her quickly through the jeep's window. "We keep
callin' till yo' reach home."

Zosia sat up in the back seat and stared at Estelle and Nat as they
hurried up their front steps. She had known Catholics who thought their
God would save them. She had known Jews who thought their God
would save them. But she said nothing.

As Karl drove out of Frederiksted toward Centerline, Angelique
turned around to check on Zosia and smiled with surprise. "You're up!
You look much better. But we're going to stop at the hospital so we can
have you examined. Dr. Schroeder is on duty tonight and—"

"Nogh. I am fine. It took me by surprise, but now I've got my box-
ing gloves on. Try the radio to see if there's any news."

"Zosia, you must—"

"Nogh! You two go straight to that boat of yours."

Karl clicked on the radio.

"—of the island's northwest corner. Specifically, the territory north of Centerline Highway, including Frederiksted, Grove Place and Fredensborg, and west of the highway running from La Reine Shopping Center to Salt River Bay, including Glynn, Mon Bijou and the entire length of Scenic Road, is to be evacuated in an orderly manner. Police and National Guardsmen will provide transportation to those needing assistance. Overnight camps will be established on the southern and eastern sections of the island, their whereabouts announced by signs posted along the major highways. There is no need for panic. We repeat, there is no need for panic. The Navy is presently searching for the missile and will remove it from St. Croix as soon as possible. A naval spokesman has assured the governor that the missile can *not* explode, and poses no threat to the island's population. This evacuation has been ordered by the governor only as a precaution.

"To repeat tonight's bulletin, the Navy has announced that it accidentally launched a Tomahawk-type cruise missile at St. Croix. The missile, which may carry a nuclear warhead, crashed in the vicinity of the northwest rainforest at nine-forty-five this evening. The governor has ordered an immediate evacuation of the island's northwest corner. Specifically, the territory north of Centerline Highway—"

Karl clicked off the radio.

"We do *not* stop at the hospital," said Zosia.

Angelique protested, "But the hospital is east of La Reine."

"You fool! Think of your child. Don't waste your time on a wheezy old lady."

"Angelique, what about your parents?" asked Karl. "Holy Cross Church is inside the evacuation area."

She argued no further with Zosia, nor did she answer Karl. She stared out the windshield and knotted her hands in her lap as he drove a little faster.

When they turned east onto Centerline, the late Monday night traffic was light in both directions. But within minutes, cars began to pour from side roads onto the highway, nearly all of them heading east. A minibus was packed with passengers, the rack on its roof heaped with baggage. The rear of a pickup truck was loaded with worried evacuees and their suitcases. People rode bicycles, motor scooters; they trotted on horses. People on foot waved desperately at passing vehicles. If a truck slowed in the backed-up congestion, roadside pedestrians jumped aboard. Cars trying to pass formed a second lane heading east, and a police car traveling west, its siren wailing and blue light revolving, had to drive along the gravel edge.

By the time the jeep was creeping past the University, Centerline had become a clogged river draining the western end of the island. Karl turned to Angelique. "You've delivered babies on every back road. What's the best route home?"

"Try to get into the right lane. We'll turn at the road to the airport, then take the Petrox highway to Sunny Isle. The roads through Christiansted will be impossible. Best to keep angling toward South Shore. We can cross north again at Seven Hills."

"Sounds good." He flicked on his blinker to change lanes, but though the traffic barely crawled, a garbage truck beside the jeep would not stop long enough to let him move over. He honked his horn, raised his arm out his window and pointed that he wanted to shift to the right.

Looking up from her window, Angelique saw the driver glance down, but he kept nudging forward. She called to him, "Stop! Why won' yo' stop?"

He pretended not to hear.

She turned to Karl. "Stop so I can get out."

"Anglique, don't be crazy. Maybe I can get in behind him."

"*Please*, Karl." She opened her door.

"Angelique, you stay right here! It's bedlam out there. You'll get run over in the dark."

But when she reached one foot out the door, he hit the brakes. "Angelique!"

She jumped out, lifted her skirt and ran between the lanes until she was ahead of the slow-moving truck. She turned and shouted up at the driver, "Stop!"

He gave her the finger and rolled past her.

A mix of rage and panic in her voice, she screamed at him, "Move yo' ass, motherfucker!" Again she ran ahead of the truck, though this time she turned and stood a few feet in front of its massive bumper, her blue sarong lit in a headlight beam. She held her hands out like a traffic cop and shrieked, "Stoooop!" The diesel horn blared so loud that she could hear nothing else around her, and for a moment she thought the tall chrome grille was never going to stop as it crept toward her. But the truck halted, a foot from her, its horn deafening. With her hands pressed over her ears, she glared up at the driver, who shook his fist at her. She did not budge until Karl had changed lanes in front of the truck.

Then she stepped aside and shouted at the driver, "Yo' belong in the back, trash!" She returned and amplified his scatological reply as she walked to the waiting jeep and got in.

Karl scolded her severely. "Now you fasten your seatbelt and you stay put."

Zosia chirped from the back seat, "I didn't know you could speak such good French."

Karl turned south at the airport road, where traffic was moving slowly in both directions. As he drove past the Agricultural Research Station, its rows of banana trees faintly silvered by the moon, he thought of Victor and his ponds of tilapia. The African bass, the Crucian Cooker, Professor Van der Voort, a project on Haiti. Tonight, those plans and high hopes seemed of another world.

Suddenly he could smell the barn back home. The hay in the bins, the cow slop plopping on the concrete floor, the sharp tang of the disinfectant for teats. And he could smell the cows themselves in their stanchions; he loved to take deep breaths of their warm bovine fragrance. He envisioned Pop and Mom joking back and forth between stalls as they attached the milking machines. And then he imagined Angelique standing beside him in the barn, wearing bib overalls and rubber boots as she watched Mom cup the milkers over a swollen udder. And Zosia was there in her wheelchair, pointing at a buff-and-white Guernsey as she laughed and began a tale about some cow in Switzerland. Yes, he would take Angelique's hand and whisper in her ear, "Would Mother like a drink of milk?"

"Pardon?" asked Angelique, looking at him. "What about mother?" Her tired eyes smiled faintly.

"Oh, I was just thinking how nice it is that we're going to be parents."

"Is it?" She reached for his hand on the steering wheel.

He took her hand, drew it to his lips and kissed it.

The lights of a small plane lifted into the sky ahead of them; the plane banked steeply and headed south.

Before the jeep had moved another hundred feet, a private jet shot across the stars; it too veered south.

Angelique sneered quietly, "The rats are fleeing the ship."

"I'll bet there's a crowd at the airport," said Karl. "Somebody ought to get an air taxi going between St. Croix and St. Thomas, to ease the strain."

When at last they reached the divided superhighway that linked the airport with the refinery, Karl saw that all four lanes were pouring east. He merged with the flow. Traffic bunched, then rolled a short distance, cars barely keeping up with bicycles. He looked at Zosia's haggard face in the rear view mirror, then called over his shoulder, "How are you doing, Zosia?"

She replied, "You're doing fine, Karl. You're doing fine."

Half an hour later, less than two miles down the highway, he pointed at a small road that angled south. "That's an access road to the refinery. A shortcut." The road was empty, though several cars followed behind as he exited.

The dark lane snaked up and down a bushy hill, then ran parallel to the cyclone fence along the refinery's perimeter. He drove slowly to see if he could spot any of the night crew; the cars behind him roared past. Searching the complex of cracking towers and storage tanks, lit by spotlights and the glow of burn-off flames, he spotted only two workers, one racing west through the steel jungle in a Petrox pickup truck, the other kneeling as he turned a valve on a major pipeline. I'll bet Ed's shittin' in his pants tonight, he thought. Time bomb ticking in the hills, and he's down here babysitting enough gayzoleen to blow him to the moon.

Staring through the chain-link fence, Angelique searched for a guerrilla in camouflage. Nick had the maps, and now he had the opportunity. Had he really put Vietnam behind him, or had he brooded and festered since she left him? She recalled the pain and rage burning in his eyes when she said her final good-bye in the hospital parking lot. Had he really become a college man? Or had she been deluding herself, hoping the best for him, and wishing as well to isolate her own little love nest?

Where was Nick tonight?

As she gazed at the giant, roaring, sulfur-stinking monster that Nicholas hated, she did not know. In her stomach she felt that knot of dread.

Nick found a grassy knoll near the edge of the cliff, the trees of the forest close behind; boulders jutted from the land, several large enough for him to hide behind. On the horizon stood the lights of the destroyer: the unsuspecting enemy.

He opened the aluminum case, opened the wooden crate, then assembled the shoulder-held, anti-aircraft missile launcher. To the grip-stock with its battery and coolant unit, he fitted the missile in its five-foot launch tube. Looks like a bazooka, he thought, marveling at the progress in weapons design since his days in Nam. He hefted the unit to his shoulder. All right, Big White Sam: Fort Maroon be ready.

He had planned to prepare the Stinger, then to leave it in the bushes while he returned to the nuke and examined its components; he could work until he heard company coming. But as he stood with his combat boots spread a yard apart on the land he loved, a sea breeze cooling his sweaty body, and thirty pounds of high-tech power perched on his shoulder, he felt the best he had in years. So he lingered, enjoyed the moment, shifted his feet against the earth.

He would have liked a little company. He would have liked a platoon of fighters who could talk terrain and weapons and strategy. And then he realized, as he watched the lights of the warship, that what he really wanted was to be standing here tonight with Leroy. Defending their island together. Fighting a war that made sense. Talking about old times while they waited. About the days when they roamed through the mahogany forest with peanut butter and jelly sandwiches in their backpacks, and slingshots in their pockets.

His sharp eyes detected a moving light, so far away and faint it might have been a blinking star drifting away from the ship and toward the island. He took long slow deep breaths, for that moment when he would hold his breath and pull the trigger. The light climbed high into the heavens and swept further east, wary of pistol shots from Maroon Ridge.

He waited until the chopper was a half-mile offshore, coming in toward Fountain Valley at roughly three thousand feet. Then he aimed his pea shooter and visually acquired his target. Leroy, here be one from the both of us. He squeezed the trigger: ROOOOOSHSH! The tiny missile roared upward like an angry hornet with its tail on fire. He watched the dual-thrust rocket curve across the stars as its infrared homing system guided it toward the flying bus loaded with combat-ready GI Joes . . . The blinking, droning helicopter erupted into a boiling orange fireball, BOOOOOOGHGHGH! He shook with an ecstatic thrill. The fireball fell out of the sky in a long downward arch toward its blazing reflection on the black water. The two fireballs collided and splattered on the sea.

As he lowered the launcher from his shoulder, he whispered with amazement, "Works like a charm."

The mass of oily flames was swallowed by the deep water off Davis Bay, leaving bits of burning debris strewn across the surface, not more than five hundred yards from the balconies of Casa Columbus.

Brimming with exultation, he packed up his artillery, then hiked back into the murky, moon-speckled forest. He figured he had at least an hour before Roosevelt Roads launched a full assault.

That gave him plenty of time.

CHAPTER THIRTY-FIVE

Tinkering

BOOOOOOOOOGHGHGH! Angelique whirled in her seat and spotted a fireball dropping out of the sky; it disappeared behind Blue Mountain.

"What was that?" cried Karl as he pulled to the side of the road.

"That was not the warhead," said Zosia. "It was too small."

"Maybe they were lifting the missile with a helicopter," he guessed, "and a fuel tank exploded."

They searched the sky, the dark hills; heard a distant ambulance siren, heard the roar of the refinery.

"So," he said, "the warhead's either still in the forest, or it's at the bottom of the ocean."

Feeling nauseous, Angelique sat back, closed her eyes and breathed deeply. She was amazed that she was still alive, that the world was still around her, that Karl sat next to her, Zosia behind her. They had not yet vanished in the flash that any moment would incinerate them. At any moment. Any moment now.

Where was Nick?

Once past the refinery, they reached South Shore Road and drove through pastureland along the island's coast. Traffic again became heavy, diverted from the bottleneck at Christiansted. As the jeep crawled in the sluggish parade around Great Salt Pond, the moon shone through her window onto her lap.

At the Seven Hills junction, most of the traffic continued toward the end of the island. Karl turned north and drove over the island's longitudinal hump toward Candle Point. As they approached North Shore Road, the three stared aghast at the exodus of refugees sweeping east. Between bumper-to-bumper cars rumbled National Guard trucks; hundreds of faces stared out from beneath the camouflage canopies. Crowds on foot moved across fields of guinea grass. "My gosh!" ex-

311

claimed Karl, "I didn't know there were this many people living on the island."

As the jeep was swallowed into the slow-moving stampede, he leaned out his window and asked a family walking beside him, "Where's everybody going? Are there camps set up?" No one answered as they trudged with their bulging plastic bags. He reached from his window and tugged the sleeve of an old man. "Excuse me, where's everybody going?"

Walking stiffly, the man with white stubble on his chin mumbled, "To de yacht club. Dey got boats out dere."

Karl wondered what these thousands would do when they discovered that the few dozen yachts had already left most of them behind. As the throng shuffled forward, he became increasingly anxious to get Angelique inside the four stone walls of Zosia's house, away from the warhead, away from this mob.

Angelique watched a woman walking just ahead of the jeep, her broad bottom spotlit by one bright headlight. Wary of the cars and trucks, the weaving bicycles, a scooter that roared and braked, the woman herded her five children with quick grabs of her hands if any strayed from their group. She yanked at the arm of her oldest boy, who was as tall as she. He scolded her, "Quit yo' fussin'!" She raised her hand as if to slap him. Angelique felt pity for the woman: the midwife had seen many women frightened at childbirth, but she had never watched a mother frantic for all her children at once.

Zosia stared at the faces outside her rolled-up windows. She knew too well the panic in the eyes, the terror of becoming trapped with no escape.

Piotr, I don't have the strength to live through this again.

At the cache, Nick unearthed one of the demolitions crates, lifted off its lid and quickly transferred five sticks of dynamite into his rucksack.

Digging up another crate, he took out a detonator.

No need for a timer; Ackerman would flip the switch.

He hurried back up the hill to the spot where the giant arrow had fallen to earth. It still seemed too good to be true. But as he put on his gloves and began with the tin snips to cut and peel back the jagged aluminum, revealing the broken cylinder inside, he knew his luck had also brought him a possible instantaneous trip to oblivion. "Oh sweet baby," he crooned as he reached into the fuselage and wiggled the end of the canister like a loose tooth, "just yo' behave yo'self a little while longer."

He heard a car. He froze, elbow deep in his work. A blue light blinked in the trees: the whirling blue beams of a police car. He held his breath. If they stopped, he'd drop them with his Colt. Then he'd have a squad car, fully armed, at his disposal.

But the car raced past on Scenic Road, filling the forest with its eerie twirling blue light . . . It disappeared to the east.

He smirked, They sure ain' want to find what they lookin' for.

He continued his tinkering.

Estelle hurried to the kitchen and phoned Rosemary.

Rosemary answered sleepily, "Hello?" When she heard the news, she cried with disbelief, "A nuclear bomb! On St. Croix?"

Estelle made plans to meet Rosemary, Cyril and Chester "in our pew."

Then she phoned Nat Junior.

He was awake, for Suzanne had just received a call from her mother in Strawberry Hill. Elouise had been listening to a late-night talk show, heard an emergency bulletin and she was frantic. Suzanne was desperate to rush to her mother; she was dressing the twins now, James and John were carrying groceries out to the car, Tyrone hadn't come home yet, he was off somewhere tonight with his friends. "Ah been phonin' everywhere, tryin' to locate that boy. Pray for us in church, Mama. Ah got to go now."

As she hurried with Nat back out to the car, she looked at her watch: 10:27. A twenty-minute trip down Centerline: they should be at Holy Cross by eleven o'clock. Good, she thought. An early midnight mass to ask de Lord for He protection on dis night of worries.

Nat turned on the radio to hear the bulletin. As they listened, he frowned, then turned to his wife. "De governor say Holy Cross ain' safe."

She asserted, "Ah put meh faith in God, not de governor."

"Chess, wake up! We goin' to church. Get up now!"

Church? He groaned and rolled over.

His mother tore the covers off him, hauled him out of bed and stood him on his feet. "Do as Ah say, Chess! There a bomb on the island and we got to meet Grandpa and Grandma at church. Take off yo' pj's. Where yo' sneakers?"

A bomb? Now he perked up. "What kind of bomb? Where it be?"

But she would say nothing more as she struggled frantically to get him dressed. Then she rushed off to dress herself, so he went outside, his sneakers untied, to see if Dad knew anything about the bomb. "Hey, Dad, what's goin' on?"

His father did not answer; he sat in the car, listening intently to the radio.

"Cyril Moorehead!" Ol' fat Mrs. Williams came shuffle-running across the lawn in her nightgown, a suitcase in each hand. "Kin Ah ride wid yo'?"

His father looked up. "Certainly, Grace. We leavin' for church in about a minute." He climbed out of the car and took her bags.

"Church? They evacuatin' people from de pier. Ain' yo' hear?"

"From the pier? Who's evacuatin' people?"

"De Navy! Dey sendin' a ship to take all de folks in Frederiksted."

His father frowned, puzzled. "But the radio say we supposed to clear out of Frederiksted, and that surely mean the pier too."

"Never mind de radio. Meh niece Liza-Anne just phone and say her boy Louey, he work at de pier office, dey got a crowd already gatherin', gon' be first come, first serve when de boat pull in."

"What's this?" asked Chester's mother as she came out the door with a Bible in her hand.

His father said, "Grace say the Navy gon' evacuate people from the pier."

"Well," she looked at her only child, "then Ah say we head for the pier. If we can get Chess on a ship, then *that* be what we ought to do."

His father reminded her, "Mama gon' be lookin' for us at church."

"Ah call her back. If she gone already, Ah call church and leave a message. Church does be fine for them, but Ah want meh boy *off* this island."

"All right. Then maybe we should pack some blankets, a little food, somethin' to drink. Grace, yo' have a seat in the car. We be ready to go in ten minutes. Chess, yo' come help carry tings out."

Chester was thrilled. How could anybody think about sitting in church when everybody else was out on the pier, waiting to be rescued by the Navy?

He helped his mother pack suitcases, then helped his father roll sheets inside blankets and tie the bundles with pieces of clothesline. While his parents were loading the car, he ran to his room, undressed from the church clothes his mother had forced on him, and jumped into his Kaptain Kommando camouflage suit. He was in the kitchen stuffing his pouch pockets with cookies when he heard his mother calling from the driveway, her voice shrill. He ran out and jumped into the car.

They were able to drive only as far as the ball park, where the road from La Grange into town was blocked by abandoned cars. Chester and his mother and father loaded their arms with as much as they could hold, then his father locked the rest of the bags and boxes in the car. Fat lady Williams carried her wicker suitcases. As they struggled on foot through the jam of vehicles, his mother argued that they should have driven around town and come in the back way. His father argued that all the roads were probably blocked. His mother set her bags down and leaned against a truck and said they should have at least tried to see what the back roads were like. His father said it was too late now, and told her to leave the lemonade jug, there would be juice on the ship.

They trudged and rested and staggered on again until they passed the walls of the fort, no longer ox-blood red as in the sunshine, but now a strange maroon-gray in the glow of the streetlamps. Chester's arms ached. He wished he had brought his roller skates: he'd be at the pier by now.

Finally they reached the waterfront, where they stared in dismay at thousands of people already crowded on the long concrete pier. If it was first come, first served, there had better be more than one ship. But though he scanned the sea from one end to the other, Chester saw no Navy vessel. He saw only the lights of small fishing boats heading toward the horizon.

The pier's gate was closed to traffic; only its door for pedestrians was open. He gaped at the frenzied mob trying to push through the entranceway. People he knew, kids from school and their parents, Jeffrey the barber, the skinny guy at the gas station: people shouted at each other and ignored each other.

His father said, "Ah go first. Chess, yo' stay between me and yo' mother."

"Aw right."

As they joined the funneling swarm of people, he nearly stumbled under the feet of a man who pushed past him.

"Chester!" shrieked his mother. "Yo' all right?"

Grabbing the arm of a stranger to keep from falling, he dropped his blanket; it fell outside the gate as he was pressed through by the people shoving behind his mother, who almost trampled him.

She cried, "Cyril, yo' got to pick him up!"

His father twisted around, his arms full. "Chester, grab meh arm, son."

"Okay, Dad. But Ah lost meh bedroll."

"Never mind. Stay on yo' feet. Just stay on yo' feet."

Once through the gate, they had room to pause and catch their breath. Fat lady Williams had disappeared. Though they looked around briefly for her, they couldn't spot her on either side of the barricade.

Picking up their bags, the three shuffled and jostled through the crowd. The further out on the pier they pushed, the more tightly people were packed. His mother argued that they had walked far enough. His father argued that people at the end of the pier would get on the ship first. She argued that the ship would dock broadside and people could get on from all along the pier. He argued that if it weren't that big a ship, it would dock at the end and take what people it could.

They soon confronted a solid, unmoving mass of people who either stood restlessly, or sat wearily on boxes and suitcases. His father unrolled two bundles of blankets, claiming a small patch of pavement for the family. He set suitcases as barriers at both ends.

"Chester, yo' climb into bed now," said his mother.

Bed?! "Aw Mom, we just got here!"

But she was in no mood for an argument. "Yo' get in that bed 'fore Ah warm yo' backside! Tis hours past yo' bedtime."

"But Mom—"

His father snapped, "Chester, do as yo' mother say."

Grumbling, he took off his sneakers and tucked them under the blanket as a pillow. Then he slid into the emergency evacuation bed and reveled at the discomfort of the hard concrete. Tonight Ah got to be tough! He fished a cookie from his pocket as he listened to the worried, whispery talk around him.

His mother asked, "Sally, where this ship comin' from?"

He lifted his head to look at Sally, the old witch whom he had never seen anywhere else than in her rocking chair on her front verandah, spitting evil threats at the boys who dared to run across her lawn. Now she was sitting on an upturned fruit crate; the moon turned her white hair into a halo around her dark face. She chuckled, "Ship?"

"The evacuation ship. How big a boat it be?"

"What yo' t'ink, gal, some fancy tourist liner gon' make Frederiksted a port of call? Yo' waitin' for de Navy to make a courtesy visit? Maybe yo' waitin' for de sea to open so we can just walk out of here."

"But we hear that the Navy comin' to—"

"Yo' hear dat from de Navy?"

"No, it been a neighbor next door who tell us a ship be on its way."

"A neighbor who spread de rumor. Rosemary meh chile, say yo' prayers. Ask de good Lord to send another ark."

Minutes after the radio bulletin, dinghies scurried like water beetles from Christiansted wharf to yachts moored in the harbor. Skippers hoisted sails with a rapid cranking of winches: white triangles sprouted and grew tall in the moonlight. Wordless crews readied the lines. Engines rumbled. Captains backed their jibs and cast off. Luminous sails paraded across the dark harbor and out the channel: soon they became pale specks on the open sea.

A catamaran tied to the wharf became so overloaded as forty, fifty, sixty people jumped from the dock onto its deck that it threatened to swamp. Those aboard hoisted sails and untied lines, found a pair of oars and beat back those on the dock who still fought to get on. The sails bellied in the breeze; the listing vessel pulled away from the pilings. Anyone who attempted to leap across the widening gap was beaten down by fists and dumped overboard. The catamaran left behind a dozen people flailing or limp in the water.

As the craft lumbered across the harbor toward the channel, it passed a dinghy with a lone white rower. A boy and his father, crouching on one of the catamaran's pontoons, quietly slipped into the water and swam toward the squeaking dinghy. The boy shouted to the rower for help while his father dove underwater, surfaced behind the dingy and, heaving his weight up on one gunnel, easily overturned it. Father and son kicked the owner away, then threatened to drown him. They righted the dinghy, tipped out most of the water, and hauled themselves into the wobbly vessel. The father rowed with powerful strokes while the boy in the stern whispered directions toward a sleek white fiberglass yawl no one had yet claimed.

Upstairs at Alexander Hamilton Airport, in an empty Eastern Airlines office, Ed Ashley spoke on the phone with the Petrox home office in New York. "Listen, David, I've got all our top managerial people here, with their families. Are you or are you not chartering a plane to pick us up?"

"We're trying, Ed, but Miami, Atlanta, Kennedy, LaGuardia, New-ark, they won't have anything to do with a flight to St. Croix until they get confirmation from the Navy that the nuke's been removed. I can't even get a bush pilot to go down. Especially one with a plane big enough to hold you all."

"David, are you offering to *pay* these people?"

"Of course. Ransoms fit for a king. They just won't do it. Every-body's spooked, Ed. Nobody wants to get near a loose cannon on deck, especially when its thermonuclear. But I'm trying, I promise you, I'm trying."

"All right. I'll see what I can raise from this end."

"Ed, keep your chin up."

"Thanks, David. The next beer's on me."

Ed hung up long enough to clear the line, then he dialed Informa-tion back home in Houston. "Operator, would you give me the number for an aviation outfit called The Flying Longhorn, please." He wrote the number on an Eastern memo pad. "Thank you very much, opera-tor."

He dialed, then waited anxiously while the phone rang, and rang, and rang. He knew his friend was often up on a ladder, tinkering under a cowling. C'mon, Longhorn ol' buddy. Be there. Please be there.

"Longhorn Aviation. What's up? We are! Can I help y'all?"

"Longhorn, ol' buddy! It's Ed Ashley, down in the Virgin Islands."

"Ed! How're them virgins treatin' ya? Ho *ho*!"

"Yeah, Longhorn, fine, fine. Listen, you want a job tonight? We're in kind of a jam down here, and we want to get our top men off the is-land as soon as we can. With their families, we've got a group of forty-six. You name the price tag, Petrox pays the bill. Can you do it?"

"Waaaallll, what's the problem down there? Natives restless?"

"Very. Things are falling apart pretty quickly. No rioting yet, but—"

"Riots? Say, what're y'all tryin' to get me into? Get the damn Air Force to evac y'all out."

Ed took a deep breath. "Longhorn, we've already contacted the Air Force. And the Navy. They both refuse to evac anyone off the island. It wasn't like that when you and I flew in Korea. We'd do anything then to keep our people safe." He paused. "So I'm counting on you, ol' buddy."

"*Why* won't they evac y'all out?"

"Well, to be perfectly honest, we've got what may be a nuclear warhead on the island. The Navy accidentally launched a missile at us. You know the damn Navy."

Longhorn whistled with surprise. "Y'all just upped the stakes, ol' buddy."

"Listen, Longhorn, the Navy's retrieving the missile right now. It'll be gone by the time you get here. That's the straight nuts and bolts. There's really no danger. But the natives *are* a little restless and I want to get our people off the island until all this blows over. So I'm calling on you, pal, to bail us out. Don't worry about the paycheck. You can retire after tonight's flight. Whatdya say? You got a plane big enough to carry forty-six red-blooded Americans who just want to go home?"

"Lemme check." After a long silence, Longhorn mumbled, "I'm lookin' at my clipboard." Another long minute passed; despite the air-conditioned office, Ed was damp with sweat. Finally Longhorn spoke, "Charlie's due back with the clipper in about twenty minutes. If she's in good shape, I'll gas 'er up and bring 'er down myself."

"Great, Longhorn. Thanks a million. And I mean that, thanks a *million*."

"But I'm reservin' the right, Ed, and Lord help me, I don't want to say this, but I'm reservin' the right whether or not I land. I ain't tanglin' with no revolutionaries. Not with a civilian plane. Gimme an F-16 and I'll clean up that island in no time."

"I'll have everybody out by the runway. You won't be on the ground for more than five minutes."

"Fine. Y'all got the Trades down there, right? Park your gang at the east end of the runway, so I can pick 'em up soon as I taxi to a halt. Gimme your number there, Ed. I'll check in with y'all before I leave Houston."

Ed gave Longhorn the number on the Eastern phone. "Thanks again, Longhorn. I knew you wouldn't let us down."

"I'll do the best I can, ol' buddy."

Ed hung up the phone and let out an enormous sigh of relief. Then he walked down the hall to a conference room where his forty-five were bivouacked. When he opened the door, his men and their families turned toward him expectantly. He closed the door quietly behind him, held a finger to his lips and pointed at the floor, indicating the mob loitering downstairs in the lobby, waiting for a plane, any plane, to save them. Then he informed his people, "I've contacted an old friend, a top pilot, who's coming to airlift us out of here."

Several men held up triumphant fists and mouthed a silent cheer.

Ed looked at the map of North America and the Caribbean on the conference room wall. Spreading his thumb and finger to gauge 300 miles on the scale at the bottom, he plotted the distance from Houston to St. Croix. "Depending on headwinds, he'll arrive about five-thirty, quarter to six. Right around dawn."

"Dawn?" exclaimed Harry Sullivan. "Ed, that's the best you can do?"

"Harry, we're damn lucky for that. Now listen, people, here's the plan. At four a.m., we start trickling in groups of two or three down the stairs. Disperse from the lobby unobtrusively, so we don't have a thousand tagalongs. Work your way to the *east* end of the runway. That's the pick-up point. Look for bushes to hide in. Then just sit tight and keep quiet until the plane's ready for us."

With a rescue mission on the way, the crisis turned into high adventure. One of the wives brewed fresh coffee in an office coffee machine. Children sat around the conference table and pretended they were having an important meeting. Harry found a bottle of Cruzan Gold in a cabinet, and a package of Eastern paper cups. Opening a half-size refrigerator, he discovered several cans of papaya juice, and ice cubes! With a grin, he cleared the papers off a desk, lined up a dozen cups and whispered, "Harry's Harbor is open for business."

Carefully, Nick placed the fifth stick of dynamite into the cavity where the guidance system had been. He completed the job of wiring his charges to the detonator. And finally, he tied black twine to the detonator pin, trailed the line down through a slot he had cut in the fuselage, then fed the line around a series of notched wooden pegs, forming a rectangular trip-string around the missile.

Working with a nimble deftness he had not lost these twenty years, he traced the twine through underbrush, over twigs and leaves. Then he set the tension—the precise tautness—and tied the knot. He had learned his tricks from a close examination of the handiwork of the experts in black pajamas.

Leroy, when them Marines come tip-toein' t'rough the tulips, let's hope they be a full battalion strong.

He swung on his backpack, picked up the Stinger case and crate, then blew a kiss to the Tomahawk. "Good night, sweetheart. Ah be hearin' from yo'."

CHAPTER THIRTY-SIX

Decision

Four miles southeast of ground zero, Holy Cross Church housed more parishioners tonight than it had even on Christmas.

Looking down from his pulpit at the throng of anxious faces, Father Abrams felt the great need of his congregation. He spread his arms and called to the spiritual pilgrims and seekers of refuge, "The Lord is my shepherd, Ah shall not want."

At the sound of his voice, talking diminished up and down the pews until silence filled the church.

His words reached out, "He maketh me to lie down in green pastures."

Standing with the choir, Estelle began to sing, repeating the lines of the psalm. She raised her eyes to the rafters and struggled to find her faith as she sent her voice heavenward.

Father Abrams pointed toward the nearby hills. "Yea, though Ah walk through the valley of the shadow of death, Ah will fear no evil."

The choir filled in behind Estelle, bolstering her spirit.

"For Thou art with me," boomed Father's voice. "Thy rod and Thy staff they comfort me."

"Speak, brother!" called a voice from the congregation. "Speak de holy word!"

"Thou preparest a table before me in the presence of mine enemies: Thou annointest my head with oil."

"Yas, Lord, O yas!"

Vehemently, Father declared, "My cup runneth over!"

Estelle sang with her fullest self-convincing power.

"Surely goodness and mercy shall follow me all the days of my life."

Her shimmering soprano spread as a benison of peace upon the worshipers.

"And Ah will dwell in the house of the Lord for ever."

Now the organ played the opening bars of a familiar hymn. Fortified by the rumblings of the pipes, the choir led the congregation in a sturdy, slow-paced rendition of "Rock of Ages."

Her heart battling between her abiding trust in God and her relentless worry about her family, Estelle looked down at Nat, standing alone by the family pew. She could hear his confident monotone, and loved him profoundly.

Following the hymn, Father Abrams bowed his head. "As we have often called upon Yo', Lord, in time of hurricane, to deflect the raging winds from the shores of our tiny island . . . so we call upon Yo' for protection tonight. We are small, and the ways of evil are mighty. We place ourselves in Yo' hands. Amen."

A multitude of fervent voices echoed, "Amen."

When the organ began another hymn, Estelle left her place in the choir and walked with quiet dignity through the door at the side of the altar. In the robing room, her quarter lay atop the pay phone. For the fifth time tonight she dropped it into the slot and dialed Zosia's number, then Angelique's number, then Karl's. She listened to ten, twenty, thirty rings before, nearly frantic, she hung up.

With a silent prayer of thanks, Karl turned off North Shore onto the Candle Point road. As the jeep topped the crest of the hill, he looked down at the tranquil, moon-glittering bay. Zosia's round, stained-glass window shone with reassuring familiarity. "Home sweet home," he called over the seat to her. "It never looked better." He drove down the slope toward the beach, leaving trucks and sirens and the river of humanity on the other side of the hill.

They passed cars parked along the beach. A campfire burned; sleeping bags were stretched out on the bright sand. A voice spoke on a radio. Hope we don't have company out on the point, he thought, suddenly faced with a new worry. Had anyone broken into the two houses? What about his cottage?

He turned onto the peninsula and drove slowly, his brights on as he searched the rocks for hidden strangers. He saw no one. Nor were there any cars in the driveway. Everything looked wonderfully normal.

As he parked in front of Zosia's sidewalk, Angelique exclaimed, "I hear the phone ringing!" She jumped out and ran to the house. He could hear her voice through Zosia's living room window, "Mama? Oh

Mama, Mama, Mama! Yes, we just got home. It seemed an eternity on that road."

Karl looked at his watch. "Two oh five, Zosia." He turned around, saw her face sagging with fatigue. "You can crawl into bed now and sleep until noon."

She stared at him with a strange look, but said nothing.

He got out, opened her door and suggested, "Let me fetch your chariot."

"Where's my cane?" She peered over the seat into the back, wrapped her fingers around the crook. "We can't forget Oppy."

She insisted on walking; he thought it best not to upset her with an argument. Along the moon-dappled tunnel, dead leaves crackled beneath their feet, he stepped and she shuffled.

Angelique appeared at the door. "That was Mama," she said, her voice buoyant with relief. "She and Papa are safe at church. Suzanne and Nat Junior and the four youngest are with Elouise at Strawberry Hill. Tyrone is helping refugees at the Boy Scout camp. Rosemary, Cyril and Chester are being evacuated from the pier by a Navy ship."

"Evacuated?" Karl said as he stepped with Zosia through the door. "Well, that's good news. But I'm surprised anybody is still in Frederiksted. Seems the Navy ought to bring a ship into Christiansted." He relished the CLUNK of the heavy door as Angelique closed it behind them: his girls were safe. Angelique locked it.

Zosia sat in her chair, then she looked up with fierce urgency at Angelique and Karl. "Now you two take your sailboat and you get *off* this island."

He stared at her with shock. "But . . . we're home now."

"You go!" ordered Zosia. "You can't feel it, but I do. I feel it exactly as we felt it coming in Berlin." The fervency he saw in her eyes was mixed with fear. She was not hysterical; she was as strong as ever, though terrified. "You are *not* safe here. You get into that boat of yours and you flee."

He glanced at Angelique; she seemed unable to speak. So he tried to reason with Zosia. "That Tomahawk is at least ten miles away, and downwind. We're perfectly safe here."

"What do you know about the things terrified people do?" Her eyes blazed with impatience bordering on contempt. "What do you know about war?"

He asserted, "That's all the more reason for us to stay with you.

You may need a man here to protect you."

"Yagh, I have no doubt you would do your best to protect us. And get yourself killed in the process. Leaving a fatherless child."

Angelique laid her hands over her belly. "Zosia, the three of us can sail to Buck Island. You can manage in my boat that far. We'll bundle you in warm clothes, put a life jacket on you. Pack blankets, food and water—"

"Nogh. Piotr insisted that he finish in his home. If it comes to that, I insist too. I want to be here with him." She nodded at her mermaid standing in the jungle of ferns. "I want to be here with my sculptures. And my paintings. Proszę, before I die of nerves, I want you to *go*."

Angelique shook her head, adamant. "For almost six years I have never defied you. But tonight I will. I cannot leave you alone."

Zosia glared at her with scorn. "Are you going to be a mother?" She scowled at Karl. "And you, do you call yourself a father?" She gripped the crook of her cane with both hands, raised it over her head and brought it down flat on the table, BANG! Angelique jumped with a cry of fright. Zosia commanded her, "Take your child and escape!"

Moving in an anguished fog, Angelique walked to the porch door and stared at the lights of Christiansted down the coast; and in the distance behind town, at the jumble of black hilltops silhouetted against the stars.

Where was Nick?

He won' hurt Zosia. It ain' Zosia he jealous of. It ain' Zosia he blame.

She leaned her forehead against the glass and closed her eyes. If Zosia know the child be safe on Buck Island, she survive the night. If we overrule her, we drive her to a collapse.

Angelique turned and faced the woman she loved as much as her own mother. "You are certain you won't come."

"Absolutely certain."

"I can put you on Buck Island an hour after we set sail."

Zosia pointed at the nurse's bag on the table beside the Doptone stethoscope. "Before you go, I need my sleeping pill, please."

The nurse was comforted by the image of her patient asleep in bed. The mother was desperate to protect her child, and the father of her child. But the almost daughter still needed to ask, "If that horrible thing in the forest explodes . . . even if it doesn't touch you . . . you can endure that alone?"

"I will hate it. But I will survive, if I know you are safe."

Angelique looked to Karl, but he looked back without a word: the decision was hers.

Going through the motions, delaying the good-bye that she felt more and more inevitable, the nurse opened her bag and took out the bottle of pills. Walked to the kitchen, tried to shake one pill from the bottle onto a cutting board; her hands were trembling so hard, half the pills spilled out. She gathered all but one back into the container. Broke the one pill in half. Took a knife from a drawer and cut the tiny white semicircle in half. Filled a glass with water. Returned to the table, dropped the bottle into her bag, placed the quarter-tablet on Zosia's tongue and helped her hold the glass while Zosia swallowed.

"Yagh, that'll knock out the old girl. Now will you please, please, *please* get in that boat and sail away, so I can get some sleep."

Nick be afraid of the sea. But Elly Zosieňka ain' afraid. She rock in that boat like a cradle.

"All right," she said quietly. "We make sure you have everything you need, then Karl and I pack blankets and food and we sail to Buck Island."

"Yagh, pack enough so you can honeymoon for a week."

The decision made, Karl said, "Zosia, we're going to prepare here as if a hurricane were coming. Candles, flashlights, bottles of water in case the power goes out."

"Yes," agreed Angelique. "I'll put plates of food for tomorrow in the refrigerator."

"Never mind me!" implored Zosia. "Get what you need and go!"

But she could not deter them as they went to work in her kitchen. She fumed with exasperation while they laid things out, gave her instructions, precautions, advice. Angelique peeled hard-boiled eggs; Karl filled glasses with water and set them in a row along the counter. On a pad beside the phone, Angelique wrote the number at church, at her parents' home, at Elouise's.

"Zosia, I have half a chicken in my refrigerator. And some cheese. I'll bring them over for you."

"Nogh, nogh, nogh! Take them with you. Pack a picnic, put it in the jeep, drive to the beach and *go*! Psiakrew!"

As Angelique hurried out the door, Zosia said, "Karl, you can't wear your coat and tie out in the boat. Look in my bedroom closet, bottom shelf, and see if you can find Piotr's bathing suit and a sweatshirt."

While he was in the bedroom, she grabbed Angelique's black bag, snaked her hand into it and clutched the bottle of pills. Glancing about for a hiding place—she had no pockets in her red gown, Karl would be back before she could walk to the kitchen, nothing on the table but a candlestick—she reached to the window ledge and dropped the bottle into a brass watering can.

"Found it," he called.

"Good," she called back.

She set Angelique's bag on the table, folded her hands in her lap.

When he returned, wearing the old baggy blue sweatshirt and even baggier blue trunks, she felt a shiver: Piotr came walking down the hall, ready to take her to the beach. She forced a laugh. "Where's your bushy white beard?"

He wiggled his jaw. "What, a bushy brown one isn't good enough? Let me dip it in the flour bin." Then he held up the flashlight from her night table. "Battery needs changing."

While he was fussing, Angelique returned in her red bathing suit, a plate of chicken in one hand, a papaya in the other. "I'll slice this for you for breakfast."

Zosia nodded impatiently. "Yagh. Thank you."

When finally everything was ready, Angelique said, "Zosia, let me help you into your pajamas."

"I don't want my pajamas. The queen likes her gown." She held out her arms with the red sleeves and frilly white cuffs. "Let me dream tonight about the wedding."

"That's right," said Karl. "Soon we'll all be gathered again at the wedding."

"If you will bring my wheelchair, I can bolt the door after you, then wheel myself to bed."

As Angelique helped her into the wheelchair, Zosia told her, "Tomorrow morning, you raise that rainbow sail of yours. I'll look with the binoculars and I'll see it waving like a flag on the Buck Island beach."

"That's right," said Karl. "Tomorrow morning, after the governor gives the all-clear, we'll come sailing past your porch. You can be out there waving your scarf, welcoming the homeless and tempest-tossed."

Zosia swiveled her chair to face the door. "Now out with you."

Angelique hesitated. For a long moment she simply stared at Zosia, her eyes welling with tears of love. Then she looked down; her red bat-ing suit bulged slightly over her belly. "Elly Zosieňka wants a kiss good-bye."

Zosia leaned forward, wrapped her arms around Angelique's waist and pressed her lips against the precious treasure. Then she sat back and complained with a smile, "She kicked me in the nose!"

Angelique began to sob, "Oh Zosia, Zosia . . ."

Zosia swept her hand toward the door. "Out!"

Karl took Angelique's hand. But when he tried to say good-bye, he discovered he was unable to speak. He nodded with confidence that everything would be all right.

Zosia pointed at the black leather bag on the table. "Take your tools, nurse. There might be people on Buck Island who need you."

Angelique took her bag, then walked with Karl to the door; but neither touched its brass handle. As they stared back, Zosia sat up tall, her wheelchair a throne, her jaw clenched against all further argument, her dark eyes filled with resolute strength. She raised her arm and toasted, "Na zdrowia!"

Angelique smiled despite her tears. "Na zdrowia, Zosia."

Karl managed, "Na zdrowia!" Then he opened the door, he and Angelique stepped out, and without looking back he closed the heavy door behind them. He held her hand as dry leaves crackled beneath their feet.

CHAPTER THIRTY-SEVEN

Hat Number One

The U.S. Navy Sonobuoy Facility was situated on the coast between the Twining Vine Restaurant and Hamm's Bluff lighthouse. It monitored a series of underwater microphones suspended from offshore buoys. Because there were no islands west of St. Croix to impede pelagic sound waves, the facility's ears were able to track both surface and subsurface movement over a significant portion of the Caribbean.

Two technicians were working tonight's graveyard shift: James ("Jimmy") Sanders wore headphones as he listened to the approach from the southwest of an unidentified submarine with dual drive shafts, cruising at a speed of 31 knots toward St. Croix; and Douglas ("Big D") Learner, who also wore headphones as he synthesized and coded the data, then relayed it via military satellite to the naval wing at the Pentagon.

Neither of the two dedicated specialists heard the snipping of the cyclone fence outside. They did not hear the sound of combat boots on crushed gravel.

They certainly did not hear the ticking of a U.S. Army demolitions timer.

Zosia's heart sank when she heard the jeep circle around the driveway and stop at the end of her sidewalk. Had they changed their minds? The fools!

But only one door opened and shut, and then Karl called through a window by the door, "Everything's fine, Zosia. We're ready to launch. I brought the jeep back because I thought it'd be safer here than down by the beach."

She wheeled herself to the bedroom window. Through seagrape branches she could see his silhouette, and a sheen of moonlight on the jeep's hood. "Good. Don't worry about me. I'm snug as a bug in here."

"Angelique says not to forget your vitamin in the morning."

"Tell her thank you. Tell her I'll take two."

"And don't hesitate to phone the police if for any reason—"

"Go! Go! Go! The police don't have time tonight for one wheezy old woman. All I need is to see you two go sailing past my porch."

"All right. Dowidzenia."

"Yes, dowidzenia. Until we meet again." She watched his dark form disappear into the night. Thank you, Karl, she thought. My brave, naive, big-hearted boy, thank you so much.

Wheeling herself to the closet, she found her red silk scarf. Then she rolled through the house to the porch door; she switched on the spotlight, opened the door and rolled out on the weather-worn boards, ready to salute her family as they sailed past.

With one green eye and one red, the sloop approached. The jib was a small pale triangle, the mainsail a larger dark triangle with a white light at its peak. She grabbed hold of the railing, pulled herself up until she stood, then she waved her scarf. "Ahoy!"

The two on the gunnel looked up and waved, Karl with a light face and dark shirt, Angelique with a dark face and light shirt. Angelique warned, "Don't catch cold out there. You wrap yourself in a blanket if you stay outside."

Zosia called down, "Bon voyage! Have a wonderful honeymoon."

Beyond the point, the boat heeled steeply. Angelique turned her attention to the sails; Karl waved a final good-bye.

Zosia wheeled herself back inside, closed the door and turned the lock. She rolled down the hallway, put the red scarf on its shelf.

Then she reached to the back of the shelf and lifted a sweater from the lid of a small pine chest that Papa had built in Bydgoszcz, eons ago. She set the box in her lap, raised its lid and took out the bundle of Piotr's love letters, tied with an ancient brownish-red ribbon from Berlin. She set the bundle on the shelf. Pinching her fingers onto a strip of leather that Papa had tacked to the bottom, she lifted out a small thin board. Beneath it lay a leather pouch. She lifted out the pouch, hooked her thumbs into its neck and pulled against the drawstring, then she reached inside and wrapped her hand around Polish steel. She drew out her father's Radom semi-automatic pistol, an ugly, brutish thing; it smelled of gun oil. She laid the pistol on the shelf, reached back into the chest and took hold of a cardboard box of 9 mm cartridges. The cardboard fell apart in her fingers, spilling shells into the chest. Picking up the gun again, she checked its safety. Then struggling as she had struggled with Piotr's pills, she filled the magazine with eight shells.

During the summer before the war—the summer of 1939 when they felt "it" coming, though they knew not what—Papa had taught her how to load the gun. She had a girl's hands then, a painter's hands, as she pressed the shells one by one against the spring in the magazine. "Never hurry with a pistol," he told her. "What you do, do well." Then on the first of September, after Hitler had thundered on the radio that Poland had attacked the Fatherland, and that Germany had therefore defended itself, gentle Papa hung himself in his library. Leaving her an orphan. With a pistol. And Piotr.

She swiveled her wheelchair so she faced the bedroom, then held the pistol with both hands and aimed it at the lamp by her bed. The barrel shook. "Psiakrew!" If anybody tried to harm her tonight, she would have to wait until he was very close before she pulled the trigger.

Laying the pistol in the chest in her lap, she wheeled across the room to her bed. Once again she checked the Radom's safety, then she slid the weapon beneath her pillow.

She returned to the closet, placed the empty chest on its shelf, closed the door.

Angelique and Karl were safe.

And she was ready for bed.

She wheeled around the house, checked the locks on both doors, turned out lights. When finally she turned out the lamp by her bed, she discovered how brightly the moon cast a circle of blurred colors on the hardwood floor.

She set the handbrakes, stood up from the wheelchair, pivoted slowly so the backs of her knees touched the mattress, then sat. Sweeping the folds of her beautiful red gown up with her legs onto the bed, she lay back with her head on the pillow and felt wonderfully comfortable.

"Piotr, do you remember our garden in Davos? The daisies and the lupine and the columbines were like a palette outside our cabin window. Kochany, we were safe then. We were safe."

She closed her eyes; utterly exhausted, she was soon asleep.

Looking over the stern, Angelique and Karl watched Zosia's red scarf flutter against the black sky.

"Karl, if the Tomahawk explodes, we go straight back to her."

"*If* the island is safe. She would never forgive us if we jeopardized the baby."

"I hate this." Angelique glanced up at her telltales, cast a look over her shoulder at the stars in the east. "I hate it."

Karl watched Zosia as she wheeled herself back into the house. He gazed at the golden rectangle of her dining room window; inside was the table where they had sat together so many times. He sent up a silent prayer for the woman to whom he owed so much.

Turning forward, he noticed that Angelique was not tacking northeast toward Buck Island: straight ahead of the bow shone the polar star. To the left, the dolphin was diving into the sea. To the right, campfires fringed the Buck Island beach like a necklace of sparks. Other evacuees were already there.

"Karl, I don't want to go to Buck Island yet. I don't want to talk to anyone."

"But Angelique, you need to sleep." He looked at his waterproof, luminous-dial watch. "It's almost three in the morning. You've *got* to rest."

"No." Her feet under the strap, she leaned out far enough to stare past him at the dark water ahead. "I just left behind my best friend to possibly finish her life alone. I left Mama and Papa in a church where the governor says they should not be. I left behind a helicopter that unexplainably exploded in the sky. And I left behind a hundred and fifty kiloton monster in the forest. Hideous. *Hideous.* I am helpless, waiting to wake up from a nightmare I know is real." She sheeted in the mainsail, gaining speed. "So I want to sail this boat, which I know how to do, and which is a good and normal thing to do. I want to sail with my friend the wind, and my friend the sea and my friend the moon. And with my good friend Karl."

"You don't think the baby needs you to rest?"

"The baby needs a mother who stops dashing like a terrified rabbit. The baby needs a cradle away from crowds and radios. The baby needs a world that makes sense."

"All right. But let's not go too far out."

She stared ahead without answer.

Looking over the stern one last time, he discovered a small constellation he had never seen before, low in the sky above Zosia's tiny window. "Angelique, is that the Southern Cross?"

She glanced back. "Yes. Papa calls it the Kite."

"It looks like a kite." He imagined Zosia out on her porch, laughing while she held the string.

Her heart filled with peace, Estelle lit fresh candles on the altar. She and Nat helped Father Abrams to distribute blankets and pillows from the rectory, and Girl Scout sleeping bags from the vestibule. There were not nearly enough blankets and bags for the hundreds who sought shelter in the church, but people gladly made do with a jacket or a beach towel brought in from the car. Father dimmed the chandeliers. The moon shone through windows along the nave, casting its pale peaceful glow on people stretched out on the pews, on the carpet around the altar, and on the stone floor.

With her choir robe for a blanket, a rolled-up towel for a pillow, Estelle lay down on the family pew. Nat rolled his coat for a pillow and lay with his head nearly touching hers.

"Good night, Nat. We in God's good hands now."

"Good night, Honey. Yes, yo' family safe, praise God."

She could hear people whispering their prayers. She too folded her hands and sent up her heartfelt prayer of gratitude.

Among the thousands of people milling aimlessly in the streets of Christiansted, with neither a yacht to sail away on nor reliable information to ease their minds, one gray-haired woman, believing the bomb would have exploded by now if it were going to, picked up a good-sized rock, cast it with all her strength through a storefront window, reached through the jagged hole and grabbed the bottle of French perfume that had taunted her for years.

At the sound of crashing glass, others in the street looked for a rock of their own. The atmosphere of panic and anger turned rapidly into the festive mood of a carnival as a frenzy of looting spread throughout the town's shopping district. People paraded up and down King Street with cameras and telephoto lenses, Danish porcelain, gold earrings, silk dresses, blue ribbon Scotch. Gathering around newly acquired cassette recorders, they danced and strutted. Cheers of approval accompanied each smashed window-front. Black fists shook in the air. For justice had at last prevailed.

In Caravelle Arcade stood a farmer, unable to pay the increased taxes on his rezoned land. He picked up a HELP KEEP YOUR PARADISE LITTER-FREE garbage can, raised it over his head and hove it with all his might through the photograph-filled window of Holiday

Horizon Real Estate. The crash was answered with a shot from inside the office. People screamed and dashed for cover, clearing the courtyard. From an alleyway, a voice taunted the real estate agent, challenging him to come outside.

Suddenly a young man carrying a bottle with a burning rag sprinted across the courtyard. He cocked his arm and hurled his homemade bomb through the hole in the window. Three shots chased after him, but the owner must have been caught off guard, for the shots were late and the man dived for cover behind an ornamental fountain gurgling in the moonlight. Flames blossomed inside the office. As the fire rose higher and higher, so did the roar of the crowd.

Several men circled around the block toward the office's back door.

In his office at Government House in downtown Christiansted, Governor Harper wanted to wring the neck of the admiral on the phone at the Pentagon. "Listen, pal, I'm not requesting an evacuation, I'm *demanding* one. I've got riots in the streets. People are killing people over a two-bit life raft. The hospital can't possibly cope with the injured coming in. All I need are two ships, at Frederiksted and Christiansted. If people know there's at least an effort to help them, they'll settle down and wait their turn."

"I repeat, Governor, we have no vessels available in the Caribbean sector."

"No vessels available? The *Defender* is sitting on its ass ten miles offshore. It could be docked at Frederiksted Pier within the hour."

"That ship has a job to do, Governor."

"It certainly does. And it's not doing it." Staring out the window at dark rooftops, he was ready to explode with exasperation. "What about the rest of your barges at Roosevelt Roads?"

"I'm sorry, but at this point in time our Caribbean fleet is on full alert."

"Why?"

The phone remained silent.

"I'm asking you *why.*"

"I can say only that we are cognizant of Soviet activity, and that we are responding accordingly."

"So what am I supposed to do? Wait for World War Three to be over before I get some help?"

"Governor, I've just been notified that Rapid Deployment Forces are on their way to help maintain order."

"Hey, I don't want a war. I want an *evacuation*."

"With all due respect, Governor, we find it somewhat reprehensible that with both a police force *and* National Guard, you are unable to control the situation."

He slammed his fist on the desk. "With all due respect, Admiral, nobody dumped a nuke in your back yard, did they?"

"What is it, exactly, that your police are doing?"

"Oh, nothing much. Just directing traffic for a panicked mob of twenty thousand. The Coast Guard is calmly plucking bodies out of the harbor. The National Guard is idling away the hours setting up boy johns and girl johns so we don't all die of typhus."

"Once the Soviet threat is contained, we will do everything in our power to assist you."

"Can you at least send a hospital ship?"

"One moment please."

He listened to muffled voices in the background: the gods discussing the fate of mere mortals. Finally the admiral answered, "I understand a hospital ship is on its way from Honduras."

"Honduras? That's the other damn side of the Caribbean. Don't you clowns have a map up there?"

"Governor, you don't seem to recognize the difficulty of our situation. Your particular island is only one point in the Western Atlantic Theater and—"

He heard no more as he stared aghast at flames rising over the rooftops outside his window. "I've got to go. But Lord Almighty, Admiral Barnes, when this mess is over, I'm on the first jet to Washington and I will personally fry your bovine butt before a congressional investigation."

"Good night, Governor. Please keep us informed."

Swiftly down the narrow, dark, mangrove-lined river, the Witherspoons paddled their Carib canoe. Albert in the stern, Cecil in the bow, and four of the older children drew six paddles in silent unison. Edith leaned against a burlap sack of yams as she nursed the infant Elspeth.

Sabrina rode in the middle of the hollowed-out log; Charles squirmed in her lap as he tried to reach over the side. She allowed him to dip his fingers in water so smooth that ahead of the canoe, the surface reflected the stars. The vessel seemed not to glide on water, but to sail across the heavens.

The river widened into Salt River Bay. Albert peered ahead at a pale white line that stretched across the mouth: the moonlit froth of waves crashing over the reef. He spotted the black cut through the coral where waves rolled in without breaking. Though he and Cecil had guided the canoe through the slot many times, never had they attempted the passage at night, or with such precious cargo. Albert swept his paddle with long deep strokes and tillered with the blade, pointing the needle-shaped craft toward the button hole.

Noise of car horns and shouting drifted across the bay from the road that skirted its western shore. Albert listened to the pandemonium, then listened to the rhythmic dipping of six paddles; he smiled with satisfaction.

Now he could hear the growing thunder of white water boiling over the reef. He watched shiny black waves as they billowed through the slot. "Keep low," he warned his passengers. They hunched their weight lower. His paddlers leaned forward and dug harder. He aimed toward the center of the cut, where a sheen of moonlight danced on the smooth swells.

Sabrina hugged Charles tightly in her arms.

The vessel shot through the turbulent passage, slicing the chop as smoothly as a needle piercing rippled silk. On both sides of the boat a comber exploded over the coral, dousing the Witherspoons with spray as it roared past, but none of the paddlers missed a stroke. The canoe rode up the wave's black belly, teeter-tottered over its top, then glided down its backside to the safety of open water.

"Good wo'k, crew!" Albert called.

Cecil called back, "Nice job, Papa."

Edith surveyed the rolling sea, then turned to her husband. "What yo' t'ink?" Elspeth, oblivious to her treacherous voyage, continued to nurse.

Albert could see the glow of the lights of St. Thomas straight ahead, forty miles north. He could also see, to the northeast and nearer, the lights of the destroyer. "We gon' make de crossin'. We gon' paddle 'round to de back side of Sain' Thomas. We runnin' for cover till dis war does be over."

Edith nodded with approval, then reached into a bag between her feet and wrapped a blanket around herself and the baby.

While Charles twisted in her arms until he could look over her

shoulder at the moon, Sabrina stared across the water at the lights of
the ship that had stolen fire from the sun.

Albert paddled and tillered, paddled and tillered, keeping his craft
as steady as the needle of a compass.

The U.S. Navy Radar Facility, a complex of reception and trans-
mission towers perched on a hill behind Frederiksted, traced both surface and airborne movement over an extensive area of the eastern Caribbean.

But the far-reaching eyes failed to note someone snipping the
peripheral fence. Nor did the towers detect a box placed at their feet—a
box wrapped with a strip of camouflage tarp and covered with cut
guinea grass.

His preparations with Hat Number One completed, Nick looked
down from the hill at as much of the pier as he could see beyond the
rooftops of Frederiksted. The town's entire population seemed to be
jammed on that strip of concrete jutting into the sea: people fleeing
from the missile had piled against each other when they came suddenly
to a dead end.

The lost leaderless masses.

But soon he would liberate them. And afterwards, as teacher, as
representative to the Crucian Congress, and perhaps one day as governor, he would lead his people toward a future of prosperity and dignity.

He swung on his backpack and was ready to hurry down to the
plain and Hat Number Two, when he caught sight of something beyond
the pier, its progress toward the island marked by moonlight on a huge
V-shaped wake. He stared with astonishment as a ship, showing no
lights, steamed past the end of the pier. He could hear a cheer from his
people, and discerned ripples of movement in the crowd as thousands
stood up.

The vessel reversed engines; white froth washed forward alongside
its hull as it came to a halt a few hundred yards from shore. Then from
her stern, the mother ship spawned a brood of amphibious landing
craft. He grinned at the stir he had caused: one successful hit with the
Stinger, and Big White Sam was pouring in troops, but not by plane.

Through the gap between rooftops where a street led to the waterfront, the lone guerrilla watched a landing craft race to the beach: its
bow dropped open and soldiers surged out in full battle gear. The

troops climbed the sea wall and dashed into town. The forces would no doubt sweep through the mahogany forest to clear it of enemy fortifications and to secure the endangered missile.

Good luck, suckers.

With a stiff middle finger he saluted the mother ship; then he hurried through the hole in the fence toward his olive-green mobile demolitions taxicab.

Seated on his father's shoulders, Chester watched with frustration and envy as people near the pier's gate swept across the beach toward the emptied landing craft: not only would they be rescued, but they would be transported out to the Kaptain Kommando battleship, where they could roam the armored decks for the rest of the night.

He was startled by shots from the landing craft. The crowd halted, then backed away. He could hear angry shouts. And then the long flat boats closed their bows, roared backwards and raced out to the ship, empty!

"Goddamn those bastards!" he heard his father say. He had never heard such words from his father, had never even known his father knew such words as some of the boys used at school.

Adults were always telling him what to do, what not to do. But he wondered if they knew themselves what they were doing.

CHAPTER THIRTY-EIGHT

Rescue

One hand on the tiller, one hand holding the sheet, Angelique looked back at her island. The fire raging in Christiansted had cupped the entire bay and was now climbing into the hills behind town. By morning there would be nothing left of the old seaport but ashes, and the stone arches of Danish arcades. Sick with grief, she turned and faced the ocean where once she had felt so happy and free.

She peered over her shoulder: stars clear in the east. The sloop was out as far as Buck Island; on top of the dark hump, a nautical light blinked with slow regularity, as if ticking off the final seconds.

Even if they escaped, even if the flash merely lashed them with a moment of purgatorial light, what would they go back to?

Mama and Papa buried alive in the burning wreckage of their church?

Zosia gone mad in an empty house. Or more likely, her battered body floating beside the Candle Point cliff, her spirit at peace with Piotr.

And Chester? If a ship had come to evacuate people from the pier, it must have come from the south, for she saw no large vessel other than the destroyer, parked on the horizon like the devil in a grandstand seat, waiting for his Big Show to begin.

No, Chester was still on that pier, protected by two parents who had loudly and steadfastly refused to come to even one of her Monday evening classes.

She wondered what a hundred and fifty kiloton nuclear explosion would do to a white marble marker. Turn it black? Shatter the stone? Melt it? Would the earth tremor heave bodies up out of the ground, so that generations of Frederiksted dead would rise to witness the extinction of their town? Yo' lucky, Leroy. Wherever yo' lie, at least yo' ain' here tonight. This be one war yo' can miss.

"Did you hear something?" Karl asked, looking over his shoulder.

She listened carefully, heard only waves washing along her boat.

"There it is again," he said. "Somebody's calling for help."

She swept her eyes back and forth across the water until she sighted a low black hump that appeared and disappeared in the glimmering waves: the hull of an overturned boat. And now, yes, she heard a faint, desperate voice. "Karl, we've got to help them."

"We can take them to the Buck Island beach."

"Ready about."

He readied the jib lines. "Ready."

"Hard a-lee." The two ducked under the boom as the sloop tacked toward the wreck.

They approached what looked like an enormous turtle. People waved and shouted in the water around it, many more people than she could take aboard her sloop. She would have to make several trips to Buck Island. But at least now she knew what she was doing out here tonight. No longer fleeing, no longer hiding, no longer lost, she called, "Is anyone hurt?"

A chorus of voices pleaded for help.

The only place she could see to tie the painter was to the propeller shaft. Someone was clinging to it, a boy with a cluster of people around him. "Karl, can you secure us to the propeller shaft, please. Ask them if they can give us a little room." She let out her sail to slow the sloop. Karl climbed onto the bow and readied the line. She tillered into the wind; the sloop glided toward the propeller: a black three-petaled flower.

"Got it," he called.

People splashed toward the sloop, reached up to its gunnels and began to heave themselves aboard. "Wait!" she cried. "Yo' can't all come at once. Let me help those who—hey!" She was nearly thrown overboard by a man hoisting himself up beside her.

Karl scrambled down from the bow, cocked his arm and swung a punch that flopped the Crucian into the sea. His eyes wild, he shook his fist and shouted, "You wait for the captain's orders, Mack!"

Though hands now gripped the gunnels from stern to bow, no one else tried to come aboard. But others still paddling fought for a grip on the rescue boat. "Move over! Gimme a place!"

"Dey ain' no place!"

"Hell dey ain'! Move de fuck over!"

She and Karl were ringed with anxious faces staring up at them. He pointed to the group still clinging to the propeller shaft, the only people who had not rushed to her sloop. "There's one dead," he whispered with shock. "And a bunch of kids. I think we ought to take them first."

She called to the group, "Yo' people gathered around the propeller, can yo' swim back to me, please?" She pointed to individual people gripping the starboard gunnel. "Would yo' help them, please."

Three children came dog-paddling toward her, assisted by arms that passed them to her waiting hands. Karl hoisted them one by one into the sloop, the three youngsters silent, frightened and cold, but apparently uninjured. Then came a women with a little boy in her arm; people along the sloop turned to help her, passing her back. The boy's teeth were chattering. The desperate woman looked up at Angelique. "The baby shivers. Have you a blanket?"

Karl gripped the child under his arms and lifted him into the boat. Angelique took off the boy's wet clothing, then bundled him in her sweatshirt.

Now the oldest boy let go of the propeller shaft. With his arm around the body of a man, he was passed back. Angelique stared at the upturned face, a mask of death wallowing in the water, and saw with horror that it was Raphael. Who had risked his life to help Karl find her in the storm. Raphael, who refused to be paid even for his gas. Raphael!

Summoning her strength as a professional, she said, "Karl, can you lift him into the boat, please. It's Raphael."

"Raphael?" He stared with disbelief as he reached his hands toward the drowned man.

She balanced her weight against Karl's. With a heave that rocked the sloop, he hefted Raphael aboard, then straightened the corpse along the deck, its head close to the four petrified children huddled around the mast. Karl took off his sweatshirt and spread it over Raphael's face.

Then he helped Raphael's wife as she clambered over the gunnel. The woman sat on the deck beside her husband and sobbed. The littlest boy stared at his mother, and at his father, and began to wail. The mother looked up from her husband long enough to take the child back into her arms; she stared down again at Raphael and through her sobs began to pray in Spanish.

Karl helped the oldest boy aboard. The sloop lay low in the water, a very heavy boat for tacking upwind to Buck Island. Angelique scanned the twenty or more faces that surrounded her, pleading faces, threatening faces. "Ah can't take all of yo' now," she said with an air of authority. "Ah bring other boats from Buck Island, enough to fetch all of yo'"

"Yo' ain' leavin' me behind!" shouted a man as he hoisted himself onto the bow.

Others followed his example; they yelled, cursed, kicked at each other. "Lemme up. Goddammit, lemme *up*."

Karl roared in a fury, "Get down! Get down!" He swung his fists, but stumbled over Raphael's legs. The bow sank lower with three, four, five men climbing onto it; the next large wave would surely wash over the sloop.

"Ah come back!" she shouted. "Ah promise! Ah come back!" But her voice was lost in the din.

Helpless as the frenzied horde overwhelmed her boat, she saw from the corner of her eye something large and white on the water to the north. She stared transfixed at the square-rigger with full canvas spread in the moonlight as it sailed toward St. Croix. "Oh tank yo'," she whispered, and in that moment of awe and gratitude, the towering sails seemed to her like the white robe of Christ as he walked across the water toward her.

The chaos around her quickly diminished to total silence as the mob discovered the *Danmark*.

Stepping over the living and the dead, reaching past the children huddled around the mast, she removed the hatch and rummaged in the dark hold until she found her flare kit. She took out the pistol, loaded it, held her hand high toward the ship, and fired. A red meteor arched across the stars.

She watched the square-rigger closely, but saw no change in its course toward Christiansted. She loaded and fired a second flare. Then she saw a signal light blinking. "Karl, they see us!"

But another flare shot up to the west, a tiny stitch of red over the black sea. Several flares etched the sky outside Christiansted harbor. Further down the coast, flares rocketed up and faded, most of them where the offshore water turned rough.

She watched the *Danmark* . . . "Please," she whispered, "please." She loaded and fired a third flare . . . until she saw it was changing course toward her sloop. "Yes! It's coming to *us*."

The three-masted vessel slowed as it approached. On its deck, cadets in white uniforms stood at their stations. An adult called through a megaphone, "I am Captain Larsen of the *Danmark*. How can we help you?"

She cupped her hands and called back, "Can you send your launches to pick up about twenty-five people?"

"Ja. We lower the boats."

He called orders in Danish. Cadets scurried up the rigging and spread themselves across the spars, where they furled some sails and reset others as the square-rigger hove-to and slowed to a halt.

Crews of cadets launched two of the ship's tenders and motored to the sloop. The boys in one launch lowered ladders and assisted the survivors, who, quietly and orderly, let go of the sloop and climbed into the boat. The other launch drew alongside the sloop so that Angelique's passengers could step aboard. Raphael's wife and children huddled together on a seat in silence. Angelique asked the cadets to come back a second time, with an empty boat, to pick up Raphael.

As the tenders motored back to the *Danmark*, Captain Larsen called, "We have heard emergency bulletins on the radio. And we have received many distress calls. Is there no rescue effort under way? Are we the first ship to arrive?"

"The only ship," she answered angrily. "Have you a doctor aboard?"

"Ja, we have a surgeon."

"There seem to be at least a dozen wrecks further west. We will pick up what people we can and bring them to you. With your four tenders, we make five ambulances serving the hospital ship."

Karl whispered with surprise, "Angelique, what about you? I think we should get you to Buck Island."

Ignoring him, she called to Captain Larsen, "Do you have charts? You must stay outside the reef."

"Ja, we know of the reef. But what about the missile? I risk my crew."

"That you must decide for yourself," she answered. "Try to radio the Navy for information."

"Ja. One minute, please." The captain turned from the rail and disappeared into a cabin.

Karl sat on the opposite gunnel, balanced with her. "Are you sure we want to be doing this? We've done our part. They've got four boats, they don't really need us. And I'm worried . . . Well, I'm worried about the danger of a miscarriage. It's been a long hell of a night. I think you ought to lie down on the Buck Island beach and get some sleep."

She shook her head, dismissing his concern for her. "Karl, any sailor who fails to answer a call of distress, any nurse who turns her back on people who are hurt . . . No, I cannot."

"But what about our child? You're endangering her, aren't you?"

"No. I'm a strong, healthy woman, sailing my boat. I'm doing none of the heavy lifting, you're doing that. Karl, there is no danger of a miscarriage, I assure you."

He pointed to the west. "If we help those people, we're going to be drifting down the coast toward the mahogany forest. What if Zosia is right? She told us to get as far away from that missile as possible."

Mindful of her nightmare, the flash of unearthly light and roar and blast of wind still as vivid in her memory as they had been in that dream, she hesitated. Had it been a warning?

Hadn't her Monday night classes been a warning?

Hadn't that Harpoon a decade ago been a warning?

"Of course Zosia is right. One day the bombs must explode. There are so many of them, and so close, that one day they must let us know they are there. But maybe not tonight. Maybe that Tomahawk is safe, as you kept telling us it is. In any case, we'll heed the governor's warning. Centerline is three, four miles from the ridge. We'll try to stay at least four miles out from the coast."

He frowned. "I still don't like it. Rescue at sea is a job for the Navy, not a pregnant civilian."

She laid one hand over the other on her belly. "Please understand, Karl, I think of Elly Zosieňka every moment. But I could not live with myself if I heard tomorrow how many people drowned out here, while we did nothing. That's not the kind of mother I want to be. This little one inside me is going to learn that either people live together, or we die alone."

"Coming alongside," called a blond cadet as he motored his launch toward the sloop. Karl helped to fend off. Then he grimaced as he reached his arms beneath Raphael, lifted the limp cadaver and passed it into the arms of four sick-faced boys. Behind them, a flare rose into the sky, a lone shooting star that scribed a red arc before it burned out its brief life.

The captain called across the water, "Your Navy assures us that the weapon presents no danger. In that case, we are glad to assist you in a rescue operation."

She called back, "We are grateful for your help. But we feel that to be safe, we should stay at least four miles out from the coast once we pass Salt River Bay."

"Ja, four miles. So do we too."

The tender pulled away with Raphael. Karl sat again on the gunnel opposite her. The two studied each other while the sloop tugged at its painter, still tied to the propeller.

"Are you ready?" she asked.

"Angelique, I ought to grab that tiller from you and sail us to Buck Island. I should mutiny, is what I should do. I ought to overrule all your arguments and take you to where I know you'll be safe."

She gathered the sheet and neatly coiled it in her hand. The sails luffed in the wind.

He continued, "But you'd leave me tomorrow if I did. You'd say I wasn't worthy to be the father of your child." He paused, waiting for her to confirm what he had just said.

"Are you ready?" she asked.

He nodded, with conviction. "I'm with you, Angelique. Give me a kiss, then let's go to work."

They leaned toward each other over the tiller and pressed their lips together with a kiss of love, and commitment.

Then he climbed onto the bow and untied the painter; the black three-petaled flower was only inches above the water.

She set her sails wing-and-wing and ran with the wind toward the faint white speck of a shirt someone was waving above the dark sea, half a mile west.

The sloop approached a swamped rowboat. Five adults were gathered around it. They stared toward the rescue team with happy relief, profound exhaustion, and blank despair.

Inside the rowboat floated a body, face down in its watery coffin.

CHAPTER THIRTY-NINE

Nicholas

Worried that troops might soon arrive to guard the refinery, Nick worked as quickly as he could manage. He had planned ten detonation points, but limited himself now to six. Driving along the perimeter road with his lights out, he made three stops, cut three holes in the outer fence, three in the inner fence, then gloated, on each of his sorties, at how well his memory of Hard Hat's maps corresponded with the actual layout of the towers and fuel tanks, pipelines and electrical switching stations.

He saw only one guard, with a dog on a leash; but Nick was downwind, and silent.

He had set the sonar clock to make its wake-up call at 0413 hours. The radar clock would cock-a-doodle-doo at 0414 hours. And now, his watch reading 0353 hours, he set the last of the six Petrox tickers at 0415. He wanted to hear a sequence of boom-booms. Twenty years ago, he had always enjoyed that extra touch of precision.

At 0401 hours he scurried out through the hole in the fence, jumped into the taxi and drove east. He could barely restrain himself from tooting the horn.

At 0412 hours he pulled to the side of South Shore Road, stepped out of the car and leaned casually against the tailgate, listening, for one minute, to the crickets in the fields, and the waves rolling into Ha'penny Bay.

Boom! on the far side of the distant hills. He trembled with excitement.

BOOM! on a hilltop: he could see the orange flash! Too exuberant to stand still, he strode in his combat boots along the deserted highway for about fifty paces, his eyes flicking back and forth between the luminous digits on his watch and the night sky straight ahead.

BO-BO-BOO-BOOM!! BOO-BOOM!! Shaking fists of victory

overhead, he savored what sounded like carpet bombing of a tightly defined target. Boiling flame bulged upward, as if an angry sun were rising in the wrong part of the sky. Volleys of secondary explosions spewed fiery geysers into the night. An enormous smudge of smoke blotted out the stars.

While he gazed at the work of his magic wand, he wished Leroy were standing there beside him. Or Andy. He regretted that he was alone, with no one to share his victory. But perhaps on the pier they were cheering.

Though he could have stood there and watched that fireball—his masterpiece—for hours, he forced himself to return to the car. He had seen no planes landing; he'd delay his turkey shoot until later. So there remained one last mission: he had an appointment with a whigger, a whore, and a half-breed bastard.

"My God!" exclaimed Karl as he stared over the stern toward the thunder of explosions. On the far side of the island, a wall of oily flames erupted into the sky: the refinery! A long narrow cloud above St. Croix, invisible a moment ago, now glowed a ghostly orange. "Who would do such a thing?"

She knew at once that tonight, Nick was fighting Vietnam's last battle. And he was winning.

She knew too that Karl would be in danger on St. Croix, until Nick was in jail. In a federal penitentiary. Serving time, after having served twenty years already as an untreated psychiatric outpatient . . . after serving twelve months in Vietnamese hell.

Traitor. She would have to be a traitor to the man who loved her. To the man who had loved Leroy. But the decision was unavoidable: as soon as possible, she would notify the police and set them after the soldier who would stop at nothing until all his enemies were destroyed.

Karl turned to her. "You don't suppose, that guy who broke into my cottage and took the maps?"

She shook her head; she could not answer. She remembered Mr. Adam's high school history class, when she had stood on the chair with a BIC lighter and set the American flag on fire. Staring now at the flames consuming one tiny corner of the American empire, she could have stood up in her sloop and cheered. For Nick.

Zosia sat bolt upright as bombs from Stukas crashed outside her windows. Only after she saw the nightlight in her bathroom, and her paintings on the walls, did she realize that what she was listening to was a nuclear explosion.

But she heard a long and erratic succession of detonations, not a single blast. Was the destroyer firing salvos at the island?

She struggled into her wheelchair, rolled to a window and saw the flames were not in the western hills, but closer, across the island to the southwest. Nor did the vast conflagration form a mushroom. Her sleep-clouded mind finally understood that she was watching the refinery burn. But the Tomahawk?

She rolled down the hallway to the living room and pinched her fingers on the toggle to the radio. "—citizens are warned not to return to the evacuated area until the governor has declared the area safe. We repeat—"

"Psiakrew," she muttered as she flicked off the radio.

She wheeled herself to the dining room window and saw sparks of bonfires brightening the Buck Island beach. She would wait here at the window to watch the colors in the sky at dawn. And to see the rainbow sail, waving like a flag that proclaimed survival.

He parked at Chenay Beach, left the Stinger hidden under a tarp. His last four sticks of dynamite weighted his backpack as he hiked through guinea grass and tantan up Green Key Hill.

The cottage was locked, the jeep gone. He shone his penlight through the windows: the bed was empty, couch empty, walls bare except for a bluish painting over the desk. And on the desk, a picture of— he squinted—the lovebirds standing together in their Sunday best, beaming with smiles.

He set a trip-wire across one of the steps leading to the front door; the detonator and single stick of dynamite he hid beneath a fallen banana leaf.

Then he hiked down the hill to the beach where she kept her boat: it was gone. He looked out at the two dark houses at the end of Candle Point. As invisible in the night as the shadow of a ghost, the guerrilla headed toward his final target.

Her dog did not bark. Hard Hat's jeep was in the driveway.

He climbed her steps. The house was locked. He shone his light through a window: her blue sarong lay in a heap on the floor. She had left in a hurry. With Hard Hat and the Hound. They probably out at

Buck Island, toastin' marshmallows.

But the old lady? If they took her with them, then he could go to work.

She heard footsteps crackling on dry leaves; her skin prickled with fear. The footsteps approached her door. She saw the brass handle slowly dip—she held her breath, her heart thumping in those moments before the Gestapo beat down her door. The door nudged, but it was bolted, and after a second nudge, the handle raised up and the leaves crackled again.

She pivoted her chair and rolled on silent rubber wheels across the living room and down the hall to her bedroom, where she reached under her pillow and willed her fingers to wrap around the Radom. She laid the black pistol in the lap of her red gown, then wheeled back to the hallway, where he could not see her from any of the windows, but she could see him if he tried to enter from either direction.

She saw a spot of light on the dining room table: he was at a window with a flashlight. The spot traveled along the kitchen counter, then it zigzagged across the floor. It searched among the ferns, swept over the mermaid; the spot of light traveled slowly down the sculpture and lingered on the belly. Then the beam rose and shone on the figure's dreaming face.

The light disappeared.

She heard crackling like fire moving slowly along the side of her house.

The flashlight shone on her messy bed. On her night table, on the mahogany cradle, and on Karl's white suit neatly folded over one side of the cradle, his turquoise tie laid over his coat. The light darted around the room, but returned to the cradle, shone again on the turquoise tie, then vanished.

She heard her visitor stepping through the seagrape bushes to the driveway, . . . and heard nothing more.

Would he go away? Would he try to break in? Was he alone?

"Thunk."

She froze, listened.

She heard the metallic creak of someone lifting the hood of the jeep. She rolled to the bedroom door, turned and rolled slowly to the window at the foot of her bed. Peering through the open wooden lattices, she could see in the faint gray light of the moon that the hood was up. Beneath the hood, on the fender, was a dark lump, that moved. Someone was leaning over the engine.

Now he stood, his clothing dark, the hood angling across his face. He opened the door on the driver's side, then knelt down, disappeared. He was not sitting in the car; was he working beneath it?

He reappeared, walked to the front of the jeep, bent down. When he stood up, her heart jumped with horror, for she could see three pale cylinders in his hands: unmistakably, sticks of dynamite. He leaned again over the engine and now she knew exactly what he was doing.

She looked down at the pistol in her lap, wrapped both hands around its handle and picked it up. Pressing with her thumb, she pushed off the safety. She set the muzzle on a wooden lattice, sighted down the barrel and saw with satisfaction that it was fairly steady; only the gun's handle shook in her hands. She hooked her finger through the trigger socket, and waited.

He stood, leaned down for something beside the car, stood again. With the nub and notch atop the barrel aligned on the center of his chest, she willed her finger to pull the trigger. PANG! The gun almost jumped out of her hands.

"Ayy!" cried her assailant briefly, and then he dropped out of sight.

She listened: waves beat against the rocks at the bottom of the cliff.

She clicked on the safety, set the gunpowder-reeking pistol in her lap and wheeled herself down the hall. Quietly, she unbolted the door, swung it open on the hinges Karl had oiled. She peered out, listened for a voice, a breath, a scrape of a shoe on pavement. Heard the dawn twittering of a sugarbird.

She rolled out the door and through the shadowy tunnel, leaves crackling beneath her wheels. Psiakrew! she cursed, though she was certain the noise did not matter.

From the mouth of the tunnel, she looked at a soldier in camouflage lying on the pavement beside the jeep, a stream of dark red blood trickling across the concrete as if a snake were creeping out from under his chest.

"Forgive me," she whispered.

She felt sick, and thought for a moment she would have to lean over the armrest and vomit. She breathed deeply, inhaling the fresh morning air.

The nausea faded. But in its place she felt a disgust, a loathing; not for the man she had killed, but for the gruesome world she lived in. A world which had forced her to end a man's life, that most hideous of Nazi crimes. She had joined their ranks. For as long as she lived, she would feel filthy. Her hands were unworthy now of holding the child she had protected.

But as she rolled herself back toward the house, she grasped at that justification: she *had* protected the child. She wheeled herself through the door, shut it and locked it, then wheeled herself down the hallway to the bedroom, where she reached her hand to the cradle and gave it a little push. Watching it rock, she heard a voice, her grandmother's voice, her Babka's sad tender voice singing a lullaby as Zosieňka snuggled beneath her down comforter on a cold wintry night in Bydgoszcz.

Singing the words aloud, for she remembered them clearly, each line beckoning the next to follow, the rhymes falling into place, she wheeled herself down the hall to the porch door, which she unlocked. She rolled out to the end of the porch, then swiveled so she faced the breeze, faced Buck Island, faced the northeastern sky where she could watch the colors of the approaching dawn.

CHAPTER FORTY

Dawn

Second Lieutenant Jeffrey Baker, United States Marine Corps, confident of his training though never tested in combat, led his patrol into the rainforest at the first light of dawn. Their faces streaked with brown and green camouflage paint, the Marines advanced cautiously through the dim, gray-green jungle.

They met no resistance. Baker distrusted the ominous silence, broken by the unfamiliar cries of tropical birds greeting the new day. His eyes sharp, his rifle at the ready, he ached for whatever was going to happen . . . to finally begin.

But the patrol encountered no enemy fire, no bunkers, no supply trails. Sheeyit, he thought with disappointment, this ain't nothin' but a Boy Scout hike.

"Tsst!" Butt-Brains Bradley pointed toward something ahead, a little to the left. Butt-Brains whispered, "There's yer Tommyhawk, sir."

Baker peered through the tangle of trees and vines, and spotted it: a long battered blue cylinder lying in the bushes, its white nosecone crumpled, its red tailfins bent. "Look sharp," he called to his men. "Objective at eleven o'clock, thirty yards." He scanned the branches overhead for snipers.

Awakening on the hard concrete of the pier, Rosemary reached for her husband, felt nothing and sat up with a start. "Cyril?" Then she remembered that he had left when the sky was still full of stars to make his way back to her parents' home to fetch something for breakfast. She scanned the mass of people blanketing the pier, lit now by the gray light of dawn; she realized she had little chance of spotting Cyril before he returned.

Chester was still sleeping, curled against a suitcase.

Standing up stiffly, she stretched her back and groaned, "Ooooh,

351

meh bones!"

She glanced at the transport ship, still anchored beyond the end of
the pier. She searched the sea from horizon to horizon, saw no evacuation ship, then she looked again at the lifeless Navy vessel . . . and
sucked her teeth.

Cyril stood on a stepladder in Estelle's garden, picking papayas. He
set each fat, golden beauty into a burlap sack hanging from his shoulder. The bag bulged with fruit, for after the long night, he wanted to
treat his friends on the pier to a good breakfast. When he had plucked
all but the small green ones, he started down the steps, careful of his
balance with the heavy load.

Estelle lifted her head to look at the windows behind the altar: the
tall rectangles, facing east, glowed with the dawn. She sat up on the
pew. Nat was still asleep, his big feet in black socks sticking out from
the end of a towel. Others around the church were awakening. People
stretched their arms, waved good morning to each other, and whispered
quiet prayers. Up in the balcony, children were giggling as they played
a game. In a back pew, a baby wailed with hunger.

God in His great mercy had watched over His flock through the
night! She stood up and shook out her maroon robe, then put it on. Ad-
justing its shoulders, she began to sing, "My Lord, what a morning . . .
My *Lord*, what a morning!"

Facing the congregation, she let her voice ring out, "My Looooord,
what a moooooooornin'! When that sun begin to shine!"

The *Danmark* rocked gently as it drifted west, four miles offshore
from the lighthouse. Its rigging was manned by a new shift of cadets
who searched the sea for boats in distress.

On the afterdeck, bodies lay in rows, covered with sails. Raphael
lay among the dead.

Below decks, survivors filled the bunks. Concepcion slept with
Julio in her arms. In the bunk above her slept Pedro, Juanita and
Theresa-Maria, huddled beneath a single blanket.

On the foredeck, Arturo was awake. Had he rescued his father half
a minute sooner, surely he could have saved him. But no, when the
boat capsized, he had thought nothing of Padre. He had thought only of
himself.

He did not see the gray-green hills beyond the bow. He did not see the first pink flush of dawn in the east. He saw only his father's lifeless face awash in the dark water.

Hidden in the tantan bushes at the end of the runway, the Petrox families searched the sky for a plane. Ed glanced anxiously at his watch: 5:31. Any moment now, he thought. Any moment.

He worried about the oily smoke snaking into the sky over the runway. The refinery, upwind, burned with undiminished fury as tanks and towers continued to explode, fueling the flames. Longhorn could certainly land, but no pilot wanted to share his airspace with a gigantic oil smudge.

Those explosions meant a complete upheaval of his career. And the careers of a dozen good men hiding in the bushes beside him. It also meant a tremendous loss for Petrox. And a giant step backward for St. Croix. "Those damn Crucians," he growled, blaming the whole ungrateful lot. "They've destroyed the only stable economy on this rinky-dink rock."

"There it is!" whispered Harry. He pointed west.

A shimmering liquid light hovered in the lilac sky like a morning star. It drifted slowly, growing in brightness, until it lined up with the runway.

Ed cheered under his breath, "Longhorn, ol' buddy! Bah doggies, you've come!"

But the passenger jet did not land; it thundered overhead at two thousand feet, well above the smoke. "He's just checking things out," Ed reassured the consternated group. "He'll be back."

The jet banked to the north, circled over the hills, then descended on a second approach, this time with its landing lights on. Ed heard a shout from the crowd at the airport, half a mile away. He warned his people, "We gotta be quick."

The airliner maneuvered around the writhing cloud of smoke until it flew beneath it. The plane's wheels touched and squealed on the concrete. As the jet taxied to a halt, the Petrox families surged from the bushes onto the runway. An emergency door over the wing swung open and Longhorn stepped out, a short stout man in blue overalls, wearing a white ten-gallon hat. "Howdy, y'all! Longhorn delivers!'

Jubilant, Ed called up, "Thanks, ol' buddy. I knew you wouldn't let us down."

354 • *Children of the Sun*

Longhorn lowered a rope ladder. "Women and children first, then the rest o' you buzzards." He cocked an eye toward the clamoring mob, a quarter-mile away. "Y'all got company coming?"

Ed asked, "Got any firearms on board?"

"The Winchester."

"Go get it. I'll hold 'em off while we load."

"Okeydoke." Longhorn disappeared into the plane.

Ed climbed up the wooden rungs, crawled onto the wing, then stood and helped the woman behind him. "Upsa daisy, Gladys."

Crawling hurriedly toward the door, she called over her shoulder, "Edward, you're our knight in shining armor."

Longhorn appeared with his antelope rifle. "It's loaded, Ed. Here's a box of shells. Sight's set for two hundred yards."

"Thanks. You be ready in the cockpit. We'll holler when we're all aboard."

"Tell your folks to hang on tight during takeoff. I want them in their seats with belts buckled. There's thermals over that refinery, so we'll be banking sharply to the left. Tell 'em not to worry."

"Gotcha. Sharp bank to the left."

Ed ran to the tip of the wing; it bobbed with a slow rhythm as he lay down, set the rifle to his shoulder and peered through the scope at dark faces a hundred yards away. Raising the crosshairs, he fired a warning shot.

Screaming with panic, the would-be intruders fled toward the bushes. Suitcases littered the grass. A bewildered child in a red dress shrieked for her mother.

Ed called to Harry, stationed at the top of the ladder, "How we doing?"

"About half way."

Through the scope he saw frantic, furious, desperate faces peering from the brush. No one chanced a dash toward the plane. And no one returned his fire. He squeezed off another warning shot.

Finally Harry shouted, "Okay, big guy, let's *go*."

Ed sprinted along the wing, ducked through the door and called toward the cockpit, "All right, Longhorn, flap'em." Harry pulled the door shut and locked it. The Petrox families waited in tense silence as the engines on one wing rumbled and the plane pivoted. Then all four engines roared as the jet taxied toward the far end of the runway, leaving the mob behind.

Ed stood in the aisle and addressed his people. "Good going, gang. Now I want everybody to buckle up. Don't be alarmed by a sudden turn to the left. We'll be banking safely past poor ol' Petrox." He sat next to the emergency door and gripped the rifle between his knees while he fastened his seat belt.

As the plane pivoted a second time and roared its engines for take-off, he looked out his window and discovered hundreds of people along the edge of the runway. They were shouting, pleading, shaking fists. Then he saw a Crucian climbing from another man's shoulders onto the wing! The man scrambled on hands and knees to Ed's window, slapped his hand on the plexiglass and begged, "Take us! Please, mahn, yo' got room. Take us!"

Ed called, "Tell Longhorn to wait a minute. There's a guy on the wing."

The engines whined with power.

He cupped his hands and shouted, "Hey, tell Longhorn to wait!"

The engines thundered; the brakes released and the jet rolled forward. Ed gaped out the TV-sized window at the man's face, a foot from his own; the eyes stared at him with disbelief and terror. Ed cried toward the cockpit, "Stop! Goddamn it, tell him to *stop*."

Then he heard shots from the other side of the plane, and he no longer called to Longhorn.

As the jet accelerated, the Crucian spread himself flat on the smooth aluminum skin, clutching at it with his dragging fingertips. Ed watched with horror as the man slid slowly backward in the growing wind. Halfway down the runway, the man, screaming, was swept off.

"You damn fool."

The plane's wheels lifted from the ground; the Petrox families filled the cabin with cheers, whistles and applause. When the jet banked sharply to the left, the celebration grew even louder. "Ride 'em, cowboy!"

He looked out his window at the jumble of jungle-covered hills, but saw no sign of the Tomahawk, nor of any naval search operation. Well, the damn Navy never could hold a candle to the Air Force.

Now as the jet banked over the silver-pink Caribbean, he could see the lighthouse on a cliff. With profound relief, he thought, Thank you, Longhorn, ol' buddy. And good riddance to the rock.

Zosia watched the incremental changes of color in the sky over

Piotr's grave: lavender-gray melted into rose-petal pinks as the dawn blossomed. "Good morning, my husband," she called. "Your Polish bride has survived another night."

She lifted his binoculars from her lap, leaned her elbows on the railing and looked at the Buck Island beach: she saw a cluster of boats, their masts spiking the sky, but no rainbow sail. Good, she thought. My Angelique needs to sleep until noon.

She swept the round field of vision across the horizon to the destroyer, its gray shape now visible, its lights fading like stars at dawn. The ship worried her, for it had not moved. If the Navy had retrieved the missile, surely the warship would have departed.

Moving the binoculars further along the horizon, she discovered the three-masted *Danmark* off the northwest coast. Perplexed, she wondered if it was helping to search for the missile. Or didn't its crew know what had happened?

And then a tiny patch of bright color sailed out from behind the *Danmark's* white hull: Angelique's rainbow sail. "Nogh!" she cried. "*Nogh.* You fools."

"I haven't thanked you yet for whatever you did that enabled your Mom and Pop to write that letter." Holding the tiller and a slackened sheet, Angelique leaned against Karl, her head on his shoulder. "It was a wonderful letter, a very beautiful letter."

"Where is it now?" he asked, his arm around her waist.

She frowned with regret. "I must have left it on the restaurant table. I ran off in such a hurry."

"Doesn't matter. The important thing is we know what it said."

She lifted her head to look at him. After working together through this long, gruesome night—he as tough and uncomplaining as the best of the staff at the hospital—she loved him a thousand times more than before. She closed her eyes and lifted her face for a kiss, then melted at the touch of his salty lips.

With tired eyes, they searched the sea one last time. "I think we've made a clean sweep," he said. "I'd say the ambulance and hospital ship might as well head for the pier. We can phone everyone from the harbormaster's office." He looked warily toward the hills. "But I still want to keep our distance as we hook around the end of the island. I don't know what's taking the Navy so darn long."

She stared at the thread of smoke from where the sonar station had once stood, and knew that Karl would not be safe on the pier. Or in Frederiksted. Surely Nick—sooner or later—would be watching her house. Better that they sailed to Buck Island and spent the day there, sent a message to the police with someone heading back to St. Croix. Better still if they sailed all the way to St. Thomas, and stayed there, until she knew the police had Nick. But first she would sleep on Buck Island. Send messages to the police, to Mama and Papa, to Zosia. Then sleep in the sun, in the warm wonderful sun, until—

"Hey, take a look." Karl was peering over his shoulder.

She turned toward the brightest spot on the horizon, a brassy red glow where the sun would soon appear. "Oh, at last," she sighed. She gazed at the crimson-bellied clouds, their upper tufts tinged with gold. "I hope Zosia is out on her porch, watching."

"Would Mother like a sunrise picnic?"

She looked at him; his tired, beautiful green eyes were full of love. She suggested, "Shall we cut open a papaya?"

He gave her a squeeze with his arm, then he shifted forward, crouched by the aluminum mast and reached for the toggle of the hatch.

Stepping through ferns toward the Tomahawk, Lt. Baker turned to his radioman. "McQuade, tell 'em we found it and that the area is secure."

Lance Corporal McQuade spoke into his transmitter, "Hound Dog, Hound Dog, this is Tootsie Roll. We have located the missile. Area secured."

A crackly voice answered, "Tootsie Roll, this is Hound Dog. Congrats. Can you fire a flare up through the trees so we can locate you?"

"Roger. Roman candle coming up."

Baker wished he had brought his camera. If he couldn't rack up a body count, he could at least have McQuade take a photo of him leaning against the nose cone. Sheeeeeeeyit! I coulda sent a snapshot home to Betty-Lou. Wouldn't she be impr—

His combat boot caught the trip-string.

BO-BOO-BOOOOOOOOGHGHGHGHGHGHGHGH!

Eighteen pounds of supergrade plutonium progressed through sixty generations of chain-reaction fission in less than a millionth of a second. The pulse of liberated energy radiated outward at the speed of light, followed by a shock wave and high velocity winds. A half-sun

358 • *Children of the Sun*

nearly a mile in diameter cupped over the hills: the fireball vaporized the bedrock beneath it, burning a crater four hundred feet wide and a hundred feet deep into Maroon Ridge.

Second Lieutenant Baker and his platoon of Marines vanished. The molecules of life became fractured atoms, particles of particles, carried upward in the fist of a red-brown mushroom that punched the lavender sky.

In the flash of stellar light, the letter addressed to Angelique and Karl turned instantly to ash. One hundred seventy-mile-an-hour winds blew the powder over the stone wall and spread it across a boiling sea. An earthquake shook the greathouse to rubble that avalanched down the hill: square-cut stones crashed onto a beach where sand was popcorning.

The gray sea in front of Rosemary suddenly turned white. Before she had time to wonder why, she arched her back with searing pain and screamed, "Ayyyy!"

Chester heard his mother's voice. Looking up from the shadow of a suitcase, he saw with baffled horror that her dress and hair were on fire. She danced berserkly over other people; they too were on fire. He cried, "Mom!" From the edge of the pier, she plunged out of sight. He fought his way through the frenzied crowd—burning his hands as he pushed people aside—until he stared down at her, floundering and choking in water that shimmered with a strange red glow. "Mom, Ah comin'!"

But before he could jump in to save her, a blast of wind hurtled him from the pier, carried his twisting body beyond her and dropped him into the sea. Dazed, he gasped for breath. Dog-paddling back toward the pier, he stared awestruck at a fiery cloud billowing above the hills as if a volcano had erupted. But the cloud mattered nothing to him as he swam in his cumbersome camouflage toward his mother.

Hundreds of people leaped from the pier in a waterfall of flames, oblivious of the child beneath them.

The shock wave cannonballed through the gingerbread houses of Frederiksted. Fierce winds that followed flung burning rooftops into the sky.

The wind slapped Cyril from the ladder and slammed him against the side of the house. The wind abruptly stopped. Wild with pain, he crawled toward a garden hose: a wreath of charred rubber. When he grabbed the hot nozzle and turned the spigot, he saw the skin was peeling off the backs of his hands.

The ground shook crazily.

Water dribbled from the nozzle.

The eye of the hurricane lasted mere moments, then the wind reversed, heaving the fiery wreckage of the house on top of him. With his last breath, singeing his lungs as he took it in, he shrieked, "Rosemary! Che—"

High above the western hemisphere, the Soviet geostatic satellite detected a nuclear blast on the American island of St. Croix.

The Early Warning Tracking Station in Moscow received the information at 1146 hours and immediately notified the Kremlin.

Light shone through the tall windows of Holy Cross Church as if a thousand suns had suddenly risen. Estelle stopped singing. She looked at Nat, yawning on the pew when wind exploded through the windows, spraying the congregation with shards of stained glass. At the same moment the roof crashed down as if a giant boot had stomped on it. Crushed beneath a beam from the rafters, unable even to crawl, she cried, "Nat! . . *Nat!*"

If he answered, she could not hear him through the screams.

"Jesus," she moaned. "Jeeeeeesus! Where Yo' be, Jesus?"

Charred spars on the *Danmark's* masts supported draperies of orange flame. Cadets shrieked as they fell burning to the deck.

The square-rigger lurched in the shock wave; hurricane-force winds snapped its masts and thrashed the sails to rags.

Hurled across the deck, Arturo lay crumpled against a steel cleat, his neck broken.

Concepcion, thrown from her bunk to the floor, terrified by the clatter overhead, frantically climbed the steps up to the deck to be sure her son was safe.

Blinded by a flash through the window, Ed knew the shock wave would hit them in seconds. He cupped his hands and yelled, "Starboard, Longhorn! Bank starboard!"

But Longhorn was blind at the controls.

The airliner's fuselage, broadside to the blast at 2.9 miles from ground zero, sustained an overpressure of 3.6 pounds per square inch when the shock wave hit like a baseball bat smacking flat against the length of the plane. The riveted aluminum ruptured and wind blasted into the cabin, wrenching the tube into two plummeting pieces.

Ed's seat tore loose from the floor and pitched out of the fuselage. Like the good pilot he had been in Korea, he fought to maintain consciousness while he spun in the buffeting wind.

He was still awake half a minute later when he hit the water at over two hundred miles an hour.

The flash penetrated the ocean to Piotr's coffin and briefly illuminated the red mahogany box where it lay dusted with silt.

A sharp tremor triggered a slow-motion avalanche down the slope. The coffin rolled and tumbled deeper and deeper into the frigid black abyss.

The hundred-fifty kiloton explosion produced an electromagnetic pulse that spread across the eastern Caribbean and southwestern Atlantic, overloading electronic circuits with a surge ten thousand times the power of a bolt of lightning. On dozens of islands, lights went out, cars stopped, phones went dead, radio stations became silent. Hospitals lost power; their back-up generators failed to function. Computer screens at Roosevelt Roads went blank.

Only submarines remained uneffected by the electronic blackout.

When the light of a gigantic flashbulb filled the *Defender's* bridge, Captain Fremont clapped his hand over his eyes. "Dear God, no!" He thought of the young servicemen who had landed that night on St. Croix. Then, vividly, he remembered the first casualties he had ever seen: men thrashing in burning oil on the surface of Pearl Harbor. Men he had loved; as he had loved these men tonight.

His eyes dazzled with bright spots, he stared at the fireball rising over the island. That disaster had originated from his ship. Under his command. And it had killed how many people? People he had dedicated his life to protect.

He maintained sufficient self-discipline to formulate an immediate report for Roosevelt Roads. But he was informed by his operator that the *Defender's* radios were dead.

Ahead of the Carib canoe, both sky and ocean turned daytime blue.

The Witherspoons continued to paddle with unbroken rhythm as they looked back over their shoulders at a fiery mushroom that grew and grew and grew until it stood like a giant burning kapok tree over their island.

While Sabrina stared with eyes that saw everything and revealed nothing, tears trickled down her cheeks.

Baffled that the Americans would destroy their own island, the Soviet president telephoned the president in Washington for an explanation.

The American president informed him, "The launching was accidental, and the explosion seems to be the work of terrorists. In any case, I assure you, the situation presents no threat to the Soviet people."

The Soviet president tended to believe this information; he had met several times with the American president, and thought he could trust him. Nevertheless, he was well aware that the Americans had never agreed to a no-first-strike policy; they had always clung to the option of being the first to launch their nuclear missiles. As Soviet president, he could trust; but as his nation's commander in chief, he must remain wary, alert to every possible threat. Accident, or decoy? A diversion in one corner of the world, while Washington prepared a surprise somewhere else?

The Soviet president returned the American president's assurances that his country too desired only peace.

Moments after hanging up, the Soviet commander in chief, dutybound to protect his people, ordered the two fleets of Typhoon-class submarines, one in the Atlantic, one in the Pacific, to prepare for possible launching of their SS-20's toward American targets.

Deep in the night-dark waters of the Pacific, deep in the morning-dim waters of the Atlantic and Caribbean, the electronic eyes and ears of the twin fleets became acutely alert. The nuclear pincers were readied.

The flash of unearthly light reached Zosia's eyes through the lenses of the binoculars. She screamed as two spikes pierced her brain.

"Angelique! My Angelique!" Hysterical, she shook her head wildly and wailed for the mother, for the father, for the child.

Then she turned her scorched eyes toward her husband. "Piotr, I come."

Wheeling blindly, she pivoted her chair, then rolled, bumping twice into the railing, toward the door. A monstrous clap of thunder boomed behind her; it rumbled, miles away yet close upon her, as if the god of war were roaring with laughter.

Inside the house, she wheeled around the end of the table—banged her knees into her chair—to the window ledge, where she felt with the vaguely sensitive skin of her forearms until she found the watering can. Fumbling in the can, she clutched at something, held it to her forehead and felt the hard round shape of the bottle. She swept her hand across her lap, heard both pistol and binoculars clatter to the floor. Then she set the bottle carefully in her lap so she could wheel with both hands to the sink.

She wrapped her thumb around the cap and twisted it open. Raised the bottle to her lips and poured the pills into her mouth. There were so many, she almost choked. But she was determined the job would not be half-done. Gripping the edge of the sink, she stood from her chair, then fumbled with the faucet until she heard water running. She cupped her hands to catch the water, and taking drink after drink, washed the bitter mass down her throat.

The rest was easy. She sat in the chair, wheeled blindly through the kitchen and along the hallway, scraping the wall, until her knees bumped the foot of the bed. She wheeled around the bed, set the brakes, stood up, pivoted on her feet and sat on the edge of the mattress. She lay down in her gown for the second time that night.

Raising her voice above the thunder of human savagery outside her window, she called, "Kochany, do you remember the day we were married in Davos? We rode in the sleigh up and up and up into the mountains, the horse's bells ringing, until all we could see were the snowy Alps around us and the blue sky above us. We got out in a fluffy white meadow with just our skis and a bottle of champagne. The driver wished us well, then down he went on that long winding road. Leaving us alone in such splendid solitude. I remember the air was so still and clear, that when you opened the champagne, we heard an echo of the POP from the mountains! Just you and I, Piotr, and the white world that reached its arms up to the blue heaven."

She felt a wave of sleep rise over her. She reached for the goose-down comforter on their bed. They pulled it up every night in the Swiss cabin and snuggled together while far away, in that insane world at the foot of the mountains, the cannons thundered. But under the comforter, oooh, when she and Piotr kissed under the comforter . . .

Writhing in heat that seared through her skin to the flesh—for one, two, three, four seconds—Angelique thought with some distant part of her brain still attached to the normal world that she should jump overboard.

But before she could control her burning body long enough to plunge over the gunnel, before she had time to stop her screaming to take a breath and hold it, before she even realized she was blind, the shock wave hit the sloop. She heard the mast crash against the deck; the hull flipped stern over bow in the blast of wind, catapulting her, arms and legs flailing.

Her back hit the water so hard, her screaming stopped while she choked for air. Instinctively swimming to keep her head above the waves, she wondered if the heat had burned the elf-child inside her. She was no person anymore, only the damaged package wrapped around that little life. She rubbed one hand over her belly, relieved that her belly was still there, beneath shreds of melted nylon.

"Angelique!" Her nurse's keen ears knew from the pitch of that voice, the tremor of desperation, that the person calling to her was badly hurt. "Karl!" she called back, then she began to swim with her head raised so she could listen for him, her child safe, safe.

"Angelique," he called, closer, but his voice fainter.

"Karl, I'm coming. Are you all right?"

He did not answer.

"Karl!" she shrieked.

He called "Angel" so faintly she knew that life was ebbing from him. Her sight slowly returned: she began to see blurry patches of water. "Karl? *Karl!*"

She spotted his face, his beard barely above the surface. She swam furiously, casting her pain aside, and grabbed him before he sank. Wrapped one arm around his chest with a lifeguard's grip, swam side-stroke beneath him so her hip lifted him: she brought his body up flat to the surface, his face raised to the sky.

Then she saw a cloud of blood between his legs. Shifting her grip, she hunted for the wound and grimaced with horror when she discovered a long gash in his thigh; she clamped her fingers over his femoral artery.

"Angelique," he said, rolling his head to look at her, "I think the mast gave me a kick as it went down."

"Karl, let me try to get a tourniquet on you." She looked desperately around her at the ocean that stretched in rolling ragged waves to the horizon. She saw pieces of jagged red fiberglass. The charred hull of the *Danmark*, masts gone, deck covered with flames. And then she spotted an orange life preserver, patches of it black but with a belt around it, ten yards away. She towed him toward it, scissor-kicking with all her strength while she held his pressure point.

He said, "I'm sorry to miss the wedding."

"Karl," she panted, "can you put your fingers where mine are? Can you stop the bleeding? I need my arm to swim."

He reached down, his hand feeble. She grabbed his fingers and pressed them over the artery. "Push! Push hard!" Then she swept her arm and kicked the last few yards to the preserver.

"You better . . . give me a kiss," he said, slurring the words.

She grabbed at the life jacket, ripped the belt free and tied it tightly around his upper leg with a neat professional square knot.

But when she looked at his eyes, they were dull. "Karl!" She grabbed his shoulders and shook him, laid her mouth over his and puffed air into him. She stared with disbelief at his slackening face. "Karl, I do," she called to him.

"I do. I take thee as my wedded husband. To love and to cherish. To have and to hold, in sickness and in health . . . until . . . " She shook him frantically.

"*Karl!*"

She turned toward her island, looked up at the boiling incandescent cloud that towered miles above her, then shook her burnt fist at the thundering monster. "You bastard!" she screamed. "You *bastard!*"

The red disk of the sun rose above the sea like an unblinking eye that stared.

CHAPTER FORTY-ONE

November

He sat in the same hospital waiting room where he had sat thirty-four years ago, waiting for Karl to be born. But now his wife sat beside him. The two of them held hands and said little, though he had silently prayed through most of the night. The strange Negro woman whom fate seemed to have brought into their lives, as fate had taken away their son, a woman whom he hardly knew how to love, though she was family now, or almost family, certainly the mother of his son's child . . . he prayed that she would survive the delivery, and asked too, dear God, that the child, after all it had been through, would be healthy.

She held her husband's hand, and though she tried to project her mind into that delivery room where she herself had lain thirty-four years ago, she could not. The Negro woman on the other side of the wall, her brown face and arms mottled with pink burn scars, her eyes so fiercely determined, was too foreign for her to take into her heart. No, her heart was still out in the cemetery, and she could not cast from her mind the image of the two black stones beside each other. Her two sons. She was still standing in front of those stones, still asking, Why? She had found it easier, in her initial gut-reaction rage, to blame Karl's death on this colored woman, who had beguiled her boy, led him into sin, had even conceived a child before the two had been blessed in the holy sacrament of marriage . . . and then that night in the sailboat had taken her son close enough to an atomic bomb that he was killed. That he was killed.

But she hid her rage from her houseguest. She listened, with her mind if not with her heart, as this Negro eight months swollen explained while they stood together in the cemetery, "He was helping to rescue people dying at sea. Nobody else was helping, except a crew of Danish boys. Your Navy certainly wasn't there to help. Your Navy was busy saving America. But Karl . . . he was helping."

She read the newspaper accounts, read the report of a congressional investigation, and listened to the quiet, guiltless, determined voice of the Negro woman who during the past month had slept in Karl's bed, had helped in the kitchen, had stared out the window at the bleak November cornfields. And slowly, when her rage subsided, when she finally allowed herself to understand that military officials had not ordered an evacuation, had not even tried to help those struggling to flee—she realized that her son had died a hero's death. And that this Angelique Nielsen, whom, though it seemed impossible, her son had loved, had that night in the sailboat simply been doing her duty as a nurse.

But still she asked, Why? What had the world come to, that these bombs could fly off a ship and land among people? And that when such a disaster happened, officials had no idea what to do about it. So she blamed the Navy and her rage kindled anew. Though it was an uncomfortable rage for a woman who truly, deeply, and everlastingly loved her country. Gradually, while she too stared out the window at a pair of crows buffeted by the chill wind blowing over corn stubble, the two silent women at the same window that afternoon on Veterans' Day, the question reformulated in her mind, and she began to wonder, Why have people allowed these wars to go on forever?

He couldn't help but smile as he waited on the couch, thinking of the many evenings this last month since they first met her at O'Hare Airport, tense, awkward evenings at first, then easier, the three of them a little more talkative, and then that one special evening after she'd been in the house for about a week, the only Negro ever in their house, carrying their son's bastard child . . . yes, he had to smile, because all of a sudden she looked at him, her scarred face more frightening than any Halloween mask, but her eyes gentle, forgiving him, yes, forgiving *him*, and she asked, "Ah wonder if we might make a bowl of popcorn."

Well, the ice broke then. And how she could eat popcorn! It became a ritual, every evening around the kitchen table. She told them how she and Karl had often done the same. She told them that POP'S POPCORN was surely the best in the world.

He turned now to his wife, squeezed her hand. "She sure does like popcorn."

She looked at her husband, his pale blue eyes smiling at her. "Yes," she said, and then she added, because it was true and it was time they admitted it, "I believe that she's come to like us too."

Angelique wanted to be sure. Virgin Islanders could not vote for the American president, so after her five months in a Puerto Rican hospital, she did not go back to St. Croix to stay with Nat Junior and his family—they had an empty bed, Tyrone's, for the boy had disappeared that night. No, she wanted to be sure, so she took a plane north, from San Juan to Miami to Chicago, bolstering her courage by telling herself that even if they didn't welcome her, they must at least welcome Karl's child. Because she was determined that her offspring would be endowed with the full rights of American citizenship, not simply so he could enjoy those rights, but use them.

Her feet in the delivery stirrups, the doctor and nurses a blur around her, the contractions worse than she had ever imagined and yet welcome, oh so welcome, and certainly nothing compared to the pain of third-degree epidermal burns . . . she envisioned Karl's face: tanned, his nose peeling, his tousled hair bleached by the sun, his Viking beard so handsome, and his green eyes filled with love as he looked at her across Zosia's table in the candlelight.

And Zosia, her olive-black eyes lit with an impish sparkle as she told her tale about riding the horse while it pulled the sleigh on her Babka's farm in Bydgoszcz.

And then she saw Nick, son of an African king, standing tall and regal on Maroon Ridge, a prince without a kingdom to inherit. Her brother's failed keeper, victim of the wrong war in the wrong country in the wrong century. His name on the registry books at the University, until the building collapsed and vanished in flames.

Leroy, Mama, and Papa, even Rosemary—smiling now because at last Angelique was going to have a child of her own—and Chester fishing from the pier, they all floated through her mind as she gripped the handles on the sides of the bed and cried out at the awful pains. And then she remembered the one silent delivery in Witherspoon's house, when Sabrina lay on the bed, her face contorted as she gripped the edges of the mattress, her mouth working, crying out her own silent words that maybe were not silent, but heard by an ear in heaven.

Sabrina's eyes when she saw her child and reached her hands to hold it: eyes radiant with such love, though her ears could not hear the child's wail. She hoped Sabrina had not disappeared that night when the sun grazed the earth.

"Crowning," announced the doctor. "Give a good push."

She clenched her teeth and pushed, looked up at the large round mirror over the bed, and began to cry, not with pain, but with overwhelming, exultant joy, as the elongated, black haired, dark skinned head emerged. She watched the doctor's hands perform with professional skill the same movements her own hands had performed so many times, and she called out, "Yes! Yes!" as the small brown body emerged between her pink-scarred thighs, first one shoulder, then the other, then into those white, glove-covered hands the torso, and arms that moved, and legs that moved! Then all the world stopped for a moment, and she held her breath, waited, waited.

"Yaaaaahhhhhh!" wailed the infant, and she knew her little fighter had made it.

"Oh Karl," she called through her tears. "Oh Karl oh Karl oh Karl. We come visit yo', Karl. Soon as we can, we come visit yo'."

"It's a boy, Mrs. Jacobsen," announced the nurse. "You've got a healthy son." The woman held up her child, squalling and waving tiny fists, and she saw Karl's cheeks and nose, and Papa's eyes.

They visited her in the recovery room, hesitant, awkward as they came through the door, though both broke into smiles when they saw the infant nursing at her breast. This ain' easy for them, she knew. They stood together beside the bed, still unsure what to say. Sally was the first to reach her hand and rub the baby's dark hair. "Angelique, he's a wonderful boy. We're so happy."

She told them, "His name is Karl Junior." She touched her son's sucking cheek. "One day your grandson is going to run for president. He can, because he was born in the Land of Lincoln."

Grief overshadowed the brief joy in Sally's eyes, for her son was not here to see his child.

"Yes, one day," said Angelique, her voice empowered with conviction, "one day your grandchild and a thousand thousand thousand others like him are going to refuse the shame of war."

Ole did not speak as he gazed at his grandson, but then he leaned over—she saw his face coming toward her, Karl's face thirty years older—and she felt his lips as he gently kissed her on the forehead.